# FANFARE FOR A WITCH

# fANFARE
# FOR A WITCH

*Vaughan Wilkins*

*New York*    THE MACMILLAN COMPANY    *1954*

FOR CORA MCGRAW LAW
OF NEW ORLEANS, LOUISIANA,
IN ADMIRATION

# Contents

# *Foreword*

'I HAVE LOST my eldest son, but I am glad!'

Such was King George the Second's epitaph on Frederick Prince of Wales. In conformity with this sentiment he interred his heir with the minimum of ceremony and, as Bubb Dodington glumly records, 'without either anthem or organ.'

The similarly unnatural hatred displayed by the mother of the unfortunate prince is chronicled again and again in the *Memoirs* of Lord Hervey, Queen Caroline's gigolo, with venomous glee. As you read the pages you know for a certainty that the writer was licking his carmined lips as he composed such sentences as the following:

> They [the Queen and Princess Caroline, one of Frederick's sisters] neither of them made much ceremony of wishing a hundred times a day that the Prince might drop down dead of an apoplexy, the Queen cursing the hour of his birth.

The original cause of this hideous passion of hate for a generous little fellow—who had a most un-Hanoverian taste for music, art, and literature, for cricket and tennis—is one of the unsolved mysteries of history.

Sir Robert Walpole, the cunning and coarse-mouthed statesman who was Prime Minister for twenty-one years, presumably knew the beginnings of this story; for on September 5th, 1737, Lord Chancellor Hardwicke made this mysterious entry in his diary:

> This day Sir R. W. informed me of certain passages between the King and himself and the Queen and the Prince, of too high and secret a nature even to be trusted to this narrative; but from thence I find great reason to think that this unhappy difference between the King and the Queen and his R.H. turned upon some points of a more interesting and important nature than have hitherto appeared.

Whatever the cause may have been, however, it was well known many years earlier that George—an ugly little man who devotedly assured his wife on her death-bed that he would never marry again, but content himself with mistresses—was all set to disinherit Frederick if he could, and supplant him on the throne of Britain by the younger son, William, Duke of Cumberland, the 'Butcher' of Culloden.

For long Frederick's reputation has lain under a cloud, due largely to the malignancy of his enemy, Hervey, whom Pope styled a 'painted child of dirt and stinks and stings,' and nicknamed 'Lord Fanny.' A reassessment of the Prince by the late Sir George Young, in his biography, *Poor Fred: The People's Prince*, would seem, however, to show that he might well have proved a far better, more democratic, and more popular monarch than any of his dynasty until the coming of Victoria. It is fascinating—if unprofitable—to speculate what the course of history might have been had Frederick lived to be king and to educate his son, afterwards George the Third, in the art of Kingship. The American Revolution even might never have taken place—or might at any rate have been postponed for a generation or so.

It may be added that most of the utterances of the royal parents regarding their son, in the pages that follow, have Hervey's authority.

As for Shems-ed-Douha, a parallel to her early history may be found in a letter to Sir Walter Scott from Mr. Andrew Rutherglen of Dalkeith, published in that fascinating volume, *Sir Walter's Post-Bag*, edited by Wilfred Partington. It is just possible that some similar story may be behind M. Henry Bordeaux's reference in his book, *Le Visage du Maroc*, to the English favourite of the Moroccan *Roi Soleil*, the Emperor Mulai Ishmael.

*V. W.*

# I

## *Commination Service in a Palace*

NOTHING YOU CAN TELL ME about Frederick will ever surprise me,
said Frederick's mother with bitter emphasis to the gentleman in
pale blue velvet standing opposite her. 'My dear firstborn is the
greatest ass, the greatest liar, the greatest *canaille,* and the greatest
beast in all the world. I heartily wish he were out of it.'

After that comprehensive statement of opinion she raised her cup
of morning chocolate to her lips—to set it down again at once with
an expression of disgust.

'*Pfui!* This chocolate, Purcell!' she complained in guttural accents. 'It is not merely lukewarm, but positively undrinkable.'

'La! Madam!' sympathized Purcell, a pretty, pert-nosed creature
in the filmiest of aprons, floating into the royal presence on felt-soled
slippers from the background whence, as usual, she had been de-
vouring the three gentlemen in attendance with the regard of eyes
as hard and bright as though they were of stained glass.

It was nine o'clock, and the Queen sat at breakfast at a small
round table in one of the sunny window embrasures of a long gal-

lery hung with the amorous pictures of rosy-limbed nudes so much appreciated by her husband—pictures of substantial Venuses, nymphs chased by satyrs, and vine-wreathed bacchantes. By way of contrast, she herself was a shapeless woman in the early fifties with a determined Germanic face, her greying hair almost completely hidden by a close muslin cap threaded with a dark blue ribbon.

'When I said that I would have fruit for breakfast, Purcell, my good soul,' she continued her chiding, 'I did not mean melon. *Fi donc,* you know well enough that I never touch the stuff! At least I haven't since the late King got his death from eating it! Bring me some oranges, and tell Teed, that *dumme Teufel,* to make fresh chocolate!'

Purcell curtsied to the cap, and the loose, unbecoming négligé of golden brown edged with dark blue, and the white silk fichu, and departed with the rejected tray.

Lord Hervey, the Queen's vice-chamberlain, slim and effeminate, his face most delicately tinted with cosmetics, waited before her in the window-place with the air of being reverentially grateful for the privilege. His coat, his ruffles, and his cravat were superb. The toupet of his powdered wig rose in two little curls in the centre as though he were about to sprout horns. He resembled a Dresden figure of a faun masquerading as a man. He said now in his neat, mincing voice with the licensed assurance of a favourite:

'I presume, madam, that you forswore melon in gratitude for its part in the happy removal of King George the First?'

'His father's death could never have happened too soon for the King or myself, as you very well know, my little one! But I am sick, *teuflisch* sick, of all this gabble-gabble about the family, or, at any rate, *some* members of it. Tell me, instead, what scandal about *other* people you have gathered for me on this fine morning! Open the window, *mon enfant,* if you please! It is already very close in here!'

My Lord opened the window on to the inner courtyard. . . . Caroline, a hawk-faced young princess who passionately adored him, remarked with concern from her post behind her mother's chair, that even such very slight exertion brought the perspiration to his brow. . . . He proceeded to display his wares.

'I hear that the Duke of Grafton, madam—'

'If you are going to tell me about Princess Emily's fat friend's latest folly, then I heard it at half-past eight. It is already *une vieillerie.*'

'I am sorry, madam. Then I suppose you have also heard about Lord Liffard?'

'Child, this is 1737. The old devil has been dead without knowing it since the beginning of the century! Nobody cares what happens to him!'

Caroline intervened eagerly—

'I know it's about the family, Mamma, but all the same tell Lord Hervey to read to you what he's written about Frederick! It compares him with Nero! *Nero!* He let me just peep at it. It was so amusing and so true! Do tell him that he *must* read it!'

The Queen clapped her hands with every appearance of extreme pleasure.

'So you've finished the opus, have you, Johnny?' she exclaimed. 'That's a different matter altogether. You have it with you? You shall amuse me with it whilst I drink my chocolate, instead of boring me with old stories of old fograms.'

Yes. He chanced to have it with him, admitted my Lord, putting a long white hand to the buckram-stiffened skirts of his blue coat, and producing several closely written sheets of paper.

Lord Dunscore, who had been standing at a respectful distance, twitched his companion's sleeve, and both ventured a trifle nearer to the lector.

Caroline was wont to call the man in yellow damask—trusted companion of her younger brother, William, Duke of Cumberland—'The Minotaur'; for there was something violent and bull-like about his heavy body and his large, bitter, smallpox-pitted face, and about his habit of hunching his head down between his shoulders and then suddenly thrusting it forward.

The presence beside him on this occasion of Mr. Standring—in a rose-pink coat with gold buttons—had, however, utterly astonished her; for that romantic young man, with the face of a patrician as portrayed by one of the Italian Old Masters, was of the household of the Prince of Wales, and members of that little court would ordinarily have no more ventured to wait upon her mother than to enter a lioness's cage.

But the Queen nodded most graciously to the man from the enemy camp.

'That is right,' she said. 'Come nearer, and hear what the good Hervey has to say! *Cela promet bien!* . . . You've not forgotten about them both being fiddlers, child, have you?'

Indeed, Lord Hervey had not forgotten.

The mother of the subject of this study settled herself into an attitude of benevolent attention. Dunscore and Standring approached still nearer. Purcell swam silently to the table with a renewed tray, set it down before her mistress, and withdrew, nominally out of earshot. Hervey unfolded his paper, exchanged a quick smile with the gratified Caroline, and then in his affected voice proceeded to read out the title of one of the most astonishing literary compositions ever submitted to a Queen of England for her approval.

'It is called, madam, "The Character of Frederick, Prince of Wales, and Parallels Between His and That of Nero." ' *

With malicious relish he proceeded to develop at length his thesis. With ever-increasing malignancy he piled up his charges against her elder son, and expiated on them.

Fretz was avaricious and yet a spendthrift. He was lewd and hypocritical. He was proud and a coward. He was unwashed, faithless and unfilial. He was (it was inferred) a potential matricide . . . How like Nero! He was also a buffoon . . . How like Nero!

A buffoon!

The monster of ancient Rome had flattered himself upon his ability as a harpist, and had played, sung, and acted in the theatre. Frederick—declared the essayist—similarly prided himself as a 'cellist and would most certainly have performed in public had he been permitted to do so. As it was he would fiddle for an hour or two of an evening at his open window in a blaze of light, accompanying himself in French or Italian songs, whilst in the courtyard beneath an audience would assemble of 'all the underling servants and rabble of the palace . . . How much does such a buffoon fiddler debase the title of a Prince of Wales!'

A buffoon!

'If Nero,' continued Hervey, sketching faint gestures as he read, 'drove chariots and performed other exercises for prizes in the Circus

---

* LORD HERVEY, *Memoirs of the Reign of George II*, Vol. III: 'Her Majesty and the Princess Caroline . . . made him read it to them so often that—what rarely happens—the writer grew more tired of reciting his own work than his auditors of hearing it.'

Maximus and amid all the scum of Rome, the Prince's cricket-matches—in which he performed, himself, among a less numerous, though not a more creditable, throng upon public commons—are in the same style of character, and considering their different situations may be justly reckoned alike.'

The Queen nodded her gratified approval throughout the performance. Once or twice she even sharply rapped out her concurrence in an argument with her knuckles upon the edge of the silver tray.

Not until a quarter of an hour had passed did my Lord draw rein. Then he read the last breathless sentence almost in the manner of a malignant spirit thinly disguised as a man rather than that strange creature to whom his fellows sometimes referred as 'Lord Fanny.' He read:

'. . . and this puts me in mind of another circumstance in which these two princely blessings to the world will, I hope, resemble one another, which is that of Nero's rejoicing mankind with his death—the only way he ever did rejoice them—when he was but thirty-two years old; and as they were both born in the same month, so I hope that they will both die at the same age.'

He folded the paper with the air of one modestly satisfied by a competent piece of work. So satisfied was he with it, incidentally, that he preserved it for posterity, fortified by an acre of Latin quotations. His enormous eyes turned confidently towards Majesty for applause.

Majesty did not stint it.

Majesty found a dozen adjectives—garnished with a little French and German—wherewith to express her genuine appreciation of my Lord's defilement and execration of her son.

Did not my Lord Dunscore think it a remarkably just assessment of Fretz's character and nature? My Lord did.

Did not her dear Caroline think that every word that dear Johnny had written was Gospel truth? Caroline loyally joined in the chorus of hate.

'Fretz is only thirty now,' she said with vehemence. 'There are still two years to go. I grudge him every breath he draws!'

She was no longer shocked at herself for saying such things about her brother. For if dear Mamma, and dear Hervey, and Papa, and all the family said Fretz was an abomination, then an abomination he must certainly be. And everyone had been terribly worried of late by the conspiracy in Parliament to make Papa give Fretz a much larger allowance. What was it to do with anyone else how much money Papa gave him? And Papa was being caricatured and lampooned right and left in the most indecent way all because of him.

She suddenly became conscious that the intent Standring had shifted his dark gaze from her mother to herself, as though he would satisfy himself of the genuineness of her emotion. In a flashing second of insight she realized that he was there then because he was an integral factor in an episode that was as yet to be unfolded. She realized that ever and again Hervey had underlined a word, a phrase, a point for his particular attention. The idea occurred to her that perhaps her mother's favourite had even arranged this commination service in conjunction with Dunscore for his special benefit.

The thought intrigued without alarming her, and she dismissed the matter from her mind just as 'The Minotaur,' in response to some whispered message, sought and obtained permission for himself and his companion to withdraw for a moment.

Majesty made a small hole in a third orange. She inserted a knob of sugar in the orifice and proceeded to suck. It was altogether rather a noisy proceeding. Meantime my Lord, posturing finger to forehead, meditated what other of entertainment he had to offer. Then his face lightened.

'I have it, madam!' he exclaimed. 'I heard last night that the Moorish envoys have landed and are now on their way to London by slow stages to negotiate the new treaty. They escorted the Empress here.'

'Empress?' inquired the Queen. 'What empress?'

'Both England and France have recognized the imperial title of the ruler of Morocco. This lady is the Emperor's consort.'

Her Majesty expelled a couple of orange pips from her mouth in a natural but not very elegant manner.

'But what brings her, child, and without him?'

'Sir Robert Walpole told me, madam, that our consul at Rabat gathered she was suffering from gall bladder trouble and was coming to consult Dr. Cheyne of Bath. The first authority on the subject. An admirable physician, as I know personally! I was, myself, under his care for two years. Whilst I do not agree with all his treatment—'

'My dear soul,' interrupted Majesty, who well knew how prone the delicate creature was to stray from the subject under debate, at the first excuse, into descriptions of his many ailments and their nauseous symptoms, 'we discuss the Empress and not your favourite Aesculapius.'

'Your pardon, madam! I gather that after consulting Dr. Cheyne, the Empress may undergo a treatment and take a course of waters at one of the spas. Actually last night one of Sir Robert's agents in the City told him privately, however, that her visit had to do with the investment of the bulk of the Emperor's fortune over here, because of the risk of civil war in Morocco. But neither he nor I could see why she should be employed in such a mission. She is, of course, travelling incognito.'

'How I should adore to see the creature!' exclaimed Caroline, who had been enchanted by the seraglio tragedy of *Zara* some few months before. 'Do you suppose that she wears a nose-ring and pantaloons?'

'I do not opine that nose-rings are worn by the *ton* of Morocco, your Royal Highness,' said Hervey, taking a pinch of snuff in the sublimest fashion.

The Queen counted her orange pips. Apparently they amounted to a satisfactory total. She made ready for departure just as Dunscore reappeared with the romantic Standring—

'Purcell, my soul, warn my ladies that I am now going to the dressing-room!'

She drank the last of the chocolate, and wiped her lips on a small napkin. As she rose to her feet she glanced out of the tall window at her side.

Sunshine flooded the palace courtyard, was reflected in the many-paned windows. Pigeons strutted on the cobbles, and then suddenly rose in a whirring cloud as a small man, accompanied by a couple of excited greyhounds, emerged from a low archway in the wine-red brick building opposite, and walked briskly across. The Queen remained looking out. Her face changed; it seemed to swell, and the greyish rather greasy skin darkened to a dusky crimson. So inordinate a hate possessed her that she could barely give utterance to the extraordinary words she spoke—

'Look! There he goes—the wretch! The villain! I wish the ground would open this minute, and sink the monster in the lowest hole in Hell!'

Hervey, who had followed her gaze, realized that the Prince of Wales had crossed his mother's line of vision—'Fretz,' who stood in the way of all her hopes and plans for that dearly loved younger son, William. Used as he was to the ugly and unnatural hatred of their son that filled both father and mother, yet even he was taken aback by the vehemence of the fury that seemed to burn the Queen up. He made mental note for his journal, and Dunscore, as Caroline remarked, cast a quick, sly, significant look at Standring, as if to say, 'You see! I did not exaggerate, did I?' and the other gave a tiny nod of comprehension and agreement.

'What are you staring at me for?' asked the Queen, turning from the window. 'I mean what I said. If my prayers and curses had any effect his life would be neither happy nor long.'

Once again the princess gathered the impression that some wordless message passed between the three men.

At that moment there came an imperative knock on the great double doors at the far end of the gallery.

The leaves flew back, and a small square gentleman with a flowing wig and a leathery face—ornamented by a large nose, a palely tight-lipped mouth, and a jaw as undershot as a bulldog's—bustled in as though there were not a moment to be lost. He wore a dark brown coat and primrose-coloured stockings, and was followed by two rather dowdy elderly gentlemen. They approached under the indifferent regard of the rosy-limbed nudes upon the wall, at so brisk a trot that their heels rattled on the bare polished floor of the long gallery with a tapping as of hammers in a busy workshop.

The Queen and the princess dropped deep curtsies; the gentlemen, fingertips to heart, bowed very, very low before the ineffable majesty of the King—George the Second, by God's Grace, King of England, Elector of Hanover.

'Frittering the morning away as usual—and in a stink of oranges. Pah!' he gobbled at his wife when he was still an appreciable distance off. 'Caroline, for God's sake, hold yourself up, instead of hunching like a sack of potatoes! Hervey, your friend Bishop Potter is a blockhead, a *Dummkopf*! My Lord Dunscore, I heard reports this morning of an adventure of the Duke of Cumberland and yourself at Vauxhall last night. Pray be more circumspect in future! . . . I hope Cumberland gave a good account of himself?'

'His Royal Highness laid out two of the mob very prettily, sir,' reported Dunscore. 'I assure your Majesty that we were not—'

'I know all about it,' said the King indulgently, 'I have heard. Chasing ladies in the alleys—privateering the townspeople's girls in the Dark Valk, I gather. Still Villiam behaved like a man of mettle in the *Verwickelung*—the embroilment—that followed. But no more puppy play, my Lord! No more of it, whilst you are avay in the country. I shall hold you responsible, you understand?' He turned his attention to his wife as he came up to the table. 'My God, you are as red as a turkey-cock! What the devil has put you in such a pet?'

'I was cursing Fretz!' replied the Queen simply, as though that were of itself a perfectly adequate explanation.

'Fretz!' said the King, immediately accepting it as such. He thrust out his lower jaw more than ever. 'Fr-r-retz—that—*Wechselbalg!* That unspeakable thing! Why speak of him? *I* do not—will not—choose even to see him, though he may stand as close to me as you are!'

'And *I* have said no word to him at all for three months,' said Fretz's mother.

'Incidentally, sir—since you are speaking of his Royal Highness—the Prince has desired me to ask your permission for himself and the Princess to leave Town,' said the larger and the more untidy of the two gentlemen who had accompanied the King.

'No,' said the King rapidly. 'No. No. No. No. *No!*'

The large and untidy gentleman continued in an unflurried manner:

'The reason for his request, sir, is the Princess's health. A short course of the waters at Crosse Wells has been recommended in view of her condition.'

'Her condition!' exclaimed the Queen in bitter scorn. 'How long do they propose to continue the legend that she is breeding?'

'It might be good policy, madam, to let them off the lead for—say—a month,' suggested the untidy gentleman, ignoring the gynaecological problem and taking his snuffbox out of a snuff-stained blue and silver waistcoat. 'Otherwise his Royal Highness may make capital out of it. A month would be long enough.'

'I don't like them out of my sight whilst they spread the report that she is with child,' said the Queen. 'When she is brought to bed, I am going to be there. Fretz is sterile as a mule. He is *not* going to impose some charwoman's baby on me, Sir Robert!'

'There are several months to go,' said the Prime Minister, helping himself rather loudly to snuff, and then blowing his nose on a yellow bandanna handkerchief. 'With all respect, madam, I think it would be a mistake not to give their Royal Highnesses permission to absent themselves from Court for a short time.'

'It is true that she can't be brought to bed as quickly as one can blow one's nose,' said the Queen thoughtfully.

She glanced at her husband for instruction, but all he did was to grunt afresh 'That *Wechselbalg!*' casting the burden of the decision upon her.

She glanced at Hervey, and Princess Caroline—whose surreptitious regard rarely left his handsome face—observed a quick indicatory flicker of his large and overbright eyes in the direction of Dunscore and Standring.

'Perhaps after all we might risk it,' said the Queen, her expression suddenly lightening.

She had risen too quickly, had curtsied too deeply. A sharp stab of pain reminded her of the secret enemy within her body—of the constant fear that she might die before her son. The flush died down on her face. It grew grey.

# II

# *Dilemma of a Two-Tailed Pasha*

'The Emperor of Morocco, sir, has some five hundred brothers,' said the blue-coated stranger in a nonchalant manner, setting down his tankard on the trestle-table, at which he sat with Mr. Tuke, beneath the shade of a pair of Spanish chestnut trees.

'Five *hundred*!' exclaimed Mr. Tuke after a long pause. '*Five* hundred!'

'Perhaps I should have said "had" and not "has," ' admitted the other. 'I fancy that the number may have been considerably reduced of late years. But there were five hundred and twenty-eight of them at one time.'

'And sisters—t'ch-t'ch—in proportion?' queried Mr. Tuke dubiously; and prodded with the butt of his otter-spear at a scratching hound which lay on the grass beside his feet.

'Not quite so many, I understand,' said the man in the blue coat, helping himself to snuff. 'I believe that a census of the acknowledged family of the late Emperor Mulai Ishmael once established the total at just over the thousand.'

Behind them the imposing sign above the door of the Maid's Head Inn and New Wells creaked concurrence with Mr. Tuke's unspoken doubts as it swung in the warm noonday breeze.

That gentleman undid the last brass button of his baggy green coat and very thoughtfully contemplated the mud on his shoes and high gaiters—which was all he had to show for a morning's otter-hunting.

Then suddenly he slapped down his three-cornered hat on the long bench, and removed the red cotton nightcap that he wore under it, revealing a bald, brown head. In a very deliberate manner he opened a leather case beside him and extracted and assumed the bushy white clerical wig which he invariably doffed before indulging in field sports.

He was a square-cut man of medium height, with a ruddy, weather-beaten face dominated by a jutting chin, large hooked nose, and bright grey eyes. Until he donned the wig he had looked like a buccaneering sea-officer rather than a parson.

The implications of the otter-hunter's metamorphosis were comprehended, and with inward amusement, by the younger man, although his attention appeared to be concentrated upon the sunlit panorama spread at his feet; the wide valley—a patchwork of silver river and dark woodlands, green meadows and golden cornfields, of orchard-guarded farms—tilting gently upwards to blue hills that rose tier beyond tier to a smoke-grey jagged wall of mountains.

Mr. Tuke rumbled at length—

'And may I ask, sir, what reliable—t'ch-t'ch, t'ch-t'ch—information you have in regard to the matrimonial arrangements that resulted in such a monstrous brood?'

The other withdrew his regard from the prospect: he surveyed his companion for an instant almost with amusement before he replied:

'There is always, of course, an empress whose position is usually unassailable. As for the others—who can tell their number? It is not well to pry too closely into the secrets of a royal seraglio, or, in fact, to pry at all. But this I can truthfully say: With my own eyes I have seen the King of Dar-Fûr go forth to war attended by two hundred spouses—of a sort.'

'With your own eyes!' exclaimed Mr. Tuke in a sudden access of excitement, his face no longer overcast. 'By Old Gooseberry, an Eastern traveller! Why, do you know, sir, that for a horrid moment —forgive me!—I feared that your information had been extracted from books and the gazettes! I am no great believer in either, sir. They can cause—t'ch-t'ch—a great deal of trouble. In fact they often do.'

He scrubbed his chin with a large and well-kept hand, and then abruptly doffed his wig and pulled on the red nightcap again. The tassel of it fell over his left eye. Quite clearly he had decided that, in the circumstances, the requirements of decorum and truth no longer demanded emphasis upon his ecclesiastical character. He took swift new survey of his companion.

The man was unquestionably a person of quality and distinction; tall, perhaps about forty years old, and garbed in a night-blue coat— a sober, but a very beautiful coat. He had something of the bearing of a soldier, and his hair was dressed with a military formality, its powder emphasizing the deep tan of a face marked by irregular features, high nose and determined chin. He was a notion whimsical in expression, and when he smiled—as now—he did so in a lopsided way, the right corner of his lips curving upwards whilst the left curved down. The daughter of the British ambassador to Turkey had once said to him that he always made her think of Don Quixote, a crusader, and King Charles the Second. He felt that he owed it to himself to protest—

'Madam, I can assure you on the contrary that there has never been a Dulcinea del Toboso in my life. Or a Zuleika. Or a Nell Gwynne.'

The desultory conversation of two strangers over their tankards had drifted to the present juncture from casual comment by the parson on the latest war news from Constantinople and St. Petersburg.

'So when you spoke a while back of the qualities of the Mussulman soldier—' began Mr. Tuke, and then decided to leave the sentence unfinished.

'—I had not obtained my information from books, the gazettes, or even the coffeehouses,' said the other, completing it for him with quizzical amusement manifested in eyes which were of an almost startling blue in contrast with his mahogany skin—of a blue such as

that of the bloom on damsons. 'No, sir, I have only recently arrived
from Sallee in Morocco.'

'Morocco! My dear sir! Barbary corsairs and Sallee rovers!'

Mr. Tuke heaved himself upright in his seat. He hammered
loudly with his pewter mug upon the table to attract attention from
within-doors.

'You will not refuse to join me in a bowl of punch? A bowl of
East India punch—t'ch-t'ch—I suggest. You really must do me the
honour. In fact, I insist. The Maid's Head is noted for its liquors. I
assure you of it. Pray, *pray* give me the pleasure. Morocco, indeed!
It *must* be punch! . . . You will permit me to present myself, sir—
the Reverend Abel Tuke, of Crosse.' He paused; added so that there
should be no misconception, 'I am a nonjuror, and so hold no cure
of souls.'

The man from Morocco bowed to his bench companion in
acknowledgment of the introduction and the proffer of hospitality.

'And I, sir, am Javan Tierce, of Constantinople, an officer in the
service of the Grand Turk, who has been loaned temporarily to his
Shereefian Majesty, the Emperor of Morocco.'

Mr. Tuke reddened with excitement as might a child on its first
sight of a giraffe, an elephant, or some other almost fabulous creature. He almost stammered when he spoke—

'Constantinople—the Golden Horn! T'ch-t'ch! Sallee! But you also
mentioned Dar-Fûr. Where on earth may that be, sir?'

'It is a kingdom considerably larger than Great Britain,' Mr.
Tierce informed him. 'It lies south of the pashalik of Egypt. A jour-
ney of some sixty or seventy days from Cairo by way of Assiût and
Sheb.'

Mr. Tuke nodded so vigorously in token of comprehension that
the red tassel of his nightcap joggled against his beaky nose as
though he were a highly animated punchinello. He battered once
more in heavy summons upon the table—so sturdily, indeed, that the
tankard crumpled in his hand; and then commented:

'A rather remote place of resort, sir! If it is not an impertinence
—t'ch-t'ch—may I venture to ask what made you visit it?'

Mr. Tierce threw back his head and laughed, revealing the most
excellent teeth.

'I have no disreputable secret,' he said easily: explained in mock
heroic tones, 'I was for a season in command of the armies of

the King of Dar-Fûr—the Mighty One, the Buffalo-Son-of-a-Buffalo, Bull of Bulls, Elephant of Majestic Strength, whose life may Allah preserve.'

The clergyman listened with fascinated attention. His long, capable fingers still clutched the battered pewter, but he made no attempt to renew the onslaught. Instead he asked, almost breath-lessly—

'And in Turkey?'

'I was—am—also a general. In fact, sir, I hold the rank of pasha of two tails.'

'Pasha of two tails!' echoed Mr. Tuke in a perfect ecstasy, his eyes shining like those of an enraptured schoolboy. 'By Old Goose-berry, sir, one would be less astonished to find a prince of the blood-royal drinking ale on the grass before the Maid's Head at Crosse Wells than—t'ch-t'ch—a Turkish pasha of two tails! Much less indeed, for there are actually at this very minute a brace of princes —Hanoverian princes!—staying at Barrington Court near by.'

Having pronounced the word 'Hanoverian' with a fine scorn that affirmed his adherence to the unfortunate Stuart dynasty, he shot to his feet, raising his voice in an enormous bellow. Then he swung round and with most astonishing accuracy projected his tankard across the roadway between green pleasance and inn—and through the open door of the taproom, fully thirty yards away. Its crash upon the flagstones within was followed by a high feminine cry of dismay.

'An infallible method of commanding attention, sir,' said Mr. Tuke, with naïve pride in the performance.

A moment later, a pretty, flustered girl in a pink spotted dress and ribbony cap came hot-foot from the inn, to be greeted with objurgations by the clergyman.

'Susie,' roared he in conclusion, 'if it's Joe standing—t'ch-t'ch—between the general and me and our potations, then Heaven help Joe! I'll read the cursing psalm over Joe! I'll denounce Joe in the commination service! I'll excommunicate Joe! I'll—'

'Joe isn't there, your honour's reverence,' said Susie in a small voice, pleating her apron.

'Then somebody else is, I'll swear to it!'

'I should opine,' remarked Javan Tierce, after a not unsympa-thetic look at the downcast face, 'that our Susan has also been listen-

ing to a traveller's tales. If I know anything about him, my man has
probably been commenting, too, most favourably upon local beauty
as against Moorish or Ottoman.'

Susie flushed more deeply, but ventured to cast a sidelong and
appreciative glance at the good-looking ugliness of the lean, dark
man. She departed at speed to fulfil Mr. Tuke's order of the ingredients for a punch-bowl.

The pasha of two tails pushed back his admirable blue coat;
thrust his hands into the pockets of a sprigged waistcoat of pale
green silk, and produced two flat gold boxes, which he laid on the
table before him.

'Snuff,' said Mr. Tuke, agreeably surprised. 'Is that also among
the pleasures of the East?'

'Indeed it is, sir. I beg you to adventure on a *prise*.' He opened
and pushed the boxes towards Mr. Tuke. 'The nearer is a Turkish
snuff flavoured with attar of roses from Damascus . . . I prefer it
to the perfume of Shiraz . . . The other is Egyptian with which is
blended the natron of Bir-el-Malha. I can recommend both.'

'Natron!' reflected Tuke. Recalling that the mummies of Pharoahs
were pickled in such an ingredient, he took a pinch of the Turkish
mixture, which was dark and very aromatic. 'Most subtle, indeed,
sir! But I fear you will find difficulty in getting fresh supplies.'

'I have brought quite a liberal provision,' said the other easily,
dusting his fingers, 'and a member of our mission has also imported
a considerable consignment as a commercial venture.'

Mr. Tuke, who in moments of self-abasement confessed himself
the most inquisitive man in the country, remarked the words 'our
mission' with intense curiosity. He was not a reader of the news-
papers, and they meant nothing to him. He realized, however, that
the time was yet hardly ripe for him to venture upon inquiry, and
so embarked upon a close cross-examination of his new acquaintance
on the subject of Morocco generally, until the punch arrived.

'You ask what the position is today, sir?' said the pasha, watching
him ladle out a very pleasant-seeming beverage. 'That's easily told.
Almost perpetual civil war. The royal brothers of Morocco have
been engaged for the past ten years in cutting one another's throats.
When they have not done so, then their father or uncles have done
it for them.'

'Father!' commented Tuke reflectively.

'From what I've heard tell, family hatred, sir, does not appear to be confined to Africa.'

'It is not indeed. There's a royal father not so very many miles away—t'ch-t'ch—who, I'll sweer, would give his right hand to be able to indulge in a little throat-cutting. These Hanoverians—'

Tuke did not conclude the sentence, but once again signified his attachment to the exiled Stuarts by raising his glass, passing it over a small jug of water on the table, and drinking in silence to 'the King-over-the-water.'

The two-tailed pasha was spared any possible embarrassment, for at that moment a near-by church clock sonorously struck the hour. With an exclamation in a strange tongue, and then an apology, he took a handsome gold watch from his pocket and confirmed the announcement, with an appearance of some disquiet.

He opened a traveller's pocket-size book of road-maps lying on the table before him, and followed the spidery line of a highway across its pages with his forefinger. Mr. Tuke remarked once more how long and lean and brown was the hand, which was set off at the wrist by a ruffle of white lawn.

'I had not realized what o'clock it was,' said the general in explanation. 'My companions are over two hours late at the rendezvous here. I came ahead of them to make various arrangements. I'ld return now and look for 'em, but there are alternative routes from our last halt. When I left, it had not been decided which they should take. It depended on the weather and the state of the roads.'

'The highways in this country are notoriously—t'ch-t'ch—among the worst in Britain,' confessed Mr. Tuke. 'On the other hand, generally speaking, there is little to fear from footpads and highwaymen.'

'It 'ould be a desperate fellow, indeed, who tried to hold up our convoy,' commented the general grimly. 'There are five carriages in it, and a considerable number of armed servants in attendance.'

A passion of curiosity about this mission, for which a two-tailed pasha acted as advance-guard, burned fiercely within Mr. Tuke's breast. It was only by a great effort of will-power that he restrained himself to the comment—

'A very sizable caravan! Pray let me help you to another glass of punch, and let us drink to its easy passage!' . . . And diverged into other matters.

And so whilst his excellency awaited the arrival of his mysterious companions, he allowed himself to be led on to talk of dancing dervishes and the Cairene dance-girls; of the Grand Signior and his ladies; of his own insigne of rank on state occasions—a crescent-surmounted lance adorned with two horsetails; of bakers' shops in Constantinople decorated with the ears of their owners; of the imperial palace at Meknes—the Versailles of Morocco—where there was stabling for a thousand horses; of the secret worship of Venus by the Ansariés of Keftin and Martrawan.

Even when the pasha embarked—as delicately as possible—on explanation of some of the very peculiar rites of this race, Mr. Tuke made no attempt to assume his wig, the insigne of his priestly office. He sat, open-mouthed, nodding his head all the time so that the red tassel of his nightcap was never still. He looked—Tierce thought—like a rather innocent pirate.

'From all you have seen and done,' he commented at length in an interlude in cross-examination, 'I gather it must be a very long time since you were last in this country.'

'I have never set foot in it before.'

'But—'

'Sir, I am not English,' said the pasha, evincing no regret at that fact. 'My father was Irish, my mother a Scotswoman, and I was born in Virginia. I suppose you would call me an American.'

With his head a little to one side, like a puzzled dog, Mr. Tuke contemplated this remarkable hybrid for a few seconds of silent amazement.

If he had never met a two-tailed pasha before, neither had he ever to his knowledge clapped eyes upon an American. What in the name of Old Gooseberry could such a hybrid want in Crosse?

But the general obviously considered that it was his turn now to be given information, and Mr. Tuke found himself embarked upon explanation of the recent regrettable development of Crosse—on the outskirts of which the Maid's Head was situated—from sleepy market town to fashionable spa.

'It was old Preece's doing—father of the present landlord,' he concluded.

'It was he who first discovered all the virtues in the world in the filthy well in Pagan Street. T'ch-t'ch. I wouldn't wash even my feet in the fluid. The old man made a large fortune. I can remember the Maid's Head when it was half its present size. Just look at that assembly room he built!'

Both gentlemen turned and surveyed the inn on the other side of the road; a long flat-fronted building of wine-red brick, with rows of glittering windows and a magnificent signboard, depicting a smug young woman wearing a crown, over its hospitably wide-open front door.

From an archway leading presumably to the stables, some hundred yards or so away, a small gentleman in a green coat appeared at that moment, closely followed by two companions. He carried over his shoulder an implement which to Tierce's eyes seemed to be a clumsy imitation of a scimitar made of wood.

'A cricketer!' exclaimed Mr. Tuke with surprise. 'Now I have heered of no match today. How can that be? Who can be playing? I wonder what the stakes are?'

But the game of cricket was obviously a closed book to a gentleman whose lifework had lain in the art of war in Turkey, Morocco, and Dar-Fûr. Realizing this, Mr. Tuke returned his regard to the inn—

'One of the largest in the country, sir,' he proclaimed rather proudly. 'They have accommodation—t'ch-t'ch—for fifty visitors and their servants. The cooking is excellent. T'ch-t'ch.'

Tierce had by now realized that his companion's t'ch-t'ch-ing was not indicative of any emotion, but had an involuntary nervous or physical cause. It sounded rather like a tiny escape of steam from something such as Mr. Newcomen's patent atmospheric engine.

'Preece has imagination—for an innkeeper. For example, he always mixes his mustard with sherry instead of water. Not merely is it an improvement in flavour, but, he assures me, more digestible.'

'We should not consider it a large establishment in Turkey,' said the general with a twinkling eye. 'I know personally of one caravanserai, at Burgas on the Black Sea, where a thousand travellers and their cattle can be put up!'

'The Gooseberry you do!' exclaimed Mr. Tuke.

'Aye,' affirmed the general. 'That is perfectly true. And I have also taken coffee at a coffeehouse in Damascus where a similar number of customers can be served at the same time. Possibly a little rough, of course, for European tastes, but—'

Susie paused from her duties in the taproom to step out of the doorway and survey the world.

Three gentlemen were walking towards her from the direction of the stables, one of them—dressed in green—carrying a cricket bat on his shoulder. She found them very unimposing compared with the tall dark stranger who Mr. Williams, his groom, said was a great general in foreign service. He and Mr. Tuke were still sitting in the shade of the chestnuts on the grass verge across the road. Both of them had turned and were idly scanning the façade of the inn.

When she had brought out the punch to them, the stranger had presented her with a big silver coin covered with writing that looked like the sort of tangle into which a ball of wool spread if the kitten played with it. He said it was a piece of goodness-knew-what. It would make a very nice brooch: perhaps Joe might be brought to do something in the matter!

Mr. Williams said that the gentleman was called 'Lord' and 'Excellency' in Turkey, and lived in a fine palace with forty servants. Mr. Williams said that, though a man could have several wives in Turkey, the gentleman was a bachelor. Mr. Williams said that *he* was a bachelor, too; but she was more than a little doubtful about his veracity.

She had got thus far in her reflections, when, far away and sweet, she suddenly heard the call of a hunting horn. Mr. Tuke also heard it, for he turned his red-nightcapped head sharply in the direction from which the music came, and was quite clearly listening with an expression of surprise.

The gentleman in green with the cricket bat heard it too, for he came to a full stop, and said something to his companions. Then all three of them looked back.

An instant or so later the quick drumming of hoofs at the gallop sounded in the distance along the main road to the town; approached rapidly. Then a man on a white horse flashed before her across the background of valley and smoke-coloured mountains and shimmering sky.

The foreign gentleman gave a sudden loud exclamation and

sprang to his feet. He raised a silver whistle to his lips; but before ever he blew it, with a scufflle and clatter, the rider swung his horse round on its haunches and rode back to the little pleasance in front of the inn.

The man was a young Negro in a blue livery with golden shoulderknots . . . Susie, who had never in her life set eyes upon a coloured person, was unable to suppress a small squeak of excitement . . . The youth dropped his reins on the horse's neck and leaped to the ground, bowing very low from the waist to the general.

He spoke—and rapidly—in a foreign language, spreading abroad his pink-palmed hands deprecatorily as he did so. Whatever he said, it was clear to both spectators that the news was most disconcerting to his superior, who snapped out two or three abrupt questions before dismissing him to the stables with his horse.

Mr. Tuke rose. He said:

'I fear, sir, that something has gone wrong with your plans. If I can be of assistance to you in any way, pray command my services!'

'A rather perplexing situation has arisen, Mr. Tuke. I should be grateful if I may call upon your moral support if necessary. You may, indeed, hear the perplexity approaching at this moment!'

'Moral support!' echoed Tuke.

With astonishing celerity he doffed the nightcap and assumed the round wig; even more than this—he whipped off his neckerchief and from some part of his person produced white clerical bands which he fixed at his throat with great speed.

As he did so, he became aware of rapidly nearing uproar—the clatter of many hoofs, a babble of cheerful voices, loud laughter, stray notes of a horn, cracking whips, baying of dogs and the noise of wheels. He realized, too, that the fellow in green with the cricket bat had disappeared from view—had vanished like a rabbit down its burrow.

Now suitably attired to lend the support of the church, he cast a glance at his companion. Tierce with an uncommonly grim expression bowed acknowledgment of his courtesy.

'I think, sir,' said he, 'that I shall best receive the arrivals at the door. I am afraid that I must defer an explanation for the moment. In any case, I, myself, am somewhat in the dark . . . Pardon me, sir!'

He put on a three-cornered hat bound with silver galloon, and, hand on sword hilt, stalked with jingling spurs to the semicircular flight of shallow steps that led up to the wide entrance of the inn. Tuke followed, admiring the cut and sleek polish of his immaculate riding-boots.

By Old Gooseberry, a very distinguished-looking fellow; but why—

They had barely reached the steps when, amid a hurricane of noise, a considerable cavalcade swept into sight along the tree-lined road towards inn and town. The disorderly procession was headed by a canary-coloured travelling-carriage drawn by six grey horses, the postilions on the broad grin. A very large, very young gentleman, hatless and in a gala dress of violet embroidered with silver rode by the door, and a cloud of boisterous young gentlemen—gay as a flower bed, in coats of every conceivable hue—followed.

'God!' exclaimed Excellency. 'What is this damned menagerie?'

'I opine, t'ch-t'ch, that the Duchess of Winterset's ball is merely ending in its usual disorder,' said Mr. Tuke, recognizing the flushed faces of a number of youthful acquaintances.

'At noon the next day?'

Before Tuke could reply, the high carriage—gaudy with gilding and heraldic blazonment—had swayed to a standstill before the inn. The lumpish youth in violet immediately vaulted from the saddle and made for the door, leaving his horse to its own devices. But Tierce was already there, his fingers closing over the silver-plated handle.

'By your leave, sir!' peremptorily cried the large lad in violet, pushing forward in a very determined manner.

'Without yours,' snarled Tierce. 'Stand aside, sir!'

He flung wide the door, forcing back the other, who all but lost his balance and staggered against a dusty wheel. The general remained squarely before the opening, holding the door with one hand, whilst he bowed very deeply to whosoever it was within.

He spoke quietly in an unrecognizable language and was answered by a woman's voice—a silvery voice in which Mr. Tuke thought to detect a note of anger.

He spoke again; was answered; and then a tall figure, swathed from head to foot in a long, hooded mantle of fine, ivory-coloured wool, appeared in the opening; rested slim, orange-tipped fingers upon his extended hand, and stepped lightly down. Her face was veiled by a muslin yashmak so that all that was visible of her was a pair of bright grey eyes.

By the Great Gooseberry, an odalisque! thought Tuke, being considerably disconcerted. The man has brought his seraglio with him!

# III

## *Affair of the Veiled Lady*

Mr. Tuke was, however, permitted no time for reflection upon the problem of a clergyman's correct behaviour when confronted by the inmate of an eastern seraglio. His hand was indeed forced, for his new acquaintance—the lady's finger-tips resting lightly upon his own —abruptly turned towards him and said:

'May I ask you, sir, to conduct this lady to a private room? I perceive that I am likely to be detained. The landlord is acquainted with my name, and her companions should arrive at any moment.'

There was nothing for it, therefore, but to make a polite bow and diffidently present his arm. What would not his neighbours say— particularly old Captain Tregallion—if they were to see him squiring an odalisque, a harem lady delicately perfumed with—sandalwood, was it?

He felt the lightest possible pressure upon his sleeve, and proceeded to lead the way to the door, conscious that the red cotton nightcap was trailing from the pocket of his baggy coat, and that his high gaiters were masked with mud.

24

The whole business of whisking away the new arrival took but a matter of seconds. The pasha now turned the glacial regard of his strange blue eyes upon the throng which was assembling about the steps and by the carriage, and had been momentarily surprised into silence by this unlooked-for development.

There were about a dozen of them, mainly young men, some very young, and most of them flushed with drink. They were all attired in the extreme height of the mode, although equestrian exercise had played the very devil with the set of curled and powdered wigs, and with the embroidered coats, silken breeches, and clocked stockings of high occasion. In varying degrees their faces expressed the mutinous discontent of children interrupted in their revels. It was as children that they would have to be dealt with, Tierce supposed.

A babble of angry protest immediately broke out. Someone dug him sharply in the ribs. Tierce swung about.

The violet-coated gentleman stood in front of the yellow panels of the coach, plainly in a towering rage. The left side of his dress was covered with dirt where it had been swept against the high rear wheel. He was even younger than Tierce had first thought—merely a boy, but a corpulent, unprepossessing boy with a scowling, arrogant face.

'Demme, sir, d'you know who I am, sir?' demanded the fat boy, tapping himself on the left breast where glittered the great star of a chivalric order. 'Tell him, someone! Demme, sir, I'm not a teetotum! Most ungentlemanly conduct! An explanation, if you please!'

'I require one, myself, sir,' said Tierce with savage contempt; remarked a sudden faint blurring of the angry expression on the other's face, and turned to the crowd, raising his voice: 'Perhaps someone will explain to me why this lady has been brought here without her companions and in these very peculiar circumstances?'

'Ask the girl!' cried a voice at the back.

'Ungemunly conduck!' complained Violet-Coat behind him in a more subdued tone.

Tierce said unpleasantly—'I am still waiting!'

An older man with miniature features set in a lard-coloured face —which was pitted all over by smallpox so that it resembled the wax of a honeycomb—and splendid in a pale green coat with cut steel buttons, demanded:

'And what in hell business is it of yours?'

'The lady happens to be in my charge.'

'Ungellemly—ungentlenamy—ungelemonly—' grumbled the large lad, who now appeared to have forgotten his complaint in preoccupation in the search for an elusive word.

'In your charge! Oh!' commented the lard-faced man in a knowing tone. It was clear that he would have elaborated on the subject, had not a neighbour put a restraining hand upon his arm. After an instant's pause, he added: 'And how are we to know that, curse me?'

'Even if I were acquainted with your name, your rank, or—your reputation, I should refuse to admit your right to ask any questions of me. Let it be enough for you that I say I *am* responsible for the lady. I am still awaiting an explanation. I *demand* an explanation.'

A certain shuffling unease now began to manifest itself among the revellers. Two or three of them muttered awkwardly together; one even shouldered his way out of the throng, nonchalantly sauntered off, and took his horse from a groom standing in the mob of servants that had gathered a short distance away.

'No harm has come to her, and no harm was intended,' said the lard-faced man sullenly.

'You are still not telling me why she was abducted.'

'Abducted be damned! Oh, God, she came with us of her own accord!'

'What are you telling me?' exclaimed Tierce, taking a half-step forward.

'Ungentlellelly!' commented the fat boy in an absent-minded tone, and sat down, and forthwith rolled under the carriage wheels.

'God! Billy's down!' cried someone.

Amid immense confusion the recumbent figure was hauled out of danger by its large elegant legs—silk-stockinged legs ending in pink-heeled shoes—and removed by two of its companions to the safety of the bench under the chestnut-tree.

'Send your damned waggon off, Winterset,' said the lard-faced man to a lad with a rose-coloured coat and the chubby face of a choirboy. 'There's no blasted reason why your infernal postilions should listen to every damned word that's spewed out, curse me!'

With an oath the youngster dismissed his carriage. As it moved away the older man returned his attention to Tierce, who stood rigidly waiting during the interruption.

'I said to you'—and he emphasized each word he spoke by stabbing into the air with a forefinger—'that she came with us of her own accord. Now give me the lie and be done with it!'

'In that case she came with you under a misapprehension. It is impossible that she should have left her companions intentionally behind.'

'You—' began the other fiercely; and was again restrained by his neighbour.

'For God's sake, my Lord!' he pleaded. 'This must not go on! An explanation is undoubtedly due. Let me make it!'

My Lord meditated uncertainly for a few instants. He carried his head a little sunk, and thrust forward from his wide, square shoulders, so that as he swung his regard from one to other of the group he resembled some beast of prey considering attack.

'Dunscore, you and I—' the would-be mediator started a fresh plea.

'Very well,' said my Lord at length. 'Have your say!' And thereupon he relaxed as quickly and completely as might any creature of the wild.

The spokesman was tall and slim, with an eager, Italianate face that was a trifle too good-looking and a trifle too poetical for Javan's taste; but he was obviously by far the most sober of the crew.

'I am, sir, John Standring of Doveton,' said he, in introduction, addressing the general. 'Is it permitted to inquire to whom I am speaking?'

'I am Javan Tierce, a general officer in the Ottoman service.'

'Ottoman?' echoed Mr. Standring, somewhat perplexed.

'The imperial Turkish army, sir.'

'Turkish!' exclaimed Standring in almost a tone of stupefaction.

A momentary expression that flitted across his handsome features suggested a mental inquiry why Tierce was not arrayed with the curved scimitar, high cap, baggy trousers, and red boots of a Turkish cavalryman. Then immediately afterwards his whole face lightened as though some problem had been solved.

'Turkish!' said Mr. Standring again. 'My God, that explains it! It has been a deplorable mistake. They—we—took your—lady to be a member of a—forgive me!—travelling company.'

'Travelling company!' repeated Tierce in considerable astonishment, and studied the face before him. 'In the name of the All-Merciful, a travelling company of what?'

'Strolling actors, sir! . . . Again forgive me! . . . Mummers—jugglers—mountebanks—dancers—merry-andrews—tightrope walkers. You *must* know, sir!'

'I don't,' said Tierce. 'I have never been in England before.'

'Never in England?'

'I am not an Englishman.' This time the tone suggested deep thankfulness.

'Well, sir, they walk from town to town, giving performances *en route*. Many of them are foreigners, and they often march with their make-up on and in their gaudy stage dresses.'

'But why should anyone think that this lady was one of them? Did not the gentleman who was with her explain?'

'I will tell you, sir, quite honestly what happened. I will then offer the humblest apologies. For myself. For my friends.'

Standring had raised his voice above conversational level, and looked round as he spoke, gathering nods and murmurs of agreement from his fellow revellers with the single exception of Lord Dunscore.

'Well?'

'After the ball—after cards and dice until noon—we decided to set out on a frolic. None of us, you know, had been to bed and none of us had breakfasted. So we were going to breakfast at the Maid's Head on salmon fry and cherry bounce, and afterwards watch the cricket in the Three Oaks meadow—there's been some pretty heavy wagering on the match. Most of us, sir, you may realize, were more than a little lushy—'

'I deny that,' interjected Dunscore.

'You were as corned as anyone!' protested Standring half apologetically. 'Pray let me continue to explain, my lord! . . . Well, when we turned into the highway from Winterset's place, there they were —three of them—walking just a little ahead along the road to Crosse.

'The first we overtook was a vast jelly of a coffee-coloured man. In a dark blue petticoat with a white turban on the top of his head. I'll swear he was the biggest and fattest creature I've ever clapped eyes on. Then, a bit in front of him, there was the lady, all in white, like a nun, with a veil over her face. Accompanying her was a queer little fellow wearing a wig that was twenty years out of date, and a black velvet coat that was thirty years out of date, and a hat that Noah might have worn in the Ark.' . . . Tierce inwardly cursed the antiquated little curio who had been sent from London by the government to greet them on their arrival in England. . . . 'Sir,' continued Mr. Standring earnestly, 'you must admit that they were an odd trio to find walking along an English road on a summer day! Admit it now!'

'I am prepared to admit that you might find the circumstances rather more bizarre than they would appear to me. But were you not informed that a carriage was close behind—and servants?'

'I recall now that the man in the wig—who seemed confoundedly flustered—said something about one. He also said something about a wagon having broken down. I—we—imagined then that it was the cart in which their equipment was carried. But there wasn't a wheel or a hoof or anyone else in sight at the time.'

Tierce shook his head as though he were a schoolmaster mourning over the crass stupidity of his form.

'The facts are very simple. A heavily loaded wagon—an eight-wheel affair—had broken down, completely blocking the road. This lady—a foreign lady of distinction—decided to walk on with an escort and an attendant until the obstruction should be removed so that her carriage could pass. And what happens in this civilized, eighteenth-century England of yours? She is grossly insulted by a posse of drunken roisterers in broad daylight. She is treated as though she were a romping pothouse wench. What have you to say?'

The other reddened from a consciousness of misbehaviour—Tierce realized—rather than from resentment at his language. He said very earnestly:

'I deeply deplore our lack of perspicacity, sir. The appalling fact remains that we did indeed take them for strolling players of a sort. . . . Well, when we saw them everybody stopped, and someone asked where they were going. The man with a wig—'

'He is the Honourable John Gellibrand, of the Secretary of State's department.'

Mr. Standring was manifestly taken aback by this announcement. There was a pause whilst he digested it, before he continued—

'Mr. Gellibrand replied: "To the Maid's Head." We'd got the Duke of Winterset's coach with us—God alone knows why, unless to pick up any of us who fell by the wayside!—so we offered to take them in it as far as the inn. The man refused at once, but the lady—who seemed to have understood what was going on—disagreed, and

they argued for some moments in a language I didn't understand
. . . There was a good deal of confusion at the time—our horses
were fresh and restless—and I was not in front. The next thing I saw
was the lady walking to the carriage and getting in. There was no
question whatever of any force being used, upon my honour.'

'It did not occur to you that she was making the best of a bad
business?'

'And then Little Billy pulled back the fellow with the wig just as
he was about to get in after her,' said the lad in a rose-coloured coat
maliciously. 'And then he himself tried to get in, and she pushed him
out, and then someone gave the word "Go" to the postboys. So
away they went! And away we all went, too!'

'Shut your trap, you fool!' exclaimed Dunscore fiercely.

The general ignored the interruption. He addressed Standring—

'But what was the purpose of this extraordinary exploit? For it
must have had a purpose.'

'I think that the idea was to persuade her to preside at our *con-
vivium* here,' admitted Mr. Standring slowly.

'Little Billy swore—'

'I should be greatly obliged, sir,' said Tierce to the dissipated
choirboy in rose, if you would refrain from interjecting remarks
about "Little Billy," whoever he may be. I shall doubtless discover
in due course if there is any reason why I should demand any particular explanation from him or any other gentleman.'

'In God's name, sir!' protested Standring, and fumbled with an
uneasy hand at the fine lace of his cravat, at the embroidery of his
grey brocade coat, at a silver button.

'The matter is considerably more serious than you might suppose.'

'It is also,' replied Standring, 'more serious than *you* might suppose!'

The two men remained silent for a moment, exchanging a long
direct glance. The little throng about them fell silent, too. The only
sounds were made by the restless horses, held at a discreet distance
by the waiting servants, and by the fat boy in violet who was being
violently sick on the bench under the trees. Even as Tierce, who was
a head taller than the rest, took note of this fact, he perceived the
small cricketer in green approaching the group by the chestnuts.

Dunscore had been looking at his watch with every sign of impatience. He now exclaimed:

'For Christ's sake don't stand there all day in a stupor, Mr. Standring! We shall have the Griffe here any minute now, and then the fat will be in the fire with a vengeance.'

'He wouldn't take any advantage of a thing like this, my Lord. Even you must say that for him.'

Dunscore gave a noncommittal grunt; and Standring turned to Tierce—

'Cannot we speak somewhere in private?'

'I can procure a room here,' answered Tierce, 'but you will perhaps arrange that these gentlemen do not disperse about their pastimes until we have reached an agreement.'

'You'll see to that, my Lord?'

Dunscore nodded at the same time as a fruity voice insinuated in Tierce's ear—

'The rooms that your Excellency has engaged have all been made ready for your Excellency. For a small personal conference I should recommend the "All's Well" to your Excellency!'

Mr. Preece, the landlord, a little man with the fluid pale face of an actor and a coat which might have been a theatrical property, stood just above him on the broad flagstones on the porch, bowing at each mention of the title 'Excellency.' Having once upon a time trodden the boards in minor roles, he permitted himself to display to the world his interest in the stage by naming the private sitting rooms of his inn by the titles of his favourite Shakespearean comedies, instead of—as was the custom of the day—after heraldic devices, monarchs, or popular admirals.

Accordingly the words 'All's Well That Ends Well' were painted in bold characters on the door of the room in which, a few moments later, the two men confronted each other—a small pale blue wainscoted room with a single tall window looking out upon a rose garden and a green bay tree stippled with blossom.

Standring made certain that the door was fast shut, and then said without preamble in an almost desperate manner:

'I throw myself entirely upon your mercy, general. In the name of God, don't let us have any scandal!'

'For the lady's sake?' inquired Tierce with irony, and sat down at the small round table in the centre of the room, and reflectively contemplated his riding-boots.

The younger man also dropped to a chair—wearily. He said—wearily:

'I put my cards on the table. As a stranger to the country you would be unlikely to recognize his Majesty's second son, the Duke of Cumberland. The—our—conduct was inexcusable, but you will realize why there *must* be no more trouble, don't you?'

' "Little Billy," the fat boy?'

'Yes. And he *is* only a boy, sir. And a very young boy!'

'But he is man-size and apparently old enough to wear the insignia of some high order!'

'Nevertheless he is extremely young.'

'You suggest that he is not old enough to give the satisfaction of a gentleman? I infer then that you consider that a birching of the royal posterior would meet the occasion!'

'I know that I am speaking for my companions as well as for myself when I present to you, as the lady's representative, our humblest and most abject apologies for what has happened, and beg that she will be pleased to accept them. All we ask is that his Royal Highness be not brought into the affair.'

Tierce delayed his reply. He shifted his regard from his own boots to Mr. Standring's nether man: noted that satin breeches, silk stockings, and lacquered shoes were pale shadows of the glory that they must have been the night before.

'So I see "why there *must* be no more trouble," do I?' he commented at length. 'Are princes then—however young—in this highly civilized western world above the ordinary code of honour and decent behaviour?'

Standring said nothing, but continued to look pathetically at him.

'It is quite clear that your "Little Billy" was principally responsible for the lady being abducted . . . One of your people said so . . . I presume that it was he also who tried to wrest the veil from her face. An unpardonable insult.'

'I swear, 'pon honour, that I know nothing about it.'

'The incident occurred. The lady is my informant.'

'Damn the fool!'

Tierce considered the matter. He felt in a pocket of his long waistcoat and produced a snuffbox: put it back again: felt in the other pocket: repeated the operation: disengaged his sword from the skirts of his coat and laid it across his knees. Mr. Standring noted that the scabbard was of morocco leather of precisely the same shade of blue as his coat.

'Well,' said Tierce, 'there is nothing for it, sir. The prince is too drunk and too royal to apologize, and too young and too royal to give the satisfaction of a gentleman. I have no alternative but to call out the rest of you in turn—in your case, Mr. Standring, with regret.'

Standring rose to his feet without protest; he recognized the inevitable.

Said Tierce, contemplating his sword:

'It is, perhaps, only fair for me to add, sir, that the consequences will not stop there, either; and they will be very serious consequences, indeed. Your drunken, fat prince may be sobered by the reflection that the royal papa will indubitably have something to say about it, I can swear, when Mr. Gellibrand makes his report. It is possible he will think that his little pet has been led astray by evil companions.'

'Good God!' exclaimed Standring, aghast.

At that moment the latch behind him rattled, and, as both men turned about, the door was gently opened and a nose came poking round the panels. It was a pug nose so very large that the flabby face—which also like a pug-dog's—was a mere dependency upon it. Even the semicircular eyebrows seemed to exist as a garnishment for the nose rather than as auxiliaries to the little round grey eyes beneath them.

'We are engaged, Mr. Dodington,' said Standring stiffly.

'I know, I know. I do apologize, I am sure,' said the Nose. 'I would not intrude for the world, but Dunscore asked me to let you know, Mr. Standring, that—er—that—the Griffe is here. He said that he proposed to leave everything to you. Desolated to have interrupted. Desolated. A million pardons!'

With each expression of regret Nose gave a little peck in the air, which was presumably indicative of the fact that the rest of him was dipping in a bow. Having made his three pecks, Nose popped out of sight, and the door was closed as gently as though it were the door of a sickroom.

'The—Griffe!' said Standring thoughtfully. 'The Griffe! Perhaps—May I plead for ten minutes' grace, your Excellency, whilst I consult with my friends?'

'Very good, sir,' said Tierce, rising. 'I will give you ten minutes. If you are not here by then, I shall understand that you are leaving a list of names, folded and sealed, with the landlord for the attention of my second.'

He drew a gold watch from his fob, and presented the dial to the other's view.

# IV

# *Affair of an Unveiled Lady*

THE 'AS YOU LIKE IT' was the largest private room at the Maid's Head and New Wells Inn. Its white panelled walls had yellowed with time to the colour of old ivory, and were hung with dim and rather crude oil paintings of sleek horses, fat cattle, and sporting dogs as well as a mezzotint of Kitty Clive as Rosalind in the comedy after which it was named.

At one end, facing the window embrasure, was a big sideboard, crowded with a hugger-mugger of toast-racks, urns, salvers, wine-coolers, and the like. There was a well-worn red Turkey carpet on the floor, and a platoon of chairs, upholstered in crimson, was ranked about the dining-table. It was altogether the sort of room in which, the day's sport done, the local gentry could loll, did loll, and would continue to loll, with outstretched legs in noisy talk after dinner, over bowl and bottle.

It was an odd setting, reflected Mr. Tuke, for an odalisque.

Her slim form shrouded by the ivory-coloured mantle, her hair hidden by the hood, and her face—but for the grey, long-lashed eyes

—invisible behind the white muslin veil, she sat demurely on the window-seat at the far end of the room, her hands folded on her lap, the immense stones in her rings burning with blue and green fire in the sunshine.

Knowing no living language but his own, he had not essayed any conversation; had led her in silence to her seat, and then returned to post himself before the door—an ecclesiastical angel at the entrance to a Mahometan Eden.

What would his sister, Catherine, say when she learned that Brother Abel had been acting as doorkeeper to an odalisque? Although she was an elderly maiden lady with a frosty nose and hands the pale mauve of primrose-stalks, yet she had on occasion a pretty Rabelaisian mind. It was inconceivable that she would fail to recall that such officials of the harem were invariably eunuchs. Without question she would have some pertinent comments to proffer. At this juncture he realized with dismay that the door of one of the side-cupboards in the buffet was wide open, revealing a remarkable array of a variety of chamber-pots, kept there—as was the custom of the day—for the convenience of winebibbers. The odalisque could hardly fail—

There came a sharp rap on the panels at his back. He opened cautiously and looked out.

Tierce Pasha stood outside, accompanied by two men whom he had never seen before.

One of them was a large, fat-faced youth in a violet satin coat stiff with silver embroidery, wearing the great badge of the order of the Garter upon his left breast. The shoulders of his gorgeous coat were soaking-wet, and his lace cravat was a mere damp rag from which water still trickled on to his green and silver waistcoat. It looked to Tuke as though his wig might have been doffed and his head soused in a horse trough, or put under the pump—as had indeed been the case.

The other stranger was an extremely elegant little man in olive-green, of rather oriental mien—for he had a hooked nose that drooped at the tip, a yellow complexion, very full lips, and round grey eyes, which reminded Tuke for some reason of a cat's. Despite his unprepossessing appearance, however, he had a not unpleasant, slightly melancholy expression.

'I am much indebted to you for your courtesy, Mr. Tuke,' said Tierce, after he had bowed low to the lady and ushered in his companions with whom he remained halted by the door. 'May I now call on you for another small service—as a neutral witness of an act of reparation? You will, of course, treat the matter as confidential in the highest degree.'

Tuke acknowledged the injunction with a bow.

'His Royal Highness the Duke of Cumberland is about to express his own regret and that of his companions for a regrettable lapse in good manners towards'—Tierce paused for a suspenseful second—'her Imperial Majesty, the Empress Shems-ed-Douha, consort of the Emperor Mulai Ali of Morocco. I regret, Mr. Tuke, that obvious circumstances prevented me from presenting you to her before. I should add that she desires merely to be known as the Princess Shems-ed-Douha whilst she is in England.'

Excellency then said something in what was presumably Arabic ending with the word 'Tuke.'

Mr. Tuke bowed deeply.

Excellency said something ending with the word 'Griffe,' whereat the ugly little gentleman in olive-green bowed even more deeply.

In spite of the wild confusion in his mind as he made his reverence, Mr. Tuke noted a slight narrowing of the grey eyes that regarded him, as though the Empress-Princess were smiling because she had read something of his thoughts. She inclined her head in acknowledgment of the salutes.

The expression of sullen resentment in the fat boy's face—like that of a child who considers his punishment unduly severe—had become one of utter consternation when Tierce addressed him again.

'I ought to inform you,' said Excellency in a rather lofty and pedagogic tone of explanation, 'that a special mission arrived in this country from Morocco with the Princess. The ambassadors are now on their way to London for negotiations over the renewal of a treaty signed in the time of King George the First. If this affair gets noised abroad, what d'you think will happen to those negotiations, may I ask?'

The royal examinee was unable to answer this question. He glanced round at his olive-green companion, presumably for prompting. But Mr. Griffe, whose air was one of respectful attention and surprise, proffered no advice; he obviously looked upon himself as no more implicated in the affair than was Tuke.

Tierce went on:

'It may be news to you that your father's government pays very large sums of money every year to Morocco and the other Barbary states to ensure the safety of his ships and cargoes from the pirates of Sallee and elsewhere. If the negotiations are broken off, British shipowners will have you to thank for their losses.' He paused for a few seconds to let this sink in and added, 'You will realize now, Mr. Griffe, that I was very much in earnest when I spoke—as I told you— to Mr. Standring of the possibility of "serious consequences."'

Mr. Griffe bowed.

The Duke's jaw dropped, and his unpleasant face, blotched from the night's dissipation, was glistening with sweat as though it had been oiled.

Tierce permitted himself to survey the portraits of Miss Clive, a fat bull, and a pointer at work in the stubble, before he turned his regard upon the royal culprit with an expression which seemed to imply that he found him a considerably less pleasant object to view.

'I am certain, sir,' he remarked icily, 'that your father would not fail to reprobate your conduct, both on the grounds of ill manners and of policy.'

On this score William Augustus, Duke of Cumberland, had no doubts at all. Although he was his father's favourite—as well as his mother's pet—there were many occasions when he, like the rest of the family, trembled before that small, fiery-tempered tyrant. He shot another swift, sidelong glance at the rather Hebraic countenance of Mr. Griffe. It was quite expressionless . . . Of all witnesses of his humiliation, Griffe was the last one that he desired.

Tierce surveyed the horrified boy for a moment with patently sardonic appreciation of his discomfort. Then he approached the upright figure seated composedly in the sunlit window-place, and spoke to her in Arabic. She answered him in a low voice, and after a brief interchange, Tierce beckoned to the Duke to approach.

'The Princess is prepared to accept an apology,' he said. 'She is also prepared to forget the incident, and to instruct Mr. Gellibrand

and her entourage to forget it. They *will* forget it. I suggest—for
your own sake—that when you leave this room you also forget what
I have told you of the identity of the personage whom you have
offended. I suggest—again for your own sake—that none—not one—
of your companions shall be told of her quality, if you wish to avoid
lamentable consequences. If any questions are asked, you must say
that the person concerned was one of her Highness's women attendants—one of the Harriffa. You will remember the word "Harriffa"? It is important. Mr. Griffe—Mr. Tuke, may I beg your concurrence, if you please?'

'Harriffa!' repeated Mr. Griffe, as though to impress the word
upon his memory, and bowed from the waist in token of assent.

Tuke followed suit—with considerably less elegance.

It seemed to him, stealthily watching the Princess, that the faint
amusement in her eyes had been momentarily intensified. How old
was she? he wondered. He had thought that the long slim hands, glittering with diamonds, were the hands of a young woman, but now
they were withdrawn from view within her ivory-coloured mantle
so that he could not render considered judgment.

There was a brief ceremony of presentation. Tierce said in his
soft, drawling English: 'If you will address the Princess, sir, I will
translate.'

Mr. Tuke contemplated the violet back and differentially bowed
head of the royal fat boy; heard his stammer of excuse and apology
with an inward feeling of satisfaction that even Hanoverian princes
occasionally had to take their gruel. It was, indeed, a sad business
that he would only be able to impart a censored version of this story
to sister Catherine.

The princess said something in Arabic and extended a white, be-
jewelled hand. The Duke of Cumberland bowed over it: he took it
clumsily on his finger-tips; he bent to kiss it.

Mr. Tuke saw that other long white hand suddenly flash from
out of its hiding-place in the voluminous mantle, and heard the
hearty crack of the box-on-the-ear that it administered to the unsus-
pecting prince; saw and heard with an inward, unpitying mirth. In
such fashion might the young Queen Elizabeth have demonstrated
her active displeasure in the olden days. With so swift a movement
might a justly incensed cat dart out a velvet paw with unsheathed

talons, and then resume its composure. Tuke was interested to note that he felt that no dignity had been lost by the Princess in the delivery of the blow.

Cumberland started as though he had been spat upon. A hand flew to the stricken ear—was withdrawn. He glanced round, as if for instruction, to Griffe: then—in response to a gesture—with a crimson face, he bowed formally to a figure that now to all appearances might never have stirred, and backed, unescorted, somewhat unsteadily to the door.

'You may even venture to say, sir,' said Tierce, watching the retreat, 'that her Imperial Highness, having been informed of the incident, was pleased to find something ludicrous in it.'

Cumberland fumbled behind him for the handle: found it; paused on the threshold to bow yet once more: was gone.

Then suddenly the Princess-who-was-an-Empress rose to her feet —and, despite her voluminous robes, Tuke realized that she was slim as well as tall. She spoke in a clear, high voice to him and to Griffe who was standing beside him.

'I think I did that very well, didn't I?' she said. 'I was afraid that he was not going to come near enough, indeed. The apology was for an offended Princess: the blow was for an insulted woman.'

Tuke was so taken aback at being addressed in English that he was unable to make immediate reply. For the great lady, that figure from an eastern fairy-tale, had not even spoken with the accent and painstaking language of the foreigner, but in the English of a native of the island—and not merely that alone, but also with a trace of the lilting speech of western Wales.

Griffe was the first to answer; replied in an accent which missed being that of an Englishman only by reason of its perfection. His voice was singularly pleasant.

'That,' he averred, 'should complete the cure, madam, on top of the application of pump water, and a draught which the landlord assured me was infallible.'

'It served him very—t'ch-t'ch—right, madam,' Tuke managed to remark.

But did it? Was it possible, he asked himself, that he had been made a partaker in some appalling hoax played upon a prince, son of the *de facto* King of England? The face of Tierce, the pasha, was not, however, the face of one given to practical jokes, though even the sanest men were known to commit preposterous follies for a woman's sake. Suddenly he felt quite sure that the disconcerting eyes above the muslin veil were reading his thoughts with a certain malicious amusement. He also noted a wisp of a smile flicker across the tanned face silhouetted against the open window with its sunlit background of rose-garden and flowering bay tree.

It was then that the Princess broke into laughter—a rippling, silvery laugh, melodious as the song of a nightingale. She was a witch: she *had* read his mind!

Tierce said:

'During our very pleasant talk this morning, Mr. Tuke, you remarked that you preferred men to books. You said that your reason was that it was impossible to check the truth of the printed word, whilst anyone of intelligence could reasonably estimate the veracity of the person with whom he was talking. Veiled ladies are a rather different proposition, aren't they?'

There was more than a hint of amusement in the quiet voice. So Tierce, too, had penetrated his mind! Mr. Tuke produced an immense and rather snuffy handkerchief in which he buried his nose and his embarrassment. The Princess laughed again; and Tierce continued:

'Her Imperial Highness will, I know, condone your suspicions, sir. They are but natural. You have my word of honour, however, that here is no bam! With her permission, indeed, I will show you a letter from the Duke of Newcastle, the English Secretary of State, delivered on our arrival.'

His hand went to the pocket of that admirable blue coat.

'*Diw!*' said the Princess, 'it is not necessary, Javan, so far as Mr. Tuke is concerned. I have looked on him and seen that he is an understanding man. We'll let him exercise his judgment in the way he is used to.'

She raised her hands swiftly to her head as she spoke with a graceful, flowing movement . . . Tuke noticed that Tierce began a quick gesture as though of protest, and as quickly suppressed it . . . The next second the hood of the ivory-coloured mantle had fallen upon her shoulders, and the veil had disappeared.

'Well, and is this the face of an honest woman, would you say, Mr. Tuke?' she demanded.

After a short pause—

'With humble duty, ma'am, it is a face which, I would sweer, is as honest as it is beautiful. I must respectfully decline his Grace's letter.'

It was in truth a face full of beauty and eagerness and youth; rather wide across the temples and cheekbones, with a firm chin, and yet without heaviness. The nose was straight and short, the mouth well-shaped and not too small, the grey eyes singularly lovely, the braided tresses as dark and shining as the midnight sea.

Such ladies as she might have sat, in the days of legend, at the table of the High-King of Ireland in the Hall of Visitation on the hill of Tara.

When she had gathered all his tribute, the unspoken tribute of his regard as well as the spoken, she gave him a small, grave smile, and inclined her head to Tierce, standing respectfully at her side.

'I think, Javan,' she said, 'that Mr. Griffe is not so readily influenced as Mr. Tuke. Show him the letter!'

But the little man shook his head. A singularly charming smile transformed his ugly face.

'Would not an apology have been equally due, madam, if you had been a—a Harriffa, or even a washerwoman?'

'That is true,' said Shems-ed-Douha, 'but I still see no reason why Tierce Pasha should suggest that there is any resemblance between me and a woman of the Harriffa.'

'Nobody in this country,' protested Tierce, 'knows what the Harriffa are, madam. I doubt if anyone does outside Morocco. Have either of you ever heard of them, gentlemen?'

Mr. Tuke definitely had not. He attended explanation, his head a little to one side so that his best ear was foremost.

Mr. Griffe was equally ignorant.

'They are an Amazonian bodyguard in the imperial household— a sort of corps of women police. Ordinarily they are more remarkable for their physique than their looks. Kadijah of course is an exception. May I summon one for these gentlemen's benefit, madam?'

'Your manners are those of an Algerine, Javan,' said the Princess frigidly.

'That's as may be, madam, with all respect. The situation, however, is that if nobody knows what the Harriffa are, they can't refute
our story—if they wanted to. On the other hand if any report of the
incident were to reach Morocco, it would only cause infinite laughter at the idea of the infidels trying to abduct a singularly unglam-
orous policewoman. It would be a joke at which the Emperor himself would be the first to laugh. You've got to see that side of the
matter, madam. Actually, Kadijah looks about your build—at any
rate when she is wearing a haik.'

'Kadijah is *not* about my build,' said the Princess indignantly.
'You lie, Javan! You lie like an Abyssinian dog, you brute! You
do indeed!'

'So will Kadijah. We can be certain that she'll swear on the
Koran to anything your Imperial Highness chooses to tell her. And
that is all that matters.'

Mr. Tuke remained near the door, awkwardly rubbing one
muddy shoe against the other. It appeared to him that he was hearing matters which he had no business to hear; that Mr. Griffe and
he had been forgotten. He debated within himself: Had his hearing
deceived him, or had he really heard Highness pronounce the word
'indeed' with all the light singsong of the Welsh mountains?

Shems-ed-Douha turned again towards him . . . He wished, indeed, that someone had remembered to shut that indelicate door in
the sideboard! He would give Preece a piece of his mind about it
when he left . . . She addressed him directly, reverting to the
original subject of discussion—

'You cannot really tell me, Mr. Tuke, that you find anything more
peculiar in a Moroccan empress speaking English than in an English
king speaking German? I can indeed talk both Arabic and Berber
fluently, whilst on the other hand I am told that the late King had
no word of English at all!'

'Perhaps a word or two, madam,' suggested Mr. Griffe. 'But certainly not more. And the present King, with all due respect to his
Majesty, still has great difficulty with his *th*'s and his *w*'s.'

'You see, Mr. Tuke?'

'It is an open secret in this town, madam,' said Tuke, drawing
himself up and obviously feeling romantic despite muddied gaiters
and the red cotton nightcap peeking out of one of his coat pockets,

'that I for one—t'ch-t'ch, t'ch-t'ch—do not recognize that king.'

'A Jack, by God, madam!' commented Griffe, not in a tone of disapprobation, but of vast interest as though surveying for the first time an entirely new political species.

Whilst Tuke was turning over in his mind the question whether or no he cared for the term 'Jack' as description of a Jacobite, a follower of the exiled House of Stuart, Tierce said—

'My father was one. He fled the country over forty years ago.'

'You are a Hanoverian in a hornets' nest, Mr. Griffe, you see,' added the Princess. 'For *my* father, too, was a Jacobite. Yes, indeed!'

Did she say 'Yes'? Did she say 'Inteed'?

Mr. Griffe explained that he had little opportunity for engaging in politics, and that much of his spare time was devoted to literary pursuits, to music, to art.

The Princess looked at him with wide, smiling eyes.

'Those, surely, are not the usual activities of an English gentleman! I should very much like to hear more.' (Did she say 'fery'?) 'We must exchange our histories, I think.'

Tuke was aware that Tierce was regarding Imperial Highness with a quizzical expression of inquiry; but Shems-ed-Douha was moving across the room towards himself and Griffe, walking slowly with a graceful, slightly swaying carriage.

'I will not detain you any longer now. I hope, however, that you will give Tierce Pasha the pleasure of your company at dinner here next week. Shall we say Monday?' Then, *à propos de bottes* she added the surprising statement: 'I propose staying in the town for a time whilst I take the waters.'

Mr. Tuke was shaken out of his good manners.

'Stay in Crosse?' he gasped almost incredulously.

'Mayn't I?' inquired Shems-ed-Douha. 'It's only for a time.'

'Not at Old Palace by any chance?' said Tuke, and added, recollecting local gossip: 'I heered it was being got ready for some West Indian plantocrat.'

'It is being got ready for *me*,' said the Princess. 'You are quite at liberty to say so. But I should be glad if both you and Mr. Griffe just for the present would not mention the fact that you have seen and met me, or know anything whatever about me. You are dining, you recollect, with Tierce Pasha. Neither of you are to know that

I may possibly join you. By then I may have arranged my plans somewhat. By then I may have decided whether I shall be a secluded Mahometan empress, a socially minded princess, or— Well, I want you to give me a free hand for a little. I know I can trust you.'

By the Horned Gooseberry, he was commanded to dinner by the consort of an emperor who was—in Heaven's name, why?—about to take up residence at a remote market-town and spa! He caught sight of the amused eyes of the pasha in the window-place. He heard Mr. Griffe promising delighted obedience. He pulled himself together. He bowed very low.

'I am honoured and gratified, indeed, by your command, ma'am,' said he, 'and would gratefully obey, but—'

There he paused, embarrassment clouding his frank countenance. Shems-ed-Douha's eyebrows rose a little, but she said nothing.

'I am, ma'am,' he set out on explanation, 'a martyr—t'ch-t'ch—to the risings. A great affliction. Our friends are used to it, but to strangers—'

' "Risings"?' said Highness in a tone of sympathetic inquiry.

Mr. Tuke sought delicate exposition of the matter.

'I was shot by one of the unspeakable Campbells whilst attending a dying man, ma'am, at the battle of Sheriffmuir in '15. In the stomach. Ever since I have suffered from uncontrollable inward—inward—t'ch-t'ch—rumblings and—t'ch-t'ch—whimperings at mealtimes. They cause me mental distress, particularly when they reach a climax in hiccoughs and—t'ch-t'ch—eructation.'

The Princess seemed to think little of this failing.

'Be assured,' she said, 'that in some parts of Africa to belch after a meal is the greatest compliment that you can pay your host. . . . Tierce Pasha will expect you.'

As he gratefully kissed her hand, she said over her shoulder, 'You will order a thoroughly English dinner, Javan. Salmon and roast beef and green peas. And plum pudding with brandy sauce. And "Everlasting" sillabub. You will see to all that, of course—and the wine. Zadana will make arrangements for the service.'

'You think that a suitable summer diet, madam?' asked the pasha.

'I do,' said Shems-ed-Douha.

Mr. Tuke, who had half feared such Arabian delicacies as kid stewed with dates and eggs, and mint tea, felt very considerably relieved. He made his congé and backed from the room after Mr. Griffe as gracefully as he could. He had recognized that small gentleman almost immediately as the cricketer who had so quickly vanished on the approach of the riotous cavalcade. He would have liked to question him now on the subject of cricket. Was there a match being played today—and where—and when—and by whom?

But Mr. Griffe seemed to have the gift of disappearance, because outside the door he bowed very politely, expressed his pleasure at acquaintanceship and at the prospect of its renewal so very shortly —and then was gone, before ever Mr. Tuke had assembled the questions in his mind. . . .

Shems-ed-Douha was standing in the window, looking out upon the garden and the flowering bay tree, when Javan Tierce returned from the door. She remained there, still and silent for several instants, like a priestess wrapped in prayer or a sorceress engaged in her witchcraft. Then she said without looking round:

'What don't you approve of now, Javan?'

'It's not for me to approve or disapprove, madam. I am certain that you have judged these men aright. I cannot think, however, that it was necessary to assume a Welsh accent for the occasion, if I may presume to say so.'

'Just practice for another identity, Javan,' she explained almost casually. 'I have not had much practice so far. Judging from Tuke's reaction I did quite well.'

He had always known, without being told, that she had had some other and very personal purpose for this voyage to Europe, beyond the mere putting in safety of Mulai Ali's enormous hoard. But this was the first time that she had ever, even indirectly, referred to it. He knew nothing more of her antecedents today than when he first had seen her riding out of the desert fringe of Vled de Non, wrapped in her haik, upon a white horse at her husband's side over seven years ago.

That strange and unhappy prince—at times as much a European as his English mother; at times as much a savage as the father who had slain her in one of his murderous frenzies—had explained nothing then. Neither had he explained anything when he had written last year to him, whom he had always regarded rather in the light of a guardian angel than an earthly friend, beseeching him to return from Turkey and fulfil a mission of the highest importance. Javan had not discovered the full nature of the errand until he had taken the most solemn oath for its fulfilment.

'Who is the small person in green?' asked the Princess, still looking out into the magic of the garden, her back to all the commonplace of the 'As You Like It'—cattle pictures, red carpet, multitudinous chairs and overcrowded sideboard with indiscreet cupboard.

'He suddenly appeared with Cumberland in tow,' explained Tierce, 'and said, "I think Mr. Standring mentioned me," or words to that effect. I said naturally, "Mr. Griffe?" which was a name that had been mentioned—whereat he bowed. That's all I know about him, madam. I take him to be the prince's bear-leader.'

She turned round now and surveyed the tall man in silence for a second before she said:

'The moment he came in something told me that here came danger—great danger!'

'Danger to whom!'

'I don't know, Javan. I think the danger is both to himself and in some way to one of us. That's why I asked him to dinner, so that we could find out more.' Her instincts were usually right, for had she not summoned him just in time on the night of swords in the gardens of Meknes? 'I am not a witch, Javan, whatever they may say about me in the bazaars of Marrakesh and Sallee!'

He allowed himself to say, with a slight smile—

'Are you not, madam?'

For how else had she subdued Mulai Ali to the condition of her slave so that she sat at his councils, and rode by his side, and made this unheard-of journey to the West? Why else had he himself fled from Morocco five years ago but to escape from her enchantment?

# V

## *Confessional*

'THEY TOLD ME that I should find you here, general,' said Mr. Griffe. 'So I followed you to make my confession. I should have come two or three days ago, but my wife has been unwell.'

The little gentleman stood silent for an instant, large three-cornered hat under his arm, tall cane in hand, staring at the long wall of pinkish sandstone that hid all behind it but the swaying tops of trees and the low battlemented roofs of the house known as Old Palace.

It was a blank wall except at this end where there was an imposing gateway through which Tierce had just appeared. It stared aloofly across the wide stretch of cobbles at the row of lime trees masking the gardens at the back of the high street. Palace Yard itself was a cul-de-sac, and ended abruptly just beyond the gate in low, crumbling ramparts, which overhung the wide sunlit valley and the curving river far below. There was an air of remoteness about the place as though it were on a cliff-top at the end of everywhere.

'Yes, I've come to confess and apologize,' said Griffe again, his

48

bright, round eyes studying his attentive auditor. 'I am—the Prince of Wales. I ought to have told you before. The Hanoverian Prince of Wales, of course!'

'You hadn't been gone ten minutes the other afternoon before I learned it,' said Javan with his slow lopsided smile. 'Preece, the landlord of the Maid's Head was my informant. I'll own that previously I had been a bit puzzled, sir, by your obvious influence over a young man for whom his friends had hesitated to take responsibility. But I imagined that you were either the governor to the Duke of Cumberland—'

'He's fully emancipated, I assure you,' interjected the former Mr. Griffe. 'With an allowance of £8,000 a year.'

'—or else some high official of the Court.'

'I have no power at Court,' said the other very earnestly, 'and no influence there except when people occasionally remember that one day I may be—*may* be—King of England! I'll frankly admit that when you addressed me by the name of Griffe, I leaped at the opportunity of keeping my name out of Cumberland's deplorable mess. It was up to me to see that he behaved like a gentleman. That was all.'

'It would have been my own reaction.'

'After I had realized your quality and her Highness's—I mean quality, I don't mean rank!—I fully intended to explain myself. But the conversation took such a Jacobite turn that I was afraid the revelation of my identity might be a little embarrassing. I didn't want to embarrass you. I wanted to be friends with you. And friendships are not well founded on initial embarrassments, you know! . . . I came back a little later to explain myself, but the whole of your party had arrived by then.'

Javan found himself liking the little fellow. He bowed his acknowledgment of the compliment.

'You do me a great honour, sir,' he said.

But Mr. Griffe was patently anxious that there should be no possible misunderstanding.

'Apart from the trade treaty, which I know the British Government is most anxious to conclude—'

Javan shook his head. He interrupted:

'Her Highness has no concern in it,' he said, 'and certainly not myself.'

The little man appeared to be relieved.

'It is only right,' said he, 'that you should realize that any degree of acquaintanceship with me—is—is—would be—would occasion regret to—the—the—powers-that-be.'

'Her Imperial Highness,' returned Javan drily, 'would be caused no sleepless nights by such a thought, I make bold to believe. Speaking personally, I should rejoice to cause regret to anyone attempting to influence me in my choice of friends.'

Mr. Griffe held out a small, yellow hand; and the two men exchanged a hearty clasp. Then Javan said, in self-exculpation:

'Your Royal Highness was referred to by no fewer than three different persons in my hearing by the name of Griffe, and so I addressed you as such.'

'*The* Griffe, usually,' corrected that personage, his sallow face flushing. 'I did not know until then that this appalling nickname was in use outside my family.'

'Appalling?' questioned Javan with a cocked eyebrow.

The other hesitated before replying in a matter-of-fact tone:

'My father is always inventing nicknames for me. "The Griffe" is his favourite and the one that has stuck. It—it is a West Indian term meaning a low-class half-caste!'

'Good God, sir!' ejaculated Javan; and restrained himself from examining that rather pathetically alien face with long dropping nose and full lips.

'Oh!' said the Griffe, who had been patently watching to see whether there would be any such examination. 'My father can do better than that when he is really irritated. My brother-in-law, the Prince of Orange, for example, is "The Baboon!" It's only his way, of course, and one gets used to it in time. It might have been all right if I had grown up with the family, but I didn't. I was left behind in Hanover—God knows why!—when they came to England. I didn't see any of them, for fourteen years, except my grandfather. From the time I was seven.'

Javan asked himself why the heir to the throne should have been thus left orphaned on the Continent.

He offered the little man his snuffbox with the aromatic mixture of Turkey.

'Alas, I always sneeze!' said Mr. Griffe, declining. 'My nose is too long or too curved for snuff, I suppose. Anyhow it is neither a useful nor an ornamental organ.'

From a pocket in the wide skirts of his coat he produced a round box of gold and blue enamel, from which he popped—rather apologetically—a rose-coloured comfit into his mouth. Javan noted an immediate intensification of the faintly floral-cum-apothecary aroma that he had previously remarked about him.

'You would like me to explain the position to her Imperial Highness?' he suggested, as the thought flashed through his mind that comfit-taking was really a cleaner and comelier habit than either snuff or tobacco.

'If you would be so very good,' replied Griffe; hesitated, and added awkwardly enough, 'I hope—er—the dinner engagement this afternoon—er—'

'W-Alláhi, sir! I can assure you that her Imperial Highness is as little interested in British politics as I am. Our fathers may have been Jacobites, but we are now inhabitants—practically—of a different planet.'

Mr. Griffe found this highly satisfactory. He nodded his neat white wig several times—the queue was set off by the most enormous black bow that Javan had ever seen—and repeated the phrase 'different planet' with evident appreciation.

'And Mr. Tuke?' he queried. 'If I keep to my incognito, or at any rate don't claim to be anything more than Prince Frederick of Hanover in his presence, do you think all will be well?'

'A hundred to one on it, sir. I'll make it my duty to explain to him.'

Mr. Griffe beckoned to the equerry waiting for him with his carriage under the shade of the lime trees across the road.

'I am glad that I have got that off my conscience,' he said to Javan. 'I hope that we shall be able to make an expedition or two together, you and I, now that Dunscore and my brother have gone back to Town. We are at Barrington Court, you know, three miles away. My wife and I have been released from the treadmill for a month. On the score of her health. She's *enceinte*. Rest for her, and country sports for me. Without surveillance—at least we hope so! You cannot possibly imagine what it is like to be free from the constant stare of unfriendly eyes after months and months of it? . . . When do you move in here?'

'I don't,' said Javan. 'The Princess will inhabit the house with her ladies and attendants, and I shall have lodgings near by in Vicar's Close. The Princess takes up residence tomorrow.'

'It's a gloomy-looking hole,' commented Griffe, looking up at the crumbling outer wall as his postilions mounted and prepared to bring the carriage across the cobbled roadway. 'What made her take it, I wonder?'

It had occurred to Tierce that if Shems-ed-Douha desired a secure retreat from which to conduct experiments in 'another identity' she could not have chosen better. He did not say so, but merely remarked—

'Arrangements for renting the house had been already made before I reached Marrakesh in January.'

'I'm told,' said Griffe, shaking his head deprecatorily, 'that Old Palace used to belong to Madame von Pfullingen, an ancient favourite of my grandfather. A very particular favourite, indeed! And equally a thorn in the flesh of my father!'

It did not appear to Javan that the younger man displayed any filial sympathy. 'The major-domo at Barrington says that after his death she tried frequently to raise the old man's ghost there. It gave the place a very bad name. She is said to be still playing the same pranks now at Hampton Court, where she lives in one of the "grace and favour" houses. My father has been trying to get her out for the last ten years.'

He was helped into his carriage by the romantic and poetical Mr. Standring, and drove away with a farewell wave of the hand.

Javan walked slowly down Palace Yard inquiring within himself what quality it was in the little man that excited not merely his friendship but also a feeling of compassion. He was ugly and small —rather like a yellow punchinello; his eyes were as round as a monkey's; and his costume today, as it had been on the last occasion, rather emphasized his shortcomings by being in the extremest of fashion. That was true enough, but nevertheless he was a prince and heir to one of the greatest thrones in Europe. Why had he been left behind by his parents for fourteen years in Hanover so that he had become a stranger to them?

At the further end of Palace Yard a wrought-iron gate and a short flight of shallow semicircular steps led up to a flagged walk known as Vicar's Close; in which a row of ancient houses, displaying every possible irregularity of architecture, drowsily regarded the greenest of graveyards set about with silver birches and weeping ash trees, and an old grey church with a tall spire.

There he found Mr. Tuke, hat pulled down meditatively over his nose and cane shouldered like a musket, contemplating two small boys seated on the bottom step intent on a game of 'conkers' played with snail-shells, which they pushed over the smooth worn stone against each other until one broke.

'An extremely popular pastime—t'ch-t'ch—among the juveniles in this part of the world,' said the old gentleman, greeting Tierce. 'With a highly developed ritual. Well, Coppie, don't tell me that you are risking Old Ironsides today!'

'Pax!' said Coppie to his rival, and rose to his feet, removing his floppy wide-brimmed hat as he did so. 'No, sir, it isn't Ironsides. He's a hundred-and-fiftier, and George's conker here has only got twenty wins.'

He was an engaging child with a wide mouth and ruffled yellow hair, dressed in a blue jacket and the loose wide petticoat trousers of a sailor. He answered Tuke, but his eyes were fixed on the tall Virginian.

'You'll have to risk Ironsides some day,' said Mr. Tuke.

'Yes, sir. But "Lumpy" Nichols is going to make a match with his two-hundreder. Ironsides will win. I know he will. But it 'ull be a fight. It 'ull make him a three-hundred-and-fifty-oner!'

Having gathered this latest information about local sport, Mr. Tuke listened to Tierce's account of Mr. Griffe's confession and plea with much benevolence. His parting remark obviously was a defence of the proposed hobnobbing with a member of the usurping dynasty—

'But of course he *is* a cricketer!'

'He is . . . Until three o'clock, then!'

Tierce gave Mr. Tuke a bow and a sweep of the hat that greatly gratified old Mrs. Garlicke, the apothecary's mother, sitting as always, throughout the daylight hours, in the bay-window of the upper floor of the house opposite, whence she could command the entrance to Palace Yard, the activities of Vicar's Close and the to-and-fro of the short, prim street that sloped steeply from her door to the centre of the town.

Looking like Grandmother Wolf in the tale of Red Riding-Hood, in her big mobcap, spectacles, and cream shawl embroidered with wild strawberries, she watched Mr. Tuke stamp homeward over the flagstones to his small green-shuttered house in the Close. She watched Javan Tierce, Pasha of two tails, general in the armies of the Turkish Emperor, guardian of the consort of his Shereefian Majesty, set off briskly towards the high street and all the turmoil of market day followed by his groom leading a pair of light brown Arab mares with ivory manes and tails.

With tiny, snuff-grubby talons she put a pinch of coarse black snuff to her right nostril, a pinch of fine yellow to the left, and meditated profoundly. . . .

An enormous black man with a wide grin, dressed in a dark blue robe with a red sash, and a white muslin turban, stood—as usual—before the entrance to the west wing by the main stairhead on the second floor of the Maid's Head, and—as usual—resolutely denied access to everybody.

Even Mr. Preece, looking more like a stage version of one of his own fashionable clients than a landlord, might not pass, although, as everybody knew, his Royal Highness the Prince of Wales was beneath the roof, dining incognito in the apartments of the Empress of Morocco. Even Henry, the waiter, and his underlings could get no nearer to perform the service of the table. The trays, the dishes, the salvers, were spirited from their reluctant hands to the imperial quarters by veiled women—with enormous eyes, they said—who were shrouded in white and slid silently to and fro in yellow slippers.

Williams, the Turkish general's groom, was therefore in great demand as a purveyor of information. He was actually given the entrée to that privileged resort, the landlord's 'Snug'—an unheard-of concession to a menial—owing to the insistence of the frequenters. Stimulated by the flattery of their attentions, and still more by the tankards of October ale thrust into his willing grasp, he embarked on bizarre and lurid stories of life—and death—in Morocco to an audience that included the exciseman, the parish clerk, half-a-dozen substantial farmers, an usher at the grammar school, and Mr. Garlicke, the apothecary, returning from attendance at a confinement.

He told of men being sawn in half; of marabouts—'Them's their saints, your honours!'—ravishing women in busy streets amid the

plaudits of their devotees; of tattooed girls; of the fantastic powers
and riches of the husband of the lady upstairs—Emperor of Morocco,
King of Sus and Tafilet and Fez, and Lord of Vled de Non.

'And what o' she?' asked the exciseman.

'The Empress? They says that the Emperor do be worshipping
the very ground she walk on. They says that even her little finger-
tip is like sunshine to him. Her name is meaning sunshine, too!
Sunshine-of-the-Morning is what it says. A fair mouthful, ain't it?
She's not like 'er old mother-in-law, the old Empress, what had
her women's breasts cut off and made 'em eat them! They do be
saying—'

But there he pulled up and said no more on the subject of
the Empress. For he remembered in time the ban imposed on any
revelations of what he knew or guessed about Imperial Majesty.

Susie, the barmaid, was a spellbound auditor; she heard much
that she had no business to hear; also she gathered that the name of
the big man on guard over the imperial quarters was Yusuf. At a
propitious moment she withdrew from the 'Snug.'

He was still standing there, a black giant, as big as Goliath, a
red sash girdling his enormous belly. At the moment no one else
was in sight.

She walked straight up to him. She poked him in his vast middle
with her forefinger. She looked up into his huge ebony face with a
smile. She said in her most winning manner:

'Yusuf!'

The giant widened an enormous mouth, showing enormous white
teeth in an enormous smile. He poked her gently in the stomach with
a finger thicker than a candle and raised his eyebrows.

'Susie,' said Susie in self-introduction.

Accordingly it was only a minute or so afterwards that she was
tiptoeing along the passage towards a door which had been left
slightly ajar. It was plainly understood that she should only peep
through the crack.

She did so.

Someone robed in pale and shimmering green was sitting by herself at the far side of the table, under the picture of the longhorn
bull Bashan, which Mr. Arrott had bought for one hundred and fifty
guineas from Mr. Jessup. Two ogres in blue robes, like Yusuf, stood
a little behind her on either side. Susie could not see her face, or

anything else, indeed, except a decanter and a man's dark coat-sleeve and lace ruffle. She heard Mr. Tuke say deferentially:

'And so, ma'am?'

Then suddenly she found herself looking into a pair of fierce black eyes set in a dark blue hood, into an otherwise invisible face that thrust itself towards her through the opening in the doorway.

Fierce-black-eyes-in-invisible-face said in a bitter whisper:

'Run away, my good girl! Run away! Prying and spying and peeping are things that I *will* not stomach. Be off!'

Susie went off. On tiptoe. At high speed.

'That woman,' said she in recounting this adventure, 'spoke English every bit as good as me. You would have thought she was a duchess.'

'That 'ull be Lady Zadana,' said Williams. 'God save us from her! . . .'

Javan Tierce shot a surreptitious glance from the weather-beaten face with jutting nose and chin on his right to the yellow, intelligent face with the oriental nose on his left.

About Mr. Tuke there was a faint air of unease which puzzled him a little until he recalled a conversation on the subject of 'risings.' Then he remarked that a small silver pouncet-box was half secreted beneath the rim of Tuke's fruit plate; that his fingers hovered uncertainly near it.

Mr. Griffe, receding chin on small yellow hand, quite at his ease, listened intently to the Empress-Princess's every word; watched intently every change of expression with the melancholy regard of luminous grey eyes.

In that rather stuffy picture gallery of fat stock, still redolent of the savours of roast beef and the burnt brandy sauce which had accompanied the plum pudding, Shems-ed-Douha was obliging her guests with a brief account of her antecedents.

She sat with her elbows upon the table and her chin propped on her hands. Under a short embroidered jacket of emerald silk she wore a filmy kaftan of pale green that caught and held the sunshine which filled the room. The great jewels on her long, narrow hands —the finger-nails dyed orange-red with henna—glittered like the rainbow spray of a sunlit waterfall. The shining midnight of her tresses was not quenched by the silver mist of the scarf wound about them. Above her the clumsy ugliness of Mr. Arrott's bull lowered in sinister sidelong fashion out of its tarnished frame—Javan had already traced a resemblance to Lord Dunscore. On either side, behind her, the enormous figures of the eunuchs, Selim and Ibrahim, stood as motionless as though they had been embalmed.

'. . . I will not tell you the names now,' said the Princess. 'One day, yes—for I think we shall be good friends, shall we not?'

The devoutness of his companions' assurance advised Tierce that even in Europe the enchantments did not fail that had enabled her to entangle Mulai Ali, Emperor and King, in the meshes of her magic.

'And so,' continued the Princess in a voice that was full of music, 'after being betrayed in such a way by the Judas, his younger brother, my father fled the country. He was attainted for high treason; my uncle succeeded to his estates.'

'He was betrayed by his brother who succeeded to his estates,' repeated Mr. Griffe below his breath, not in mere comment or criticism, but as though in echoing antiphon.

Shems-ed-Douha glanced at him. She nodded, and continued— 'He fled with my mother to America, where I was born.'

'Forgive me, ma'am, pray, for a question,' begged Mr. Tuke, taking advantage of another pause by the Princess. 'But I presume that it was in America, then, that his Excellency first—t'ch-t'ch—had the honour of making your Imperial Highness's acquaintance? He tells me that he is, too, a native of the New World.'

'Her Highness was born in Massachusetts,' said Javan, who had been listening with interest and composure to Shems-ed-Douha's appropriation of his own family history. 'Whereas I am a native— as I think I told you the other day—of Virginia. A matter of many hundred miles away. In fact I did not have the honour of presentation to her Highness until after her marriage to Prince Mulai Ali, the present Emperor.'

'Seven years ago,' said Shems-ed-Douha, as though calculating whether that estimate were right, and then went on with her autobiography: 'After my mother's death, my father became very restless. He returned with me to Europe, and after many wanderings eventually came to Fez in Morocco, where he took service with the

Emperor Mulai Ishmael. I never saw the Emperor although he was my husband's father. He died before my marriage. He was a very, very dreadful old man, indeed!'

Tierce annotated:

'He once sent ten thousand heads to Fez and Marrakesh as token of victory and warning.'

'My father quenched a rebellion raised by one of his sons—'

'Sons!' echoed Mr. Griffe.

Again she looked at him and slowly nodded.

'—and so secured the Emperor's confidence which he never lost. He was made a Bashaw, and given a province to govern as big as Scotland. My father once showed me the comparison on a map.'

'The empire of Morocco is at least twice the size of Great Britain!' interjected Javan who, as a matter of principle, would never permit Europeans to believe that they had a monopoly of the big and the beautiful.

'But what happened to the rebellious son, madam?' asked Mr. Griffe, leaning a little forward.

'I do not know. I was only a child.'

"It is easy to guess,' said Tierce Pasha. 'His best-loved son, Mahomet, was mutilated before his eyes and died. The next favourite, Zidan, was suffocated by women at his father's command. There were others.'

'His best-loved sons!' said Griffe almost in a whisper. 'His *best*-loved sons!'

There was so long a silence that Tuke feared the Princess of Morocco had ended her story.

'And where were you during these years, ma'am, if I may—t'ch-t'ch—ask?' he ventured, discreetly opening with one hand the little box wherein he carried medicaments against the 'risings.'

'In Morocco with my father, Mr. Tuke. He had a house within the palace enclosure at Meknes, which was furnished in the European fashion. There were one or two English servants, and our meals were most usually such as the English eat.'

Tuke's invincible curiosity was unbaffled by his inward disorder.

'So that explains then, ma'am,' he said, inviting further confidences, 'why you speak English like a native—t'ch-t'ch—and are so completely acquainted with western customs.'

'I can eat roast beef quite politely, I trust, with knife and fork in the English fashion, and sitting on a chair—as you have seen. I can also help myself to couscous with my hands, squatting on a cushion. I have been brought up to a life that is a mixture of East and West.' She paused for the barest moment in which, Tuke noticed, her eyes left his face and sought the four veiled women in white ranged before the dish-covered sideboard at the far end of the room. A fifth, who wore a blue hood, stood a little in advance of the rest as though she were officer in charge of the detachment. 'I had an English directress for my studies. I owe much of my education to her.'

There was no doubt—Javan Tierce reflected—that the woman known as the Lady Zadana had been an excellent instructress, but the pupil had been very apt. One of the English merchants at Rabat had once shown him a list of the books that his London agent had been ordered to provide for her. It had astonished both of them.

'I cannot say that she taught me to stitch a sampler and make "pinprick" pictures,' said the Princess of Morocco. 'On the other hand I learned by heart all the answers in *The Young Lady's Mentor*. I was not instructed in the use of fan and quizzing-glass, I am sorry to say, but I am acquainted with the history of Europe. And then, although I know my Shakespeare yet also I can, even now, recite twenty-nine suras of the Koran.'

She broke off. Her bright grey eyes travelled from the Reverend Abel Tuke to Javan Tierce Pasha, and from him to the yellow Hebraic face of Mr. Griffe: in their depths, too, lurked more than a hint of mockery.

In the very act of discreetly conveying a pinch of coarse brown powder from his little silver box to his mouth, Mr. Tuke suddenly realized with surprise that there had been no trace whatever of the Cambrian accent which he had remarked in the Princess's speech at their first meeting. He wondered whether Mr. Griffe had observed this.

The Princess's eyes returned to Javan, and, still regarding that dark Quixotic face, she concluded:

'I have studied magic and astrology under the most famous of all African magicians, the Sheikh Abd-el-Emir of Fez, the city of magic. On the other hand, I have also read all the works of Addison and Steele, some of Pope, and Locke's *Essay Concerning Human Understanding*. So I am not completely orientalized. I am also sufficiently acquainted with the rules of European society to know that the time has come when I should leave you to your wine. Yusuf will summon you to the teaboard in due course.'

# VI

## *Coppie and the 'Eunoxes'*

THE ROOM lost its bizarre enchantment.

'*Ya bauwâb!*' said the Princess to the veiled women. One moment the chamber was the anteroom of an oriental fairy tale, peopled by strange figures in strange attire; the next, the magic had deserted it, and the three gentlemen were left by themselves to sit over their wine, as everyday gentlemen had sat over very ordinary wine in a commonplace room under the pictures of Mr. Arrott's bull and old Sir John Taylor's celebrated pointer, Salad, and the rest of the static menagerie any time these last twenty years.

Mr. Griffe sighed for the lost fairy story.

The Reverend Abel sighed, too, as he leaned back in his chair, thrust out sturdy silk-stockinged legs, and undid a waistcoat button —sighed because the premonitory symptoms of serious after-dinner 'risings' were steadily mounting. He moistened his finger-tip and dipped it into the snufflike powder and put it to his lips.

'Wine,' averred Mr. Griffe, holding his glass up to the light, with the appearance of a man emerging from a daydream, 'should always be drunk like this—in the sunshine. General, Mr. Tuke, I give you the toast of that lovely and royal lady, the Princess Shems-ed-Douha —and no heeltaps!'

'She is more than just that, sir,' said Tierce after the health had been honoured, feeling that a little truthful biography might well follow the fictional. He set his wineglass upon the table and looked down into it as though it were a diviner's crystal in which he saw pictures out of the past. 'She is a lady of the highest courage. She has even accompanied her husband to war, wrapped in a hooded jelab of a man. There was a battle near Fez when Mulai Ali's cavalry wavered—were on the verge of flight. She rode down from the hillock where she had been watching at her husband's side, with her hood thrown back and her long hair streaming about her. She shamed them into charging with her into the massed ranks of the enemy. She was unarmed. It was she who won the vital battle.'

'Good God!' said Griffe. 'I was under the impression from recent authors I have read that the women of Morocco were most strictly secluded: Windus—Jean de la Faye—Braithwaite—'

Tierce interrupted a recital of authorities with his lopsided smile of apology:

'You will forgive me, sir, but there have been exceptions. Shems-ed-Douha is one. Her husband is at times a man of furious action. At times he's sunk in the dreams of a hashish-eater. But at *all* times he believes in her devoutly. This journey of hers to Europe is sufficient proof of that, surely?'

Mr. Griffe—in a dark red coat heavily embroidered with gold— nodded agreement.

Mr. Tuke took yet another and larger dose of his powder.

Tierce went on—

'The people in the bazaars credit her with magical powers. In Meknes and Fez and Rabat they think that she is a witch—a beneficent witch! They call her the Witch of the Atlas.'

'A Witch-Empress!' exclaimed Griffe, savouring the phrase with obvious delight.

Mr. Tuke felt it became his cloth to look rather grave.

'There is no question but that she has powers out of the ordinary,' said Tierce, 'because I have seen her use them. She once described to me quite clearly, for instance, through the medium of a small boy looking into a crystal, an event of which I was the only living witness. An event of which I had never spoken. It was very astonishing, of course, but then what do we know of the mysteries of the human mind and spirit?'

' "There are more things in heaven and earth, Horatio—" ' quoted Griffe.

Tierce nodded.

'And then she seems able sometimes to sense the approach of events. I don't mean that she can divine the future; she is just aware of its shadow. A sort of foreboding. She sent for me once—it was shortly before I left Morocco for Turkey in '32—just because she had an inner warning that something desperate was about to happen. It did happen. She sent only just in time. The professional storytellers in the coffeehouses, of course, have woven an epic about her calling djinns to her aid—but there were no djinns, only myself!'

'Is it permissible?'

'It was a murder plot against the Emperor,' said Tierce, circulating the wine, 'hatched by conspirators of his own blood. With the connivance of his guard. Shems-ed-Douha saved his life and was seriously wounded in doing so. If I had arrived a minute later—'

Was he ever likely to forget that cypress-sentinelled pavilion in the imperial gardens at Meknes, bright with coloured lanterns, under a moon golden and round as an orange? Or the slim girl, with a scimitar in her hand, defying the knives of murderers over the fallen body of her husband, her almond-green kaftan dark with blood? Or the dead prince lying in his silks by the blue marble rim of the fountain before her? There had been other princes, too, who had died that night in the battle which raged in the horseshoe courts and cushion-strewn halls of the palace; he himself had killed one of them; and there were yet others who died later, and less mercifully.

Something of the story of the night of swords at Meknes he recounted to the two gentlemen as they sat over their wine in that very ordinary inn room in Crosse.

'I take it,' said Griffe thoughtfully after a while, 'that Mulai Ali—is that his name?—is the Emperor Ishmael's eldest son?'

Tierce shook his head.

'The eldest son was tricked out of the throne and murdered by his brother Achmet. Achmet died and was succeeded by Abdullah, another of the present Emperor's brothers, whom he has defeated and deposed.'

'What has happened to the Empress's family, whilst she is away? I presume she has got one?' asked Tuke who had been burning to ask questions about the imperial home life for some time.

Tierce shook his head again.

'There is no family,' said he. 'Mulai Ali's father, in a spasm of quite unjustified suspicion towards the end of his life, deprived him of the ability to sire one. That is not generally known, so please keep it to yourselves.'

Griffe turned a shocked face towards the pasha.

'Father and son!' he said very softly, almost to himself.

'Father and son,' agreed Tierce . . . His eye caught Mr. Arrott's bull lowering at him out of the tarnished frame above the mantelpiece . . . 'It is the old bull becoming jealous of the young one and driving him out of the herd.'

At this juncture, the conversation was fortunately interrupted by the arrival of Yusuf to summon them to tea.

Through the open door in his hand came all the homely noises of the inn.

A stagecoach was changing horses, and its passengers flocking to refreshment: an old lady argued with a postboy about a shilling in the hall: 'Drawer!' 'Ostler!' 'Where's the landlord?'—and a background of immense and earthy conversation from the vaults, and an unmusical tintinabulation of bells.

As they proceeded to the tea-table Mr. Preece's treacliest voice could be heard in a momentary lull in the uproar downstairs protesting—

'But, my lord, there is not a room in the house, my lord! Not one, my lord! Her Imperial Highness, my lord, the Princess of Morocco, is staying here, my lord. There are five coach loads of her Imperial Highness's entourage, my lord.'

When they reached the 'All's Well,' the small blue, sunshine-filled parlour where tea awaited them, there was little of the exotic East about it either.

The Princess was not present, but a fierce elderly lady with powdered hair—garbed in an iron-grey and silver dress with an uncommonly tight corsage and uncommonly wide hoops—rose from her chair before the small round table upon which the tea-tray was set.

'General Tierce,' said the fierce lady with a small dip, "her Imperial Highness has instructed me to beg these gentlemen to excuse her for a few minutes. A small matter has arisen which demands her personal attention. Pray introduce them!'

'Permit me,' said Tierce dutifully, 'to present to your ladyship the Reverend Abel Tuke, of Crosse Wells, and Mr. Griffe, a visitor, like ourselves, to this town. Gentlemen, this is the Lady Zadana, chief of the Princess's ladies—shall we say, Mistress of the Robes?'

The great lady acknowledged their deep bows with a curtsey nicely adjusted to the disparity between an imperial court official and a country clergyman and a casual visitor. Neither then nor afterwards did she display any token whatever of her knowledge that the rather Jewish-seeming Mr. Griffe was actually the Prince of Wales.

'I think, general, it will perhaps be best,' she said, indicating that they might be seated, 'that use should be made of my English patronymic whilst we are in the society of English people and in England. The name is Mott. Miss Augusta Mott.'

With that she proceeded to dispense tea, sugar, milk, cream, and hot water in the Maid's Head's best Delft ware, as though she were a textbook on the art of tea-serving.

She also assumed complete control of the conversation. She seized any subject presented to her by the nape of its neck—so to speak—gave it a couple of sharp shakes, and slew it on the spot.

Morocco? She really knew little or nothing about the country. They put mint leaves and sugar *in the teapot*, and ate with their fingers!

'Fingers—t'ch-t'ch—were made before forks, ma'am,' said Mr. Tuke tritely.

'Fiddlededee, sir! Fig leaves were made before satins.'

England? Really her duties had left her little time to pay heed to the countryside.

Literature? She did not wholly approve of Mr. Pope. She did not at all approve of Dean Swift. Or Mr. Dryden. Or Mr. Defoe. Shakespeare was not always suitable for a lady's reading. Give her Addison and Steele.

'But what about Monsieur de Montesquieu?' suggested Mr. Griffe, an intense admirer of the *Lettres Persanes*.

'I do not approve of French literature,' said Miss Mott.

Travel? She could not approve of sea travel. It was not natural to journey on water. Sailors were rough, vulgar persons, and ships only fit for the conveyance of cargo. Coaches were an abomination, suitable but for visits in Town. Horses were the most unreliable of creatures.

'But how, ma'am, would you—t'ch-t'ch—journey then?' said Mr. Tuke.

'Ladies should not travel, sir, except for an extreme urgency,' said Miss Mott primly. 'It is usually quite unnecessary for them. It is lowering to the female dignity. It is a business that should be left to the gentlemen—like politics and horse-riding.'

In the momentary silence that followed, Mr. Tuke's unfortunate postprandial failing—so long threatened and so long held at bay—overtook him, before he could set his cup down, before he could even turn his head. He hiccoughed, and then he belched—with great violence. The tea was slopped on to the floor. With scarlet face he sought his pouncet-box; fumbled at the lid; in his confusion let it overset and fall so that the dark brown powder it contained was spilt all over his black silk breeches and the carpet.

'And what are the constituents of that nostrum, sir?' asked Miss Mott, ignoring his apologetic mumblings, and broaching a subject of her own accord for the first time.

'I believe, ma'am, that it is a preparation of fennel.'

Miss Mott snorted.

'It was strongly recommended to me—t'ch-t'ch—by Mr. Garlicke the apothecary of Palace Street, ma'am,' said Tuke defensively.

'Fiddlededee!' said Miss Mott decidedly. 'The man cannot know his business at all. Fennel, indeed! A small dose of dried watercress seed taken in port-wine is infallible. Quite infallible! Mark my words, sir!'

The sufferer thanked her with deferential gratitude. He vowed immediate essay of the remedy, and Miss Mott then unbent so far as to volunteer a dissertation on the remedial value of herbs.

Fennel—she admitted—was valuable as a treatment for corpulence, although she personally believed in parsley seed. It appeared that a course of asparagus-root tea and horse-radish poultices had lately cured her sciatica. One writer had recently advocated nettle poultices, but she concluded from certain remarks that he was a Dissenter, and thought that his remedies would inevitably prove as wrongheaded as his religious principles.—Mr. Griffe and Mr. Tuke gravely agreed with her.—It was as a hair tonic that nettles were most valuable. She recollected when the Princess was little more than a child—

'You have been with her Imperial Highness for a considerable time then, ma'am?' ventured the ever-inquisitive Abel, when she had narrated certain events illustrative of the benefits that spring from combing the hair with nettle juice.

'I have been with her since childhood,' said Miss Mott. 'I had the privilege of being her instructress.'

Listening to the anecdotes of the Princess's early years which followed, Javan inquired within himself whether they were as apocryphal as Shems-ed-Douha's own autobiography sketched for her guests' benefit earlier that afternoon. Like her imperial mistress, Miss Mott had appeared, antecedentless, out of the wilds of the Vled de Non.

That lady broke off in the middle of a tale, rose from her chair with stiffly rustling skirts, and dropped a profound curtsey as the door suddenly swung open and the Princess entered.

Mr. Tuke, bounding to his feet with the agility of a boy, saw that one of the big eunuchs had taken up his stand in the passage, and sensed the presence of other attendants near the door.

'Kadijah has found a man under my bed,' said Shems-ed-Douha, rather with the air of being pleased than otherwise.

'Good God!' exclaimed Javan. 'What can Yusuf have been doing, or the others, to let that happen? There are only two stairheads for them to watch, and I gave them the most precise orders.'

'The man under my bed was only a very little one,' remarked Shems-ed-Douha with a smile, and seated herself in an elbow-chair near the tea-table. She clapped her hands.

The door swung open again, and two tall women of the imperial Harriffa guard in dark blue haiks, unveiled, entered with the prisoner.

He was, indeed, only a very little one. Javan Tierce recognized him at once as the small boy with ruffled hair whom he had seen earlier in the day playing 'conkers' on the steps to Vicar's Close. Now he stood uneasily between the Harriffa, nervously twisting his fingers and looking from face to face of the tribunal by which he was confronted.

Before dealing with this criminal, Shems-ed-Douha desired, however, to be satisfied on another matter.

'Mr. Tuke,' said she, 'would you not say that Tierce Pasha was a liar when he said that Kadijah is about my build? That is Kadijah—the younger one with the hazel eyes. Say what you think. Neither of them can understand a word of English.'

Mr. Tuke threw the general a reproachful glance.

'I should suggest, ma'am, with all respect—t'ch-t'ch—to him that Tierce Pasha needs attention to his eyesight. By—er—I should! And now, Master Coppie, may I ask what you were doing under the Princess's bed? Do you know that if you had done so in her own country, having your head chopped off would have been the least thing that could happen to you?'

'Don't frighten him!' said the Princess. 'I'm not angry. Now tell me, Coppie—'

'Are you the Princess, ma'am?'

'I am.'

'A real princess, ma'am?'

'I am, Coppie.'

An infectious grin of gratification widened Coppie's already wide mouth, and beamed from a face adorned by a pleasantly snub nose and bright grey eyes.

'Now tell me why you got under my bed. It is no place for a gentleman—under a lady's bed.'

'I wanted to see you, ma'am. So I've won my bet, ma'am!'

'The essential thing to know, madam,' interjected Tierce, 'is how he succeeded in getting there.'

'How did you, Coppie?'

'Climbed up the tree by the window in the passage, ma'am. It was easy. "Lumpy" Nichols's got to give me two fifty-er conkers, ma'am. He betted I'ld never see you.'

The game of 'conkers' as played with snail-shells was a mystery to the Princess; she did not seek to resolve it; she continued her cross-examination—

'But how did you know which was my room?'

'I didn't. I went into the nearest one when I heard somebody coming along the passage.'

'But why should you bet about seeing me? It sounds as if I were a wild beast on show!'

'Everybody's talking about you at school, ma'am. Some say you're black, and others say you're brown. But really you're a lot whiter than'—he surveyed the occupants of the room—'than Mr. Tuke, or the other gentleman, or anybody here.'

'That is highly gratifying,' said Shems-ed-Douha. 'But will your friend—"Lumpy"—believe you?'

'He'd better!' said Coppie grimly.

'You shall be able to show him proof. Kadijah will give you some sweetmeats that come from Morocco, and then everybody will know that you have indeed seen me, won't they?"

He was quite at his ease now, very upright, with his legs apart and his hands behind his back, gazing at her loveliness with evident admiration.

'Thank you very much, ma'am,' he said, and then passed on to a problem of urgency. 'Please, ma'am, is this a harem?' he asked.

Mr. Tuke snorted appreciatively.

The Princess gave the question her most serious consideration. No, she thought that it could hardly be called a harem. Gentlemen were not allowed in harems, and, as he could see for himself, here were Mr. Griffe and Mr. Tuke visiting her to talk business—to say nothing of Tierce Pasha.

'But the very big men—the black men—in blue, they are like they have in a harem, aren't they? Eunoxes they call them, don't they?'

The big men in blue were her guards, it was quite true.

'Why then,' said Coppie, 'didn't the eunoxes stop the Prince of Wales carrying off your lady-in-waiting?'

From his post of vantage behind the Princess's chair, Javan Tierce shot a glance at the Prince who was sitting next to her. He was looking at the child with an expression of almost ludicrous astonishment.

'Wherever—t'ch-t'ch—did you hear that, Coppie?' asked Tuke.

'Everyone in the town knows about it,' said Coppie. 'Old Mrs.

Garlicke told me. You see, I am the only person she ever tells any-thing at all of what she sees and hears from her window.'

'But how did she know?' inquired Tuke.

'She heard someone telling Lady Morfa the other evening by the steps. He said Lord Somebody-or-other had told him.'

'Was the name Lord Dunscore, Coppie, by any chance?' asked Mr. Griffe, rubbing his chin thoughtfully.

But Coppie had no idea.

'I don't think that the Princess would invite the Prince of Wales to dinner if he had tried to run away with one of her ladies-in-wait-ing, do you, Coppie? Because you see, as a matter of fact, between you and me, I am the Prince of Wales. At least'—he hurriedly amended for Tuke's benefit—'I—er—am called the Prince of Wales by —er—the Hanoverian party.'

Coppie was obviously interested, but equally certainly not much impressed by the heir to the throne; for he said—

'Do you want me to say he was here, ma'am? Or don't you want me to say anything? Would you like me to say you're black and talk Chinese or something? I don't mind a bit. I always keep my word of honour—Mr. Tuke will tell you so—but I don't mind telling a lie now and again, if they're necessary—not evil lies of course, I mean.'

He certainly might say that he had seen the Prince of Wales hav-ing dinner with the Princess of Morocco. He might say, too, that really—

Shems-ed-Douha turned her lovely head in inquiry to her neigh-bour. He shook his head very slightly; and she concluded—

'—really it was somebody quite different who behaved so badly. The Prince came to say how ashamed he was of any Englishman who would do such a thing!'

'He should be put in a barrel of nails and rolled into the river,' said Coppie severely.

He departed a little later, more gratified by a silver coin of Moor-ish provenance supplied by Tierce than by a small basket of strange candies at which he had looked with some suspicion; and most of all gratified by the suggestion that he might be invited very shortly to pay Imperial Highness an official visit when Imperial Highness had taken up residence in Old Palace.

'My circle of admirers is enlarging,' said the Princess, examining the tea-leaves at the bottom of her cup. 'Who is this latest one?'

'An orphan, ma'am,' Mr. Tuke informed her. 'Copernicus Tregallion. His father was a naval officer. His maternal—t'ch-t'ch—grandmother is that strange termagant, Madame von Pfullingen, who once owned Old Palace.'

'Old Antonia!' exclaimed Griffe in surprise. 'I didn't know she had any grandchildren. Odd!'

'You are acquainted with the lady? A friend of hers, perhaps?' asked Shems-ed-Douha quickly.

'Hardly, madam,' he hastened to inform her. 'As a child I remember her well years and years ago in Hanover. But I've never seen her since—just heard about her.'

'The boy lives a few doors from me in the Close,' said Tuke, when it appeared that the Princess had lost interest in Madame von Pfullingen. 'With an aunt and his grandfather, Captain Tregallion.'

'My landlord-to-be,' supplemented Tierce; and addressed himself directly to the Prince. 'Have you any idea at all, sir, how this extraordinary story can have arisen? It is such a perversion of the truth that it would appear to me to be deliberate.'

'It *is* deliberate.'

'Then it must be challenged, and the truth told.'

Griffe shook his head.

'I'm not going to pretend that my brother is a pleasant lad,' he said. 'But I am absolutely certain that he would do nothing deliberately dishonourable. He's had no hand in this, and it wouldn't be fair to drag him in, when he isn't in any way responsible. It can't do me much harm. I'm used to slander.'

'But it's a barefaced, unnecessary lie,' protested Tierce. 'At the very least a couple of dozen people must know it to be untrue.'

'A brisk lie will always overtake the truth,' said Tuke, sententiously. 'The issue will get so involved that before you know where you are, sir, most people will be under the belief that it was your Royal Highness who was concerned.'

'It was for that very reason that I didn't claim my name and rank at the outset. All the same I think it best to let sleeping dogs lie.'

'That's preposterous,' said Shems-ed-Douha. 'You don't have to drag your brother into the matter at all. To start with, everyone will know before the day is out that you have been dining here. If that isn't enough, give the world good measure by airing yourself in the town and the Outlook Gardens tomorrow with Tierce Pasha in his best coat with the order of the Seraphim upon his breast. As a final touch, and to set the seal of my approval on the affair, you shall have a couple of my "eunoxes" in attendance in full regalia.'

# VII

## 'Non Sine Pulvere'

AGREEABLY to the suggestion put forward by Shems-ed-Douha, Royal Highness and Excellency promenaded together through Crosse Wells on the day following their encounter at the dinner-table.

They made their appearance at noon—the spa's high tide of fashion—followed by two exquisite gentlemen-in-waiting; by superb lackeys in crimson liveries with the Hanoverian black cockade, and carrying long gold-headed staffs; by Yusuf and two of his fellows, blue-robed, white-turbaned, enormous, with curved scimitars in their sashes.

Royal Highness wore a coat of green-blue watered satin and—very much to one side—a hat bound with gold. He thrust a hand, encased in a white glove embroidered in silver, through the arm of his tall companion and made brisk conversation during all their parade.

He stopped at Mr. Toller's library in the market-place to point out a print—especially displayed in the window in honour of the eastern visitors—depicting a Turkish army on its line of march, and another portraying the celebrated Grand Vizier, Kara Mustafa Pasha.

73

Royal Highness insisted on buying these and presenting them to Excellency as being also a Turkish general and pasha. The latter tactfully refrained from mentioning the fact that the late Kara Mustafa had been strangled and beheaded for incompetence on the field of battle as a punishment and as a warning to other commanders.

The pictures, however, served the Prince's purpose as a *point d'appui* from which he could proceed to draw Javan out on the subject of his profession, and the fascination of the study of the strategical and tactical problems involved in a campaign.

They navigated the Close, where six sundials placed like street posts before the house of Captain Tregallion provided further subject for conversation. The spiring fifteenth-century church, set amid the shivering foliage of the birches, brought them to architecture—Moorish architecture—the Mansur Gate at Meknes, and the shrine of the Saadian dynasty at Marrakesh.

At length they reached the Outlook: a garden with a noble prospect of far-distant hills, smoke-blue and grey under the clear midday sky; a garden whose walks were thronged this day with old ladies in chairs, old gentlemen hobbling on sticks, young ladies with sallow complexions, and young gentlemen with red noses, as well as the usual collection of the *ton* suffering from nothing except lack of heart or lack of head.

What a bowing and scraping there was—what a sweeping of elegant hats from elegant heads—what a curtseying of elegant gowns and flirting of elegant fans! The royal face-saving expedition had all the publicity it required.

At the street entrance to the gardens, on the way back, Royal Highness paused by the rank of sedan-chairs awaiting their passengers, and collogued for a minute with one of the chairmen, a fiery-faced person with a bottle-nose and a bunch of greasy blue ribbons as a shoulder-knot. An itinerant dealer in secondhand wigs, sitting on a handle of his barrow, watched the proceedings, sucking at the stub of a clay pipe. Money changed hands.

'Poor fellow,' said the Prince when they were out of earshot. 'His appearance is against him, I know. Appearances often are against people.'—He spoke in such a tone that Javan realized, not for the first time, that Royal Highness was very conscious of his own lack of physical attractiveness.—'Eight children, another on the way, and a very sick wife. It's been a bad season for the chairs, he says. Too many people prefer to walk . . . My family are all great walkers: my father—my grandfather—my great-grandmother, even in her eighties! Augusta, my wife, fortunately likes walking, too, although now of course— Does your Excellency indulge in that exercise?'

Excellency did: accordingly found himself engaged to walk with Mr. Griffe—there was much emphasis on the incognito—on the morrow, at the time agreeable to himself, subject naturally to any unexpected call on his services by Imperial Highness.

But Shems-ed-Douha made no demand whatever upon the services of Javan Tierce Pasha. She remained, in fact, practically invisible in her new quarters at Old Palace. On the rare occasions that he saw her, she staved off discussion of the business that had to be done with regard to the immense funds lying in her husband's name with the various London bankers, on the ground that it must wait until she 'was settled down.' On the other hand it was impossible not to notice that great activity of some sort was going on in her private apartments. Messengers were always coming and going, and even Miss Mott's habitually secretive air took on something extra in the way of mystery.

Javan did not so much resent being left out in the cold, as feel anxious. It was true that Shems-ed-Douha had triumphed over every tradition and convention of Morocco; but if she were to set out on a course that ran counter to the traditions and conventions of eighteenth-century England, he was not so certain of success. The reference she had made a day or two before to 'another identity' with all its implications worried him extremely.

For ten days, however, he was left free to join the Prince on his incognito expeditions as Mr. Griffe.

They walked unattended along the river; watched a gratified Mr. Tuke angling—and talked politics.

'The present British government is the most corrupt in the world,' said the little man.

'You wouldn't say that, sir, if you had any experience of Turkey or Morocco,' said Javan.

They proceeded accordingly to instruct each other on the prevalence of bribery West and East.

On another occasion they walked to an outlying church or two and discussed the ecclesiastical architecture, Christian and Mahometan.

They walked to a neighbouring country-house, in the absence of the owner, and studied the picture gallery. Mr. Griffe was already starting a collection, he said. In his house in Constantinople, on the other hand, Tierce Pasha had assembled some particularly fine Persian rugs and Turkish pottery of the sixteenth century.

They walked to the Three Oaks meadow below the town, by the river, to see a cricket match between the Gentlemen of Crosse and a team raised by one of the local squires—a match for one hundred pounds a side.

Javan thought it a deplorable game—one man trying to hurl a ball into a hole in the ground between two upright sticks, another defending the wicket with the flat side of an instrument like a wooden sabre, and others standing about in various attitudes of expectancy. He dozed in the sunshine through most of the match, to be aroused at intervals by Griffe shouting himself hoarse at a good hit, a smart catch, or clever bowling.

On cross-examination Javan confessed that he would prefer any day to see a jereed game of (say) twelve a side.

As they made their way townwards, he was called on for a full description of that violent sport, performed on horseback with blunt throwing-spears.

'One wouldn't have thought that there could be much demand for secondhand wigs in a rural district!' interjected Griffe suddenly. He pointed downwards with his gold-knobbed serpentwood cane.

They had turned off the highway and were taking their usual short cut to Palace Yard and Vicar's Close—up a narrow footpath which climbed steeply athwart the reddish face of the bluff above the valley to a wicket in the old town wall. At a bend in the main road below, the itinerant salesman whom they had seen before had halted, presumably to recover his breath. In the prow of his barrow, above the hairy foam of its cargo, a gigantic flaxen peruke of very antique cut rode upon a wig-stand like a ship's figurehead.

'The wig business is completely mad,' said Javan. 'It is a European lunacy, more foolish and even less sanitary than the beard of the Moslem. At any rate a beard is supposed to be a sign of virility. Nobody could say a wig was that; and I have never heard of anyone in Turkey or Morocco wearing a false beard. I used to sport a rather imposing beard and mustachios. I really regretted having to remove them before I landed in this country.'

Griffe crowed with delight at this thought. He scrutinized his friend's visage, which was tanned to the hue of old oak, as though trying to visualize it *à la turque.*

'Your own hair is black, I suppose, Javan?' he queried.

'As black as your hat, sir.'

'Not "sir." Fred.'

'Fred.'

'That,' said Fred, 'is what I like about you, if I may say so. Being friends with you is like being friends with the Man in the Moon. We are inhabitants of different planets—is the moon a planet?—with all the information of two worlds to exchange. We can be friends without having ulterior motives.' He paused, and added gravely, 'Which is a change for me.'

At that moment some small sound or some secret instinct suddenly made Javan look upwards.

The cliff-top, thirty feet above them, was crowned by the dilapidated ramparts of the town which were completely hidden under a dense tapestry of ivy. Even as he stared, the top of the wall directly overhead began to bulge out, whilst just a little further on a capstone from a crenellation of the rampart hurtled outwards, smashed the guard-rail at the edge of the path, and plunged fifty or sixty feet down to the highroad beneath, where it burst like a bomb.

Javan had already flung his arm about his petrified companion and violently forced him face forward against the earthy face of the cliff upon their right.

'Press yourself in! Press yourself in!' he cried, praying that the concavity might be sufficient for their protection.

For the space of a breath there seemed to be utter silence. Then, after a loud report followed by a violent rending noise, an avalanche of stone descended with the roar of a sea breaker smashing itself against the rocks. The air was fogged with dust, and a hail of broken stone beat up from the path about them like a ragged volley of musketry. The cliff—against which they were pressed as though they would force themselves actually within its shelter—shuddered; the powdery earth poured down its surface, against them and over them, as though it were water running from a wave-drenched embankment.

Once more there was silence, broken only by a trickle of lesser rubble, and then by distant shouting.

Javan looked cautiously about him.

The avalanche appeared to have expended itself. A section nearly forty feet long of the wall above them had disappeared—lay in rubble on the path, or in fragments on the main road. The dust was still rising like smoke.

'My God!' said Griffe uncertainly, his face grey with dust. 'And so we are still alive!'

'Apparently,' said Javan drily. 'Are you hurt?'

'Something like a blacksmith's hammer hit me on the left shoulder, and I feel battered all over. That's all. And you?'

'Nothing to speak of. My chief feeling is one of surprise.'

'Surprise?'

'Surprise at our survival.'

'I was so frightened,' said Griffe honestly, 'that if you hadn't pushed me against the cliff, I should have run for it. Then I should undoubtedly have been killed. I owe you my life, Javan!'

'Nonsense, sir.'

'Fred.'

'Fred.'

In a rather serious, anxious manner the grimy Mr. Griffe scanned the grimy countenance of Tierce Pasha. He vigorously dusted himself.

'Whatever they may say about me—and they say some pretty terrible things, Javan!—I am really not a coward. My nerves are not at the moment at their best. This is the second time that I have escaped with my life in just over twenty-four hours.'

'W-Alláhi!' exclaimed Javan. 'Why did you never tell me? What happened?'

'My favourite mare bolted with me yesterday morning. A thing she's never done before. Up by the quarries near Barrington. I threw myself off in time, just before she went over the edge. I hope to God it isn't true—as they say—that these things happen in threes.'

With both hands he started to wipe the dust off his face. Javan noticed that they trembled a little. For some odd reason the small man, thus engaged in makeshift toilet, reminded him of a tame chipmunk he had had as a boy in America many, many years ago.

' "Non Sine Pulvere," indeed!' quoted Mr. Griffe, and grinned at his serious companion. . . .

'The old tower at the West Street end of the Wall fell in exactly the same way in February,' said Mr. Tuke, after hearing Javan's account of the catastrophe that evening over a game of chess in what he called his study—a very small room without a book in it, and completely dominated by an enormous glass case containing a stuffed seventy-pound salmon.

'It was a market day,' he continued, 'and two old women were killed. There was no warning at all. The town council—t'ch-t'ch— have been arguing ever since about the cost of demolition. When they hear what might have happened to—er—Prince Frederick, they will—'

'They won't hear,' said Javan. 'We got back to Vicar's Close un- observed, I don't know how; and he wants his name kept out of the business. He's afraid his wife might get to hear. He thinks it might be bad for her—in her condition. I gather she is an exceptionally nervous young woman.'

'The town council wants shaking up. It wants hanging. Do you know, sir, that Price, the builder, actually told me after he had in- spected the wall, that there were places where it would collapse if it were given little more than a hearty shove?'

'For that in Morocco, in the days of Ishmael, Mr. Mayor and his corporation would have been dragged naked through the streets at the heels of mules until they lost all human resemblance and died. Or else would have been impaled alive.'

Tuke relighted his long clay pipe at one of the pair of candles on the table. Stopped with the operation only half performed—

'By the Great Gooseberry,' said he, 'I remember now—t'ch-t'ch— that the stretch along Fewter's Passage, which has just come down, is one of the places he particularly mentioned.'

# VIII

## *The Unexpecting Uncle*

THERE WAS NOBODY youthful among the gentry who resided in
Vicar's Close except Coppie Tregallion; from the flat-fronted, red-
brick mansion sentinelled by the six sundials at the top of the steps,
where he lived with his grandfather, to the small white house with
green shutters, at the far end, inhabited by Mr. Tuke and his sister,
Catherine.

In the daytime, if it were sunny, most of the residents might be
observed taking gentle exercise along the flagged paths of the
churchyard, or in the adjoining public gardens, the Outlook, which
had a highly approved view. 'Quite Attic,' is how the Close described the prospect, employing the strongest term of polite praise
in its vocabulary.

At night no indecorous sound disturbed the almost cloistral
silence. Of a summer evening, perhaps, the faint music of a harpsi-
chord might tinkle through the open windows of a drawing-room
and lose itself amid the silver birches of the churchyard. A passer-by

with sharp ears might possibly catch the hospitable jingle of glasses as negus and sandwiches were brought in to refresh the players at the weekly quadrille party at the Misses Grenville; or might hear the muted hum of elderly conversation at the Honourable Mrs. Foley's small fortnightly soirée.

In the winter, however, the windows were all so closely curtained and shuttered that no sound could escape, and only a faint glimmer from the fanlights of the Close fell on the grey flagstones of the path, the mist that haunted the whispering trees, and the ghostlike shaft of the memorial to the victims of a long-ago pestilence before Mr. Tuke's front door.

Vicar's Close may have been geographically in the town of Crosse, but it was very definitely not of it. It was an oasis of the genteel in a desert of indeterminate persons such as attorneys and apothecaries, to say nothing of innkeepers and tradespeople, and of the lower orders. As for the summertime invasion of octogenarians and valetudinarians seeking lost youth and health in the nauseous waters of the spa, it ignored them.

It was a self-sufficient community acknowledging only the social authority of Mrs. Foley—the Honourable Henrietta Foley—a thin old dowager with a melancholy sheeplike face the colour of cold veal, who bathed once a month in hot cider for her rheumatism, and took air in an immensely heavy and very ancient sedan-chair covered with black leather studded with brass nails. The one remarkable thing about her household was the unfailing regularity with which her maids slid into irregular maternity—to the old lady's equally unfailing consternation and surprise.

It was Mrs. Foley's cordial approval that had reconciled Miss Letitia Tregallion to the scheme of renting rooms on an upper floor of her father's house to General Tierce, although she never failed to demand confirmation of that judgment on every occasion on which they met.

So on this bright morning, Miss Letitia pounced out on her friend as the old lady—enveloped in a fur-edged pelisse of grey tabinet and wearing an enormous hood—came slowly down the path to the chair which awaited her at the foot of the steps to Palace Yard.

'My *dear* Madam,' said Letitia in a conspiratorial whisper, 'Papa was in an exceptionally good mood last night. So I *asked* him. And he *had* asked the general before he ever came here. Asked him point-blank, dear madam, whether he had more than one wife. Because it wouldn't have done—not in the Close—even if they *weren't* with him. Would it now? But he assured dear Papa on his honour that he was completely unmarried. "Completely unmarried" were his very words, Papa said.'

'I could wish,' said Mrs. Foley, 'that Harriet Slebbage were not so completely unmarried! Would you believe it, Letitia, that that girl is breeding *again*! At this time every year, as regularly as clock-work, she has to let out her stays. The devil seems to possess her whenever spring comes.'

Everybody in the Close, with the exception of her mistress, knew that it was not the devil who possessed Harriet Slebbage in the springtime, but Letchworth, Mrs. Foley's middle-aged manservant, who combined the decorous and demure aspect of a bishop with the amativeness of a he-goat.

'I am so glad,' said Letitia, referring, of course, to her conversation with Papa. 'I assure you after Julia Grenville made the suggestion last night, I could not sleep a wink. He could not *possibly* have stayed—though poor Papa has been so terribly extravagant lately. He paid twenty guineas for a horologe only last week! Twenty guineas!'

'I think, Letitia,' said Mrs. Foley, preparing to move on, 'that you are taking the business altogether too seriously. So far as the general goes, I cannot see anything ungenteel in providing accommodation to a person of such distinction, a member of an imperial entourage. I should not, indeed, have seen anything not *comme il faut* in your lodging him, even if he had owned to four marriages, so long as he did not expect us to receive any but his principal wife. In reality, my dear, you are obliging the Princess, you know . . . Perhaps you will be so good as to ascertain from the general what etiquette should be observed in the payment of our respects to her Imperial Highness. I should imagine that by now she may be ready to receive.'

At this precise moment Javan Tierce himself appeared on the doorstep of Tregallion House. He was turned out to a nicety in a coat of dark green, black silk breeches, and white stockings. His hat was under his arm, his hand was on his sword hilt so that the weapon stuck out from between the buckramed skirts of his coat in a very military and rather belligerent fashion. His tanned saturnine face, set off by his snowy wig, appeared even more purposeful than usual.

Javan was feeling, as a matter of fact, both belligerent and purposeful. He was setting out to insist on audience with Shems-ed-Douha, who had now been invisible for three days. He was not so concerned about having few duties to perform, as by the fact that the Princess did not entrust him with her confidences at all. He was utterly in the dark as to any of her projects.

He had already exchanged a few banalities with Miss Tregallion —whose face and clothes appeared simultaneously to have faded in the wash—on two occasions of ceremonious tea-drinking in his host's parlour; had already been presented to Mrs. Foley. So now he saluted the ladies with much *empressement*—to the delight of Mrs. Garlicke who was already ensconced in her window opposite the steps.

Mrs. Foley's sad face poked forward from the shelter of her vast hood—like a tortoise's head peering out of its carapace.

'Ah, general,' said she, 'how fortunate! I was just this moment asking Miss Tregallion if she knew whether her Imperial Highness is to receive company yet awhile.'

'It is a matter to which the Princess's attention has been drawn, madam,' replied Javan. 'You will realize that until we had obtained a suitable English staff it was impossible to make any plans for receiving company. Now, however, that we have succeeded—'

'I heard so. I heard at Laycock's—the pastrycook's—that old Robbins who used to be parish clerk had been given some appointment at Old Palace. He is, of course, Mrs. Laycock's stepfather, but she appeared to have no notion of what his duties might be.'

Javan explained that Robbins would act as a sort of usher. One of the Moorish servants would be the actual door-porter, whilst Robbins would deal with visitors according to certain standing instructions. Likewise two elderly and highly respectable women had been engaged—

'Mrs. Feare and Mrs. Wells,' said Mrs. Foley.

'I believe so,' said Javan. 'They will do all the marketing for the household under the direction of an English lady who is at the head of her Highness's personal establishment. Little by little we are becoming organized, you see, madam!'

'And is her Imperial Highness likely to receive company soon, sir?' persisted Mrs. Foley, emerging still further from her hood. 'I have heard many inquiries by friends in the county. My cousin, Lady Morfa, was asking but yesterday.'

Of that Javan said that he could not be sure; but a visitors' book had already been established, in which callers on Imperial Highness might inscribe their names.

It was at this juncture that Mrs. Garlicke became aware of the arrival of newcomers upon the scene—that two ladies were ascending the steps to Vicar's Close—two strangers dressed in the height of elegance.

Javan Tierce knew nothing of this until he found himself clasped round the neck, and fondly—and far from silently—kissed by a lovely young woman, who exclaimed in the tenderest accents—

'My dear, dear Uncle Javan! Dear, dear uncle!'

She released him; withdrew a little from the astonished group; displayed herself with an air of innocent coquetry—

'Don't tell me, sir, you've quite forgotten your niece, Jane from Carolina! I know I have grown up, but you *must* remember me, Uncle Javan!' said Shems-ed-Douha.

She wore an extremely modish lavender gown revealing in front a sprigged underskirt of light green. A wide 'milkmaid' hat of straw, which was tied beneath her chin with cherry ribbons, hid all the midnight glory of her hair but for one jetty ringlet. She might have been attired for a party at the duchess's rather than for a morning call in Crosse, but nevertheless both older ladies silently admitted that she was certainly the loveliest creature that had been seen in Vicar's Close within living memory.

'This is certainly a surprise, my dear Jane,' said Javan, quickly pulling himself together. 'It is a very long time, indeed, since I last saw you. Bless me, you are really getting almost good-looking although no one will ever come up to—to Kadijah, naturally!'

He held her by the shoulders at arm's length and subjected her to a close inspection; a secret smile lurking in his dark blue eyes, in the compression of his lips, in the lopsided lift of an eyebrow. He kissed her then in an avuncular fashion most decorously upon the forehead.

'And what is the meaning—Forgive me, ladies! Permit me to present to you my brother's daughter, Miss Jane Tierce! What she is doing in Europe—in—England—in Crosse—is beyond my present comprehension. Elucidate, Jane!'

Jane proceeded to do this, having swept the most beautifully managed and reverential of curtsies to her elders.

'We landed from Charleston last week, Uncle Javan.'

'Why?'

'The Assembly is at snick-and-snee with the governor. Papa has been sent over to ask that he shall be replaced. The day before yesterday he saw in the *Evening Post* that you had arrived here from Morocco, so he packed me straight off to you. He said it was to welcome you back to civilization on behalf of the family. But *I* think it's because he's got to go immediately to Paris about some property he's bought in Louisiana, on the Charles River, and doesn't want to take me. I have a letter for you in my baggage. I arrived here late last night.'

'Late last night!' echoed Javan in a voice of expressive consternation. 'But where on earth have you been ever since?'

Miss Mott suddenly materialized at the side of his newly acquired niece, in a dark green dress, and rather resembling a ladylike cobra.

'Miss Tierce has been with us, as her Imperial Highness's guest,' she announced with a dragon grin.

Fresh introductions:

'The Lady Zadana, of Her Highness's—'

'Pardon me, general! I do *not* approve of using that title in English society.'

This difficulty having been satisfactorily overcome, and her exalted position in the Princess's household revealed, Miss Mott expounded the situation.

Miss Tierce had arrived at Old Palace late the previous night. By post-chaise from London with a lady companion. She had expected to find her uncle domiciled there. She—Miss Mott—had thought it better that the young visitor should remain till the next morning, rather than all Vicar's Close should be disturbed by the process of knocking up General Tierce. Her valises and other impedimenta should be brought across as soon as it was convenient to receive them.

After Miss Mott's thoughtfulness and kindness had been duly acknowledged—

'I do not know, my dear Jane,' said Javan with ironical propriety, 'whether it would be strictly correct for you to become a member of my bachelor establishment, even though it is at Tregallion House.' And he bowed to Miss Letitia as to the tutelary spirit of that mansion . . . How could Julia Grenville ever have dared to suggest that such a man might have four wives? . . . 'In any case I do not even know that it could be arranged.'

'But I want to stay with you, Uncle Javan,' protested Niece Jane in a voice that suggested tears.

Miss Lavinia was as favourably impressed by niece as by uncle.

'I am certain, sir,' she ventured, 'that we can arrange for Miss Tierce to be at Tregallion House, if you approve. The Blue Room has only recently been aired, and the bed, I *know*, is comfortable, for Papa slept there recently whilst his own apartment was being painted, and he is *most* censorious.'

'Oh, thank you, madam,' said Jane gratefully, and shot a quick glance of triumph at her 'uncle.' 'It is most obliging of you. If Miss Tregallion is agreeable, uncle, as she says she is, then surely I may come? And— Oh, isn't this the sweetest retreat imaginable! There is nothing like it in America. I could live here for ever and ever!'

She would not live there for even a single day, if Javan could help it. Under no circumstances should any woman—princess or niece—encroach on his private life. Shems-ed-Douha should not engage in her preposterous masquerade beneath his own roof. In any case the position she had created was going to be fantastically difficult if she persisted in it. What was the purpose behind it? For some deep purpose there was, he felt sure.

'It is most kind of Miss Tregallion,' he acknowledged, 'but I am really too set in bachelor ways to surrender 'em. And I am equally not going to inflict them on you. No, Jane, we will find you accommodation and a chaperon elsewhere. Under another roof. I am sure it will be best.'

Jane pouted. She was ready for further argument.

'But I've got a chaperon already—a regular duenna. Mrs. Crawford isn't here only because she was sick in the carriage all the way from London, and is now in bed with the vapours.'

'Furthermore,' said Javan, ignoring the question of chaperons, 'when I come back at night after dealing all day with an extremely obstinate and self-willed young woman—for, charming as she is, I will not hide from you ladies that her Highness is as difficult on occasion as a princess can possibly be—I am sometimes out of temper and far too grumpish to be a pleasant companion to anyone. I am better alone. I want you, my dear, only to see me at my best.'

His charm was positively Attic, thought Miss Letitia, observing the pleasant and rather weary smile he bestowed on his niece. Shems-ed-Douha, however, recognized the determination in his tone. She pouted anew, looked appealingly at him from under immense lashes; then cast a swift sidelong appeal for assistance to Miss Mott.

But that astute ally had recognized defeat to be inevitable.

'I think that your uncle is right, dear Miss Tierce,' said she with a generally ingratiating smile. 'I think that he has sound reason on his side. I approve. Let me now put forward a suggestion. Her Imperial Highness herself propounded it to me this morning. After your little talk with her, which she much enjoyed—I think you must be about the same age, you know!—she proposed, in short, that you should remain as her guest at Old Palace—'

'Oh!' interjected Jane, with the arched eyebrows and rounded mouth of pleasurable excitement. 'To stay with a princess—a Moorish princess!'

'The suite of rooms which you occupied last night,' continued Miss Mott with a sympathetic smile, 'are placed at your disposal by her Highness. It would also cause me great gratification, General Tierce, to accompany your niece on any occasion requiring the escort of an older woman during the period of Mrs. Crawford's indisposition. Always subject, of course, to my duties to the Princess.'

Javan Tierce was standing with his back to Tregallion House, facing the little group of ladies. He now perceived, with an emotion which was between consternation and an almost malicious joy, that Jane-the-impostor was between the tiger and the crocodile—and unaware of it. For no sooner had he remarked out of the corner of an eye that the Reverend Abel was advancing towards them from his house at the end of the Close, than he realized that the boy Coppie Tregallion, whistling shrilly, was on his way up the steps from the street.

Coppie swept off a singularly shapeless hat in a comprehensive salute; surveyed Shems-ed-Douha with open admiration but without a flicker of recognition; and so bustled into Tregallion House about his private affairs.

That he had failed to recognize the Princess, transformed though she was, Javan did not believe for an instant. During that week alone he had spent two entire afternoons with Shems-ed-Douha in the neglected garden of the Old Palace, instructing her in some game with a ball which had kept Kadijah and two of the eunuchs occupied permanently in fielding. 'She can throw as far and as straight as a man, sir!' Coppie had told him enthusiastically on the last occasion. It further had appeared that the Princess's sports-wear had consisted merely of loose pantaloons and a short tunic.

Mr. Tuke certainly had not played cricket with the Princess; but he, too, as certainly declined to recognize her in the slim, fashionable miss when he paused to exchange morning greetings. So he, then, had also received advance information of the metamorphosis!

'You must know, sir, that I am an uncle!' said Javan to him in prefacing an introduction; and Mr. Tuke had smiled and bowed and apologized, as though to an utter stranger, for the red night-cap revealed under his hat.

He was on his way to the stables; his favourite hunter—t'ch-t'ch —Nimrod was poorly, and wigs—t'ch-t'ch—were not suitable wear when horse-doctoring—he explained before continuing on his veteri-nary errand.

Javan found himself resenting the fact that two new acquaint-ances, a child and an elderly man, should have been given the con-fidence which she had denied to him, who was so vitally concerned. And why did Miss Mott, that model of propriety, that dragon of perpetual disapproval, promote such an Arabian Nights' escapade? He said—

'I think, ladies, if you will forgive me, that I cannot deny myself the pleasure any longer of a brief talk on family affairs with my niece. Mr. Gellibrand will be already at the palace—'

'He is,' averred Miss Mott quickly. 'Her Highness also particu-larly instructed me to say that she would not expect you this morn-ing. In fact she has a slight chill—a very slight chill. She will prob-ably keep to her room.'

'And while the general and Miss Tierce are having a nice cosy chat, dear madam,' suggested Letitia—conscious that the parlour was in apple-pie order, and that Papa was in a good mood, 'will you not step into Tregallion House with Mrs. Foley and partake of a glass of elderberry wine and a slice of seed-cake?'

After a proper amount of persuasion, Miss Mott said that she *would* step in. She approved of elderberry wine and seed-cake—early in the day though it might be for their consumption. She even almost permitted it to be understood that her main objection to life in Morocco was that the art of baking caraway seed-cake was as unknown as the art of making potables from parsnips, dandelions, and other such homely ingredients.

Letitia decided that she would not send to ask the three Misses Grenville to join them. She did not think that Julia had behaved at all well about the general yesterday. Miss Mott—she rather regretted that flat rejection of the title of 'Lady Zadana'—was her prize! . . .

'Well?' asked Shems-ed-Douha.

She stood between the two long windows in Javan's small parlour, surveying him and the prim, impersonal room that was his home. There were two pewter lamps of an unusual shape upon the mantleshelf, one on either side of a stopped clock, which was also of a very unusual appearance. A large and amateurish picture in oils of a full-rigged ship in a storm hung—slightly askew—on the dark panelled wall facing the windows and the birch trees of the churchyard.

The table in the middle of the room was completely bare; so, too, was the old oak buffet that confronted the empty hearth. There was not a thing in the place to show the tastes, or habits, or occupation of the man who had dwelled there now for nearly a fortnight; not even a book, a glove, a riding-crop—the small oddments which any traveller might toss down on entering his sitting-room at an inn.

'Well?' said Shems-ed-Douha again.

The tanned man standing stiffly before the closed door raised his eyes to her; remarked once again that splendid confection of lavender and pale green; remarked once again that victorious bearing and expression; said tersely:

'It is not well, Princess.'

'You do not admire my dress, then? It came for me from London, yesterday—with others. Many others.'

'It is utterly unsuitable to place and occasion; but I was not referring to it, madam.'

'You are calling my conduct in question, then?'

'Yes.'

'But that is not in your province, Javan!'

'I would point out to your Imperial Highness that I was hired to be your guardian—not to be your uncle!'

'You were hired, Javan—' She began in a curious tone; paused, started afresh more lightly; 'At any rate you can hardly disown me now!'

'I am responsible for your safety to the Emperor. You are making my job a hundredfold more difficult if you persist in this ludicrous adventure.'

'It would have been comparatively easy if you had let me stay under this roof.'

'You are quite mad, madam!' he exploded. 'What would have been said when the truth came out—as come out it must? What *will* be said in any case will be bad enough, but nothing to the slanders that would circulate once it became known that you had shared my lodgings in Tregallion House!'

'What *would* be said? What *will* be said?' asked Shems-ed-Douha maliciously. 'Why should it be known?'

He disdained reply to the question, and insisted:

'You cannot come to my rooms again, madam, under any circumstances whatever. I will acknowledge you as my niece—'

'Thank you!'

'—and escort you as my niece wherever and whenever you desire. The Emperor gave specific permission for you to live as a European during your stay in this country. Why you do not do so, but create a situation as complicated as this is beyond my comprehension.'

'I *had* thought of dressing as a boy!'

'Good God!'

'Zadana thought it wouldn't do.'

'It is the only ray of common sense that lightens the story, madam. For God's sake drop the business!'

'No. General Tierce's Yankee niece—'

'American niece!'

'American niece will be able to do a hundred things that a Princess of Morocco can't. She is going to do them. We shall have a wonderful time together, Uncle Javan! And sometimes I am going to have a wonderful time just by myself!'

Javan knew that he was worsted. He had fortified himself that morning—very unusual—with a small glass of brandy before he marched out of the house determined to come to a settlement with her, even to proffer his resignation. He knew now that he would never have done so.

'Shall you be able to play two parts at once, madam?' he asked. 'Princess and Jane Tierce alternately?'

'Am I playing the part of a princess, Javan?'

He hesitated before replying—

'You have been an empress for two years, madam, and a princess for seven. Perhaps I should have said "playing a version of your Imperial Highness's rôle that is completely new to me." '

'I am now twenty-four. If seven years ago—' she began; decided against self-analysis; broke off with the warning: 'I have even thought of adding a third part.'

'I hope in such case that you will not spring it on me as you have sprung my unclehood. I hope I may have as early information as Tuke and the boy, Coppie, presumably had on this occasion. It would be considerably safer.' A thought struck him suddenly. 'Has that third part any relation to the fact I remarked on before, that you amused yourself by speaking to Tuke and Griffe with an atrocious Welsh accent when you first met them?'

She did not answer his question, but eyed him in a hostile fashion for an instant before saying—

'And now, Javan, we will join the old ladies and eat cake and sip elderberry wine—if that is good for you after brandy. And I shall sit and watch you adoringly, and when you propose some plan of amusement for me, I shall squeeze your hand with youthful fervour. "Oh, uncle, *how* kind of you!" I'll say. Or am I a little too old for that girlishness? Anyhow everybody shall know how glad I am that my ugly-goodlooking uncle has come back from a savage, barbaric, and cannibal country.'

He regarded her for a moment in cold astonishment as she pulled on an elbow-length glove of filmy lace.

'After brandy? Do you suggest, madam—' he began.

'I am not suggesting anything. I just noticed that you smelled of brandy when I kissed you in the street.'

'I did not seek that honour, madam,' snapped Javan.

'I am not suggesting *anything*,' said Shems at her most irritating. 'All I did was to speculate whether elderberry wine was good for you after brandy. Javan, how can you live in this room as it is? It isn't a human dwelling-place! Throw a boot in the corner—put a brandy bottle in the middle of the table—make the clock go! A room with a stopped clock looks as if there were a corpse in it.'

'Even its owner can't set it going.'

'Then get rid of it.'

'I daren't,' said Javan, relieved at the change in the skirmishing. 'It's a Persian water-clock four hundred years old, although it looks like a squirrel's cage. There are twenty-three water-clocks in this house, thirty lamp-timekeepers like those on the mantelpiece, forty-one sandglasses—you'll see four on the chest in the entrance hall—and God knows how many pocket sundials beside the six dials in front of the house.'

She displayed no interest in Captain Tregallion's collection of early time-recorders. She said—

'You have complained of my reticences. May I remind you, Javan, that when I saw you on Wednesday evening, you said never a word to me about your narrow escape that afternoon.'

He bowed slightly in noncommittal reply.

'You might have been killed.'

'But I was not, madam. I was not on duty with your Imperial Highness when the affair occurred. Any more than I was this morning when I drank a quarter of a glass of brandy. Any more than I am when I take my ease in this private room of which you are pleased to disapprove!'

She stopped wrestling with the button of her glove. She looked directly at him as though she had never seen him before; after an instant she said—

'I am sorry, Javan, that I am not permitted to take any interest at all in your private life—or death.'

From the change in his expression she thought that he was about to speak; but he bowed to her again without a word, opened the door, and stepped aside that she might pass.

Javan's man, Williams, stood outside, his hand ready to knock upon the panels.

A little behind him, at the stairhead, waited the small, demure figure of Mr. Griffe, more splendid than usual, quite obviously the Prince, queue tied with an enormous black bow, fingers resting upon a tall clouded cane, gold-bound hat under his arm, almond-green coat gorgeous with gold embroidery and the blue ribbon and great badge of the Garter. He had presumably masked the brilliance until his arrival, for a light cloak—such as travellers by carriage used to protect their clothing from the dust of summer roads—lay over the handrail of the banisters.

# IX

## Roses for a Tomb

MR. GRIFFE's very bright catlike eyes travelled swiftly from the transformed Princess to the saturnine man at her side. Javan sensed that he was inquiring within himself whether he was supposed to recognize the vision in front of him or not. He made his mind up quickly, however, for when he spoke he did not permit the faintest recognition to appear either in his somewhat oriental face or in his speech. He said with a deep salutation—

'Forgive me, madam! Your pardon, general! I was not told that you entertained company. Pray permit me to withdraw!'

It was Jane Tierce who swept him a curtsy.

'Pray do not, sir!' she begged. 'Pray do not! Uncle Javan, please to tell this gentleman that I am even now on my way downstairs. I have but one thing to say, which is not private, if this gentleman will forgive a very small family matter being mentioned before him. It is merely a message from Aunt Evans about the Russian poodle.'

As she spoke she withdrew into the room, and when the little man had been persuaded to enter, and the door had been closed,

94

she was standing by the empty fireplace with the strange melancholy clock on the mantelpiece, facing the shiny blankness of the table and the bare buffet. The windows were viewless—filled with the shivering, sunlit pattern of the foliage of the birch trees in the churchyard.

'Her Imperial Highness,' began Javan stiffly, 'has condescended to masquerade as my niece. She has doubtless some good reason, although I am not acquainted with it.'

'Doubtless, indeed,' agreed Griffe with his rather melancholy smile. 'I remember that when I first read Galland's translation of the *Arabian Nights*, I was inspired to emulate Haroun-al-Raschid. It still seems to me to be the height of pleasure for a prince to wander in disguise through the streets of Baghdad—or Hanover, or Crosse for that matter. I must confess to sympathy with her Imperial Highness in her masquerade.'

'When you go Haroun-al-Raschiding,' said Shems-ed-Douha, 'you luckily are not handicapped by having to produce a chaperon or to adopt an extremely reluctant uncle!'

'I think I might, perhaps, be permitted to assist you in that respect,' said Frederick smiling again at her. 'But it will have to be at once. For I heard today from a sure source that my father has told my mother to see that "The *Wechselbalg* comes back to Town instanter."'

'*Wechselbalg?*' inquired Javan. 'Is that another of his nicknames for your Royal Highness?'

'It is indeed,' explained Frederick obviously asking for sympathy. 'It is a German word which suggests that my origin is somewhat uncertain.'

'Fathers can be very peculiar,' said Shems in a matter-of-fact fashion. 'My husband has only one recognized child—a son by a wife who is now dead, and to whom he was much attached. But he always addresses the boy as "Son-of-a-Cow"! He loves him very much nevertheless.'

Javan, who knew very well that the Emperor Mulai Ali had no children at all, by a flicker of expression advised Shems-ed-Douha of his admiration for her fertility of invention in the cause of consolation.

The Prince was obviously on the verge of some comment; thought better of it; shook his head over the oddities of fatherhood; and then came to the object of his visit—

'My wife has been taking an airing in her carriage this morning. For the first time she has driven into Crosse. So I called on the general to ascertain whether he thought that the Prince and Princess of Wales might be permitted to pay their respects in person to the Princess of Morocco. Now I will ask if I may have the honour of presenting Miss Tierce to the Princess of Wales, and the Princess of Wales to the Princess of Morocco. My wife is actually waiting in her carriage by the steps.'

Shems dropped a curtsy—

'If you think, sir, that she will grasp my double capacity, at the moment as Uncle Javan's unloved niece, Jane, and a little later as an incognito Empress, I should like to accompany you to Old Palace. The Princess of Morocco will be glad to receive the two of you—in private, of course.'

'Augusta is discreet although she is very young—very young indeed, madam.' He paused; embarked on further explanation. 'She barely speaks a word of the language, and French only a shade less deplorably than most of her ladies. Except for me she is utterly alone in a very foreign land. My father would not let her bring any of her friends or attendants with her. All she has got to remind her of home is a miniature of her mother which she wears round her neck, and— pray, don't laugh!—an old doll! She is little more than a child, indeed —and a rather frightened child!'

'Most of us have a talisman of some sort,' admitted Javan. 'For years, sir, I have carried an amulet compounded, so I was told, of the blood of a he-goat and a bezoar stone. It was given me by a Moorish magician who was supposed to have married a female jinn.'

'Talisman!' said the Prince, delighted at this deep understanding. 'That's the word. I have adopted the doll—Elsa is its name—as a mascot, too, because people might not understand. You know the sort of things that might be said! I declare that it brings us luck, and insist on it accompanying us on all our expeditions. We always dress it, too, in green, which, as you know, is the mystical colour of good fortune.'

He rambled for a moment into the alchemist Khunrath's eulogy of 'blessed viridity whereby all things germinate,' before they went downstairs very quietly, past the door beyond which Miss Mott sat engaged in the consumption of elderberry wine, seed-cake, and small talk with Miss Tregallion and the Honourable Mrs. Foley—past the

chest on which the melancholy hourglasses stood, Time stationary
for them in their motionless sand—and out into the sunshine and
the rustling of the birch trees in Vicar's Close.

The coach, a fairy-tale equipage with its gilding and blazonry
and cream-coloured horses, waited at the foot of the semicircular
flight of steps leading to Palace Yard. It was watched at a respectful
distance by a little crowd of goggling townsfolk, and by Coppie
Tregallion perched atop the churchyard wall, eating red cherries.
It was guarded by postilions in crimson and gold, by running footmen in jockey-caps with tall staffs, by lackeys off the footboard with
their black-cockaded hats in their hands.

The only occupant that mattered was a very young lady with a
prettyish face slightly stippled with the scars of smallpox, sitting
stiffly bolt-upright. She was laced into a wasp-waisted dress of green
and silver, which was dowdily magnificent and had been obviously
chosen for her by her elders and betters: indeed she looked as if
she had but that day come out of the schoolroom, for she seemed
all angles and bones and anxiety.

Beside her on the port-wine cushions of the carriage was propped
Elsa, a large doll with red-and-white cheeks and staring black eyes,
in attire that was practically a copy of her own.

As the Prince went down the steps to the carriage, he waved
gaily to the gratified Coppie who vigorously acknowledged the
salute.

Old Mrs. Garlicke, sitting at her window, mumbling a comfit,
earnestly watched the small pageant. She saw a doll-like figure in
stiff brocade handed delicately out of the carriage amid bows and
curtsies. Presently she saw the party move off, two by two in miniature procession, along the limetree-bordered walk towards Old
Palace.

A dapper little gentleman, whose green coat was crossed by the
blue ribbon of the order of the Garter, squired the young lady who
had recently been engaged in conversation with Mrs. Foley and Miss
Tregallion. The Turkish general followed with the doll-like figure
from the carriage. Three or four ladies and gentlemen brought up
the rear, gay in satins and silks, with fluttering fans or gallant with
swords. With a sigh she saw them pass out of sight.

So that little gentleman was the Prince of Wales, was he? She
cast her mind back half a century, and sighed again, this time at a

girlhood memory of the tall, saturnine figure of King Charles the Second, of his lean and imposing successor, King James. These German dwarfs! She swallowed her comfit, and sought consolation in her snuffboxes—a pinch of light brown for the right nostril, a pinch of black for the left. . . .

They talked endlessly in bad French in the audience chamber of Old Palace—just the four of them.

The room was on an upper floor; was bare and white, but for the few rugs upon the floor, and the bright cushions and coverings of the low divans along the walls. The windows were high and empty of a view of anything except a pale sky. In an astonishingly short space of time Shems-ed-Douha had affected a complete transformation of herself to receive her visitors: now she sat composedly in one of the windows robed in a kaftan and short jacket of the azure of a summer night, her hair hidden by a pearl-embroidered cap and a long veil of yet darker blue.

The little man almost forced his confidences upon them.

'I have to return to London in a week,' he said. 'I am commanded, so I must obey. My father let me off the leash for a little very unwillingly. You see though I am married and thirty years old I am not allowed to set up an establishment of my own. Augusta and I have to live in my father's houses, where he ordains. We would like a house of our own—wouldn't we, Augusta?'

Augusta would, indeed.

'Only a week more freedom!' she added with a sigh, and then glanced hurriedly at the Prince as though to ascertain whether she had said the right thing.

Javan was rather touched at the manner in which she constantly looked at her little husband for confirmation of what she said, and at the manner in which he beamed upon her in reply. Mr. Griffe's attitude towards his bride was wholly that of a child who has acquired a very precious possession.

'A week,' said the Prince. 'Only a week, but in that time I hope your Imperial Highness will spare the general for a whole day—if he is willing—to take a Haroun-al-Raschid ramble with me to the fair here. Nobody will recognize us if we go dressed as—farmers, perhaps. It would be immensely entertaining!'

Javan meditated that it would be impossible to conceive anyone less like a farmer than the Prince of Wales, however disguised.

'A fair!' reflected Shems-ed-Douha. 'It's—'

For a moment Javan feared that she was about to propose to dressing up as a country girl and accompanying them, but she left the sentence unfinished, and Frederick declared:

'I have never been to a country fair. I long to see a pig-faced lady, and wrestling matches and puppet-shows. In London I was able to slip away sometimes without anyone knowing. Then I used to go to all sorts of taverns, the gallery of a theatre, to Vauxhall on a one-shilling night, or a fight at Figg's. I've gone dancing at Pancras Wells, and played cricket at the White Conduit. Now that I am married, of course it is rather different. But I still think that it is the best way of learning to understand the people over whom I may reign—*may* reign! Augusta will trust me away from her for a day —just one day, won't you, Augusta?'

Augusta would—with a blush as she spoke, and a manner which held a nice balance between regret at impending absence and delight in his own expectation of pleasure.

Javan saw difficulties in companioning the small heir to the throne of Britain amid a rough, and probably drunken crowd of merrymakers.

'But—' he began, preparing to shirk responsibilities.

'I am much stronger than you think,' said Mr. Griffe, guessing the character of the impending objection. 'I play golf at Molesly Hurst, and tennis and fives as well as cricket. I'm very wiry. I have dealt with ruffians quite comfortably before now. It's settled then—'

The elegant Mr. Standring—who, it transpired, was a gentleman-in-waiting—Lady Somebody-or-other, Miss This, and Mr. That, had entertained themselves as best they might for nearly two hours when Royal Highnesses finally took their leave.

'It is a rather surprising thing to find a man of his age so extremely nervous of his parents,' said Javan, on his return from ceremoniously conducting the pair to their carriage.

Shems-ed-Douha was sitting, with her legs folded under her, on a divan covered with Kermanshah rugs, smoking a Persian *sheesheh*.

'The fact that for fourteen years he saw nothing of them at all is probably explanation enough,' she answered him, taking the amber

mouthpiece of the snaky tube from her lips. A wisp of scented smoke
rose like incense from the bowl of the crystal and silver water-pipe
on its enamelled copper stand upon the floor.

Javan scrubbed his chin. He shook his head.

'It is far more than that, madam. From small things he has said
I have gathered that he is really afraid of both his mother and his
father, as well as puzzled and hurt by their dislike of him. Whenever he talks of them, however casually, I am always aware of a
certain tensing of his mind, as though he reminded himself of the
need to be ready to meet spiritual as well as material attack. I have
heard him speak of his father—not disrespectfully—as if he were
something not human and larger than real life.'

'He's infected the girl,' said Shems. 'Her hands were never still
during the entire time that she was here.'

'I noticed that when he was speaking of their apartments in
Hampton Court Palace she shuddered. It seemed to me to be an
involuntary action and not a gesture of dislike or an appeal for
sympathy. I am sorry for her: she is the merest child.'

'Child! How old do you think she is?'

'I know, madam. She is only seventeen.'

'Only seventeen!' echoed Shems-ed-Douha in an accent of dis-
paragement. 'Only seventeen! My own experiences by then—well,
among other things, had included having boiling oil poured over
my feet. To persuade me to become a Moslem! As a prelude to
matrimony! She is, at any rate, unlikely to have to endure anything
quite so drastic.'

She had taken up the mouthpiece of the *sheesheh* again, and a
little smoke trickled from a corner of her lips as she looked at Tierce
with an ironical smile.

Although he was acquainted with the methods occasionally employed in making converts to Islam, he was completely shaken—so
shaken that it was a full minute before he exclaimed in a shocked
voice:

'Good God! But Mulai Ali—'

'It was by Mulai Ali's orders. He watched the treatment, weeping
and imploring me to give way. After I had surrendered he behaved
very magnanimously—according to his lights. He had the torturer's
head struck from his shoulders. It was the first thing that I saw
glaring up at me from the floor, when I came out of a swoon.'

'I never heard anything of this before.'

'Mulai Ali, remembering his English mother, has never cared for any of his very occasional lapses into barbarism being recalled. Besides, there's a lot about me that you don't know.'

'I only know what you have told me, madam.' He paused, and his wry and apologetical smile removed any suggestion of offence from what he went on to say: 'Forgive me mentioning it; but you know that there is the matter of a stepson whom the Emperor calls "Son-of-a-Cow"! There is also the matter of a father who was Bashaw at Meknes, and also, among many other things, the matter of a Welsh accent. Can I take it that this is not as apocryphal as the rest?'

'What I have just told you, Javan, is as true as the one fact which you know to be a fact—that I am Mulai Ali's "High Queen," Shems-ed-Douha, Sun-of-the-Morning.'

'You are indeed, madam.'

She might truly be an empress, but, sitting on that divan, motionless against the panel of pale blue sky framed in the long window, in a filmy robe the hue of a summer night, her secret eyes bent on the gently smoking *sheesheh* as though upon a censer, it seemed to him that she might well have been an enchantress from the *Arabian Nights*. None other than a sorceress from such a beginning could have tamed Mulai Ali, so that her word was his law, her least wish his commandment.

Without looking up at him, she said—

'And now forget what I have said, Javan. I merely told what is the truth to make you realize that there have been other "children" who deserved sympathy—which they did not get—far more than this princess who was born with a golden spoon in her mouth, and will one day be Queen of England.'

'May be Queen—*may* be!' he corrected her, using Mr. Griffe's stresses.

She remained silent for a little while after that, her eyes bent on a small dark bowl on a tripod-stand upon a low inlaid table before her; whilst, watching her, he speculated—as he had done a thousand times before—on what manner of woman this was, with an unknown past, who had conquered Morocco for her husband. Then, quite suddenly, he knew with absolute certainty that beneath the Empress and the enchantress there was in reality someone who might have

been like—might even yet be like—the girl she had evoked to serve
her as a disguise. It came to him in a flash of lightning clarity; and,
even as he knew this, Shems-ed-Douha raised her grey eyes from
the bowl before her.

'And now you know, Javan, don't you?' she said as though she
had read his thoughts, or, perhaps, provided them.

He was too taken aback to answer immediately, and she rose
slowly to her feet, and came across the polished floor to him in her
golden slippers. As she approached he knew that she was more than
empress, more than witch; that Jane Tierce was no masquerade.

'And now you know, Javan?' she repeated.

'All—*all* that I need to know,' he replied and bowed very low.

'You will be genteelly and affably avuncular, won't you, Javan?'
she said, tapping him admonitorily with a forefinger on his sprigged
yellow waistcoat. 'You will no longer permit yourself to feel injured
because Tuke and Coppie were let into the secret before you, in
case of a chance encounter?'

'Yes, Jane,' he agreed meekly.

'And now, I think, we had better take an airing in the town.
Zadana has returned with an invitation for me to Mrs. Foley's "evening" tonight. I should like you to escort me. Tomorrow Miss Tregallion expects me to tea in your company. On the following day
there is to be an organ recital of Mr. Handel's works to which *everybody*—including royalty—will go. The patronesses of the ball in the
Long Room at the Maid's Head on Thursday have hurried to send
us cards. By then I shall have got used to European dress and manners again. So the next day you may go Haroun-al-Raschiding with
our Mr. Griffe—and I hope that you will behave yourselves!'

'The programme appears to have been quickly arranged,' said
Javan with a twinkle of amusement. 'You have not forgotten, I hope,
that the banker, Goldstein, is due here from London on Friday?'

'I have put him off.'

He was taken aback and a trifle disapproving.

'I could have wished that you hadn't, madam. If word were to
get about of those jewels—half a million ducats' worth—'

'How can it? The house, too, is like a fortress and the men reliable, as you know. Now I shall be ready to come out with you in
less than half an hour. We will show ourselves in the Outlook first,
I think. I hope you will succeed in looking as though you appreci-

ated having a personable niece. I feel in need of admiration.'

Whilst he waited for her to return from her dressing-room he glanced idly at the books strewn upon the divan on which she had been sitting. The diversity of her interests intrigued him. A four-volume edition of Dean Swift's works companioned the very latest atlas. The plays of Colley Cibber were cheek by jowl with Ephraim Chambers *Cyclopædia* and a French history of the reign of the Emperor Ishmael. It was with something of a shock that he remarked the title of a very small volume lying beside the bowl upon the inlaid table—*The Magic Art of Artephius and Mehinius.* The bowl itself, he now realized, was made of clear glass but full to the brim of some black fluid.

She returned so silently to the room that she watched him cogitating upon the bowl of Chinese ink for some moments before he realized her presence.

'Coppie is a really remarkable partner in *darb el-mendel.*' She answered his unspoken question. 'We have made several very successful experiments.'

'It doesn't frighten him?' he asked, not altogether approving.

'But why should it? To see a picture in a mirror of ink is a very different thing from hearing a bogle under the bed, or fancying a ghost is going to pounce from out the shadows on the landing. I've explained to him that there is no magic about it, but that it is just a natural power like water-diviners have. He's seen dowsers at work. He is interested but quite unconcerned.'

'And you have never seen anything yourself?'

She shook her head:

'Only through others—just as the dowser can only sense water by means of his twig . . . The power was my mother's, I am told. And her mother's. And her mother's mother's. They came from Cloghane in Kerry, in the far, far west of Ireland where the Island of the Ever Young is supposed to float in the misty sea. . . .'

Even if Javan succeeded only in looking resignedly avuncular, Miss Jane Tierce at any rate called forth the highest expressions of admiration permissible in the Close from the very moment that she entered Mrs. Foley's drawing-room that evening, wearing a simple cherry-coloured sacque with ruffles of fine Mechlin lace.

'Utterly Attic!'—'Sweetly pretty!' whispered the ladies of the colony assembled in the low, white room whose walls were decorated very martially with swords, pikes, and suchlike garnered from the battlefields of Blenheim and Malplaquet by the late Colonel Foley.

The gentlemen were naturally far more outspoken; from the sociable and intrigued Mr. Tuke, squiring his mauve-nosed sister Catherine (who invariably wore black attire which was as invariably covered with the white hairs of a pet dog or cat) to Mr. Tudor, of Virginia Cottage, an old gentleman in incredibly tight breeches, who ordinarily said nothing unless he was spoken to, and carried a silver ear-trumpet like a large silver cockleshell.

As for Captain Tregallion, he was completely her captive—a little red-faced man with a button of a nose, wearing the scarlet coat with blue facings and the scarlet smallclothes of a naval officer in the service of the Dutch East India Company. It was never quite clear why he, a Cornishman, had gone into Dutch employment; but he enjoyed a not illiberal pension, and never failed to point out to the Close the disparity between the dividends paid by the mynheers and those of the Honourable East India Company of England.

At any rate he attached himself so firmly to Jane that nothing short of violence would have prised him from her side. Once Javan, meditating a rescue, realized that his 'niece' was listening to the captain with seriously concentrated attention. He caught fragments of Tregallion's disquisition—

'So I said to the old witch, "Madam, you can go to Hell! My boy is as good as your girl any day of the week" . . . "At any rate, madam," I said, "my boy's mother wasn't a whore!" You will forgive an old sailor's honest speech, my dear miss!'

It was clear that he was talking of Madame von Pfullingen, the Hanoverian lady who had enjoyed King George the First's favours for many years, and whose daughter had eloped with the captain's son. It also appeared to Javan that, for purposes of her own, Jane was encouraging the ancient sea-dog to every revelation possible about the strange woman who had inhabited Old Palace ten years or so agone.

'Drinks like a fish, ma'am,' said Captain Tregallion. 'Almost see me under the table, too—*me* who was brought up on "mahogany" from the time I first went to sea! It's part of the armistice between us that the boy shall spend three months every year with her. Her only grandchild. He goes next month. I don't like it, but—'

After that he had embarked on a bitter diatribe against Madame
von Pfullingen's proclivity to dabble in the black arts. Fortunetellers
and seers and geomancers, it appeared, had been the habitués of
Old Palace during her reign there. People even said that she tried to
raise unlawful spirits by charms and incantations and unholy sacri-
fices. The countryfolk, who saw her on the rare occasions when she
drove out, declared that she could cast the evil eye on them. Once
her carriage had been stoned—and serve the old devil right! To all
this and more Miss Jane Tierce listened with the most flattering
attention.

Miss Tierce's success was repeated and intensified with every
public appearance. The whole Close felt it a matter of personal pride
that she should be much caressed by Royalty itself on the occasion
of the Handel recital. The fact that she had secured Lady Morfa's
approval was utterly thrown into the shade by her promenading on
the Outlook in company with the Prince and Princess of Wales.

She was undoubtedly the belle of the ball in the Long Room at
the Maid's Head. She walked a minuet with much composure with
Mr. Standring, who thereafter never left her side, but stood looking
poetry at her, who danced looking poetry at her, and finally saw her
into her chair for the short homeward journey looking the very per-
sonification of poetical parting.

'I am not very greatly taken with that lad, madam,' said Javan,
as he bowed over her hand in the great shadowy hall of Old Palace,
'but all the same I hope that you will deal lightly with him.'

'You think that he might get hurt?' asked Shems-ed-Douha with
a rather odd expression, looking down upon his bent head.

'I'm sure of it, madam,' he answered with conviction.

'I've divined a very hard practical streak beneath the poesy,'
said Shems. 'And, as I told you a few days ago, Javan, I feel in the
need of admiration.'

He wondered a little at her small enigmatical smile as she turned
from him and slowly mounted the wide shallow stairs to the upper
floor. It still lingered on her lips when she paused at the bend and
wished him good night. The grey of dawn filled the tall window
behind her, quenched the light of the wax candles held by the
attendant Yusuf, and gave something of the phantasmal to her and
to her silver dress. Then, like a ghost, she was gone.

'Fool!' he said bitterly to himself as he took up his hat.

Upon the long oak table a great Canton bowl of roses stood beside a silver candelabra—white roses and red roses alternately, the largest that he had ever seen, the most sweetly scented that he had ever smelled.

But, when later in the day he took his morning walk to the Outlook through the misty churchyard, he saw—he could swear that he saw—those selfsame roses lying upon the flat top of a table-tomb beneath the wide canopy of a weeping ash. It was a high chest of weather-stained stone in a lonely corner, and, even in the shade of the tree and the vaporous obscurity of the haze, the great flowers—ice-white and deepest crimson—seemed unmistakable to him.

He stopped himself just in time from bending over to read the inscription on the monument, and turned away with a feeling that nearly, very nearly indeed, had he been guilty of a dishonourable action.

Nevertheless it was impossible for him not to realize, when he presented himself at Old Palace, that the roses had disappeared from the hall.

# X

## *Mr. Griffe Goes 'Haroun-al-Raschiding'*

'IT HAS BEEN A GOOD DAY,' said Mr. Griffe. 'I've never known a better. But this is waste of time. There are far too many interesting things to do.'

He was sitting on an upturned keg, eating oysters and drinking small beer from a grey-blue earthenware mug with Javan, at the counter of a covered stall which specialized in these commodities—and gilt gingerbread.

The evening mists were already rising from the river which fringed the fairground. In the distance, beyond the West Gate, the tall spire of the church lifted into the hazy twilight over the town with an appearance of insubstantiality, as though it were compounded of solidifying smoke rather than of stone. The booths, the stalls, the canvas theatres had become flower-beds of twinkling lanterns.

The noise was louder than ever; the merrymakers thronging the wide alleys that intersected the fair were more numerous than ever; the swings surged up and down faster than ever; the man outside the shack opposite—where was being performed the drama of 'St. George and the Dragon'—beat his drum more insistently than ever, to advertise the fact that real green fire was spouted from the jaws of the monster; the man with the telescope declared more loudly than ever his faith that on the moon were still visible 'The Mountains—Hi! of the Moon—Hi! . . . 'Oo'll spy the Mountains hof the Moon—Hi! Many times higher than Hararat—Hi! One half penny the go. Hi!'

Everywhere fiddling, squealing, piping, laughing, beer-drinking, shouting, and dancing.

Mr. Griffe sighed a sigh of the purest pleasure.

'Do you think gingerbread would go with oysters?' asked he; and answered himself. 'No, Javan, no! Now let's go and dance! I saw a place in one of the other alleys, called "The Temple of Harmony." There's a proclamation outside it saying—"Dance all Night for Threepence." Let's go and dance all night for threepence! . . . This has been a red-letter day for me!'

'As you will, Fred,' said Javan, unfurling himself from his barrel seat. 'At any rate I will watch you perform, for I have forgotten how. Where I come from it is only dervishes and professionals who dance. But remember that if we don't return at a reasonable hour, Standring will probably call out the military.'

'He'd better!' said Griffe.

In fact, however, Javan had long since lost any fears for his companion despite the consternation that beset him when he first discovered that Griffe had abandoned the idea of going to the fair dressed as a countryman—which was bad enough—in favour of a nautical costume to which—Javan Tierce thought—he was utterly unsuited.

The little man had revealed himself at the place of assignation garbed in a seaman's loose white breeches—so baggy that he looked to be wearing a petticoat—white cotton stockings, a brilliantly blue jacket, a yellow neckerchief, and an enormous three-cornered hat. He was also flourishing a most murderous cudgel.

Javan, inconspicuously dressed in a country coat of homespun and a round hat, felt that no one could possibly have resembled a sailor less. As the day wore on, however, he discovered that no one seemed to notice anything unusual in the appearance of that rather oriental-looking seaman.

The small man was in fact completely sure of himself. So much so, indeed, that after watching a needle-threading competition for a groat between a dozen buxom young women, he had entered—the only man to do so—for the next bout, and had won, hands down. The roars of laughter and extremely coarse jests from the male on-lookers that greeted the result in no way disconcerted him; and when he presented the disconsolate runner-up with the silver four-penny piece, she had fondly embraced him to his own and the crowd's delight.

The young lady, a strapping lass with very black eyes, in a pink cotton dress, had attached herself to them after that: had accompanied them to a shortened and definitely indecorous version of *The Beggar's Opera*, to see Cadman, the celebrated 'Flying Man,' to the juggler's—to the calf with two heads—the mermaid—the giant—the dwarf; and to drink cider and eat hot beef sausages. She had endeavoured, but in vain, to persuade them to witness a battle in the boxing booth between two women prize-fighters naked to the waist; and had shortly afterwards been lost, somewhat to Javan's relief, owing to a sudden surge in the crowd near the stage on which singlestick contests were taking place.

Griffe had watched two bouts with great interest before he said to his companion:

'I think I will take that fellow on, Javan.'

'For God's sake—'

'I know a bit about the broadsword. I've got a chance at any rate.'

With those words he had thrown his hat at the last winner and clambered upon the platform.

The countryman was a huge creature in a pink waistcoat and blue smalls, with a face like a scalded pig's. He greeted the arrival of an opponent half his size with a bellow of laughter, which was echoed by the bystanders. It was a case, however, of David and Goliath; although he began by clowning and simulating great fear, the rustic very quickly found himself in difficulties, and ended with a gory pate dizzily watching the flight of his weapon over the heads of a guffawing crowd.

Mr. Griffe was, indeed, obviously well able to take care of himself. This was even more apparent when they finished their repast and began weaving their way from the gingerbread-and-oyster stall, through the slowly moving throng, to the Temple of Harmony. Griffe

came abruptly to a standstill. Without saying a word, he clutched
a hand that was gently insinuating itself into one of his baggy side-
pockets. He held it for a second in a grip from which there was no
escape, whilst he swung round and delivered a single devastating
blow on the pickpocket's nose before letting him escape.

'There's no reason why he should go scot-free. *"Impunitas sem-
per ad deteriora invitat,"'* said he sententiously.

It was now night; the ground mist had risen, and a full moon,
veiled by vapours, ornamented rather than illumined the dark sky.
With its myriad small lights the fairground shimmered in a spectral
yellow haze along the banks of the hurrying black river. In the pri-
vacy of the shadowed alleys at the back of its booths, and in the
darkness on its fringe people whispered, danced, made love, or
settled their differences by fist or cudgel.

The Temple of Harmony was in private life a barn—and a very
large one; for the present occasion the narrow end which fronted
upon the alley had been given a gaudy canvas façade decked with
fairy-lights. At the entrance, hung with a red baize curtain, Tierce
and Griffe paid their threepences to an old lady with one eye and
a witchlike face before they edged their way in.

The interior was lit uncertainly by a large number of tallow
candles stuck in hoops suspended from the crossbeams. Music was
discoursed to a milling crowd of noisy dancers by three sweating
fiddlers on a small rickety platform, each man with his mug of ale
beside him. The onlookers were accommodated with benches placed
along the walls, whilst a row of beer barrels on trestles near the
door guaranteed refreshment.

'Ah!' sighed Griffe in an access of pleasure. 'This is what I like!
Sit as near the beer as you can, Javan, if you won't dance. Then I
will know where to find you. Will you look after my cudgel, if you
please?'

With those words, he seized upon a giggling, bright-complex-
ioned girl standing near by with a respectable elderly man and
woman, and vanished amid the stamping, perspiring, shouting hurly-
burly.

Javan found a place to sit at the end of a bench nearest the beer,
and secured a pot of very light liquor from one of the tapsters.

Whilst he watched the chiaroscuro of moving figures that ca-
vorted and swirled to the high squeak of the fiddles, he let his mind

play with the suspicion which he had conceived at the beginning of the week, that Shems-ed-Douha intended sampling the entertainment offered by the Fair. He wondered if by any chance she were dancing amid the crowd in the Temple of Harmony or elsewhere, and whether the poetically smitten Standring had escorted her.

Griffe came seeking him by-and-by, accompanied this time by a handsome young gipsy in a red gown with an aquiline nose and enormous golden earrings and a rose and a great gold comb in her hair.

'Delaia and I have decided to dance together till sunrise, Javan,' said he, mopping his forehead with a lace-edged handkerchief, which was completely out of keeping with his nautical disguise, 'She says her sister will teach you to dance, if you like.'

'She could make a dead man dance, pretty gentleman,' said Delaia.

'Sunrise!' said Javan. 'Sunrise! I'm not so young as you, Fred. So let me sit here quietly a bit longer before I test the kindness of Delaia's sister.'

'Delaia says,' continued Griffe, 'that there is brandy for those who can afford it—good stuff, too, which has paid no duty to the King! I shall enjoy drinking a measure of brandy that has paid no duty to his Majesty! Rather a pretty little piece of irony, I think, don't you? Have a tass of it with me?'

Javan shook his head.

'Give the tapster the high sign for you and me, then, my pretty,' said Mr. Griffe. 'I've only been drunk once in my life, and I don't intend to get mazed now. But I'd like to wash the taste of this dishwater beer out of my teeth.'

Delaia gave the tapster accordingly the 'high sign' and she and companion were duly accommodated with right Nantz that had paid no duty to Mr. Griffe's father's customs.

'Fred and I'll come back soon, pretty gentleman,' said Delaia, 'and then you shall learn to foot it with my sister Clevansi. After that you will want to dance with her for ever. Like those who are bitten by the spider on the Feast of St. John! Come, my little *comly*!'

She swept Griffe off with her; but an instant later he had returned and was whispering delightedly into Javan's ear the speech of that other Prince of Wales in Shakespeare's *King Henry the Fourth*—'I am sworn brother to a leash of drawers; and can call them

all by their christen names . . . I am so good a proficient in one
quarter of an hour, that I can drink with any tinker in his own
language.'

Javan had a moment of ill-ease at the thought that Delaia might
be meditating a more serious companionship with Griffe than a
dancing partnership. On the other hand the little man, whilst freely
commenting upon every instance of feminine beauty that came their
way, had evinced no amorous propensities and frequently deplored
his Augusta's absence. Javan felt, however, that it might be as well
if he were to dance with Clevansi and keep a closer eye on the
Hanoverian Haroun-al-Raschid.

The music, which had been almost continuous, stopped after a
while; nevertheless Griffe and his Delaia did not make their appearance, and he could not see them among the crowd that surged to
and fro on the beaten earth dance floor. Only immediately under
the candle-hoops, in fact, was it possible to distinguish faces at any
distance. The shadows in the high arched roof of the barn pressed
downwards like an extinguisher ready to descend upon the pale
illumination. Away from the central lights a thin dusk brooded—a
dusk full of activity and noise, of half-seen faces and half-seen gestures. The place swam in a miasma of the odours of humanity,
tobacco smoke, and beer.

He had just decided to begin a tour of investigation when the
violins struck up a lively hornpipe and dancing started once more.
At that same moment he became conscious that someone, who had
just sat down in the place next to him on the bench, was endeavour-
ing to attract his attention by gently tugging at his wide coat-cuff.

He looked, discreetly sidelong, at his new neighbour. It was a
girl—and a pretty one—in a rose-pink gown with a white neckerchief
modestly veiling her bosom. Her face was vaguely familiar, and he
had just remarked that her scarf was pinned by a brooch made from
a Moorish silver ducat, when she leaned towards him and whispered
in his right ear in self-introduction—

'I'm Susie, my lord! Susie from the Maid's Head!'

Now he recalled her, arriving flustered and apologetic in response to Mr. Tuke's summons by tankard. He himself had given
her the coin that she wore.

'It's Susie, my lord!' she reasserted her identity. 'My sweetheart
Joe's with me.' She indicated with a little nod a very large young

man with a large amiable face and lanky black hair, tied with a singularly narrow black ribbon, at her side. 'It's your friend, my lord—'

'My friend?' he exclaimed quickly. 'What about him?'

'They've just carried him out of the place, my lord. By a little door at the other end. I'd see 'ee here with him, and me and Joe didn't like the look of it, my lord, and so I—'

Javan was already on his feet, cursing himself inwardly for not having kept constant watch upon Griffe's activities.

'Thank you, my dear. I'll see what has been happening!'

But Susie detained him by the sleeve.

'Joe 'uld better go with 'ee, my lord,' said she in a low voice: and Javan thought that the company of Susie's lover might well be useful, supposing Mr. Griffe to have been overcome by anything other than brandy that had paid no duty.

He pushed his way unceremoniously to the entrance, with Joe closely at his heels.

On the other side of the red baize curtain the one-eyed witch was cackling to a group of men clustered about her lantern-lit table. Some second sense told him that the silence which fell upon them as he burst out was ominous. He knew quite well, without turning round, that their eyes were following him as he plunged into the dark passageway between the Temple and Gingle's Medley of the Dead-Alive, a waxwork show now closed for the night.

At the end of the passage the few twinkling lights of the town on its cliff above the river showed in the darkness as though suspended from the sky.

No one was stretched out on the grass by the further door to recover from indisposition or the ill-effects of uncustomed brandy. He had not expected that there would be. In fact no one at all was visible on the gentle grassy slope from the back of the barn to the bank of the fast-moving water.

Joe said:

'That black gipsy queen says he were took bad. But I sees 'im wi' my own eyes a-strugglin' wen they carries 'im out. And 'e weren't strugglin' like 'e were overtaken in liquor, your honour. 'E were sort of palsied tremblin'. There was four on 'em a-holdin' of 'im, an' the girl goes out wi' 'em. They'll have emptied 'is pockets an' knocked 'im out an' put 'im to sleep under a cart, or in a ditch—that they will.'

Searching for him in the fairground amid the jumble of tents and shanties would be like seeking a ring in a sand-dune.

Joe made further comment—

'Susie a'seen 'im flashin' of gold wen 'e was a-buying of fairings a while back. Sailormen are all the same, your honour.'

It was true enough. He himself had warned Sailor Fred to be a little more cautious on two occasions—the last only a short time before the incident with the pickpocket.

Joe continued with grim appreciation of possible melodrama:

'They'ld be hung either way. So they may have knocked 'im on the head and thrown 'im in the river. As well be hung for a sheep as a lamb, as the sayin' goes, and dead-uns aren't tellin' no tales, your honour.'

As though impelled by the gruesomeness of Joe's suggestion, Javan went swiftly to the river bank, and looked down into the inky flood in which the cloudy moonshine was all but quenched.

The smooth surface of the water was unbroken and unruffled. A hundred yards away, perhaps, the vague light revealed the squat mass of a barge drifting slowly with the current towards the curve of the big loop which the river made about the fairground meadow. Although the craft showed no lights and no sound came from her, it seemed to Javan that several men were clustered aft. His mind was seized on the instant by an utter certainty—

'*W-Alláhi*, they are kidnapping him!' he exclaimed.

'Anan?' questioned Joe, to whom only the words 'they,' 'are,' and 'him' were comprehensible.

'Hurry, man!' said Javan, setting off back to the fair.

The two men walked rapidly through the fast emptying streets of the fairground. Many of the lights had been extinguished, and only the dance-places still were in full swing. Almost every dark corner, however, held a whispering couple. Drunkards with linked arms, singing discordantly, guided one another's wavering tread towards the gate to the main road and the bridge that led to the town: others had collapsed and lay like logs where they had fallen; a dozen noisy brawls were taking place simultaneously; somewhere or other a woman was screaming persistently, but her shrieks were those of a virago's anger and not of anguish. A lost child wailed near the gatepost, clutching but uncomforted by an enormous sausage thrust into its fist by a consolatory passer-by.

In such sordid setting had the drama of a Haroun-al-Raschiding Prince of Wales reached its climax! reflected Javan as he came out upon the many-arched bridge with his companion.

The barge swam slowly into sight round the bend; came loitering towards them. A man with a pole stood in her bows, and another with a long oar aft kept her head-on to the central span of the bridge. No one else was now visible at all.

Deliberately she oozed under the arch, and then, in that instant Javan, staring over the parapet, saw in the murk below him two men stooped and hauling an inert something under the dark canvas tilt which covered most of the hold. Even the brief glimpse was sufficient, however, to tell him that his premonition had been correct and that he had found Sailor Fred.

The crew of the vessel were too intent upon their tasks to look up as they passed out of sight.

'Follow her along the bank,' said Javan to Susie's Joe.

He threw off hat and wig and leaped to the other side of the bridge. The bows of the barge had already begun to appear.

For split second he lay flat along the parapet, peering down. The next moment he had swung over, and was hanging by one arm, whistling tunelessly to himself as was his wont before going into action. Then he let go and dropped into the flat bottom of the boat aft of the tilt.

He fell on all fours; bounced up; hurled himself—it seemed to be one continuous movement—upon the nearer of the two men amidships as the fellow straightened up.

The steersman had given a guttural cry of warning, although too late to do aught except attract the attention of his comrade in the bows; but the latter equally dared not leave his post for fear lest the long craft should ground against the bank.

If Javan had dropped like a cat, he went into battle like a tiger. He tore his victim backwards with one hand, hauling him to his feet and striking him a stunning blow under the chin as he did so. Then, as the man sagged, he seized him by the nape of his neck and by his breeches, raised him above his head, and, swinging round, flung him overboard into the dark river.

The oarsman shouted. The boat lurched.

In the few seconds of swift justice the second man had disengaged himself from the folds of the canvas tilt—was already about to spring,

a knife in his fist. But Javan's plan of battle was already clear-cut
in his mind. The heavy splash of the body in the water coincided
with the completion of the swing about of his body and the first of
three panther leaps towards the stern.

The steersman gave a cry of dismay, dropped the oar, and fumbled at his belt—but too late. Javan was on him, towering over him
in deadly menace before he had collected himself for self-defence.
A hammer fist struck him between the eyes; another over the heart:
and he fell backwards with something between a groan and a cry,
his head cracking loudly against the gunwale of the boat.

They had drifted now out of sight of the bridge, and the barge
was slowly turning broadside-on to the current between banks that
were dense with osiers. The man in the bows was making frantic
efforts to keep her on her course and at the same time watch the
progress of the drama aft. His surviving mate, a square ape-man
with hunched shoulders and features hidden by a wide-brimmed
hat, had been momentarily disconcerted by the surprise shift of the
battlefield, and halted some ten feet away, his knife held against
his chest, point outwards, whilst he pondered the situation.

Javan did not particularly like that knife. He folded his arms,
and waited, and cajoled his enemy—

'Come, baboon bastard of a burned mother!' said he. 'Come and
let me push your face through your backside for you! Come, you
frog-livered son of a—'

Of all languages in the world, Arabic has established the
most potent vocabulary of invective. Javan's translation of the
choicest items lost nothing of the force of the original, and little
of the succinctness. The ape-man grunted. He took one small step
nearer. It was clear to Javan that he was no coward, but slow-think-
ing when confronted with the unforeseen.

At that moment the man in the peak of the boat impatiently
urged some course of action in the canting speech of the longshore
rogue.

Ape-man growled an answer without shifting his eyes from his
opponent.

'Come, Vomit!' said Javan. 'Let me finish you off with my bare
hands as I did the others! Let me tear out your guts and dance with
them round my neck like the girls of Footha-Yallon!'

He sprang straight into the air as he spoke, clapping his hands above his head in absurd parody of a war dance, his coat and arms flapping and flailing as though they were the dark wings of some creature from the Pit.

For a bare second the other's common sense left him, and he recoiled; then, infuriated by his own fears and by the insolence of this lunatic invitation to conflict by an unarmed man, he gave up caution. With a grunt of anger he made his rush—and was stopped beyond arm's length by a terrific kick from a long leg that caught him in the groin.

The next moment the two men were rolling over and over on the gratings in the bottom in a frenzied struggle. With both hands Javan clung to the wrist of the other's knife, and suffered the while heavy punishment about his head from a fist as hard as a cudgel. Once the threshing body heaved him over, and for a split second loosed his grip sufficiently to force the blade downwards against him. He felt the sharp bite of the steel, and the grating of it against his ribs, and the sticky wetness of blood.

With that an utter fighting madness seized him. He was no longer a battling man but an elemental force—a tornado of superhuman violence, which caught up the ape-creature as though he had been something inanimate seized by its whirlwind, and cast him down again; and seized him afresh, and hurled him away once more; and then picked him up and catapulted him overboard, with a broken arm, into the shallows wheron the barge at that moment gently grounded under a willow tree.

For a few seconds Javan rested against the gunwale breathing heavily and assessing the damage to himself. A cut on the ribs—superficial. A long wound on the right forearm whereon his sleeve hung in shreds—superficial! A badly battered face—superficial! All superficial!

The light of the declining moon fell directly on the barge, and he saw now that the man in the bows had vanished. The figure in the stern, lying in a mess of dark blood, moved its head feebly from side to side and groaned.

He staggered, more from sudden weakness than the gentle uncertainties of the boat, towards the tarpaulin-covered portion of the cargo space. He raised a fold of the sheet. He could just—and only just—distinguish Griffe's features. Mingled with the gentle wash of the stream against the sides of the barge and the sound of her nuzzling happily against the mud, he could hear his heavy breathing.

With a prayer of thanksgiving he let the flap fall.

A loud voice hailed him. It was the voice of Susie's Joe.

# XI

# A Borrowed Past

THE FRONT DOOR of Tregallion House was open to the sunshine; the wide hall, faintly scented by lavender in a Chinese bowl sentinelled by the four hourglasses, was empty; the only sound to be heard was the vague drone of organ music seeping through the whispering birch trees from the church.

Miss Jane Tierce, decked in a cherry-red gown, a 'milkmaid' hat tied under her chin with a ribbon of darker red, hesitated but for an instant. Then, unheralded and unescorted, she set off up the stairs—stairs so wide that she did not need lift her hoops or step sideways, and so shallow that Coppie complained it was impossible to slide down them satisfactorily on a tray.

She tapped once—twice—thrice—upon the panels of the door of Javan's parlour, gently—louder—imperiously. But there was no reply.

Again she paused. It was long past eleven o'clock, and yet he had not appeared, as he always did at half past nine precisely, in the gloomy entrance-hall of Old Palace to present his humble duty and to request audience of Imperial Highness.

Very quietly she turned the door handle and entered.

Javan was asleep in a high-backed chair before one of the tall windows, which was full of sunlight and the delicate, restless pattern of the birch leaves. Never before had she seen him completely off his guard. She closed the door softly, and stood by it watching him in silence.

He wore a fur-rimmed montero cap, not unlike a turban, and his head was turned away from her so that all she could see of his face was the right cheekbone and the angle of the jaw. He was dressed in a wide-skirted morning-gown of flowered silk, of which the right sleeve hung empty over the arm of the chair. Beside him was a low stool whereon were an empty glass and two small, fat books in battered red bindings.

The room was otherwise just as desolate as when she had seen it last. The meaningless face of the clock upon the mantelpiece looked across the shining desert of the table to the emptiness of the buffet. The picture of a ship sailing amid a treacly swamp of oil paint hung as crookedly against the dark panelling as it did before. Javan's parlour still told nothing whatsoever of the habits or the tastes of its occupant. It was as spotless and featureless as an inn parlour made ready for a new guest after the departure of the old. There was nothing to remember about it except the sleeping man—and, perhaps, the two books beside him!

Quenching the susurration of skirt and petticoats as best she could, she stole towards the window, cautiously seized the small volumes, and withdrew a pace or two to the table, where she proceeded to examine them with occasional cautious glances at their owner.

The first was a New Testament printed in English half a century before. On the inside of its cover was pasted a bookplate engraved with elaborate armorial bearings and a motto which she knew to belong to his family. She studied the label intently for a moment, and then idly fluttered the leaves. Between two of them she found a pressed violet like a faintly tinted shadow; and over that ghost of a flower—which must, she thought, also be ghost of a memory—she lingered for several moments more.

Dissatisfied as much with herself for her curiosity as she was with the results, she took up the other volume. It also had its ownership marked by the bookplate, but it was printed in characters entirely foreign to her, and she set it down on the table with a small sigh of displeasure.

'What—' began Javan drowsily. 'What—'

His eyes travelled from the unstirring clock over the fireplace to the girl in cherry-red standing by the table; remarked her sudden change of expression when she saw him full-face. He began to remember. He averted his gaze. He said—

'Forgive me, madam, if I do not rise. I find I am a trifle stiff. The onset of old age, I presume.'

'The Princess expected you two hours ago, Uncle Javan,' said Niece Jane; and then as he fumbled with his left hand for a watch that was not in his fob, added: 'May I ask what you have been doing with your face? There was, it seems, very boisterous fun at the fair.'

'*Very* boisterous, my dear.'

'And the other reveller?'

'Dreaming of the—revelry, I opine.'

In the search for his watch he had disarranged the folds of his morning-gown, and as he made answer, she suddenly became aware of a bloodstained bandage about his right arm, and of a white shirt dyed ominously red.

In an altogether different tone—in a tone of concern that amounted to consternation—with a catch in her voice, she exclaimed—

'Oh, God! Javan, you are hurt! You are badly hurt! Who has seen to the wound? Why aren't you in bed? Why didn't you send and tell me?'

His swollen lips writhed in what was meant to be a reassuring smile.

'It's a mere nothing. They're just scratches, but I am uncommonly stiff. It will have worn off in a day or so. My face, too, will soon be respectable enough to present myself before your hostess. She would doubtless have acid remarks to make about my appearance if I ventured within her sight at the moment. Pray tell her that I am a little indisposed! A riding accident, shall we say?'

'Where is your man? He must get you to bed and fetch the surgeon to you. At once. How long have you been here like this? Why has nobody done anything for you?'

Questions and instructions poured from her lips. She stood over him now, anxious, almost fierce in her alarm, whilst he fumbled to draw the revealing fold of the banian over the ugly stains upon his shirt.

'I sent Williams into Wales yesterday to buy horses. He won't be back for a couple of days.' Recollection of the small clash between them a week earlier came to him, and he added, with another distortion of the lips. 'Perhaps it's just as well. He might, of course, think it was overindulgence in the bottle. He might even smell brandy, you know!'

'Don't be a fool!' said Jane. 'Try to get up! I'll help you. *I must* get you to bed.'

'You can't. There's someone already in it!'

'Someone? Who? Why?'

He turned his battered face up to hers as she bent over him—

'The Prince. We couldn't get him back—to his Augusta—as he was. He is not harmed. He was drugged. He's sleeping.' An expression, the meaning of which she could not divine, suddenly came over his battered face—an expression that combined shocked surprise and intense pain. 'I am all right, too. Quite all—'

The blood ebbed from his face as he spoke, and his head fell forward upon his breast. The sound of his breathing was so strange that for a dreadful instant she thought he was dying, and that she heard life bubbling from his lips in the last rattle of death.

Even when she had placed her hand against his heart and felt its beat, and so satisfied herself that he had but fainted, anguish did not leave her.

She stood for a bare instant looking down at the man who had saved her life in the moonlit gardens at Meknes, the man whom her husband trusted alone among men, whom she trusted; and said aloud as if taking an oath, 'Javan, I think I shall die if you do not live!'

She went to the door to summon help. Somebody must fetch Garlicke, the apothecary, whilst she waited by him. Coppie Tregallion—a maid—old Captain Tregallion—anybody.

Heaven was on her side, for as she opened the door Coppie himself came bounding down from his quarters on the top floor.

After that it was only a matter of seconds before the ancient Mrs. Garlicke, sitting in her watchtower, saw Copernicus Tregallion chasing down the steps of Vicar's Close as though Mr. Tuke's Old Horny Gooseberry were after him. She heard the jangle of the bell on the

ground floor as he burst into the shop where her son's clubfooted
apprentice spent a dreary life of potion-compounding and draught
testing. Another moment, and she saw the surgeon scrambling across
the street at a knock-kneed canter, wigless, and in his slippers.

She took snuff. She meditated. She might never know what was
happening. She did not mind very much. She was used to catching
one glimpse of a drama and no more. Her active imagination would
provide her with a beginning and an end which might be far more
amusing than the reality. . . .

Javan lay in bed.

It was an uncanopied bed with four squat posts of black oak,
elaborately carved and surmounted with large classical urns. Lying
there, as he had done for a fortnight, he had acquired the positive
conviction that the tops of the urns, being unscrewed, would reveal
within mortal relics of previous tenants of the bed. Jane had not,
however, approved the fantasy; had declined to investigate.

The sunlight and the subdued chanting in the church of Kethe's
hymn, 'All people that on earth do dwell,' came streaming in
through the open window. The room glowed like the garden of
jewels in Aladdin's cave with the fruit and the flowers which arrived
every morning from Barrington Court. Between the windows also
hung a remarkable study in red chalk of the head of a shouting
warrior by Leonardo da Vinci, which had been sent from the art
collection that Griffe was forming in London, owing to a fancied
resemblance to Javan. Griffe had himself placed it in position.

Miss Mott examined it for some time when she first saw it.

'A genuine Leonardo,' she remarked at length. 'I must approve.
I do approve. Its value is doubtless immense!'

'But do you see any real likeness to me?' persisted Javan.

'I have never seen you with your mouth wide open, sir,' replied
Miss Mott in her most Attic manner. 'It is *not* a genteel expression
before ladies. I have remarked, general, that you barely show your
teeth at all, even when you are talking. Which is a habit to be com-
mended. The circumstances are rather different in the case of the
soldier in the picture. He is clearly not a gentleman.'

Miss Mott had been that day at her most ultraistical—which was
the Close's term for the holding of any extreme view on any subject.
To be ultraistical was definitely not Attic for a lady—always except-

ing Miss Mott, of course. Even the Jacobitism which permeated this
genteel enclave was not so ultraistical that its inhabitants were not
fluttered and flattered by the daily visits of a prince of the usurping
dynasty of Hanover to the sickbed of one of their number. Nay,
more—

'An old wound, my dear Julia, I assure you,' said Mrs. Foley to
Miss Grenville a few days after the calamity, 'It was opened by a
fall from his horse in the Prince's company. His Royal Highness—
for we can recognize his royalty as a prince of Hanover at any rate
my dear—told me so this morning. He did me the honour of calling,'
said she with ill-concealed gratification, 'on purpose to see the Van
Dyck portrait of my great-grandpapa, of which Mr. Tuke had told
him. He admired it very greatly. Letchworth was instructed to
announce him to me merely as Prince Frederick. A remarkable instance of Attic taste, my dear!'

Now on this Sunday morning, a fortnight after the battle on the
barge, Niece Jane had been engaged until a minute ago in reading
from one of the many books which Griffe had provided. She had
stopped in order to engage in admonishment of her 'uncle.'

'It's monstrously absurd,' protested Javan.

'It would be more absurd if you tried to get up,' said Jane.

'I *have* tried—and succeeded. I walked as far as the window
without help last night.'

'In that case someone will have to sit up with you all night.
Don't be a pig-headed fool, Javan! Somebody *shall* keep watch on
you, in this room and not in the dressing-room, unless you give me
your promise. I swear it, *W-Alláhi!* What is more, I'll have every
stitch of clothing you possess—I like that grey coat and the primrose
embroidered waistcoat!—shifted out of the house!'

'Then I'll—'

'You will not. Unless you are prepared to appear in Coppie's
breeches, or Captain Tregallion's Sunday-go-to-meeting coat of scarlet and blue.'

He groaned 'Oh, God!'

'You know very well that both Garlicke and Hope say you cannot get up for another week at least. Tierce Pasha, you are going
to do what they say, if I have to put Yusuf and Abdulla on day and
night shifts! Or send a detachment of the Harriffa over under command of Kahdijah!'

'But something has got to be done about this business of the jewels and the investments. Goldstein ought to be seen, and the man at the Bank of England. Everything has been let slide. I don't like—'

'Goldstein has waited,' she said indifferently. 'Goldstein can go on waiting. Let him earn his profits by waiting. Are you grown bored with your company—with me—with Griffe's daily visit—with Captain Tregallion on the East Indies—with Mr. Tuke on sport—with Coppie on everything under the sun—with Standring—'

'Standring! Are you—are you—being quite fair to him'—he paused for appreciable time before he concluded—'Jane?'

He turned his ruffled head on the pillows so that his intensely dark blue eyes should meet hers that were of so deep a grey. She said very soberly—

'I've always tried to be fair, Javan—even to Mulai Ali. I told Standring confidentially that I was married privately and unhappily —on the night when you got hurt. He swore that he was heartbroken. And I think, indeed, that he may have been grieved at the time. But now he has already settled down to being poetically and respectfully heartbroken for ever. Whenever he can escape from his duties, I am sure of finding him being respectfully heartbroken wherever I may be. I honestly believe that he enjoys the sensation. Being in his company is rather like being in company with the chief mourner at one's own funeral.'

Javan pondered on this psychological phenomenon, staring the while at the rose and the blue and yellow checks on his patchwork quilt.

'I don't know that it is a condition which I could ever enjoy,' he finally pronounced.

'But could you ever be—heartbroken, Javan?'

Then she remembered the violet lying in the midst of the thirteenth chapter of St. Mark in his New Testament. She added: 'Have you ever been?'

After a long silence Javan looked away and said with a faint, quizzical, lopsided smile—

'I haven't got a past—madam.'

'Haven't—got a—past.' She hesitated for a little, and then went on reflectively: 'I really don't believe you have, Javan! I *will* be honest. While you've been lying here I—I—I couldn't help realizing that you've got nothing personal here at all—apart from your clothes and your weapons. Nothing except two books!'

'My *Odyssey*—which is the finest story of all time. My Testament!'

He glanced quickly at her; and in that swift regard she realized that he well knew she had seen the flower preserved between the pages of Holy Writ. He did not refer to the knowledge, however, and she merely agreed, although she felt that a telltale flush was showing in her face—

'Just those two books!'

Then he said—and he was still smiling:

'Well, you see, I have lent my past!'

'Lent it?'

'Perhaps I should say that it was borrowed. A month or so ago. I was very glad to lend it, I assure you!'

She looked at him in puzzled fashion; and then, as realization broke upon her, looked away.

'I didn't borrow it. I stole it,' she said, and knew that her embarrassment showed vividly. 'That afternoon at dinner with Griffe and Mr. Tuke. I stole your past—the Judas uncle, and the father who was attainted of high treason and wandered about the world with his orphan and became a bashaw in the service of the Emperor Ishmael. It was easier than inventing anything. But haven't you got any more past at all, Javan?'

'That should be yours, too, madam, if it were of any use. I will get Lawyer King to draw up a deed formally investing you with full rights in and legal possession of all my past that may be of assistance. Is not the Empress entitled to her servant's past, if she requires it? Shall she not also—'

He broke off very suddenly.

She was still looking at him expectantly when, with a vigorous thump on the door and without awaiting a response, Coppie Tregallion came bustling in, full of news.

The boy gave a little bow of a tousled head to Niece Jane, and another little bow to Uncle Javan.

'Oh, do you know sir,' said he, 'Old Ironsides is a three-hundred-and-fifty-oner at last! We absolutely shamed "Lumpy" Nichols into the match yesterday. And his conker went crunch! at the first shove. It did! So I'm going to retire Ironsides now. I always said I would. Oh, and old Mrs. Garlicke was watching from her window. It was open, and she heard everything, because she's got ears like a cat's.

'So after we'd whacked "Lumpy," do you know she sent for me! And I went up to her room, and she said, "So you've got a three-hundred-and-fifty-oner, have you, little boy? When my brother was a little boy—he died young—he had a five-hundred-and-fiver. He used to play conkers on the steps across the road just like you do. That was in Good King Charles's days." That'll be quite a hundred years ago, won't it? So then, do you know, she opened a drawer in a little bureau beside her, and actually gave me her brother's conkers with the five-hundred-and-fiver! The man in the shop afterwards gave me some lozenges made of garlic and honey. He said they were for people in a decline. They are odd, but nice. Would you like to try, ma'am?'

With that he put his hand in the pocket of his yellow nankeen smallclothes and produced a sticky paper of sweetmeats and also a handful of ancient snail-shells, with the air of one who had been given access to the treasury of King Midas. From the aroma that he diffused it was clear that he had been sampling his strange confection.

He accepted a slice of pineapple, however, and was trying to wheedle Javan into permitting him to view and handle his silver-mounted French pistols, when Williams announced the arrival of the Prince. A moment later Mr. Griffe appeared on the scene in person —today a rather drooping melancholy person, though clad in a gay coat of green brocade.

He was always an object of great interest to Coppie—not so great, naturally, as those romantic, fairy-tale figures, Shems-ed-Douha, Princess of Morocco, and Javan Tierce, Pasha and general in the paynim service of the Grand Turk; but very nearly so. It was a sympathetic interest more than anything else, as was made manifest when Griffe, after greeting, lamented that he dare delay his departure for London no longer.

'I had another letter this morning,' Griffe said sadly. 'It warned me that a very serious construction would be put upon any further failure on my part to obey orders. I shall have to leave by the day after tomorrow at latest. There is no question about it. Augusta is in floods of tears. She has dressed Elsa, the doll, in black this morning.'

'And *I've* got to go away, too!' mourned Coppie. 'I have to go to my grandmother's. I hate it. I oughtn't to, I know, but—I hate—her, too.'

'You hate her, do you, Coppie?' inquired Mr. Griffe, interested in family dislike thus made manifest at such an early age in other circles than his own.

'She says *things*!' said Coppie darkly. 'Grandfather calls her a—' 'What sort of things?'

Coppie was rather hazy and embarrassed; circumnavigated the question; concluded—

'And do you know, she once told me that I was a grandson of King George the First? Grandfather Tregallion is the only grandfather *I* want. I *don't* want to be a grandson of King George the First. There's a picture of him in her room—I don't like it. He looks—'

'He was very kind to me,' said Mr. Griffe. 'You see I am his grandson as well!'

'Oh!' said Coppie, 'I hadn't thought of that, sir!' And he looked with open amazement at the uncomely yellow face with the drooping foreign nose and the thick lips and the kindly smile and the intelligent eyes; and then smiled as though gratified at realization of the kinship.

'I don't honestly see how I can be his grandson,' he remarked uncertainly, 'because, you know, grandmother isn't even a princess.'

'It's all very puzzling, I know,' said Mr. Griffe, 'but quite unimportant. It is nice to think, Coppie, however, that we are cousins. You can call me Cousin Fred, if you like, when we are alone together with friends just like this.'

After Coppie had retired, somewhat comforted, he drew up a chair by one of the funereal posts at the foot of the bed and sat down facing Javan, and Jane, who was sitting by him with an open book in her lap. He leaned a little forward, resting one pale green brocade elbow upon the quilt of rose, blue, and primrose, and interlacing the long fingers of his narrow hands.

'Do you realize, my dear friends, my very dear friends,' he asked, 'that Augusta and I are being called back to prison—for that is what we are—practically prisoners? The instructions are that from now on we must live wherever my father lives; we must occupy apartments in whatever palace he occupies; when he moves, to move with him. We must be at hand and under watch all the time!'

'Must?' said Javan, studying the little man at the bed-foot. 'Can't you break away?'

Griffe shook his powdered head, tied at the back with an enormous bow of black ribbon.

'We have been able to steal these weeks only because he has been very preoccupied lately. Augusta's ill-health was our excuse. But we *can't* break away. My father does not give us a sufficient allowance. He does not give me the half of what he receives from Parliament for us. He keeps the rest for himself. Even living in his palaces, as I must, I am most horribly in debt. If I defied him—well, my grandfather put my father under arrest once, you know! I don't think that my father in his turn would hesitate for an instant to follow the example. Why does he hate me so? I would be a dutiful—a very dutiful—son, I swear, if only he would let me. Why *does* he hate me so?'

But neither of his auditors could offer any suggestion.

# XII

# *Tradesmen in Death*

GREEN—KHUNRATH'S 'BLESSED VIRIDITY'—might be the mystical hue of good fortune, but the particular shade of that colour in his brocade coat was far from kind to the Prince's dejected, jaundiced countenance. As he brooded in the heavy silence following his remark, Shems-ed-Douha found herself sympathizing with him not merely in his unhappiness, but also in his ugliness and smallness, and with a degree of commiseration that surprised her.

It was only after the lapse of at least a full minute that he said very gravely:

'But I've something else far more serious to say. We've debated the matter often enough, but now I know for an absolute certainty that the business at the fair was not just another case of the doping, robbing, and trepanning as slave to the American plantations of a drunken sailor. It was a deliberate plot against the Prince of Wales.'

'I tried to let myself be persuaded by you,' said Javan from his pillows. 'I reminded myself of the way in which you had been flashing about a fat purse with gold in it. I warned you twice at the time,

130

you recollect! I remembered the incident of the pickpocket. Then, too, old Tregallion—who knows nothing about the matter at all—told me quite casually the other day of two cases of kidnapping at the fair in recent years. I still felt uneasy, all the same.'

Griffe put an unusually potent-smelling comfit into his mouth. 'Even if all the gang weren't aware of my identity, I know for a fact that their leader at any rate knew who I was.'

'Know?'

'Yes—know!' Griffe repeated, nodding. 'Tuke told me.'

'Tuke!' exclaimed Javan in the uttermost astonishment. 'In the name of the All-Merciful what can he have got to do with it?'

'It turns out that he was down by the bend of the river just before dawn the next morning studying the habits or the habitats of otters. Apparently that is a good time to do it. Anyway, there he found a half-conscious, half-drowned man lying in an osier thicket —or should it be called "holt"?—with a broken arm and Heaven alone knows what other injuries. Tuke took him to a near-by cottage, where they put him to bed, and sent for Garlicke. He was in a very bad way.'

'He had less than his deserts,' commented Javan grimly.

'At first he declared that he'd been set upon and robbed; but, against that, his pockets were full of money. Then last night he was convinced that he was going to die and made a full confession to Tuke, who came to me with the tale this morning. He just told me all he knew, and left it at that. It's the first time I have ever known him not to ask any questions at all. So I told him the truth about our escapade, because I am certain that he is reliable.'

'I am sure, too,' averred Shems-ed-Douha.

'Before he gave me the details, he said very earnestly in that way he has of talking—"I can assure you, sir—t'ch-t'ch—that we of the Stuart party would never engage in so dastardly a conspiracy. And if I heered of any such plan, I should look upon it as my duty in honour bound—t'ch-t'ch—to inform you." He is a chivalrous gentleman even to us usurpers, you see! Then he went on to say that the scoundrel had told him he was to be paid five hundred guineas for the job. He was given a hundred in advance.'

'One hundred pieces of gold!' commented Javan. 'And who was the Judas?'

'He couldn't, or wouldn't, say. Tuke thinks he didn't know. He mentioned none of his gang by name, and would give no particulars of them. There must have been a fair number, for all our expeditions together were known of in advance and spied on.'

'I don't like the implication of that foreknowledge,' said Javan.

'Neither do I, but the fact remains that they *were* known; otherwise preparations could not have been made to precipitate the town wall on top of us when we passed beneath.'

'So that bombardment of masonry was man-assisted, then?' said Javan startled.

'It was indeed. This fellow was the pedlar with the barrow full of wigs. He gave his confederates the signal from the bend of the road when we got into the danger zone. There seems to have been no risk of discovery to them, for the passage at the back of the wall is used practically for nothing but a rubbish dump. He also said that my horse was doctored on the morning that I rode towards the quarries, and then deliberately startled.'

'Three—*three*—attempts at murder in a fortnight!'

'The word "murder,"' said Griffe, 'always makes me think of knives, bullets, or poison. On the first two occasions regrettable *accidents* were arranged. For the third, a mysterious *disappearance* had been planned, it would seem. I was to be taken to Bristol in the barge and from there shipped to Norfolk, Virginia, and sold under indenture. At least that is what was *supposed* to happen after I passed out of the hands of this tradesman in death.'

There was a long silence in the room, with a background of the buzz and clack of gossip from the congregation now streaming through the churchyard and along the Close. Javan said at length—

'That man must be made to make a sworn statement before witnesses.'

'He can't. He's dead. Tuke left him alone in the cottage whilst he went out to send for Garlicke. When he returned a bit later the rogue was dead. Dead as a door-nail! Tuke swears that he didn't die naturally; that somebody guessed that he had started to talk—a somebody who put a pillow on his face and suffocated him. Tuke's description of his looks was rather horrible, but he says he thinks that he has satisfied Garlicke sufficiently for the thing to be hushed up.'

'These enemies of yours don't appear to stop at much,' said Javan. 'Have you any idea who they are?'

Griffe did not answer the question directly.

'As a matter of fact,' he said, 'I have often thought that something like this might occur. I am really rather surprised that it hasn't happened before.'

'But who? But who?' insisted Javan impatiently. 'Who would plan such a thing, and why?'

The Prince replied—rather reluctantly, and again obliquely:

'What you have to take into account above all else is—that my parents would not be very upset if I were to vanish from the scene completely. No, that's an exaggeration! They would not be in the slightest upset if I disappeared—so long, of course, as there was not too much fuss involved.'

'You *can't* mean it! You *can't* believe it!' exclaimed Shems-ed-Douha. 'That is simply not possible. Your mother—'

He shook his head, rather—Javan thought—like a sad small punchinello.

'You don't know my mother,' he said. 'If you did, you would realize the truth of what I am saying. Mind you, I don't mean necessarily that my parents planned—or were even cognizant—of the plan to export me. But still that wouldn't prevent them from being highly gratified by the result.

'Don't you recollect from the history books how King Henry the Second once used wild words about Archbishop Becket? And how forthwith four of his court rode off and immediately murdered the man?

'Very well then; my mother once remarked of me, "He is the greatest beast in the whole world, and I heartily wish he were out of it!" She did. *She did.* She doesn't know that I overheard! And it is nothing at all for my father to say that he wishes I were dead. Nothing at all!

'Perhaps somebody wanted to please them—like his knights tried to please King Henry. I'm inclined—I prefer—to think that is what happened, and that they did not realize that someone, like an evil fairy, would try to grant them their desire.'

He swung round in his chair and opened the carved teak chest that stood at the foot of the bed. In it he kept the violin with which he had been wont to entertain Javan ever and again on his daily visits, for he was a more than average performer.

He took the instrument out; unwrapped it; tuned it; without

word of explanation or apology embarked on a small haunting air
that was both a funeral lament and a mockery of one. He was David,
and at the same time Saul.

'That,' said the violinist when he had concluded, 'is entitled
"Cradle Song for a Prince of Wales." It was composed by one Frederick Griffe.'

Javan had lain watching, with knitted brows, the expressions
that flitted across the little man's face as he played. Now he said
abruptly and with much emphasis:

'And you seriously tell me that you *honestly* believe that your
parents could countenance so dreadful and unnatural a crime?'

'You don't know my family!' said Frederick, with the air of one
explaining things to a child. 'You don't know what they are capable
of! I will tell you something in confidence. When my grandfather
died, my mother, the Queen, found in his cabinet a document. Such
a pretty, pretty document! It was a plan drawn up for my grandfather's consideration. A plan to kidnap my father and send him
off to America, "where he would never be heard of more." * Those
were the words. Or nearly so. The plan was propounded by an
admiral, the Earl of Berkeley, and drawn up for my grandpapa by
one of his most trusted advisers, Lord Stanhope. So you see that my
father would be merely following tradition in considering an involuntary sea voyage for me, my dear Javan!'

'Oh, God!' said Javan.

Frederick fondled his violin lovingly.

'I think,' said he, 'that Mr. Griffe will have to compose a sailor's
hornpipe for the use of seagoing Princes of Wales. The sort of gay
little tune to which you might have danced, Javan, before the ape-
man on the barge!'

'This is all too horrible,' said Shems-ed-Douha almost violently.
'It's the sort of thing that might happen in Morocco, but not here—
not here! It is a treason to motherhood and to fatherhood. It's a
stain on every mother and father. It's a stain on the mother whom
I never knew and the father whom I loved, and who loved me—
and believed in me.'

She turned her lovely head a little as she spoke, so that she
looked sideways at Javan; and he knew then she was telling him

* *Reminiscences of the Courts of George I and George II,* by Horace
Walpole.

that she said the truth; that they were no borrowed parents of whom she spoke.

'Well,' answered Frederick in a soothing manner, 'I can really assure you that if my parents can stop me inheriting the throne they will do so. I can assure you, too, that if they can supplant me by my younger brother, William—the Duke of Cumberland, you know—they will do so. It's a fact that they have already tried, more than once!'

He took his violin again, and struck up a savage little air. Then he said quietly enough:

'I must tell you that immediately William was born they started campaigning to rob me of my inheritance in his favour. Even during my grandfather's lifetime! He warned me that they would. He didn't mince matters about it either. William—they said—had been born and would be brought up in England. I had been born and was being brought up in Hanover. Let him be King of England and me be Elector of Hanover when the time came. I was to be an involuntary Esau to William's Jacob. But was it my fault that I was left in Hanover for fourteen years from the time I was seven?

'Then when the old man died and I became heir to the throne, I should still have been left abroad if it hadn't been for the British government constantly reminding my father of my existence. Even so I should never have been sent for if my parents had not got to hear that I was planning to marry my cousin, the Princess Wilhelmina of Prussia. They did not want me to marry anybody—they did not want me to have a son to come after me. They did not want me to have heirs. So they sent for me in the end to come to England.'

Again he fell silent for a moment or so, plucking the strings of his instrument.

'I was not made welcome by any—*any*—of the family. I was a complete stranger. I was an ugly alien. I came to the palace in a hackney coach. I was taken to my parents' presence up the back stairs. I was twenty-one, but I was put into the schoolroom with the younglings, whilst my father tried to get the British government to alter the succession! When he failed he did everything he could to persuade me—to drive me—to force me into signing a renunciation of my rights. I would not be persuaded—driven—forced.'

Once again he stopped, this time to tune the violin. Then he went on:

'When I was only little and everybody went off to England, my father didn't trouble to say goodbye to me, and my mother didn't lean out of the window of her carriage behind the cream horses to blow me farewell kisses—like other mothers—whilst I stood weeping on the steps. Everybody I had known for all my short life seemed to disappear suddenly, just as if I had waked up from a dream. My grandfather—his ladies—his ministers—his court and their children, my friends—his servants, as well as my parents and my sisters. There were a hundred and fifty of them, all told, who set off to the Promised Land, leaving me behind. I was seven years old, an ugly little boy, and very conscious of it. Nobody loved me.'

Once again he took up the bow, and then set to playing a frantic, desperate, mocking hornpipe.

'I was left to the care of servants, and to make new friends amongst the pages and the stableboys,' he went on at length. 'Only on occasions of high ceremonial did people remember me. Then I was rigged out in splendour and made to stand beside my grandfather's portrait, which was set up in a chair of state for all Hanover to do homage to—like idolaters before a graven image. I was given a haphazard education by the schoolmasters of the town, who taught me gratis, as though I were an object of charity!'

'They seem to have made a good job of it,' commented Javan bluntly.

A flush mantled on the little man's sallow cheeks, and he nodded his appreciation.

'They were an odd lot, those tutors of mine,' he said, 'and I didn't get the sort of education that a prince is supposed to have. But at any rate I learned to like music, and painting, and literature! When I landed in England, I not only spoke and wrote English, but I thought in English.'

He added, with a rather naïve pride, 'Do you know that I hadn't been in this country three years before I collaborated in writing a play! It was a deuced bad play, of course. Wilks put it on at Drury Lane. My name didn't come out, but I'm pretty sure that people suspected the authorship. Anyhow it lasted for two nights—and very rowdy nights they were, too! Cudgel-play, catcalls, and chucking out! Now, however, I have written a book—this time in French. It's called La Histoire de Prince Titi, an allegorical fairy tale, something

after the pattern of Perrault or Madame d'Aulnoy. It's proving rather
a success in the West End of Town.'

'One day I should like to read it,' said Javan, briefly, feeling that
it was the Prince of Wales's continued existence rather than his literary career that should be under discussion. 'But meanwhile it's of
paramount importance to find out who is behind the outrage. From
the viewpoint of your future safety.'

'Today, after I saw Tuke, I told Bubb Dodington what had
happened. You have seen him, I think?'

Javan recollected an enormous pug nose, to which every other
feature was subsidiary, projecting round the corner of the 'All's
Well' room at the Maid's Head Inn. He nodded.

'Well, he swore at once that Dunscore was at the bottom of it
all. He's got no evidence, naturally, but he's a pretty astute fellow
is Bubb, for all that his appearance is against him . . . Appearance
isn't everything!' And Frederick flashed a melancholy smile at
Shems-ed-Douha.

Javan cast his mind back again to the day of their arrival in
Crosse.

'Dunscore! I remember him. An evil-tempered fellow with a
lard-coloured face? A troublemaker, I should say for the sheer pleasure of stirring up mischief, if for no other malign motive.'

'Definitely,' concurred Frederick. 'He is one of the creatures of
Hervey—my Lord Hervey—my mother's *éminence grise*, and an excessively dangerous man. Dunscore has a scabrous reputation, but
she'll hear nothing against him. He is fifteen years older than Cumberland, who admires him past belief, because he is a first-class
horseman and swordsman and an all-round sportsman. He is supposed to be making the boy a manly man.'

His voice became very bitter as he digressed: 'You see, I am not
a manly man! I am a half-man! A poor, ugly dwarf of a fellow who
is interested in womanish things like pictures and fiddles and books!
—Do you know that I've actually heard my father say that he considered the study of books "beneath him"!—And then, too, I've ab-
sorbed the most pernicious ideas about government from friends
who don't believe in bribery and corruption!

'I was able to make Cumberland behave like a gentleman on the
day we first met because a report had just come from London that

my father had been taken seriously ill at Hampton Court. Even a
blind, deaf mute could have remarked the immediate change in
people's attitude. I might be King of England the next morning! I
might actually be King of England that very moment! They weren't
running any risks! It looks now as if someone had decided to make
certain as soon as possible that the risk should not be run again.'

Shems-ed-Douha had taken no part in the discussion except for
her one protest. Now she said:

'The barge ought to be traced. It wasn't there on the river bend,
grounded, when I went to see after I had gathered what had happened. Somebody, however, must have noticed it going downstream
that morning. The murderer of the ape-man, too, ought to found.
The girl, Delilah'—'Delaia,' corrected that lady's former partner—
'ought to be questioned, too. There should be no difficulty in tracing
her at any rate.'

'It's a thousand ducats to a copper *flus* against her having seen
anybody but the ape-man or one of his gang,' wagered Javan. 'It's
ten thousand ducats to a *flus!* She'll know nothing.'

'She might,' said Shems almost violently, 'if Kadijah and one or
two of my Harriffa could undertake the questioning!'

Javan turned his head on the high pillow so that he could regard
—with a momentary flicker of amusement—the slim figure sitting
beside his bed-head, very civilized in a short-sleeved dress of rose-
patterned silk, very ladylike in a pair of green net mittens.

'There speaks a Moorish empress,' said he, 'and not a lady from
civilized Carolina.'

'The Prince was abducted. You only just escaped with your life.
And now murder has been done. Would you handle such conspirators with velvet gloves? This thing has got to be fathomed. Otherwise, Prince, life will be a nightmare in which you see murder
lurking at every corner and in every shadow. I know. In seven years
four attempts were made on my husband's life, and twice someone
tried to poison me.'

'Why you?' said Javan, startled. 'It is not as if there were other
wives or favourites.'

'I should fancy that Ali's brother, Ibrahim, was at the back of it.
He was always jealous of my influence. However, I grew used to
the sensation of murder round the corner after a while.'

Frederick drew a shocking screech from the violin, a screech as though of somebody discovering murder at a dark stair-foot or behind the arras.

'I suppose that Augusta, too, might get accustomed—in time,' he said doubtfully. 'But the atmosphere of hate that envelops us is already a nightmare to her. She dreams of murder and conspiracy; of daggers, pistols, and poisons. She wakes up at night in a panic to reassure herself that I am still by her side and alive. So I shall never dare tell her what happened after the dance at the Temple of Harmony. In fact I am certain that it will be far better to lie low—as we have done—and make no move in the matter at all, lest she should get to hear about it.'

'She should not be left in the dark as to what is going on,' said Shems firmly. 'It is unfair to both of you.'

'She is very young, and frightened enough as it is.'

Javan saw by a sidelong glance that that plea had no influence with Shems, who said nothing.

Frederick laid down the violin upon the gay silk garden of the patchwork quilt. He leaned an elbow upon the high bed, and propped his chin up in his hand whilst his melancholy grey-green eyes travelled below lids that were the colour of a bruise, from the one to the other of his companions. At length he said in a low voice:

'You remember, don't you, that Augusta is going to have a child?'

Javan remembered. He merely nodded.

'She is absolutely convinced,' said Frederick very slowly indeed, 'that she will never be allowed to have that baby. As I said before, it is not intended that I shall have heirs.'

Javan could find no suitable comment. Shems still remained silent.

'You are a married woman, madam,' went on Frederick, his yellow face darkening to a dull red as he spoke, 'so that I can say this before you: my mother and my father have decided that I am incapable of having progeny! They openly say so. They adduce that as the main reason for passing me over in the line of succession to the throne. But long before I married Augusta I had become a father. I am making no excuses. There are none possible. I was very fond of the boy. He's dead, alas! My parents weren't worried about the morality of the affair at all, but they would not believe for one instant that I could physically be responsible, so my Lords Harrington and Hervey and others politely hastened to own my—*my*—son as theirs! The world was told, "Oh, it isn't the Prince's child at all. The poor fellow is as sterile as a mule. Everybody knows he's impotent. There was grave trouble at his birth!" '

'Your mother! Your father!'

'My mother! My father!'

'I think it is a sacrilege to use those words in their regard.'

'If I ever have another child—' He broke off abruptly and reverted to his story. 'A little later, madam, I asked if they could arrange a marriage for me. I had lost Wilhelmina, my cousin, who had been the fairy-tale bride of my dreams ever since I was a child. I didn't care who the lady was. I only wanted to marry and get away from my family—to live my own life in congenial company in surroundings of my own choice, with pictures and books and music and intelligent talk. So in the end they produced the Princess Charlotte Amelia of Denmark for me! She was even less than half-witted —she was practically imbecile, and deformed as well!'

'Dear God!' said Javan, 'I suppose they thought there could be no risk of a family!'

'Precisely. I politely declined, of course. So there the matter rested until eventually Parliament got busy about the question of succession, and my poor, humble-minded Augusta was brought over to be my wife. It's rather a grim fairy-tale story for a princess, madam, with evil enchantments and conspirators and witches, and the ugly prince one who will never be turned by magic into a Prince Charming.

'How Augusta ever became aware of the dark background of the tale I don't know. Probably one of her ladies told her—Lady Archibald Hamilton would be the likeliest. So now you perceive the sequence in her mind! Firstly, it is put about that I am incapable of being a father. Secondly, and accordingly, my paternity of Vanella's son is called in question. Thirdly, I am offered a bride who's physically and mentally deficient. Fourthly, as Augusta and I, in fact, are both young and pretty healthy and should in the course of nature produce children, What (she asks herself) is most likely to be the next move?'

'After all we have heard,' said Shems, 'it seems to me that Augusta may well be justified in asking herself—and you—that question.'

'But you must have many and powerful friends on your side,' insisted Javan.

Frederick started to wrap up his violin in its swaddling clothes.

'It's true that I have friends,' he admitted, 'but they have no power at all. All the power in the country today is concentrated in the triunity of Walpole, the Prime Minister, the Queen my mother, and the King my father. They rule by the corruption of Parliament. Every worthless officeholder under them—every recipient of their bounty—knows what would happen if ever I succeeded to the throne. Every worthless officeholder and every recipient of their bounty is, accordingly, a declared and bitter enemy to me. My accession would mean the end of a Golden Age!'

# XIII

## *Observations of Mrs. Garlicke*

AND SO in two days' time Barrington Court was deserted by its exalted visitors. The emblazoned coach, drawn by four cream-coloured horses, was no more to be seen waiting by the steps to Vicar's Close, and the gratified residents could no longer watch a small royal figure in a green coat and high-heeled shoes standing with a very tall tasselled cane at the door of Tregallion House.

Despite its Jacobitism, the Close approved of the little gentleman who had respected its feelings by insisting on being known merely as 'Prince Frederick.' Mr. Tuke voiced this sentiment, shortly after the departure, in conversation with Mrs. Foley at the card-table on the occasion of one of her 'evenings.'

'If I had not known otherwise,' he said, 'I should have thought he weere wholly Stuart. He has—t'ch-t'ch—the breeding and the intelligence of that royal race.'

'He has the good heart of the Stuarts, too,' said Mrs. Foley, collecting her cards. 'I heard at Laycock's this morning that when he

142

left he paid for the release of all the debtors in the town prison. That will have cost him a pretty penny.'

'A cool four hundred guineas, ma'am,' said Captain Tregallion.

'Uncle Javan told me,' said Jane, 'that it was the Prince's favourite form of charity. He explained to Uncle Javan that he was himself always so deeply in debt that he had a fellow-feeling with all other debtors.'

'And how is the pasha today?' asked Mrs. Foley.

'He will make his first expedition out-of-doors tomorrow. He is beginning to mend very rapidly. I am glad of it. Now I shall be able to go away with an easy mind.'

'You are leaving us?' exclaimed Mrs. Foley in a tone which was filled with the consternation that was expressed in Mr. Tuke's brown face and Captain Tregallion's red buttoned-up countenance. 'Not— for good, I hope?'

'No. Not yet. For a month or so, my dear madam. My father has returned from'—where on earth had he returned from?—'returned, and wishes to see me before he sets out on further journeys. He cannot leave town at present.'

'The Princess will miss your company, Miss Jane. You are the only person from the outside world she appears to have seen since she came—except Prince and Princess Frederick. She will find it, I fear, excessively dull, unless she decides at last to receive company occasionally.'

'She is very occupied,' said Jane, 'and will be for some time—in literary pursuits. She is engaged in writing a history of the reign of her husband's father. The Emperor Mulai Ishmael, I believe she said.'—She must remember to warn Javan and Zadana of this imperial activity!—'From what she has told me, however, I do not think, dear madam, that it will be a book at all suitable for female readers.'

'He was credited with a thousand children, ma'am!' annotated Mr. Tuke, dotting Jane's *i*s.

'With you gone, dear miss,' said Captain Tregallion regretfully, 'and with my grandson away with his disgusting grandmother, and his Royal Highness no longer tripping in and out, the Close will revert to what it was before all this excitement occurred—a damned lobby to the boneyard it adjoins.'

'You have omitted to turn up the trump card, Captain Tregallion!' said Mrs. Foley disapprovingly, for the Close was not accustomed to referring to the prospect it fronted as a repository for the dead. It was not Attic to speak of it otherwise than as the churchyard.

From an adjoining table there was wafted to Jane's ears the rather flurried conversation of Miss Letitia—

'Of course, my dear Julia, the Prince was here at Mrs. Foley's last "evening." He did me the honour to partner me, you may recollect. We won half a crown. He appeared to be extremely pleased. He congratulated me on my play. Mr. Standring told dear Miss Jane afterwards that he had known his Royal Highness to win a thousand pounds at a sitting! Yet I am sure he couldn't have looked more pleased than he did over that half-crown!'

Jane fancied that those elderly voices would tinkle the story of the princely visitor through the years to come, until he became a legend in the Close—almost, perhaps, a ghost.

'When I played whist with the Prince!' 'When my great-aunt played whist with the Prince!' . . . 'They say that a hundred years ago the Prince of Wales of the day used to play whist in this very room.' . . . 'My grandmother remembers her grandmother telling her how—' Perhaps they would know by then that an empress had also played whist with old ladies and gentlemen in one of those prim houses looking on the churchyard, and the birch trees, and the memorial to the dead of the pestilence of 1637! Perhaps they would know something else about that empress in those days to come!

'It is you to play, miss!' said Mrs. Foley.

'Lost in daydreams!' averred Captain Tregallion. 'Wondering whether you will see Mr. Standring in London, I presume! You will advise us of your sailing date in due course, my dear miss, so that we may have our handkerchiefs ready. . . .'

None of those acquainted with Miss Jane Tierce were, however, to witness her departure from Crosse Wells in the veiled light of daybreak on the very next morning, excepting only Mrs. Garlicke.

That old lady had supped rather more heartily than was her wont, upon cold goose and pickled walnuts. By one o'clock in the morning she realized that she had grievously erred; and when she had to arise from her bed for a fourth time, daylight was filtering through a gap in the heavy curtains before her closely shut window.

It was intolerable! She collected her snuffboxes and her cordial, drew the curtains, and ensconced herself in her accustomed observation post well wrapped in gown and shawl and rugs and quilt. On the last occasion that her digestion had been upset—by an over-indulgence in pettitoes—a similarly early vigil had been rewarded by a sight of Letchworth slipping quietly home to Mrs. Foley's establishment after some nocturnal adventure. Perhaps she might see him again!

She had been sitting there for some half hour, comforted inwardly by Dantzic goldwater and alternate application of black rappee and the best Spanish snuff, when she heard footsteps approaching from Palace Yard echoing in the hollow silence. The brisk footfall did not in the least sound like Letchworth's furtive tread. She leaned a little forward to observe the better.

A woman came into her view—a tallish figure in a dark, hooded cloak, carrying a large bundle done up in a bright blue cloth.

It was a nuisance that the hood completely hid her face, especially as she crossed the road and ran quickly up the steps to Vicar's Close. She could have come from nowhere but Old Palace, and there was something in her bearing that was vaguely familiar. Mrs. Garlicke's brain, stimulated by a copious dose of snuff, began to get very busy.

Some minutes later Cloak reappeared, ran down the steps, turned to her right, and set off towards High Street at a businesslike pace. The hood was pulled so far over her face that even with the aid of her silver-rimmed spectacles, Mrs. Garlicke was unable to distinguish her features. Nevertheless, Mrs. Garlicke *knew*! She had studied that walk and that bearing too often to be mistaken.

Why did the Turkish general's niece wear a print dress under a country cloak—which could not have cost a penny more than four shillings—and carry a blue bundle? Why did she leave Old Palace at dawn, visit for a moment the house in Vicar's Close, and then set off to the town? She was running away: that was what she was doing.

Mrs. Garlicke sat back in her chair, her ailment forgotten. She was mentally replete. Even if nothing else of interest occurred, there was food for her imagination to mumble over and chew for a day—for a week—for a month. She would never say anything about what she saw: that was secret to her. She would ask her companions and visitors about the passers-by, but she would never say whether or no she had seen them before, and never say when she saw them again.

That, for example, had been the case when someone pointed out my Lord Dunscore to her one evening as he passed by in all his finery of ruffles and brocade on an expedition to the Outlook, accompanying a very overdressed and flashy woman, and followed by a little black page with a gold turban. He had stopped to speak at the foot of the steps to my Lady Morfa. A few days later she had seen my lord again towards dusk—this time in a slouched hat pulled down over his nose, a scarf up to his chin, and a shabby frieze coat—talking at the furthest end of the churchyard wall to a large man with a face like an ape, who had come to a rest there with a barrow full of dilapidated, secondhand wigs. Mrs. Garlicke knew him again. She was never mistaken. On no account, however, would she share the pleasure of her private discoveries with anyone, except occasionally with Coppie Tregallion.

Now she began to embroider in her mind a wonderful tapestry of adventure for the Turkish general's niece.

She was still so engaged, when the young woman concerned was climbing into the dark interior of the London stagecoach before the yard of the Maid's Head. The windows were tightly closed, the floor almost knee-deep in straw, and the smell such as indicated that the other five occupants had continually refreshed themselves on the road with beer and gin. Even as she accommodated herself as best she might on a hard leather seat between two fat women, Shems-ed-Douha found herself regretting the impulse that had made her set out on new adventure in the rôle which she proposed to play later. . . .

The heavy vehicle lurching over the rutted road like a galleon in a choppy sea had been crawling eastwards for some few hours when Williams, after pulling back the curtains to an overcast day, presented Javan with a letter, which, he said, had been found early that morning pushed under the front door.

The missive was addressed to 'His Excellency Javan Tierce, Esq., Pasha, General in his Ottoman Majesty's Service.' It was written in a bold handwriting that he did not know, and was sealed with a signet whose impress was blurred out of recognition.

He was not vastly curious, for his duties in attendance on the secret Empress, and the friendship displayed towards him and his 'niece' by no less personages than the Prince and Princess of Wales, brought in ordinarily a considerable correspondence. Letters had not so far, however, appeared under the door of Tregallion House in the small hours of the morning. He broke the seal, and unfolded the sheet, automatically glancing at the signature. It was the one word, 'Jane.'

It was the first time that he had ever, to his knowledge, seen Shems-ed-Douha's writing; and he knew, too, before he read a line —a word—that this first letter to him contained ill news.

He laid the letter down on the gay quilt, and pulled himself rather painfully upright against the pillows; summoned water so that he might sponge face and hands; donned fur-edged montero cap, and had Williams fling his gay morning-gown about his shoulders. Not until the dust of sleep had been washed aw       he had been made presentable for parade could he brir              read what Shems-ed-Douha had written.

The letter ran:

Monday<br>Midnight

Javan,

I am going away now to find n            is more important to me by far than all this business         Ishmael's treasure. When Ali found the secret hoard at Meknes, it meant nothing to me except that there was a chance of return to my own land, and the recovery of my past. Ali needed no persuading that nowhere in the world could he keep that wealth in safety for himself except in England. When he has milked Morocco dry, or loses his precarious hold upon the empire, do you know what he wishes to do?

He desires above everything in the world to become an English country gentleman!

You may laugh, but his mother—his English mother—instilled the notion in him in his earliest childhood. You will well believe how heartily he has been encouraged in it by his wife with the support of Zadana. It has been rather pathetic to watch his efforts to assimilate European culture without letting the least suspicion get abroad. He never even mentioned his ambitions to you for fear of your ridicule and because of your dislike of England.

I have done—and more than done my duty by Ali, and my plans for the future do not necessarily coincide with his.

Now I have gone to find my own, true past—not that which was forced upon me, nor that which I borrowed. Javan, you have given me loyalty and duty—and your own past. I return it to you now—and your father, and the evil uncle who betrayed him, and the childhood you spent wandering across the world. When I come back again, I will have *my own* past with me. Perhaps you will not like it. But have it I *will*.

I did not say goodbye to you, Javan, because I knew you would try to persuade me not to go where I am going, or how I am going, and I must not be persuaded. I did not want to argue with you and hurt you, and perhaps be hurt myself. I shall say goodbye to you when I push this letter under your door in a little while

use your asking Zadana where I've gone; she will Niece Jane has gone to London to meet her father. you a letter in a few days' time which you can rea gallion, and quote from to Mr. Tuke. The Princess uha will remain resolutely enclosed like a nun until nished the life of the Emperor Ishmael upon which she aged. She is improving daily under the spa water cure.

I have written to the agents in London to say that you will visit them a month from today—you should be fit to undertake the journey by then—and make final arrangements about the property they hold and the estate that is to be bought. Can you picture, by the way, Ali in topboots and bag-wig riding to hounds, or presiding at a claret-drinking, pipe-smoking symposium of local gentry?

My jewels meanwhile are safe at Old Palace in Zadana's care. You have always been so loyal, Javan, that . . .

I wonder what you will think of my past, Javan; perhaps . . .

I can't write all this letter again, and if I scratch anything out it will look as though it were worse than it is.

Goodbye for a little.

JANE

He rang his handbell to summon Williams. He was going to dress. He was going to Old Palace—if he had to be carried there. He was going to cross-examine Miss Mott—everyone; although he knew in his heart that it would be a hopeless task. And so it proved.

'I am surprised and shocked,' said Miss Mott, iron-grey as usual, sitting in the bare little office on the ground floor with a barred window looking out upon the dankness of a laurel shrubbery, whence she conducted the domestic regulation of the establishment. 'I had thought better of you, general. I cannot approve of your asking— nay, demanding—that I should betray her Majesty's confidence. You would not do so, yourself. Why, then, expect me to?'

'I am not attempting to pry into her private affairs. God forbid! I am responsible for her safety, however. I don't want to know what she is doing, or why she is doing whatever she is, but I *do* want to know where she is, so that if she lands herself in trouble, I can bring help with the minimum of delay. Even if this is not Morocco, there are many and grave dangers for a young and handsome and unprotected woman in this country.'

'It is possible,' said Miss Mott, examining an account, opening a drawer, and proceeding to count out silver from a small canvas bag, 'it is just possible that her Majesty is better acquainted with conditions in this country than yourself—who have never been here before!'

With that he had to be satisfied; but so certain was he of the direction in which his duty lay, that he felt it to be no treason to undertake a study of the problem of Shems-ed-Douha's disappearance with the same meticulously thorough care that he would have devoted to the planning of a campaign.

Fast on that determination, he limped rather painfully back to the Close and made his way directly through the churchyard to the solitary tomb, canopied by a weeping ash, whereon some weeks before he had remarked the great mound of red and white roses from the hall of Old Palace.

An aged labourer, bent and bearded like Father Time, was scything the long grass near by; paused in his labours to watch the tall, lame man stoop over the flat top of the high tomb and read the incised inscription:

Sacred
*to yᵉ Memory of*
COUNT LOUIS ANTON
VON PFULLINGEN
*Who departed this Lyfe
on Feby yᵉ 8th*
A D 1730
Ag'd 23 Yeares

'They do be sayin', my Lordship,' said Father Time, breaking in on Javan's reflections, 'that the poor young gentleman a'hanged of hisself. They do be sayin' that. And they do be sayin' that becos his old mother were a very great court lady it were kep' dark. Dark it were kep', surelie, or he'd have had a stake in his innards and bin berried at the crossroads—like Dick Tyson.'

He would have gone on further with the lamentable history had not Javan turned the current of his thoughts to astonished gratitude by a gift of silver as he moved away.

A sudden thought struck the investigator, however, and he posed one question over his shoulder, and received the answer that he expected:

'Aye-aye, my Lordship, 'twere at Old Palace, were the grisly deed. They do be sayin' that . . .'

Von Pfullingen!

He recollected one or two incidents—the merest trifles. He added them up. They made a total of a sort, whereas during the days that followed he could discover nothing else at all from which to make any other kind of logical sum. So for a fortnight he ate his heart out; and then once again the Close found that it had got to say goodbye.

After Miss Jane, the general!

He was posting to London on imperial business in one of the imperial carriages—which were all painted duck's-egg blue and heavily gilded, with an oriental crown surmounted by a crescent emblazoned on the door panels in most Attic taste. He was not sufficiently recovered yet to undergo the fatigues of horseback travel, and the hundred and twenty-five mile journey by coach would probably not take more than one day longer, and would be infinitely less wearing. He would be a great loss.

Would he be gone for any considerable time? asked the Close regretfully, when it first heard the news at Mrs. Foley's evening party.

He could not say precisely. There were many matters to be attended to.

He would be seeing dear Miss Jane, of course?

That he could not say, either. He was not sure whether his brother might not have embarked on a trip to Scarborough for the sea-bathing. He had spoken of it.

Very tonic! said the Close. Presumably there were bathing machines?

There were definitely bathing machines, said the general, who had but that morning noticed an engraving of Scarborough in Toller's bookshop in the High Street.

Would he undertake a small commission for her in matching some lace at the Misses Hogarth's shop near Little Britain-gate? Miss Julia Grenville neighed at him. Mrs. Foley, with her long sad nose looking more like a dejected nanny-goat than ever, baaed a very similar request. Captain Tregallion begged that a personal inquiry might be made about the manuscript of a volume of travels submitted to Mr. Dodsley, the bookseller in Pall Mall. The general averred his delighted readiness to undertake any and every errand desired by the Close.

'It is thirty years, dear sir, since I was last in town,' said Mrs. Foley when Julia and Tregallion had been summoned to one of the card-tables. 'In Ramillies year it was. My late husband . . .' And she gyrated into a circumambulatory account of London socialities in the reign of dear Queen Anne, from which she suddenly emerged to thrust at her auditor without warning the question:

'And dare I ask you, dear general, if it is true what they are saying in the town about the Princess?'

'About the Princess?' echoed Javan blankly, fearing what of the truth might have seeped out. 'I have heard no reports about her, ma'am. What are they?'

'Well,' said the Honourable Georgina in a very low bleat, 'they tell me in Laycock's—the pastry-cook's, you know!—that it is common talk that her Highness is contemplating conversion.'

'Conversion!' exclaimed Javan, being completely at sea. 'Conversion of what, ma'am?'

'I mean conversion from Mahometanism, sir. They even say that she is to be baptized privately next week.'

'It's the first I've heard of it, ma'am. I can assure you that there is no question of the Princess at the moment contemplating such a procedure. None at all. What on earth can have given rise to so fantastic an air-bubble?'

'They say,' said Mrs. Foley, 'that our neighbour'—and she reduced her bleat till it was barely audible even to Javan, and looked meaningly across the room to where Mr. Tuke was playing very earnest whist with Captain Tregallion against the eldest Miss Grenville and the deaf Mr. Tudor—'our neighbour calls at Old Palace almost every day. And, as I understand, her Imperial Highness has received no one at all, apart from your dear niece and the dear Prince and Princess—'

Javan had been unaware of this phenomenon. There was little for him to do at the house since Shems-ed-Douha had disappeared from his ken; he merely paid a brief official visit every morning, and advised Miss Mott where he might be found during the course of the day in the event of any message being received from Shems-ed-Douha; but there had been no word from her at all. He contemplated a daily assignation between Shems' Mistress of the Robes and Mr. Tuke with some inward amusement. Could Miss Mott be contemplating a return to the Christian fold, or was theirs an autumnal courtship?

Mrs. Foley did not pursue the matter, although after a little while she put a question that considerably surprised him by reason of the conspiratorial tone in which it was put, as she rose to greet Lady Morfa, who had just entered the room.

'How many females can a Mahometan marry, sir?' she asked.

'Four, madam,' replied Javan, getting to his feet.

'Ah,' said Mrs. Foley with a gratified smile, 'how *very* satisfactory! When you come back, my dear general—'

He could trace no possible connection between that last question and anything she had said before. The possibility of a rapprochement between Miss Mott and Mr. Tuke was, however, considerably strengthened in his mind some time later when parting from the old gentleman at the top of the steps to the Palace Yard—Tuke was going to visit a sick mare, about which he was much concerned, at the stables of the Swan Inn.

A round moon was balanced atop the weathercock on the tall spire. The leafy arcade of Palace Yard whispered to a little errant breeze. The small cobblestones of the roadway were an embossed pattern of silver. Mr. Tuke, leaning on the gold knob of his ebony Sunday-go-to-meeting cane, permitted himself to embark upon a eulogy of Miss Mott.

'Sensible woman—very!' said he. 'Done me a lot of good—t'ch-t'ch. Miss Mott, I mean. She has actually worked me out a vegetable diet from which—t'ch-t'ch—I trust I shall get beneficial results very shortly, for I will frankly confess that whilst the spirit is willing enough the flesh is singularly weak in respect to fleshpots. I am also having a cold sponge all over each morning—Catherine complains that we have to send to the well four times instead of three times a day now! The watercress seed and port wine which she recommended has worked wonders. I am now taking, in addition, a tonic of her prescription, and—t'ch-t'ch—to it I attribute a further considerable lessening of my risings. Garlicke made a good deal of fuss about compounding it—but Garlicke's out-of-date, and doesn't attempt to keep abreast of the times.'

Was the way to a man's heart through his medicines, Javan wondered. He inquired—

'What particular ingredient was it that Garlicke took exception to, sir?'

'The juice of hog-lice!' replied Mr. Tuke, looking at the romantic moon. 'The juice of thirty hog-lice; and he mumbled over the powdered crab's eyes as well. It is all stirred up with asses' milk. Miss Mott said that the medicine would sweeten the blood. By the Great Green Gooseberry, sir, it does! Indeed it does! And it needs to, too, for it tastes most infernally peculiar, to say the very least of it.'

'I recollect being given a potion when I was ill in Kobbé,' said Javan, enticed into rivalry by Tuke's naïve pride in the deglutition of nastiness. 'It proved to be a tea brewed from cow-dung gathered in May. I did not discover this until I had swallowed half the draught.'

Mr. Tuke did not take up the challenge, but merely nodded sympathetically.

'She has a heart,' he continued, still surveying the moon—or the weathercock. 'She has also an invincible spirit.' He paused rather awkwardly, and said in a low voice: 'Privately between ourselves, might the consequences be serious if she were to return to the Christian faith?'

Having had a good many opportunities of studying Miss Mott's character, Javan could perceive no reason why she should desire to return to the creed which she had abjured. If anything was at all certain it was that she would not approve of martyrdom for the sake of Christianity; martyrdom was neither a ladylike nor an essential proceeding. On the other hand, did she consider conversion as a preliminary to matrimony with a well-to-do clergyman?

'She has told me,' said Tuke, 'of her agony of mind over her abjuration. She has—t'ch-t'ch—told me of the indescribable tortures she underwent before becoming a Moslem!'

Javan, who had been led by Shems-ed-Douha to understand that Miss Mott had made her change of religion without the flicker of an eyelash, wondered whether he ought not to disillusion Mr. Tuke—if not at that precise moment, then at some near future date. He was considering this problem when, apparently feeling that he had said quite enough, Tuke wished him good night and stamped off down the steps to the street.

Miss Mott said nothing, however, of her desire to be received into the Church of England when he paid her a final visit the next morning, before setting off to London.

She was in a grey morning dress with a muslin cap ornamented with grey ribbons, sitting at her desk in the little office facing the garden, calmly studying the household accounts. She might have been—Javan thought—the wife of a lord bishop pondering the palace housekeeper's books instead of a court official to a Mahometan empress.

'There has been no communication from her Majesty, general,' she said flatly even before he could question her, and proceeded to make a sort of omnibus statement. 'As I have frequently said, I will forward any that should come, by courier and immediately, to the address of the agent in London which you have given me and I have entered on my tablets. I have plenty of money here, unlimited credit, an adequate guard, and intelligence sufficient to deal with all problems.'

'Mr. Tuke will doubtless be happy to be of assistance should any unforeseen occasion arise when masculine advice might be useful,' said Javan, a little ruffled by her sublime faith in herself.

She shot him a very quick, almost suspicious glance, and answered merely by raising her strongly marked eyebrows in restrained expression of her incredulity that such an occasion could ever arise. . . .

Mrs. Garlicke of course saw him set off a little later that morning in the blue and gilt four-horse coach, with two footmen in blue and gold on the footboard behind, and his man, Williams, and another servant following with pistols at their holsters.

She saw him come down the steps—dressed as usual in deep blue and looking, she thought, more than ever like King Charles the Second. Could he—might he—be one of the many unlawful offspring of the house of Stuart?

He was escorted to the carriage door by Mr. Tuke in his baggiest green coat, carrying fishing rod and creel, his wide hat topping his red cotton nightcap and garlanded with the flies he most favoured. Captain Tregallion—in his slippers—shouted final farewells from the archway at the top of the steps. Mr. Tuke shook hands very heartily. The carriage rattled and clattered away over the cobbles.

Was he going in search of that niece of his who had slipped off so quietly and so early in the morning a fortnight ago? They said she had gone to London to her father. With a large blue bundle—dressed in a cloak that could have cost no more than four shillings, and shoes that were not worth half a crown! Mrs. Garlicke, sipping a little Dantzic goldwater, and helping herself liberally to snuff, knew much better.

PART TWO

# I

# *Pictures in the Treacle*

'IF YOU HAF BEEN LYING to me, girl—' said Madame von Pfullingen, and left the sentence unfinished so that the menace in her deep voice was fortified by a suggestion of unspeakable consequences.

She leaned back in her chair, her large, pallid hands folded upon the edge of the mahogany table, whose shining surface reflected, like a dark pool, the lemon-coloured flames tipping the candles, the glittering decanters and glasses, the soft sheen of silverware.

As though it were of spun glass, her white wig shimmered against the purple curtains behind her shrouding the windows. On the wall in front of her at the other end of the room were more curtains; but they veiled a grim portrait of the late King George the First—a lowering personage mostly wig, ermine mantle, and lace cravat.

The picture was hidden, not because the countess was other than proud of having been intimate with majesty, but because she held that the face of a king should be withdrawn from pollution by the constant stare of menials. Indeed, when the curtains were with-

157

drawn, her servants must bow deeply to the frowning portrait, and back from out of its presence as though the ungainly dark gentleman were there in the flesh in the white supper-room of the house in the precincts of Hampton Court Palace, instead of lying, embalmed in spices, in a vault in Hanover, as he had done these last ten years.

'If you haf been lying—' said Madame von Pfullingen again, and left the sentence yet more incomplete.

Her hooded eyes in her immense, arrogant face stared, unwinking, at the girl in the blue print dress, small white apron, and mob-cap of a maid, who stood at the foot of the table awaiting her commands with an unmoved countenance.

'So the saucy, red-haired daughter of a bitch is prepared to brazen it out, is she?' said Madame von Pfullingen to herself. Aloud she uttered one single word—

'If—'

'I am not lying, inteet, madam,' said the girl. 'I did be saying what Ottilie says I said in the servants' hall. And I *can* be doing what I says I could.'

'You *vill* do it, Howell, or else be vhipped!'

Howell appeared to be unimpressed by the threat.

'Yess, madam.'

'And you vill do it here and now.'

'Fery good, madam, but it's needing I'll be someone to help me, my lady, you'll understand.'

The countess turned her vast pale face—with the heavy jowl and beaked nose of a hanging judge—from the girl towards the only other occupant of the supper-room, a dark, savagely good-looking serving-woman of forty who stood at respectful attention a little to one side of her.

'You will help the creature, Ottilie,' she commanded.

'As you wish, madam.'

'Ottilie will inteet not do, my lady.'

'Vhy not?'

'The woman, my lady, must be a virgin, or else be breeding.'

Ottilie made a movement of indignant protest: Madame von Pfullingen did not actually smile, but her heavy eyelids flickered before she said in an ominous tone:

'You vill not escape like that, Howell. You had better reconcile yourself to the rod. Ottilie, fetch Anna and tell her—'

'Madam,' remarked Howell, apparently unmoved by the imminence of punishment, 'I was going to say that a young boy is better than a woman. A boy of ten or eleven years of age.'

Madame von Pfullingen turned this over in her mind.

'Ottilie, go to the door, and tell Franz to fetch my grandson. I varn you, Howell, that you only vorsen your offence by your persistence. You had better make up your mind to the rod.'

'For yourself you shall see, madam. But I shall also be wanting a spoon, my lady. The one on the table will do. And a little of whateffer that dark stuff is in the jar at your ladyship's right hand.'

The vessel, in fact, held black treacle that, combined with two parts of gin, formed the elixir known as 'mahogany' of which Madame von Pfullingen highly approved.

The great lady nodded. She was becoming interested. The preliminaries were intriguing, and even when the performance failed —as fail it must—the infliction of the consequent punishment should prove not unamusing. She had thrashed her offspring until they rebelled. She still thrashed erring maidservants with the assistance of Anna, the brawny stillroom woman—and greatly relished the doing of it. . . .

When Copernicus made a very sleepy appearance, wrapped in a quilted bedgown, with his yellow hair more tousled even than usual, Howell's preparations were complete. The lights in the wall-sconces were extinguished. The two silver candelabra on the table had been moved to the end where the child was to stand beneath the hidden portrait facing his grandmother. Between them rose a grey-blue spiral of scented smoke from the silver chafing-dish that usually kept her morning chocolate warm.

'Vat did you put on the charcoal, Howell?' asked Madame von Pfullingen.

'Frankincense and coriander seed, madam,' she answered.

Now she took a small square of thin paper covered with writing from her pocket and placed it in the bowl of a large spoon, which she filled with slow-running greenish black treacle from the wide-necked jar of cut glass.

'Hold this spoon in your right hand, little master,' said Howell, giving it to Coppie. 'Bend your head over it, and look into it! Don't be taking your eyes from off it for a moment!' She took his left hand in hers, and added in little more than a whisper. 'Now say these three words over and over again to yourself! Over and over again! Over and over again! Over—'

What the three words were, her auditors could not hear; any more than they could make out what it was that the girl recited afterwards in a monotonous undertone.

Then presently there was silence but for the sound of rain beating against the window panes. The room was heavy with the scent of burning spices; was full of shadows except at the end of the table where the boy, his bent fair head shining in the candlelight, stared into the bowl of the spoon as though he were an acolyte with a mystic offering before some strange shrine. The girl brooded darkly over him.

'What do you be seeing, little master?'

It appeared to Madame von Pfullingen that the question came from very far away, and the answer too was no more than a whisper—

'Nothing.'

Ottilie's dress rustled as she stirred. The countess sat very still, leaning over the table, her heavy head supported on her cupped hands: she watched the girl and child with an unwavering stare.

'What do you be seeing?'

Again—'Nothing.'

Again silence: and then, with a new insistence—

'Now, what do you be seeing?'

The child began suddenly to tremble. When he answered it was in a low, strange voice which his grandmother could barely catch.

'There's a wall,' he said. 'A wall. A brick wall . . . Now there's a man. He's pulling the wall down. Very fast!'

'What do you be seeing?'

'He's taken down the wall. He's gone . . . He turned and winked at me as he went . . . Now I can see a street. A cobbled street. There are a lot of people standing in it. They look as if they are waiting for something. I don't know the street. There's snow on the roofs. There's a man with blue stockings and a crutch standing by a post—an old man.'

'Who else do you be seeing?'

'Oh, there's my grandmother sitting at a sticking-out window over a shop. She isn't so old as she is now. She's laughing.'

'Can you hear anything, little master?' asked the girl, her hand resting lightly on the child's shoulder, her veiled eyes intent upon the two watching women.

'There's a lot of noise. It's getting nearer. It's not an angry noise. It's a sorry noise. People are saying, "Ooh! Ooh!"'

'What do you see now?'

'A man is coming up the street between the people. He's leading a horse and cart. It's a yellow cart with blue and red flowers painted on it . . . Oh!'

'What do you see?'

'There's a woman tied by the wrists to the tail of the cart. She's got long, long black hair. It's hanging down in front of her. I can't see her face. Her back is all bare—and it is covered in blood—covered in blood.'

'Long black hair!' said Madame von Pfullingen under her breath, knitting her jetty brows.

'What be you seeing?'

'There's a man in a long blue coat walking behind her with a whip. He's beating her with it. Before he hits her, he runs the lash through his left hand. Why, he's got red paint on the palm of his hand! It is red paint on her back. It isn't blood. The people don't know that. They are all saying, "Ooh!"'

So the miserable Louis had managed to arrange that trick before she caught him and sent him off, captive, to immurement behind the high walls of Old Palace at Crosse!

'And now?'

'The cart's under grandmother's window. There's a woman standing in the room behind grandmother's chair. She is moving back a little . . . The cart has passed. It is turning down a street past an inn. It's called The Castle Inn. Now the woman behind grandmother has fallen down . . . She's fallen down!'

Although his voice had risen with a new excitement, Madame von Pfullingen took her eyes from the child: she turned her head very slowly and looked up from under heavy, almost lashless lids at the woman beside her.

Ottilie was deadly pale. Her eyes were closed. Her lips were moving, though no words came from them. She swayed slightly to and fro upon her feet. Even as Madame von Pfullingen watched her, with a small sigh she suddenly collapsed into a sitting position upon the red Turkey carpet, and then fell over upon her side. Without a flicker of expression the countess shifted her regard back to the child. She had not seen the faint smile of triumph that for a space of time shorter than a breath had shown in Howell's lips and eyes.

The boy was saying:

'Grandmother is getting up. She is standing at the window . . . The man with the blue woollen stockings is pointing to her. He is shaking his fist. He is an old man with white hair. He is saying something to another old man. I can't hear very well. It's something about "Jeanie." No, it's something about "Janie." The people in the street are pointing up at the window. They are shouting at grandmother. I can't hear what they are saying. It's getting dark. It's quite dark. I can't see anything. I can only hear—'

'Listen for a moment! Listen for a moment! Listen! What do you hear?'

Silence; and then the child went on—

'I can hear a loud voice speaking. It isn't in the street. It sounds as if it were in church—or in a big hall. It says . . . I can't hear . . . Yes, I can. It says—"and afterwards transported for the term of seven years to the plantations beyond the seas." It must be a very big room because there's an echo . . . Oh! Somebody said, "Six silver spoons!" right in my ear . . . Now I can't hear anything at all.'

He raised his eyes from the black-green mirror in the bowl of the spoon, and turned their candid regard on the girl at his side.

'That woman—the woman in the room—' he began.

But Howell did not answer except by a shake of the head and a smile. She let fall his left hand, and gently removed the crested silver spoon from his clasp and set it on an empty fruit plate.

'That's all, madam. Another day, perhaps! You do be understanding what he sees?'

The Countess von Pfullingen said:

'Take the boy to his bed. Send the man Franz to remove Ottilie.'

She made no comment whatever on what she had heard. . . .

The room had been reillumined, and the unconscious Ottilie removed. Franz had set the plate with the spoon on it before her. Now she leaned with folded arms upon the table looking down into the dark, viscous mirror which reflected nothing except the candle-light.

'Six silver spoons!' This was one of them! They had come from Hanover, bore her crest, a falcon on a fetter-lock. They were unmistakable; and she had but the six of them, all told.

Six silver spoons! For the theft of them, the sixteen-year-old servant girl, Jane—she forgot the surname, though she remembered that the creature was daughter of a village schoolmaster, and motherless—had been convicted; had been sentenced to be whipped at the cart-tail, and afterwards to be transported to the American plantations for seven years. It had all been most satisfactory.

Louis had pleaded with her not to prosecute; had wept; had threatened. When she had proved adamant, he had risen from the sickbed to which he had been confined for months, and had disappeared; had been found in a low gin-shop offering fantastic bribes to the turnkeys who had care of the prison in which the creature was immured.

At no time did she ever let him think that she suspected him of aught but fantastically romantic notions unbecoming to a Count von Pfullingen. At no time did she ever let him know that she had learned—just one day too late—of his secret marriage to the creature when the doctors had thought him to be dying. It was the prerogative of the young Counts von Pfullingen to seduce their mothers' maids; but it was no birthright of theirs to wed with them. So she had forthwith cooked the creature's goose! And then Louis had cooked his own—on a silken cord in his bedroom! It had been just as well. He was no von Pfullingen! He was a poor, weak-kneed, milk-spirited caricature of a man.

She took up the spoon and examined it again.

It was one of those very pieces of silver that had been found hidden amongst the girl's clothing in the garret where she slept. She herself had seen them produced by the searchers from amid the bundle. She herself had, indeed, given them to Ottilie to secrete there. She felt no more compunction about the villainy now than she did seven years and more ago. For was not the theft—that is what it was—of a Count von Pfullingen an offence more deserving of punishment than the theft of ten thousand silver spoons?

The crowd of dirty pig-dogs *had* shouted at her—as the boy said.

They had called her a 'Whore!' and told her to go back to Germany.
But that sort of thing, of course, had also occurred on occasion to
her compatriots and partners in George's favour, the Kielmansegg
and the Schulenburg. It had been thought better that she should
leave the shop whence she watched justice being done, by the back
way. The filthy, disloyal, ruffianly English!

Ottilie *had* fainted as the boy said, although there had been
nobody with them in the room to see and she had never spoken of
it. She had given the silly woman a good sharp kick in the ribs. It
was most fortunate, perhaps, that there had been no possible reason
for the fool to be called upon to give evidence. She had never suspected Ottilie until then of suffering either from tender-heartedness
or from a conscience—two imbecile weaknesses!

What other pictures from the past could the girl Howell evoke,
with her frankincense and her coriander seed, her pool of black
treacle and square of cabbalistical paper? It would be interesting to
know, for example, what had happened to Countess Louis Anton
von Pfullingen—the housemaid noblewoman. Was she a sailors' trull
in Charleston, a battered woman-servant at some plantation house,
or gone to the gallows? *The Countess Louis Anton von Pfullingen!*
She pronounced the title out loud, and broke into a cackle of laughter which Franz heard through the door panels. He hurriedly made
the sign of the cross.

There were many pictures, too, in the long gallery of her life
that she would like conjured up—some lurid, unseemly, brutal, and
some that were even dangerous to recall. Dangerous? Very, very
dangerous.

But Howell was not to know what they meant, for all that she
looked the complete witch with her tawny skin and her cheek and
neck marred by a great purple birthmark as though by the satanic
unguent of sorcery.

She had come from Crosse to warn Mary Stevens, the schoolroom
maid who had accompanied Coppie to Hampton Court, that her
mother was dangerously ill, and to take her place. Her credentials—
signed by one Miss Mott of the household of the Empress of Morocco—said nothing about her strange powers. They simply stated
that she had lived practically all her life in Morocco, and was the
daughter of a Welsh clerk to an English merchant in Rabat. She
had recently been orphaned by the death of her father, and was

returned to Europe in the Empress's retinue to find employment in her own country.

Madame von Pfullingen poured herself out a mighty dollop of gin; she laced it with treacle, and briskly beat the compound with a spoon; she drank it at a draught, and remained brooding on many strange things.

The von der Schulenburg, her aforetime rival in George's favour, had sworn that the old King's spirit had visited her in the shape of a raven; but if Howell possessed in full the powers she appeared to do, then Melusina's nose would soon be put out of joint.

She helped herself to yet another tot; levered herself slowly to her feet; unsteadily crossed the room and drew back the curtain before the portrait, and curtsied to that dark lowering face and huge peruke which she had known so well. . . .

The girl Howell tucked up Copernicus Tregallion in the vast four-posted shadowy bed, in the draughty chamber near the top of the house where he slept when he stayed with his grandmother, by the light of a single guttering rushlight.

'Do you know, it's like a fairy tale, and *I'm* in it!' he said, looking up at her with admiration from his pillows. 'Like the story of the old woman who was really a fairy-queen in disguise or Cinderella the wrong way round. An empress who—'

'Ssh!'

He beckoned to her to lean over him for an instant, and then said in the lowest of whispers—

'Did I do it all right?'

'Wonderfully well,' said Shems-ed-Douha in an equal whisper. 'But you mustn't invent things. Why did you put that in about the woman fainting in your grandmother's room? That wasn't what we arranged. I had never heard about it!'

'But, ma'am—'

'"But, Howell!"'

'But, Howell, I saw it all! I really did! When you asked me for the third time—like we said—and I was going to say about the man and the wall—like you told me to—I suddenly *did* see it all, there in the black stuff. And then it wasn't a picture any longer, but it was real, and I was there—myself. You said it might happen, you know! I wasn't in the room. I shouldn't have said anything if you hadn't kept on speaking to me. And I heard the Voice, too! Really! It said more than I said—more than you told me. I wasn't a bit frightened though.'

'Honestly?'

'Honestly. Not a bit. When I was little, ma'am—'

'Howell—Howell—Howell!'

'—Howell, I used to have a friend who played with me when I was by myself. Nobody could see him but me, but I don't know what he looked like at all. He was always different the next time. We talked a lot together, but I never knew afterwards what we'd talked about. I wasn't asleep, you know! He was quite real, though he wasn't real like us. I never spoke about him to Aunt Letitia, or grandpapa, or anyone at all. Of course not grandmamma!'

'Perhaps he was an angel.'

'Do angels talk about conkers, do you suppose? Because I think —I just fancy—that he did.'

'Why shouldn't they?' asked Howell. 'Now you go to sleep, young master!'

She kissed him on the cheek and withdrew with the guttering rushlight, to the near-cupboard opening out of his room, where she slept in her official capacity of guardian attendant.

The imperial quarters were so constricted that there was barely passageway between the wall and the narrow bed with its thin straw pallet. A window no more than one foot square faced the foot of the bed from above an old chest surmounted by a chipped basin of brown earthenware. The imperial wardrobe hung from nails in walls which might once have been whitewashed but were now the colour of stewed tea.

Shems-ed-Douha closely scrutinized the olive complexion and purpled birthmark which she had acquired, in the fragmentary mirror near the window by the pale light of the candle. Neither acquisition, she noted with relief, would need repair yet awhile. She put down the rushlight-holder upon the bare, uneven boards, and sat on the foot of the bed—which was covered by a mud-coloured blanket—to meditate.

The very first experiment had confirmed the suspicion that had been with her through the protracted agony of arrest and trial— through the humiliation of public punishment, half-naked, in the streets—in the stinking cabin that she shared with five other women transports in the brig *Anna Boult*—in the mad confusion of the wreck off Cape de Non and the fantastic seven years which had followed.

All along she had been certain that Madame von Pfullingen had done to her what George the First—according to Griffe's story—had contemplated doing to his son. All along, too, she had been sure that Ottilie was the old woman's agent in the crime. Now she was convinced.

Ottilie had fainted when the boy, Coppie, had called up the ghosts of the past, exactly as she had fainted when she witnessed the living spectacle in the streets of Kingston seven years ago! Ottilie was not ordinarily one of the fainting kind of women. Once, when they were in London, she had gone to see a hanging at Tyburn and had come back from this raree-show to recount every horrible detail of it with relish. Ottilie's conscience had betrayed her!

Sitting there in that grim closet, her head propped in her hands, staring with unseeing eyes at the feeble rushlight glimmering upon the floor, whilst the wind battered incessantly at the minute dark window, she tried to visualize the pathetic face of Louis von Pfullingen for whom she had been so very sorry that she had mistaken sympathy for love. Instead she saw only the dark, adventurously ugly face of Javan Tierce pondering over the history of a pretty servant-maid, who had won the heart of the sick, unhappy son of a great lady; who had been transported for a theft which she had never committed, wrecked on the wildest part of the coast of southern Morocco, and was now returned to civilization as the consort of an emperor.

She saw, as if he were there before her at that moment, the small twisted smile he had, which could be at the same time both ironical and tender. Would he smile like that—she wondered—over her story; over her substitution of his father for hers? From the little that he ever said, she gathered that his father had been one such as himself, whom he had happily accompanied in the silence of perfect understanding in wanderings across half a world. Her father had been a little lame, white-haired man—she never remembered him other—who was village schoolmaster and parish clerk. He had died of a broken heart before she sailed—they told her—still believing in her.

Would Javan smile in that small lopsided way, which she found somehow comforting, when he knew all about her?

What would his reactions be when he learned the secret which

she already knew—the death of Mulai Ali, the husband who was no
husband, who had tamed her to matrimony with boiling oil, and
whom she had tamed to serfdom? For she knew another secret, too
—Javan's secret. She knew why he had fled from Morocco five years
before; why he had kept at all times and places—even in the close
quarters of the crowded ship in which they sailed to England—a
rigidity of formal conduct that was almost unfriendly. She knew all
this because she had suddenly remembered the trifling history of
the violet, the shadow of a flower, which she had found pressed
between the pages of his Testament. A tiny memory, but enough.

And now that she was free?

Why, he would say—

'She is still an empress, whom the Queen of England will address
as "Madam, my sister," and I am her servant. She is a princess of
vast wealth, and I am a penniless adventurer.'

That was a thing that she also knew. It was a problem which
would have to be solved, and there was a letter beginning 'Madam,
my sister' that she had received a little while since, which might
help to do so.

By a great effort of will she had begun to concentrate once more
on the events of the evening when she became aware of a faint—
very faint—scratching on the door.

There were one or two of the forbidding German menservants
who looked as if they might venture on nocturnal expeditions, with
or without encouragement, even to a girl with a blemished face.
There was no bolt to her door. Then she remembered. She had
secured the outer door in Coppie's room.

She realized who the caller was, and rose and unlatched her door.

Coppie stood there in his long white nightgown, faintly illumined by the guttering candle against the solid darkness of his
bedroom. His fair hair was more dishevelled than ever; his eyes were
very wide-open and he was manifestly in a great hurry to speak
about something, because he started as the door swung inward
before him—

'I say—'

'Howell,' she warned him.

'I say, Howell—'

'You'd better come in, Master Coppie. Look, sit on my bed, and
wrap this cloak round you! You *must* remember always to say

"Howell" even when we are quite alone together, so that you won't make any mistake at other times. What is it? Because you ought to be in bed and asleep!'

'I say, Howell, you know I couldn't go to sleep for thinking. I honestly couldn't.'

'You must try.'

'I know I can't until I've told you something. Something very important.'

'It's very late at night to start telling me things, even important things.'

'Howell, d'you know—' He broke off, started afresh: 'You won't be cross if I tell you something? Honestly?'

'You can tell me anything you like, Master Coppie. But quickly so that you can go back to bed. Well, what is it?'

He said then very slowly:

'Do you know that that girl was—you? The girl I saw, I mean. At least it looked like you. And something told me that it was you. Was it you—Howell?'

This was a complication for which she had not prepared when she had overcome her scruples and enlisted his assistance in her scheme. It had been originally Zadana's suggestion—when she heard of the old woman's almost fanatical interest in divination and the kindred secret arts. Coppie had been enchanted to be her ally. It was just an experiment; that was all—he was told. Any explanation she chose to give him was good in his eyes. She did not hesitate now, however, to tell him the truth:

'Yes, it was I.'

'But you hadn't done anything to deserve it, I *know*,' he said, stating his faith with complete assurance.

Her heart warmed to him for his unhesitating belief.

'Of course I hadn't, my darling.'

'And you're the girl in the other story—the one we've still got to tell? The one that starts with just sea, nothing but sea; and then a ship comes sailing on it, and gets larger and larger and larger and—'

'That same girl.'

'And there's the wreck, and the Moors come galloping up over the sand—'

'Yes, I was there.'

'And grandmother laughed—just laughed when they beat you in the street,' he meditated. 'If I had been there, I would have—' His common sense refused to let his imagination depict the knightly deeds that Copernicus Tregallion, aged eleven, would have liked to perform against the forces of law and injustice. He reverted to his grandmother: 'She is an old witch. She ought to be put in a barrel full of nails and rolled downhill! Don't you think so, Howell?'

'No, Coppie dear,' she answered him gravely. She analysed her feelings for the benefit of the small figure sitting on her bed, wrapped in her cloak and regarding her with solemn eyes, almost as though she were expounding them to Javan. 'Once I would have given anything for revenge. Once I wished to make your grandmother suffer just as I had suffered. Once I planned that she and whoever had helped her should undergo the most dreadful tortures—'

'What sort of tortures?' asked Coppie with great interest.

'One day I may tell you,' she said without any intention of keeping the promise. 'But by-and-by I found that I didn't want any revenge. I found that revenge wasn't worth while. The only thing that I wanted to do, was to let people know the truth. Not just everybody, but the people who knew the girl you saw—you saw tonight. The people among whom she had lived when she was a little girl; the people who had loved and respected her father, and were sorry for him because his daughter had done—as they thought —very, very wrong. People, too, who might love her in the future. And then—'

But how could she explain to a child that she felt, too, that the comfort of her exculpation must somehow be brought to poor Louis's pathetic ghost?

'You could go down in your golden coach,' said Coppie, visualizing a thoroughly dramatic scene, 'with the general riding beside your door, and all the footmen on the running-board, and the golden crown on the door-panels, and Miss Mott and the Harriffa in another coach, and Mr. Gellibrand. You could get the town-crier to read a proclamation!'

'No, darling, not that way! The girl who used to be me isn't me any longer. Only you and one or two other people will ever know that she has been me. So all I want is a lawyer's paper telling everybody who used to know her that she was innocent of any crime and was condemned unjustly.'

Coppie did not approve of so tame an ending to the story—without the wreaking of appalling vengeance or a spectacle of the greatest magnificence.

'But you really should,' he insisted. 'After all you became all of a sudden an empress—a real, live empress over a land twice as big as this one.'

'Yes, I married the son of an emperor, Coppie.'

'By Old Gooseberry,' said her admirer—who had always been much intrigued by Mr. Tuke's favourite exclamation—'it's like a fairy-story! I've read one just like it, where a king's son—he was only a king's son, of course!—sees a goose-girl and marries her straight off.'

Shems-ed-Douha doubted very much whether Mulai Ali could ever have qualified for the rôle of a prince in a fairy-tale. Or whether such a prince would woo his bride with the aid of boiling oil. She did not say so. She took up a small hand and held it tightly in her own. Through him she knew for a certainty that Javan Tierce would have the same faith in her.

Coppie had almost done: he concluded with a wish and a profound thought.

'Of course, in a way I'm sorry that you aren't a widow—I don't mean that I want the emperor to die. You'd still be an empress, wouldn't you? But I should have liked you to marry the general, and then we could all live together so comfortably ever after in the Close.'

Shems-ed-Douha found no answer to that remark.

The candle flickered up in an ominous fashion.

'If you don't go to bed now, you'll never find your way in the dark. The candle will be out in a moment. This is the goose-girl kissing you, Coppie. And this one is for the empress.'

# II

# *In the Palace of Enmity*

JAVAN had bespoken rooms at the Toy Inn, an ancient hostelry of wine-red brick standing at the outermost gates of Hampton Court Palace, its many latticed windows surveying the wide, grey Thames through a screen of young lime trees. It was frequented in the summer by the extreme of fashion, and was celebrated for its wines, its coffee, its marrow pudding and its high charges.

He arrived on the third day of a wearisome journey from Crosse Wells; but even so he had barely supped when his servant, Williams, tapped on the door of the wainscoted room where he sat, and announced in the stealthiest manner possible:

'Mr. Frederick waits upon your Excellency.'

'Mr. Frederick' entirely lived up to the fashion of his announcing. Like a stage conspirator he was swathed to the eyes in a black cloak, and his overlarge hat permitted nothing but the merest glimpse of his nose to the world. Javan could not help feeling, however, that, like the legendary ostrich, he had hidden his identity from no one

172

except himself. The floral-cum-apothecary aroma, which generally accompanied him, was also particularly in evidence.

Of the little man's pleasure there could be no doubt. He seized both his hands, and kissed him very heartily on both cheeks.

'The last person I expected to see,' he declared, after they had exchanged greetings and fragments of news. 'Equally the first person I would wish to see! Your letter gave me no clue, however, to the reason for your visit. I am not going to flatter myself that it was for my sake.'

'To be honest,' said Javan frankly, 'it is my duty—or, at least, my conception of my duty—to her Highness that has brought me here. There is very little, however, that I am at liberty to tell you for the moment.'

'And whatever you do,' said Frederick, disembarrassing himself of his voluminous cloak, 'don't ever say anything through the post that you would not wish other people to know. My correspondence is very closely inspected. The mails are always being tampered with, and have been for a long time. A very long time!'

He dropped into an elbow-chair before one of the casements that looked on to the water. In the rapidly growing dusk a few lights were beginning to twinkle on the opposite bank; the ferryboat with a lantern in its bows, and top-heavy with a large travelling-carriage and a pair of horses, was being poled slowly towards the landing-place before the inn. The lime trees near the water's edge shivered and gossiped in a small, damp wind.

'And not only that,' he added, tossing his hat on to the window ledge, 'but I myself am under surveillance all the while. So is my wife. Our every movement is watched. Fortunately the place is a rabbit warren of courts and passages and yard and galleries so that one has discovered a bolthole or two.'

Javan sat down opposite him; poured him out a glass of wine, and helped himself.

'Why should you be so closely watched, sir?' he said.

'Because we are suspect,' answered the other, sipping his wine. 'We are here by Royal Command, and here we have got to remain. Can you imagine a more inconvenient and unsuitable spot for Augusta in her present condition? Her time's nearly up, you know! No arrangements of any sort have been made, although I have warned them, and it is a matter of the succession to the Throne.

The doctors who have been attending her—the midwife who's to look after her—are in London, fifteen miles away. The roads are appalling. If anything were to happen unexpectedly, they would probably be two or three hours too late! Perhaps they want them to be too late!'

'Why not return with the Princess to London then?' inquired Javan.

'That would be outright defiance. It would be sheer mutiny.'

'Well, what of it?'

'The King of England,' said the son of that king, 'isn't like an ordinary father, you know! He has prerogatives in regard to his sons that other fathers don't possess. *My* father was arrested by *his* father for insolence; was kept prisoner in my mother's apartments by Yeomen of the Guard, and was deprived of the custody of his children! That just shows you what can be done quite legally! And when it comes to the secret powers and influence of the Throne, backed by unscrupulous ministers, and executed through unscrupulous agents, don't forget what I told you about the First Lord of the Admiralty in my grandfather's time, and his plan for effecting my father's disappearance! If a cabinet minister would plan such a thing then, isn't it equally likely that one could plan something similar today? We still don't know who was behind what happened at the fair, do we?'

In the light of the candles that stood on the small table between them, the Prince's alien face seemed yellower than ever, his nose longer and more punchinello-like, his expression more forlorn. Then suddenly he raised his head, and looked directly at Javan from heavy-lidded green-grey eyes.

'All the same,' he said, 'I am prepared to swear that my parents weren't responsible—directly. I honestly am. I can't believe that my father would ever seriously contemplate such a scheme. But my mother— Sometimes I am inclined to think that there is nothing she might not bring herself to countenance in order to secure the succession to Cumberland! *Nothing!* You could not possibly imagine how she hates me! Is it my fault that I was born small and ugly instead of tall and blue-eyed?'

'It would never occur to me,' commented Javan, recollecting the fat boy in the incident at the Maid's Head at Crosse, 'that the Duke of Cumberland is any Adonis.'

'He may not be, but he is Benjamin all the same, the *enfant gâté*, the apple of my parents' eyes.' Frederick fumbled in the skirts of his coat for his comfit box. 'Enough of me now. Let us talk of you! Is there any way in which I can be of service to you, either personally or for your duty?'

'One of the purposes of my visit,' said Javan slowly, and then repeated the phrase with emphasis, 'one of the purposes of my visit is to ask you, sir, to do me a favour—a very great favour!'

Anything that he could do should be done at once, Griffe assured him, taking a comfit from his box—a rose-scented one of remarkably penetrating aroma.

'I want,' said Javan, 'I most particularly want letters of introduc-tion—to Madame von Pfullingen. From someone who really knows her well!'

'My grandfather's mistress?'

'Yes.'

Griffe was obviously intrigued by this request. He meditated upon it for a moment or two before he said:

'You know, I suppose, that the old woman has one of the houses on the south side of the Outer Green Court of the palace?'

'Captain Tregallion told me so.'

'My grandfather gave it to her for the term of her life, and noth-ing my father can do will dislodge her. There are half-a-dozen houses or so in the avenue from the Trophy Gates to the palace, opposite the barracks—as you'll see in the morning—and it is easily the biggest and best of the lot. She never appears at all when the Court is in residence. She's fully imbued with my grandfather's hatred of my father. I have not seen her since I was a child. Now I wonder what I can do.'

He reflected again.

'They say,' he said at length, 'that very odd things go on in that house. It's declared that she holds veritable witches' sabbaths there with a lot of old cronies, but I don't know who they are. I'll find out. No—wait! Old Duchess Sarah knows her well—the Duchess of Marl-borough—and she will do anything for me. Duchess Sarah is the woman for our money. It's as good as done, Javan! I remember now, by the way, that Princess Shems-ed-Douha seemed to be very inter-ested in her. Once or twice she asked me about her; but I had very little to tell.'

Javan did not say that it was precisely because he had also recollected that fact and several similar that he had made the journey to Hampton Court. He said instead:

'I have also my devoirs to perform. I am to make my bow to his Majesty at his levee tomorrow morning, and be presented to the Queen at her drawing-room in the afternoon.'

'Ah!' sighed Griffe with satisfaction. 'Then you will be able to see for yourself how things are. I *am* glad that you are here.'

'But of what use can I be to you—much as I should like to be? I am, as we said before, a man from another planet. Advice from another planet cannot be very helpful!'

'It isn't so much advice that I need,' said Griffe. 'I have a score of advisers, for that matter. I have even a sort of shadow cabinet!' He cited a list of names which meant nothing at all to Javan. 'But they all look upon my personal affairs as politics, and upon me not as a person but a political asset. No, you are not merely from another planet, but from my auspicious planet, Javan! I am sure of it. You are my periapt—my amulet—my talisman! You have already saved me twice—but things always happen in threes, you know!'

'I had better lend you my bezoar stone,' said Javan more than half seriously.

'I get premonitions,' expanded Griffe wholly seriously. 'And they mostly turn out to be right. When I first saw you sitting with Tuke under the trees before the Maid's Head at Crosse, something told me that you were going to have a great influence upon my life. There's no good you wagging your head at me! It's true enough! You've been taking snuff! The Turkish sort, and not the Egyptian. I didn't see you do it, but I can tell.'

This appeared to Javan to be a digression. He remarked drily—

'And you've been eating one of your rose-scented comfits, sir! Even if I hadn't seen you do it, I could most certainly tell.'

'Precisely,' said Griffe. 'You emphasize my very point! Our noses tell us about entirely invisible snuff and entirely invisible comfit. Very well, I maintain that it is no more extraordinary that we can equally sense the unseen qualities of friendliness and helpfulness in a stranger.'

'A sort of spiritual nose?' suggested Javan. 'For an unsmellable smell? I'll do anything I can, as you well know, bating my service to her Highness.'

'Whilst we are waiting for Duchess Sarah, lend me—not the bezoar stone, but yourself. Be a sort of spiritual watchdog for me, Javan! I have got a premonition about you, Javan, indeed I have.'

There was that in the small man's voice, in his restless fingers and twitching face which warned the other that he was almost on the verge of hysteria. So he said in matter-of-fact manner:

'I have been the governor of a province. I have been the commander of an army. I am now, I suppose, what Coppie Tregallion would call Head "Eunox" to Shereefian Majesty. I have never been an amulet before, but if it is any help—'

'Help!' said Griffe. 'I need help—not material help, but spiritual help, and now! I *know* that something is going to happen, and almost at once. Anything could happen here! I know it to a surety!'

'Here? In your father's house?' exclaimed Javan, not quite incredulously.

'Here, and in my father's house—yes! Most certainly,' said Griffe. He got up and started to prowl round the low-pitched room, the inordinately high shoe-heels which he wore to increase his stature tap-tapping on the bare polished floor like the light hammering of a cabinetmaker. 'It's haunted—it's thick with the ghosts of things that have happened. Far more so than the Leine Palace in Hanover ever was, even though the bones of my grandmother's murdered lover were buried under her anteroom floor.

'It's haunted, too, by my mother's hate! My mother, who will not believe that I am capable of producing an heir to rob her favourite of the succession! My mother, who has discussed with Lord Hervey —and I know this for a solid, incontrovertible fact!—the various ways in which I might have arranged for someone else to father a child for me on Augusta without her knowing it! My mother, who is quite satisfied that, if Augusta were to present a child to the world, either I should not be the father, or else she would not be the mother! In other words either a bastard or a changeling! And my mother does not mean that that shall happen. Neither, Javan, is it a far journey from "Griffe *can't* have a child" to "Griffe *shan't* have a child!" When you think of what has already happened—'

Javan, staring out upon the darkening river, saw another and smaller stream with a barge twisting sideways to the current in the moonlight: saw a crenellated wall set with a turret swaying outwards on a cliff-top. In his mind there was already forming an image of the gawky, childish princess, her mind numbed by apprehension, awaiting unguessable events in a place of ever-thickening shadows.

Griffe came to a halt again by the table in the window, and looked down upon the tall man in blue.

'Anybody might suddenly explode with anger and say, "I wish to God the young devil were dead!" or something such. And no one would give more than a passing thought to it, would they?'

'Personally I shouldn't say such a thing, but I dare say that plenty of people do so without rousing more than momentary attention,' admitted Javan.

'Well then, but if day after day, week after week, month after month, year after year, you wished it, prayed for it, as publicly as you like, would you be surprised if someone took you at your word? Wouldn't you expect it? There are a lot of people, Javan, who might like to make that wish come true—people whose future—whose fortunes and power and advancement in rank depend on that wish being fulfilled! Wouldn't you realize that when you wished and prayed before them for somebody's death?'

Griffe set his hand upon Javan's left shoulder, and gripped it very hard with long bony fingers.

'Suppose that something happened to Sylvia—'

'Sylvia?'

'I forgot. It's a pet name for her, which she likes. I've used it in one or two poems I've written for her. But suppose something happened to her! It would be so easy just now! This palace—this enormous palace, so full of enemies! I never know who are my enemies. One of my own—I thought, my very own—people betrayed me a few weeks ago. One of the politicians, he was. You might almost have called him my Minister for Personal Affairs. I found out that he was a creature of the Queen. A sister I thought that I could trust—Emily—the only one I ever gave any confidences to—proved to be utterly disloyal. I am not even sure of my wife's women, although I chose them myself. I'm only quite, *quite* sure of two people about me. One of them is my man, and the other—well, the other is Desnoyers, the French violinist who used to be a dancing master!'

Unhappy Prince, thought Javan, who dare to trust none but a valet, a dance-master, and a stranger 'from another planet.'

'Sit down!' he said brusquely; and then, as the other dropped obediently into a chair opposite him: 'You had better have another glass of wine, you know!'

'She goes about like a ghost!' said the Prince. 'She is so very, very frightened—for me—for the child to be—for herself! Although she doesn't know anything about what happened at Crosse, she won't let me out of her sight if she can help it. And she won't be left by herself on any account. And our rooms are lit up all night long. All night long!'

It was now quite dark. The small noises of the breeze had died away, and the air was so still that they could hear the faint jingle of the harness of horses that padded through the dust of the tow-path hauling a laden barge against the current. A string of gaily lighted boats came sliding down the uneasy blackness of the river. From the leading craft there rose suddenly the sound of violins, and a moment later a rocket streamed upwards into the night and burst into a cascade of gold and silver fire. The eyes of both men automatically followed the course of the projectile. . . .

Comparatively early the next morning Javan was waited upon by one of the minor hierophants of the order of almost-priests who attended upon the shrine of Majesty.

He was a retired colonel of some sort, a thin old man dressed in plum colour, with a grey face which reminded Javan of Mrs. Foley in its mixed resemblance to the countenance of a goat and a tortoise. It was his duty apparently to guide him to the Guard Room, where he would hand him over to someone else, who in his turn would hand him over at the right moment to yet another somebody—a veritable archbishop in the court hierarchy—who would proffer him with due ritual to the altar of Royalty at the most propitious moment.

The thin old gentleman took his duties as cicerone very seriously, and kept up a constant stream of information as they proceeded to the palace, although his conversation was rendered uncommonly jerky by frequent pauses when he was apparently engaged in finding synonyms for the most ordinary words.

'The largest brick building erected since Roman times!' said he with as much pride as if he had built the place himself, when they turned in at the Trophy Gates and saw in the distance the great western gatehouse and all the fantastic jumble of dark red towers, turrets, pinnacles, roofs, and gables of the palace. 'It actually covers eight and a half acres!'

'The imperial palace at Meknes covers one hundred and sixty acres,' commented Javan, with a hint at his lopsided smile, following his invariable rule of keeping Western civilization advised that it had not the monopoly of everything that was biggest, best, and most beautiful.

Colonel Sir Richard Hurrell—for such was his rank and name—was obviously so disheartened by this overwhelming comparison that Javan immediately regretted the remark, and hastened to soften the blow.

'It is, however, considerably dilapidated already, although it is only a half-century old.'

The Colonel's confidence was restored. He pointed out the barracks to the left of the avenue, and the irregular line of Tudor houses that faced it across the velvet turf to their right.

'That long house with the two gilt weathercocks,' said he, 'is Madame von—' There he halted for a second, and added rather lamely, 'A German lady, mistress to the late King. A very'—pause—'odd'—pause—'woman in her younger days. Very odd now, sir, too.'

'Madame von Who?' asked Javan, surveying the low red-brick building with its rows of irregular windows, its dormers, its twisted chimneys. Did it shelter Shems-ed-Douha, and if so why? 'Madame von Who?' he repeated.

This question appeared to cause Sir Richard much discomfort. He meditated his answer for some appreciable seconds, and then replied:

'Her name begins with the sixteenth letter of the A B C.'

It took Javan a mental recitation of the alphabet to discover that the sixteenth letter was P.

'Madame von Pfullingen?' he inquired at length.

Much relieved, Sir Richard nodded his grey goat head. He admitted to acquaintanceship with Madame von Sixteenth-letter. He was even encouraged by Javan's unruffled aspect to expound.

It transpired that he was a lipogrammatist, possibly—probably—the only one in England, and had the finest collection of lipogrammatical works in Europe. It took some time to explain that lipography was the art of writing compositions without employing one or more letters of the alphabet, as the colonel was—and had for some

time been—practising the art in his daily speech with a view one day
to translating the *Aeneid* in this useful manner without any P's, L's,
J's, and Y's. It chanced that the letter P formed the subject of the
day's exercise.

Sir Richard, who (Javan thought) was clearly a little but amiably
mad, talked of Lope de Vega—without mentioning the word Lope,
naturally—and the great dramatist's five novels from each of which
a different vowel had been excluded. That brought them to the gatehouse. He discussed various German and French professors of the
art of lipography. That brought them across the Base Court, and to
Anne Boleyn's Gate. He discussed Tryphiodorus's version of the
*Odyssey;* which brought them to the Colonnade in Clock Court. He
discussed the lipogrammatical work of the Greek Lasus whilst they
mounted to the state apartments by an enormous staircase whose
lofty walls and ceiling were a tangle of exuberant gods and god-
desses.

He parted from Javan with the regret of a missionary letting a
possible proselyte out of his clutches, and promised to take wine
with him a little later in the morning.

A gentleman in a crushed raspberry coat, with a face as smooth
and expressionless as if it had been glass-papered, convoyed Javan
across a vast room decorated with a few thousand swords, bayonets,
and pikes arranged in sunbursts above the wainscot; across a great
presence-chamber hung with pictures of ladies, who all looked alike,
and of King William the Third in partly Roman attire and a full-
bottomed wig; and across a second great presence-chamber with
more pictures of more kings. In all those rooms were knots of cour-
tiers awaiting summons before Majesty, and engaged in reverently
muted talk.

Finally Javan came to the sanctuary itself.

The audience-chamber was large and sunlit, with views from its
three tall windows of a formal garden looking like an extremely
gaudy counterpane. It was full of men and a murmur of conversation
as low as though they were at prayer. At the far end, under a canopy
of black and red damask, a square little man—with protruding eyes
and a lower jaw that stuck out like that of an ill-tempered bulldog—
sat on the only chair placed on the only carpet in all the room.

'Permit me to present to your Majesty—General Tierce Pasha,
in the service of his Shereefian Majesty the Emperor of Morocco,'

said a portly gentleman in black, who, with one foot on the sacred rug, had been talking behind the back of his hand in a secretive manner to the almost-divine.

Majesty permitted; extended a hand—which sadly needed a manicure. Javan raised the stubby fingers to his lips; made the motions of kissing without completing that operation.

'The Emperor,' said Majesty, talking down to this representative of barbarism, 'has a large army?'

'The troops of his Majesty's household brigades amount to eighteen thousand,' answered Javan, straightening himself to his full height, and well aware of the fact that the entire English standing army at the time only amounted to that number.

The King grunted. The gentleman in black—whose powdered wig set off a portwine-tinted face—asked almost dubiously:

'Regular troops?'

'Naturally, sir. There is a standing army of some one hundred and twenty thousand men.'

'I imagine, however,' said the King in his guttural speech, 'zat you are britty short of guns?'

'The country can manufacture muskets, gunpowder—and bombs —sufficient for all military needs. Our cannon mainly come from Sweden, where they make the world's best—as your Majesty is doubtless aware.'

'Better zan ours?'

'Definitely, sir.'

'Do you play cards?'

'No, sir.'

In obedience to the faintest nod of dismissal, Javan withdrew from before Majesty. As he did so, he became aware for the first time of the fact that the Prince of Wales was standing a little to the left of the King in a green velvet, gold-embroidered coat. He had been obscured to view by the large figure of the portwine-faced gentleman. He was quite by himself in a room where everyone else appeared to be engaged in whispered communion with his neighbour. Once his father turned in his direction, and looked not at him but straight through him as if he were not there. It was more than a mere contemptuous ignoring him; it was a complete refusal to admit even his existence.

Javan backed a few paces, and then took refuge by a great carved

fireplace, whence he was able to watch the wearisome business—
presentation; one, two, or three questions by Majesty; dismissal—
repeated *ad nauseam.*

The room gradually filled as the presentees were brought in from
the outer chambers—soldiers in scarlet, unwieldy country gentlemen
in unaccustomed finery, young sprigs of fashion, and sober persons
of a City cut clearly in difficulties with the conduct of their swords.

Then suddenly he sensed that he was under close observation.
He turned his head quickly, and saw Lord Dunscore hurriedly
averting his eyes. There was no mistaking those miniature features
set in a pale face patterned, like the wax of a honeycomb, by smallpox. The other had been surveying him from behind the shelter of a
large grey silk back crossed by the light blue of the Garter ribbon.

Grey-silk-back turned at this juncture and studied him for a split
second with a very juvenile assumption of indifference and non-
recognition. It was the handsome clumsy lad, William, Duke of
Cumberland.

Their glances met, and held. Then Javan saw the colour suddenly
flooding the other's face so that he turned away again quickly, as
though his attention had been recalled by some remark of his
companion.

Javan continued to observe Dunscore, and to speculate upon him.

After long years of constant peril, he recognized a potentially
dangerous man when he saw him—whether he was Moor, Turk,
Sudanese, Arab, or European. The more he looked at Dunscore the
more certainly his every instinct warned him that here was a completely ruthless creature, who could well have been responsible for
abduction and murder without any qualm of conscience whatever.
Abduction and murder, indeed, were small matters when the kingdoms of England, Scotland, and Ireland were at stake, to say nothing
of the overlordship of vast lands in America, rich islands in the
Caribbean, settlements in India and Africa, and a princedom in con-
tinental Europe! He had known men before with such sunken bull-
like heads, such glazed eyes as of wet black stone, who spoke even
as this one was doing, with barely any movement of the lips.

Majesty had had enough; Majesty rose and departed to some
innermost Holy, accompanied by the port-tinted gentleman, followed
by his sons, and saluted almost to the ground by a reverent assembly.

Javan made his way back to the Toy—very slowly as he passed

by Madame von Pfullingen's house in Outer Green Court; but no sign of life at all rewarded his close inspection of every window looking upon the avenue. Those on the lower floor were shuttered, and the others all closely curtained. Only a thin wisp of smoke from one of the twisted chimneys told that it was occupied. Was the old lady not in residence, and had his journey been in vain?

Sir Richard Hurrell was already waiting for him in his room overlooking the river when he arrived, and solved the problem for him.

At first, however, there was a small difficulty, because the old gentleman, when asked his preference, wished to drink port. Unfortunately there being a P in that word as also in Portugal, the country of the liquor's origin, it was some little time before either Javan or the drawer in attendance were able to fathom the meaning of his request for 'Lusitanian wine.'

Once the conundrum had been solved and the colonel had been fortified by that beverage, however, he willingly embarked upon a full account of Madame von Sixteenth-Letter's household and eccentricities. The ostracized letter of the alphabet caused one or two hesitations, but not many.

'When the Court is in residence, my dear sir,' said Sir Richard, 'the lady we are s—er—talking of retreats within her stronghold like a hermit crab. All communication whatever with the—er—Ham—er—royal residence is cut off utterly. She does not admit its existence. There is a narrow flagged garden at the back of her house, and she has, quite illegally, cut a doorway through the outer wall giving on to the tow—er—towing way along the riverside and the outer world.'

'What does she do that for?' asked Javan, perceiving further difficulties in making contact with Madame von Pfullingen's household.

'When the late King broke off relations with his son, the—er—reigning monarch, she naturally followed suit and has maintained invincible hostility ever since. There may be more to it than meets the eye. There is no doubt, however, but that of all his women, this lady was the most devoted to him, heart, soul, and body. If he had told her to commit suicide or murder, I am sure she would have done so. All her family, I am told, have had a very strange—strange—strange—'

The old gentleman was clearly so gravelled here that Javan inserted the word 'reputation' for him. This, however, was presumably not in accord with the rules of the game, for he still halted, until he

finally emerged a little chastened from a morass of mental research
with—

'—strange renown. There was a great-grandmother who was adjudged by her father-in-law, and burned for witchcraft. She herself
takes an almost morbid interest in the occult. She is, I am sure,
ca—er—equal to anything. When I call on her in the evening for
cards occasionally—I have a royal "grace and favour" house near the
village—she insists on me joining her in draughts of a most—er—
extraordinary liquor, of which she drinks incredible quantity.'

'Mahogany!' said Javan. 'I have heard of it. Old Captain Tregallion, whose son her daughter married, told me about it.'

'The grandson is staying with the old lady now,' said Sir Richard
with a smile. 'A very delightful small boy. I met him on his way to
raid the royal kitchens yesterday. He does *not* observe his grandmother's rules. Teed, the Queen's chocolate maker, is his great ally.
I told him I was about to conduct a Moorish general to Court.'

'I know Coppie,' said Javan.

'He gave me no hint of that, but asked many questions about you.
I imagined at the time it was because his grandmother has a maid-
servant from Morocco in her establishment.'

So Shems-ed-Douha was beneath Madame von Pfullingen's roof
as a servant! And Coppie knew of his presence in Hampton!

At this stage a terrible mishap occurred. Sir Richard began a
sentence—never to be completed—with the single syllable:

'Per—'

Oh, fatal labial! Not even another bottle of Lusitanian wine was
sufficient to obliterate in the old gentleman's mind the recollection
of that lapse. . . .

The day sped on.

He was led up more vast staircases, through more vast rooms,
into a huge, lofty drawing-room, where a large and exuberant Queen
Anne postured and simpered maddeningly in various guises on ceiling and walls. A room that was full of men and women far gayer in
their silks and satins and brocades than the formal garden, to be
glimpsed through the windows, with its funereal procession of
dwarf yew trees looking like lines of pieces on a halma-board.

He was taken in charge by the Duke of Newcastle, a middle-aged
gentleman with a hook nose and black eyebrows, dressed in dark

brown velvet. His Grace fussily introduced him to a simpering woman in apricot and a simpering gentleman in sky-blue and then left him to his own devices whilst he ambled off through the crowd, buttonholing, whispering, and scratching himself the while in every attainable part of the body with the ardour of a flea-ridden dog.

At some signal, unperceived by Javan, the entire assemblage suddenly shuffled itself into a wide circle as though about to indulge in some round game. There was a complete hush but for the rustle of dresses and the tap of high heels upon the floor as the Queen of England entered, squired by her Vice-Chamberlain—her Ganymede, her gigolo—my Lord Hervey, and followed by the princesses, her daughters. All the brilliant silks and satins and white wigs swayed in curtsey and bow like a flower-bed in a breeze.

In a workmanlike way Majesty started on her circuit. One sentence—a question—for everybody. Two for people we vaguely remembered. Three for old acquaintances. Four or even five for the important.

His Grace had returned to the side of his protégé; he refreshed his memory as to name and quality from a card in his hand: '—and Chamberlain to her Shereefian Majesty,' he announced in conclusion of presentation.

As he kissed the royal hand, Javan reflected that Shereefian Majesty might at that moment be sweeping the floors or dusting the china not a quarter of a mile away.

Majesty trusted that the voyage had been pleasant. One.

Majesty trusted that other Majesty was in good health. Two.

Majesty inquired the length of the visit. Three.

Majesty trusted that the stay at Crosse Wells had been beneficial. Four.

. . . How much did Majesty know about events in Crosse? . . .

Majesty was most affable; suggested, indeed, that Excellency should present himself at Court on future occasions. Five.

Majesty learned that he did not play cards! Six.

Majesty moved on to the apricot lady.

. . . 'Was the road from Town dusty, Madam?' . . .

Javan was aware that the willowy figure—in pale primrose—of my Lord Hervey had lingered—was languishing at him with enormous eyes—was dimpling a milk and roses complexion in an ingratiating smile.

'We appear to be two of a trade, your Excellency!'

'An amateur, or at any rate a beginner, my lord.'

. . . *'Have you had rain in your part of the country, sir?'* . . .

'We must compare notes, your Excellency.'

'It would be a pleasure, my lord.'

. . . *'Are you in Town for long, Madam?'* . . .

'I will wait on your Excellency, if I may, at the Toy,' said my lord, and would have moved on in pursuit of the Queen if he had not been reminded of another duty by a gentle tug of the sleeve. Excellency was thereupon presented to two little hawk-faced princesses in panniered dresses of flowered grey silk.

Did Excellency play cards? inquired the prettier of the two.

Excellency, wondering whether a gambling hell were part of the establishment, regretted that he did not. The accomplishment was not required at the Court of Morocco.

Prettier Hawk-Face was taken aback by this revelation, but persisted in a searching cross-examination as to the social life of the East. It was left to the younger sister—who had a rapt and serious expression—to probe deeper, for she asked in little more than a whisper:

'Does—does the Empress wear a nose-ring?'

'No, your Royal Highness, nose-rings are not part of the Imperial regalia,' said Javan, reflecting that at that very moment the lady under discussion might be engaged in peeling potatoes in the scullery of her late grandfather's mistress. 'The Empress Shems-ed-Douha, madam, is a European. She is quite definitely one of the most beautiful women I have ever seen.'

This encomium called for a detailed analysis of the appearance and bearing of the Empress. When at last the young princesses were satisfied and resumed their circuit, Newcastle—scratching the small of his back in a complicated manner—said out of the side of his mouth:

'Your Excellency has made a hit. Emily's the girl! Fast little devil! Tomorrow you will be *en famille!*'

Whatever the morrow might hold, the ritual of Javan's social baptism was completed for the day by attendance, under the chaperonage of Sir Richard, at the public dining of Majesty.

This entertainment consisted in standing with others so privileged at one end of an immense green and gold room, restrained by a crimson silk rope and two halberdiers, and watching the King, Queen, Prince of Wales, and the princesses eat their dinner. They all sat at one side of the table and were served on the knee. It was astonishingly like a stage banquet, and Javan would not have been in the least surprised to learn that the dishes were theatrical properties of papier-mâché. For a student of manners, however, Majesty's method of shovelling green peas into his mouth was noteworthy.

Javan found it a preposterous performance. He did not wait until the last crumb had been demolished, but before he withdrew he had remarked that the Queen did not address one single word to her son, who sat at her left; that his sister, on his other hand, had spoken across him to her mother, but resolutely ignored him even when he made some remark to her. It was not an edifying picture of family life.

# III

## *A Past Restored*

LORD HERVEY paid his promised visit the next morning, so very early indeed that Javan had but just sat down, wrapped in a flowered silk banian, to breakfast on coffee, rolls, and fruit in the sunny window overlooking the river.

My Lord was dressed with feminine finicality in a dark blue coat, silver waistcoat that fell almost to his knees, and partridge-coloured stockings. He was powdered, scented, possibly rouged, and lace-ruffled; he tiptoed in a springy bent-kneed prance with the studied elegance of a dancing-master; he spoke in a light womanish voice with an affectation that Javan found almost intolerable; he simpered and dimpled and used his large, swooning-away eyes like a flirtatious girl.

'Your Excellency will forgive the earliness of my descent upon you. But, Gad's life, at Court one cannot call one's soul one's own! One is at the beck and call of Majesty from her morning chocolate at nine until the last hand of cards at night. As today is Wednesday

189

it means one may have to spend four intolerable hours on horseback riding with the royal chaise while she follows the staghounds.'

He put a long white hand to his lips, masking a symbolical yawn.

'Does your Excellency hunt?'

Javan considered the chase of the stag a very tame sport, and said so.

'The only sport of that sort I enjoy is boar hunting,' he added.

Hervey obviously thought the latter a rather boisterous form of amusement, which might cause havoc to the toilette.

'Your Excellency is not, then, bound hand and foot to the Empress's chariot wheel?'

However exigent Jane Tierce might have been, it could not truthfully be said that the Empress had required the constant attendance of her chamberlain. In fact she had done her best to escape from him.

'Her Majesty makes only very modest demands on my time,' he returned.

After the exchange of a few more banalities, Hervey permitted himself to reveal the object of his visit.

'I had purposed coming to pay my personal respects to you in any event, sir,' he said. 'But, as it turns out, I have been ordered to wait on you as emissary of the Queen. It is a highly gratifying errand to me, I can assure you. A sympathetic bearer of good news must always partake of the pleasure of the recipient. I have it in command, sir, to present you with this document.'

From some part of his dress he whipped out, like a conjuror, a long folded paper which he passed across the table with a bow.

Without displaying any surprise, Javan unfolded the document, propped it up before him against the dish of oranges, and read it.

With many flourishes of penmanship, with imposing red seal and the scrawled signature 'George R', in stilted verbiage and legal jargon it announced a free pardon for his father's high treason of nearly forty years before, the extinguishing of the attainder, and the consequent restoration to himself of the family estates in Ireland and elsewhere which had been sequestrated to the Crown after the death of his uncle.

Although he let his face show nothing of what he felt, it was with complete incredulity in his mind that he regarded the lines making him master of all the domains of which his father had talked nostalgically—of the old house at Athmoney in the hills above Dublin, of the small battered castle in Galloway, of farmlands and villages, of a township, of fairy-haunted mountains and woodlands, of—

It could not be true! It could *not* be true.

He was silent long enough for the other to inquire with a slight lift of the eyebrows, a faint shadow of surprise in his voice—

'There is no point of honour, I presume, that can restrain you from accepting this act of grace? You are not a practising Jacobite by any chance?'

Javan smiled his lopsided smile.

'Indeed I am not. I have no interest in the Pretender. My rather unmannerly silence was solely due to overwhelming surprise.'

'Surprise?' echoed my Lord, taking a very small pinch of snuff from a golden snuffbox with the flourish of one engaged in an exercise of deportment. 'Do you mean that you didn't know anything about this?'

'I'm as ignorant as I am astounded. This is a thing I've never dreamed of in the wildest flights of my imagination. How could I know anything?'

His tone was such that it carried conviction even to the naturally suspicious mind of a born intriguer. Examining his overpolished fingernails, Hervey inquired within himself whether the Queen and he could possibly be wrong in their speculations about the Empress's relations with her chamberlain.

'As I understand it,' he said at length, 'the British government was very anxious to make some friendly gesture to mark the satisfactory conclusion of the treaty. The Empress herself delicately suggested this method. And there you are!'

Hervey did not add that it had been equally delicately—but very definitely—suggested by Imperial Majesty that agreement on the much-desired pact might never be reached unless her proposal were found acceptable.

Javan made no spoken comment. So this was how, then, Shems-ed-Douha, consort of Mulai Ali, Emperor of Morocco, Witch and Empress, restored to him with heavy interest the past which she had borrowed; restored it so that he had a new present and a new future!

Hervey's veiled eyes surveyed the dark, romantic profile that was reminiscent of Don Quixote, of Charles the Second, of a crusader.

'If Princess Emily—if the other women about the Court get their claws in him,' he thought, 'they won't release him in a hurry for anyone, not even an empress!'

Aloud he emphasized the fact that the making of the gift had not been unattended by difficulties—

'There was a bit of bother at the start,' he said, 'on the score of the King's strong prejudices against the Stuarts. He needed rather careful handling, your Excellency. At the moment, too, the government as a whole is exceptionally sensitive on the subject of Jacobitism. It is aware of a great recrudescence. Largely due, of course, to the King's undisguised preference for Hanover and things Hanoverian, and his protracted absences from the country.'

'I can hardly take the oath of allegiance whilst I am still employed by the Emperor,' said Javan helping his guest to coffee. 'But I am quite prepared to give the most solemn undertaking to engage in no conspiracies against the established order, my Lord.'

'I will convey that statement to the right quarter,' Hervey assured him with a theatrical gesture of the hand as though he were receiving it in a neat parcel for delivery. 'I shouldn't have mentioned the matter at all if it hadn't been that the ministry see plots, smell plots, hear plots, sense plots in every direction. One of the most celebrated of Jacobite conspirators, a man named Murphy, Doctor Murphy, was recognized in a London street a few days ago. He went to ground at once, of course, without leaving a trace. He is a professional plotter and a very dangerous man, so perhaps their anxiety is natural.'

'I will hasten to give my most grateful thanks to his Majesty,' said Javan.

'Your gratitude is in fact due to *her* Majesty,' corrected Hervey with his small, knowing simper. 'It is entirely due to her that that paper of yours has been signed. The King may reign, but she rules—although the little fellow does not know it, and would never believe it. But it's a fact, Gad's life, that the woman he teases and bullies, by day and by night, will in the end always influence him to her own way of thinking. She is the cleverest woman in the world. She loves power. She pays for it—Gad's life she does!—but she *has* it!'

He paused as though to let the words sink in, preening himself the while in an indescribable way as if he would say, 'And in me you behold the power behind the power behind the throne.'

. . . The grey-faced woman, who moved dowdily amid all the ritual and mummery of the palace—the woman who loathed her son

—had said the word, and lo! a grubby, stubby fist had scrawled a signature upon a sheet of paper which gave a landless man estates, a homeless man houses, an exile among the barbarians rank and security. What wonder that there should be very willing servants to minister to the desires of such authority—whatever they might be— when their rewards, too, might be on such a scale! . . .

Javan recalled himself to his duties. He thanked the bearer of good news. He begged advice on the correct etiquette for a reverential display of gratitude.

My Lord obliged in every particular, and then turned the conversation to other and more trivial matters—to the shade of tan attained by his Excellency. Gad's life, all the Court were talking of how well it went with hair powder! All the men would be washing their faces in walnut juice before the week was out.

He drank a little coffee as though the raising of the cup, the putting of his lips to the rim, and the sipping of the hot liquid were rhythmic motions in a courtly ritual.

He simpered and pouted into exposition of the advantages of a vegetable, seed, and milk diet for health. Gad's life, his lordship could speak about it—and most definitely did so—for he had lived on a strictly vegetarian diet for three years!

Then he embarked with gusto on an endless discussion of doctors and the diseases with which he and his family had been inflicted— principally his own.

Javan was beginning to feel that Miss Mott, or even Tuke, would have sustained his conversation with more aptitude than himself, who was never ill, when his visitor branched out into analysis of the various personalities at Court.

He painted them with pitiless malice, with all their foibles and peculiarities of appearance—from Walpole, the Prime Minister, with his unfailing store of cesspool stories, to the Duke of Grafton, fat and drowsy Adonis to the Princess Emily; from Lady Deloraine, lovely, tipsy, brainless, who doubled the parts of governess to the younger royal children and mistress to their father, down to the pert Purcell, the Queen's favourite tirewoman.

'Then, of course, there's Fretz—the Prince of Wales,' said Hervey thoughtfully. "But him you have met, I believe?'

'During my stay at Crosse, my Lord.'

Hervey nodded his head as though he knew all about it.

Javan awaited tensely the next move by the *Eminence grise* of the Queen. This man—he realized—for all his paint, his simpers, and his dimples, had brains, boundless ambition, iron self-mastery, and not a single scruple. This man, above all others, he knew to be Griffe's implacable foe.

At this juncture he realized that a face was peering through the window, behind his visitor's back, at the far end of the room overlooking the wall of the huge outer court of the palace.

It was a small face, and, although he could not distinguish the features, he knew it to be Coppie's. On the whole he was not surprised. The owner of the face nodded reassuringly when he perceived that his presence had been noted, and then popped out of view.

The next moment the mellow song of the bell of the great clock over the gateway in Clock Court sounded the hour. It was nine.

'Gad's life!' said Hervey, checking the hour by a gem-studded watch. 'That clock may stop sometimes in rather odd circumstances, but it's never wrong. Gad's life, I am already due in attendance on her Majesty. Nine is the hour, and woe betide me if I am late! You will forgive me, sir?'

He performed very exquisitely the ceremonial of departure: paused as he bowed at the door, hat under his arm, fingers touching dark blue satin coat in the region of the heart, toes as pointed as though he were dancing.

'Perhaps, sir,' he said, 'I should not have mentioned the government's concern over the Jacobite situation. May I ask you not to speak of what I have said? It might prove unsettling to ill-regulated minds.'

'I shall say nothing at all.'

'There have been already some very disturbing incidents, and our agents appear to believe that a serious coup is in contemplation, but of what nature they have been completely unable to ascertain. The return of Murphy to this country from France certainly lends colour to their belief. The last occasion that he is known to have been here was some ten years ago at the time of the Layer plot.'

'Never heard of it,' averred Javan. 'I know nothing of contemporary English history.'

'A very bloody and desperate conspiracy,' said my Lord informatively, his accent and intonation suggesting that the fluid concerned was not like his own, of an elegant old-rose colour. 'It was to have been carried through by mutinous men of the Guards and discontented old soldiers. It sent Christopher Layer himself to the gallows, the Bishop of Rochester into exile, and the Duke of Norfolk and Lord North to prison.'

'The only Jacobites of my acquaintance are a few romantic elderly ladies in Crosse and a harmless old parson, with whom the Prince of Wales has struck up a great friendship.'

'The Prince of Wales, ah!' quoth my Lord thoughtfully, but did not pursue the subject.

Javan repeated his assurances, and escorted him to the front entrance of the Toy, where an exquisite sedan-chair in pale blue and gold awaited his lordship, with two exquisite chairmen also in pale blue and gold. My Lord waved a slender hand in a ladylike farewell as he entered this dainty nest and set out on the journey of approximately one furlong, through the Trophy Gates, to the western entrance of the palace.

Javan went upstairs to his room pondering why the Queen's Vice-Chamberlain should have gone out of his way to impress upon him the government's concern on the subject of Jacobite plots.

Could it possibly be, he asked himself, that he was being proffered thus indirectly an explanation of the desperate adventure at the fair? In spite of what Mr. Tuke had said, not all conspiracies were planned to follow a strictly gentlemanly pattern, even in Europe. After all, could not the abduction of the Prince of Wales have been part of a wider project by Stuart adherents? It could have been: but he was morally certain that it was not.

He opened the door of his pleasant wainscoted apartment to see Coppie standing by the small round breakfast-table in the window wistfully regarding the dish of oranges. The knees of his nankeen breeches were very stained; his jacket was torn, his hands cut and bleeding, and his hair more ruffled even than ordinary.

'Why not come in through the front door, Coppie?' he asked, after they had exchanged the most cordial greetings.

'I got here all the way from Trophy House without touching the ground once,' said Coppie proudly. 'I like doing that. Do you know that I can actually go right round the whole palace on the roofs all the way except for one place, from the top of the north wing in Outer Green Court back to the south wing! It's miles and miles and

miles! I frightened someone at a window over Chapel Court into fits
the other day. She screamed like—like a walrus! I say, do you think
you'll eat all those oranges, sir?'

Javan did not think that he would require them all—which was
satisfactory.

Coppie made a hole in one of the golden spheres, inserted a lump
of sugar, and proceeded to expatiate upon the pleasures of roof-
climbing in the intervals of refreshment. Javan let him have his head.

'Do you know,' said Coppie, 'that there's acksherly a garden on
the roof? It's on the leads of one of the buildings over by Back Court.
There's bushes in tubs, rambler roses against the wall, and flower-
beds in boxes. There's even a trellis arbour, too! Do you know I
knocked a bit of tile or something off the roof of the lodgings in
First Court and it fell on top of the greenhouse! It made a terrible
smash, so I went down the skylight into one of the rooms. They're
nearly all empty there. I daresay it would have blown down anyhow
if there had been a gale, don't you?'

'I should think it quite possible,' Javan reassured him.

'Another time I heard a little noise, so I hid behind a chimney
stack. There were two men creeping about the roof. It was on the
new part of the palace, over the other end where the Prince of Wales
lives.'

'Workmen,' suggested Javan with a quickening of interest.

Coppie shook his head decidedly.

'Workmen talk in loud voices,' he said, 'and these were whispering. Besides they'd got list slippers on. Workmen don't wear list
slippers, do they? They went down a trapdoor.'

'They *might* have been workmen,' said Javan.

'I don't think so, sir,' insisted Coppie. 'I saw them again yesterday. They were crawling along by the parapet towards the clock
tower over the gateway in Clock Court. I didn't see where they were
going, but they wouldn't have been going on their hands and knees
when they could have walked quite easily if they'd been ordinary
people, would they? I said something to Jenkins, who knows about
me and the roof—'

'Who's Jenkins?'

'He's a sergeant and lives in the barracks. He's a very nice man.
He once let me have some gunpowder to play with. He only laughed

when I told him about the men. Do you think they can have been robbers?'

'If there'd been a robbery, Jenkins would have known all about it, wouldn't he?'

'Yes,' said Coppie doubtfully; brightened up. 'But, of course, they might have been planning one, you know. Look at Jack Sheppard!'

That celebrated criminal and escapologist was not within Javan's cognisance, so that he could not 'look at' him. Although he felt that Coppie's roof-creeping acquaintances deserved attention, he also considered that it was about time that he should learn whether or no Master Tregallion's call was one of pure courtesy or of business.

'I am going to visit your grandmother very shortly, I hope,' he remarked.

'She thought you would.'

'How on earth did she know?'

'I don't mean my grandmother, sir. I mean—I mean—well, the Princess. I told her about you, you see. I've got a letter for you from her.'

He set the orange down on the table, and fumbled under jacket and shirt with fingers that were not only grimy and bloodstained but also moist with fruit juice. It was when his body was at its most contorted and his searching hand halfway down inside his breeches, that his roving eyes apparently caught sight for the first time of the document which Javan had dropped on the table.

'I say, what a *huge* seal! I suppose you want it, sir?'

'I'm afraid I do, Coppie. It's the King of England's seal.'

'Oh, him!' said Coppie, losing interest, and simultaneously brought to the surface the sought-for paper, which was intricately secured with silk thread and small dabs of green wax.

'I had to borrow the sealing-wax from Grandmother's scrutoire,' he said proffering the little packet.

'Sit on the window-seat and spit pips into the road, or amuse yourself somehow whilst I read what the Princess has to tell me,' Javan instructed him.

'Can I have another orange then, sir? I bet I can get one into the horse-trough.'

Provided with a fresh supply of ammunition, Coppie turned his

attention to the world without. Javan opened the cover. There was
a short letter within in Shems-ed-Douha's writing; it ran:

> The Trophy House
> Wednesday

Javan,

I don't know why you are here. I don't know how you found
me out, or whether it was just by accident. I didn't want you
here, because the I that is Shems-ed-Douha has nothing to do
with the I-of-the-long-ago, and it's the I-of-the-long-ago who is
concerned here. When she has accomplished what she's got to
do, I might tell you about her before she vanishes for ever.
Perhaps, too, when I become an elderly retired princess living
with just a little state—muffins for breakfast—cards at night—neat
house—two carriages—lady-in-waiting—early hours except occasionally for a rout and the opera; then, too, I might speak of her
in confidence now and again with a retired general of my
acquaintance—if he maintains it!

At first I was even doubtful about having Coppie as her ally.
But she has done him no harm, and his mother would have liked
him to help.

I know it. You see, Javan, that other woman knew her once
upon a time—at a respectful distance. She even knew Coppie
when he was a baby.

Now I realize it's just possible that you may be able to help
the girl of long ago. So please stay on guard for a little while,
but don't make any attempt to come here unless I ask you to.—S.

Stay on guard for a *little while*! For her he would stay on guard
until the Last Trump sounded—and beyond! Castle and estate were
a fantasy—he knew that he would never quite bring himself to
believe in them—compared with the reality of his duty to her. He
was her knight, holding her in all honour until the end of time.

'I say, sir, I got one right in the middle of his hat!' said the 'I-of-
the-long-ago's' ally, evincing the greatest pleasure. 'It bounced off
the crown into the curl of the brim, and he doesn't even know!'

Besides Williams who was entirely trustworthy, Javan had taken
into his personal service Joe, the large sweetheart of Susie, the girl

at the Maid's Head. One or other of them must be on duty at the Toy all the time whenever he was necessarily absent.

'I say, sir,' said Coppie, 'Sir Richard is just coming to the door! Do you know, he isn't going to use any G's today at all? He told me so yesterday.'

'He'd better not see you. Make off now and come back when I whistle. I've got a very important message for you to take.'

'What 'ull you whistle? Something Turkish?' suggested Coppie, gladly plunging into any adventure. He could be the general's ally without disloyalty to his other and imperial ally, he felt assured. He was Galahad as well as Merlin; he was the dark plotter as well as the unequalled projector of orange pips!

# IV

## *House of Ghosts*

ALTHOUGH they had planned to make frequent excursions, as they had done at Crosse, Griffe and Javan Tierce had but one considerable jaunt—on horseback—together. It was a successful enough expedition in a way, yet Javan was conscious all the time that armed servants in scarlet coats were riding ahead and behind, just out of ordinary earshot but within hail.

'I see you've learned your lesson, sir,' he remarked as their horses ambled along the towpath of the river. 'No Haroun-al-Raschiding without an escort nowadays!'

'Anyone would be a fool to go anywhere without one in this district,' said Griffe. 'You have to travel, once you are out of sight of the palace walls, almost as if you were going into battle. From here, through Twickenham and Richmond to London, the roads are as infested with highway men and footpads as a dog is full of fleas. Eleven were strung up in one day at Tyburn at the last hanging, but the profession continues to flourish. Of course—'

He left the end of the sentence in the air, and Javan meditated that the lawlessness of the countryside might furnish as good an excuse for a crime of violence as any Jacobite conspiracy.

They rode for all a pleasant summer afternoon upstream along the river. They dined on cold boiled bacon, and bread and cheese and onions, and home-brewed beer at a thatched public-house embowered in trees. They exchanged affable banalities with taverners, farm labourers, and bargees. They discussed everything under the sun from the comparative mildness of the punishment for theft in Morocco to the mysterious disappearance of Elsa—

'Elsa?' questioned Javan, in whose mind the name awakened no echo. 'Who's Elsa?'

The small man's yellow face flushed a little. He said rather awkwardly, as though regretting having to explain a childishness:

'Don't you remember my wife's talisman?'

'Oh, the doll!'

'The talisman,' insisted the other. 'Our counterpart to your amulet. Its constituents less romantic, I admit, than a he-goat's blood and a bezoar stone.'

Javan recalled the treasured puppet with staring black eyes and red and white cheeks, dressed in green—'the mystical colour of good fortune'—which was practically all the Princess Augusta possessed to remind her of her childhood and her home in the toy, fairy-tale duchy, of Saxe-Gotha; recalled, too, Griffe's loyal adoption of the absurd thing as a mascot for himself. He listened sympathetically whilst the Prince narrated every circumstance bearing upon Elsa's vanishing from their bedchamber; debated the rival theories of theft by a jealous lapdog—by an envious child—by some hireling of my Lord Hervey!

'But why, in the name of Allah, should Lord Hervey want—'

Then, as Griffe went on, he saw that the rape of Elsa could indeed be a malicious jest worthy of the serious attention of such as my Lord or those others who might, or might not be his creatures. In the minds of the Prince and his bride it had become a crime of enormous proportions, comparable to no ordinary felony or sin of violence—but to the sacrilegious theft of a crucifix from an altar, of a locket of a dead child's hair, of hope.

'In Augusta's present condition—' urged Griffe.

His round greenish eyes anxiously sought in his friend's face for any token of inward amusement. They saw nothing but grim attention displayed in its dark lineaments. . . .

It was well past sunset when they returned to Hampton. They left their horses in a narrow lane by the outer wall, and went in privately through the huddle of alleys and courtyards of the old palace of Henry the Eighth, lying west and north of the raw, red theatricality of the new buildings.

'This is no dress in which to appear before her Royal Highness,' said Javan coming to a halt at the foot of the private staircase leading to the Prince's quarters, and contemplating his spurs and dusty boots. 'If you will give me ten minutes—'

'We'll be real people tonight, not marionettes on the strings of court formulae,' insisted Frederick, and led the way upstairs and through a fair-sized empty room, which was his audience chamber, into another in which four people were talking with lowered voices.

It was a corner room, and on two sides there were windows full of sad grey twilight. The small golden flames of a pair of three-branched silver candelabra on the high mantelpiece only served to emphasize the melancholy of day's decline. It was difficult to distinguish the faces of the women who curtsied, or the precise shades of the subdued colours of their hooped dresses.

'But where is the Princess?' asked the Prince, without salutation, coming to a halt as he entered. 'Where is she?'

Just for a moment there was a pause. Two of the women looked at the third. The man—it was Mr. Standring, the heartbroken lover of Jane Tierce—looked at his feet.

Then the older of the women—she had a pale face, clear-cut like a cameo—spoke with the suspicion of a Scottish accent.

'Her Royal Highness is abed, sir,' she said.

'Abed!' he exclaimed incredulously. 'Why? At half past eight! Where? Has—'

He made as though to set off immediately upon investigation towards a door in the far corner.

'I shouldna go to her, sir,' said the woman with the Scottish accent. 'She is asleep. She is not in labour.'

'What are you hiding from me, Lady Archibald? What is the matter? What has happened?'

'Dinna fear, sir! Dinna fear! It's just a wee dose of opium she's had, sir.'

'Opium! Why opium? Who gave it her? Not my father's damned apothecary? Not Yager?'

'No, sir. Wrede did.'

He calmed a little at that; for Wrede, his valet, amongst other unusual qualifications for a body servant, was also a surgeon. Javan, a silent witness of the scene, recalled that the man was one of the few people about him in whom the Prince had implicit faith.

The little man reached out his left hand and took the wide cuff of Javan's coat between finger and thumb, as though he felt that by that contact the confident strength and courage of the other would flow into his own frame. It was rather like a child asking for his hand to be held in a dark passage.

'But why should she need opium?' he asked in a quieter tone.

'Elspeth must tell you that, sir.'

The youngest of the three women was pale—very pale—in a gown of a grey that was shadowy. She curtsied stiffly, as though she were a puppet impelled to the movement by some other force than her own. Her wide eyes turned from one to another of the group about her. Her lips moved, but no sound came from them. . . . They moved again: they uttered the one word, '*No!*'

'Dinna be a fool, Elspeth!' said Lady Archibald harshly, and took the girl by the hand. 'The fact is, sir, that the Princess went to the chapel this evening to pray. She has been doing so lately, as you know.' He nodded. He knew of Augusta's intense prayers for the child-to-be, for him, for herself. 'Elspeth accompanied her Royal Highness. After she had said her prayers and got up— Now go on, girl! *Go on!*'

The tense tone of unexpected command in the older woman's voice awakened sudden obedience in the girl, for she continued the story in flurried sentences:

'We went to the door. I put out my hand to open it, when it shook. It shook just as if someone outside were pulling at it, and trying to get in, and couldn't. And then we heard a woman on the other side sobbing as if her heart would break. She was? She *was*, I tell you! And then the door shook again!'

Her voice rose as she spoke almost to a cry; and her eyes widened as though again she saw the door of the chapel shaking.

'Sh-h, Elspeth!' said the older woman.

'Go on!'

'I had forgotten about—about— And so I opened the door. There wasn't anybody there. Nobody at all!'

'And then I remembered—and as I remembered, there was a sort of wail some way off. A dreadful wail! Not a loud one, but dreadful! And then we both looked to the far end of the gallery—where it turns. There was something misty there in the dusk like a woman. Like a woman. It flung out its hands and cried again—it was horrible. Then it vanished into the wall. It just wasn't there any longer! . . . I can't bear it! I want to go home! I never want to come here again! Let me go home!'

She burst into hysterical weeping.

'Janet, awa' wi' Elspeth and put her to bed!' said Lady Archibald. 'Perhaps Wrede, sir, might gi' Miss Eyland a wee dose—'

'I won't go to bed! I won't have opium, my Lady! I *won't* stay! I'm going home if I have to walk!'

'Sh-h!' said the third woman, and led her away.

The clock on the high mantelpiece struck nine, and a moment later the bell in the Clock Tower sonorously announced the hour to all the palace.

The Prince said in an emotional voice:

'My poor wife! I must see her at once!'

'No, sir!' the Scotswoman denied him flatly. 'You canna. The doors are all double-bolted within. To knock wud mean wakin' her, and Mrs. Arbuthnot is sittin' by her and wull tell us when she rouses. There's every licht we can find burnin' in the room, forbye.'

Presumably the Prince brought himself to accept the Scotswoman's dictum, for he broke out only after a long pause with:

'It is an abominable and wicked hoax! This is the work of—' He pulled himself up, and ended rather lamely: 'Did nobody else see or hear anything? There is always a sentry at the entrance to the Queen's Guard Chamber, not thirty yards away. What about him?'

'When Elspeth brocht her Royal Highness back here, the Princess had swooned—'

'Fainted. Oh, God! And fell, I suppose?'

'Elspeth caught her. She has received no hurt, sir, I assure you.'

'She might have had a miscarriage!'

'She didna,' said Lady Archibald flatly. 'Weell—when they got back, Mr. Standring went to investigate. He'll tell ye.'

But Standring, fiddling with the lapels of grey and silver coat, had very little to add.

The sentry outside the Queen's Guard Chamber *had* heard an odd noise coming from the gallery like a woman crying. But the door was shut, and it was not his duty to investigate. Standring was inclined to fancy that even if it had been the man's duty he would have not performed it. For the fellow said that there were often strange sounds to be heard from what he called 'the Haunted Gallery.' None of the men liked doing guard duty anywhere near it.

'Did you investigate, sir?' asked Javan.

'I walked the length of the gallery,' said Standring, looking poetically detective, 'but the old State Apartments are not used and are kept locked. I tried them all. Only the doors to the chapel were open, and one that gives on to a winding staircase.'

'To the roof?'

Mr. Standring had not risked poetically beautiful clothes amid the prosaic realities of dust in the interests of topographical knowledge; but made the point:

'The figure—or whatever it was—was seen at the far end of the gallery. The door to the turret stairs, on the other hand, is the first one as you come in.'

'It's a hoax all the same, and a damnable one!' declared Javan, who had been watching the Prince's face.

Mr. Standring, however, was not so certain.

'Who would dare,' he suggested, 'to play a practical joke on the Princess of Wales?'

Lady Archibald, on the other hand, was concerned for the authenticity of the apparition. That the ghost of Queen Katherine appeared in the Haunted Gallery, crying to Henry the Eighth for mercy, was very well established, she maintained.

'I wud not admit it to Elspeth,' she protested, 'but there are three people of my acquaintance who have heard her before this.'

They stood, a group of four, in the middle of the dimly lighted room. Through the north windows a wing of the older buildings was visible across an open court. The cupola of a turret was outlined against the evening sky, and a solitary light glimmered in the dark mass.

'There are too many ghosts altogether in this damned house,' said the Prince, breaking the silence that had brooded for nearly a minute. 'There's Jane Seymour, another of Henry's wives, who walks about upstairs with a lighted taper in her hand. There are the two Cavaliers of the Rebellion days in Fountain Court. There's the spinning ghost in the old west wing . . . T'cha! It's dark in this room! It will be full of ghosts next—if it isn't already! Do you believe in ghosts, Javan?'

The soldier was not prepared for academic discussion on phantoms. He said bluntly:

'I don't believe in this one, sir. If it were daylight, I should wish to hunt it with bloodhounds and pistols in my hands. I *know* it is a hoax, sir!'

From where he stood the delicate, poetical features of Mr. Standring were silhouetted against the pale golden glow of the candles on the mantelpiece. He wondered if the tiny ripple of an expression upon the romantic face was due to his emphasis, to an almost imperceptible flicker of the small flames, or to some other cause.

The Prince recognized the emphasis, although he made no direct reply.

'Call a page to light me to the Palace Keeper's lodging, Mr. Standring, if you please,' he commanded. 'My Lady, be so good as to send there for me the moment the Princess wakes.'

On the way, among the chasing shadows of endless passages and the labyrinth of small courts, Javan told Frederick of Coppie's rooftop encounters—of the men whom the boy had seen descending into the upper storey of his apartments.

'They are keeping us virtual prisoners here, whilst they arrange our fate for us,' the Prince commented in a low voice. 'God knows what that fate will be! Augusta has always thought it would be poison. But now one would say that they are trying to frighten her to death. God blast them! . . . This old fellow will know nothing; neither will he be able to help.'

And so indeed it proved to be.

The Keeper of the Palace, a parchment-pale, deferential old gentleman—caught in his nightcap, and enjoying a bottle and a pipe at a table strewn with dusty papers, in a small room walled in with shelf-loads of dusty papers, the very chairs stacked with more dusty papers—expressed not the faintest surprise at anything—supernatural or human—that might happen at Hampton Court.

'There is no one who knows a tithe of what goes on in the place, your Royal Highness, or could say who is entitled to be within its walls,' he said. 'It is a rabbit warren. It is an anthill. It is a town. Apart from the royal suites there are hundreds upon hundreds of rooms. People might live here for weeks on end without anyone being the wiser. They might die, and no one would know.

'There are people living here who have been allotted apartments by his present Majesty—by her present Majesty. *I* am never told. There are others who have been given rooms by King George the First—by Queen Anne—by King William or Queen Mary. There is even one old gentleman who has a warrant dating from the time of King Charles, over fifty years ago. He actually takes in lodgers, and I can't stop him. I have no authority.

'The residents let their apartments; they make alterations without permission; they exchange rooms with one another; they snap up vacant rooms and add them to their own suites.

'There's Madame von Pfullingen for instance. She has annexed a great part of Trophy Buildings and calls it Trophy House. There is no one at all, your Royal Highness, who can do anything at all with her.'

'It would appear, sir,' remarked Javan, accepting a glass of wine, 'that a gang of highwaymen might find happy lodging here—or a Jacobite conspiracy?'

Even this possibility the Keeper of the Palace did not entirely put beyond the bounds of credence. He added a further interesting particular in conclusion—

'There are certain privileges attaching to a royal residence, such as freedom from arrest for debt, that some of the inhabitants here do not find at all incommodious.'

'And such is the hinterland of the pomp and display of my father's state!' said Frederick, as they walked back a little later without escort. 'We are prisoners, Augusta and I, in *his* palace, surrounded by *his* friends, *his* guards, *his* servants, *his* dependants, *his* ruffians, *his* doctors—*his* doctors!'

'Bolt!'

'In *his* carriage? With *his* horses? With *his* grooms? From *his* stables?'

'There are other carriages, horses, servants, and stables!'

'And be brought back under guard?'

'You will bolt at that moment, and not before, when her Royal Highness's labour pains commence. You cannot be brought back then.'

The Prince came to a halt under a glimmering oil lamp in a cavernous archway. His long, yellow face was haggard and twitching, and once again Javan was reminded of the pathetic features of a punchinello.

'And the risk of the journey to Augusta?' he asked. 'The terrible, terrible risk!'

'Is the risk as great, sir, as if the child should be born here?'

'No,' he said loudly, and again, 'No.'

'Sh-h!'

'No, it is not as great . . . Our child shall *not* be born here in this house of ghosts. I'm already a ghost! My mother cannot see me even when I kiss her hand! My father does not see me when I stand next his chair! My sisters do not see me when I bow to them! I am invisible to them, though alive. There are enough ghosts. Augusta begins to look like one. The child would be born one. I will not be father to a ghost.'

'You will let me arrange then?' said Javan quietly. 'All you have to do is to tell me what is necessary, and warn me when the time comes.'

The Prince made no answer but by a nod, and Javan saw that he wept—this forlorn and hated prince.

He waited until the little man had recovered his self-control, then he gave one last urgent instruction:

'There must be a finesse, sir. You must appear to make arrangements of your own—vague and indeterminate—for a possible escape at an indefinite date. About this plan of mine you will say nothing at all. . . .'

There had, indeed, been only one person who ever could—in the words of the Keeper of the Palace—'do anything' with Madame von Pfullingen; and he had died many years before, although Shems-ed-Douha had the fancy that at night, in her white-panelled supper-room, she communed with the spirit of the bleak king whose portrait was shrouded by the curtains of purple velvet.

Now at any rate the old woman was a law to herself, ministered to without question by a staff that was almost completely German —dourly silent men and women from a hamlet on the family estates almost under the shadow of the forbidding Hexentanzplatz, the Dance Place of the Witches, in the haunted forests of the Harz Mountains.

Shems-ed-Douha had little to do with them, for her duties were confined to the care of Coppie; accompanying him on his daily official walk in Bushey Park, hearing his lessons, and eternally mending his clothes—extremely badly, for she was no needlewoman.

'I shall always keep them as a relic,' said Coppie one day regarding with favour a pair of breeches which she was engaged in reseating.

'They are little more than a relic now,' said Shems.

'I mean,' explained Coppie, 'that I'll always keep them to show my little boys and tell them that they were mended by an empress! There are not many boys who have seats put in their breeches by an empress, you know. Do you suppose the Queen ever used to do any mending?'

Shems had been a little uncertain whether her lack of skill with the needle might not have been too apparent to his grandmother, but the old woman never required his presence except at dessert after her four o'clock dinner, when he wore his best clothes.

What Madame von Pfullingen did with herself all day long in that house with its shuttered or curtained windows staring blankly on the wide avenue leading to the palace was a mystery to Shems. Nobody ever seemed to visit it; nobody ever seemed to leave it. The saturnine menservants crept silently about its dusky passages, and in and out of its candle-lit rooms.

All the panoply and pageantry of a royal court flaunted outside; with powdered hair the Guards marched past behind their band in red uniforms faced with blue, and long white spatterdashes; a rainbow cavalcade swept by to the hunt; gilded and coronetted coaches with postilions and outriders and running footmen went to and fro. The house ignored them. Once or twice someone came rapping on the front door; the house ignored them, too. It did not admit the existence of George the Second, disloyal son of the other George, master of the old woman who drank herself into a fuddle every night on gin and black treacle.

It would seem as if Madame von Pfullingen herself or, perhaps, Ottilie, had spoken of what had happened on the night when the past had been mirrored in a silver spoon. For Shems-ed-Douha found that thereafter the atmosphere of the house was changed towards her. No one said anything, but the attitude of her fellow servants was tinged with respect as also with a peculiar suggestion of companionship in some dark and secret ritual.

For a few days after the incident Ottilie had gone about her duties like a ghost, obviously hagridden by her conscience. Then suddenly she vanished altogether, and when Shems eventually commented upon her absence, Franz, the least dour of the menservants, vouchsafed the information that she had gone back to her home in Germany. Madame von Pfullingen, it was clear, had come to the conclusion that a conscience still tender after seven years was better out of the country, and had acted accordingly.

Shems realized that it was the complete destruction of the plan with which she had come to Trophy House, of inducing Ottilie by one means or other to confess. She did not think that any pictures called up from the past by the exercise of those rites of Moorish magic known as *darb el-mendel* would affect the iron-willed old woman. She would stop at nothing, however, to extract a declaration of the truth—nothing at all, even if it meant abducting Madame von Pfullingen with the aid of Javan and the retainers whom Coppie called her 'eunoxes.'

She was revolving this in her mind one early afternoon when she was summoned to the shrouded inner sanctuary of the mistress of Trophy House.

'Vhere is the boy?' the old woman demanded as she curtsied in the doorway.

'He has gone to London for the day with the Turkish general, the friend of Sir Richard Hurrell, madam. You said he might.'

'Vhen he comes back,' ordered Antonia, 've vill try your experiment once again.'

'Inteed it will be no use, madam.' The answer was respectful but decided.

'Vhat, you dare to say "No" to me?'

'It will be the wrong time of day, madam.'

'Vhy does that matter?'

'I will not be knowing, madam; but it *does* matter. And the weather is wrong.'

'Vhat are you telling me, daughter of a pig-woman? How can the veather affect magic? If it is magic!'

'You have been seeing for yourself, madam, whether it is magic. But with a high wind and a cloudy sky, there is nothing to be seen —ever, at all.'

'Ve vill try.'

'It will be waste of your time, madam. Men have been seeing lakes and trees and cities in the bare desert, madam; but only in certain kinds of weather. There are islands and fields that have been seen floating on the sea, too; but only at certain times. The *darb el-mendel* is like that.'

Into the mind of the old woman came long-distant recollection of the vast mirages of the Brocken, near her childhood home, where a hundred witnesses could testify to the appearance of monstrous spectres above the mountain summit, but only at sunrise and in certain conditions of wind and mist. Against her will she was convinced: she dismissed Shems with a snarled warning—

'The next time I send for you, Howell, I shall have remembered about the time of day and the veather. Then if you fail—'

As she curtsied respectfully to the pale, amorphous, Buddha-like figure backed by the sheen of purple velvet, the tall woman with the blemished face said, but not out loud: 'And if I fail next time, it is you who will suffer! You will undergo what I underwent. The whip. Boiling oil. Not as punishment, but because I can think of no other form of persuasion.'

'I hope not to fail—yess, inteed, madam!' said Howell.

Coppie was still recounting to her the entrancing events of the day, which had included a visit to the royal menagerie at the Tower of London, when Javan left the Toy to report to the Prince that everything was in train.

# V

## *Three Pilgrimages to St. James's*

THROUGH ALL the sultry Sunday the interminable routine of the Court of England trailed its pageantry. They drowsed—the great ones and their acolytes—with little show of respect and less devotion through morning service and droning sermon. They displayed themselves thereafter upon the airless terraces, fluttering impracticable fans and imprisoned in hornet-waisted dresses, or adorned by lampshade-skirted coats of delicate fabrics already marred by sweat and wigs that had become intolerable. They dawdled in the heat upon the bowling-green. In presence chamber and in dressing-room they scandalized, plotted and counterplotted without conviction, or made listless love.

Javan sat at his open window in the Toy, a tankard of ale by his elbow, and waited the coming of a messenger. He compared himself in his mind to Mrs. Garlicke in her watchtower in far-distant Crosse as he watched a crew of naked youngsters gamboling in the shallows at the ferry-landing. The shrillness of their cries and the silvery splashings of their commotion in the glassy water shivered the lethargy of the heavy afternoon.

With unconcealed envy Coppie also watched the bathers when he presented himself, by way of the back window, as bearer of a letter from Shems-ed-Douha.

'I wonder—' he soliloquized aloud, and glanced at Javan; but the man with the tanned face was unfolding the message with (he thought) a queer half-smile and heedless of him.

'I wonder—' repeated Coppie in a slightly higher key. But Javan was intent on the few lines that Shems had written—

> There was no need, Javan, to thank me yet again. It cost me but the trouble of exercising a little intelligence and putting pen to paper as I said before. This is to tell you that I may have to employ other methods than I have been doing to get what *I* want. I may need your advice and help, but it will not be for a few days. Despite the stimulating companionship of Coppie I cannot pretend that I am enjoying myself—but then I did not expect to.
>
> JANE

'I wonder very much—' said Coppie desperately.

'I shouldn't wonder too much,' said Javan, realizing in an instant the course of the young gentleman's reflection. 'The path of duty leads directly to Trophy House with a message. Debate the question of aquatics with the proper authority when you get there. Meantime let me draw your attention to the dish of fruit on the side-table! Employ yourself with it whilst I write the letter.'

'Do you suppose that afterwards you would—'

'You might not think it, my lad, but I am on duty at this window. . . .'

The day wore on.

With infinite condescension the Majestic and the Royal dined in public in the monumental dining-room of green and gold and white marble. After a spectral ceremony, at which the Prince of Wales was treated as though he were invisible and his princess looked as though she were a ghost, the Court went its several ways.

In his private snuggery the King played at commerce—and gallantry—with my Lady Deloraine. In the Queen's Gallery his consort played quadrille; the Princess Caroline played cribbage with Lord Hervey—watching him rather than her cards with the anxious eyes of a spaniel; and the Princess Emily was a law to herself at a noisy round game.

Throughout the vast, rambling palace its teeming population turned earnestly to cards: they played ombre and faro, piquet and whist, gleek and lanterloo, and a dozen other games; they played for love, for farthings, for golden guineas; they played in private apartment, in kitchen and attic.

The gilding of a hazy sunset had already tarnished, and faded into grey, and deepened towards nightfall, when a small, square man in neat, dark clothes, his black hair unpowdered, paused under Javan's window. He cast one quick glance upward, met Javan's eye, and forthwith produced a large red handkerchief and blew his nose before he passed on.

It was John Wrede, the Prince's valet, who, at some time in his mysterious past, had been not merely a surgeon but also a midwife.

'W-Alláhi!' sighed Javan, rising to his feet, gratified at the conclusion of his vigil. He quoted to himself by way of asking benison upon adventure the sentence from the third sura of the Koran: 'Is not Allah the best deviser of stratagems?'

A little later when first one horseman, and then another, had emerged from the courtyard of the Toy and set off on the road to London, he made his discreet way to the apartments of the heir-apparent.

Augusta—dressed in a concealing loose sacque of dark green silk, sat in a high-backed chair in a room hung with tapestries representing a sea battle. There was a staring patch of rouge upon each cheek, and her eyes were preternaturally bright and empty. She looked, Javan thought, not quite real—rather horribly like Elsa, the doll that had been her mascot. The cameo-like Lady Archibald and the pale Elspeth Eyland stood on either side of her, and Mr. Standring was posed opposite, romantic in rose-coloured coat, beside a green lacquer cabinet supporting a tree with leaves and flowers of jade.

The Princess interrupted the ritual of greeting—

'But, Frederick, do you know the clock never struck the hour?'

She spoke in French. Her voice was very high-pitched and full of a strange excitement.

Lady Archibald intervened swiftly.

'Now, madam!' she said in a syrup-soothing voice such as she might have used to a child. 'Now!'

'But you know it did not. Mr. Standring noticed it, too.'

'What clock did not strike what?' asked Frederick, who had arrived but that instant through a further door. He looked rather nonplussed and glanced round questioningly.

'Nobody here chanced to hear the palace clock strike the hour, sir,' explained Lady Archibald in a most matter-of-fact tone.

'Perhaps the wind is in the wrong direction,' said the Prince, still very much at sea.

'I know it's stopped!' said Augusta with hysteria in her voice. 'I know it! Let Mr. Standring go and see! I can't bear it any longer! Don't you know what it means, when it doesn't strike, Fritz? that someone here is going to die?'

Her mouth stayed a little open as though she were about to scream; as though she were a talking doll, whose mechanism was out of order.

'That story's nonsense, dearest,' said the Prince, going to her side. He looked a swift question at Javan; received answer. 'And in any case it doesn't matter, because we shan't be here.'

But she was not listening to him. She rose to her feet and took him by the breast of his coat.

'Fritz,' she said, 'I am so frightened—so very frightened! Your mother—she looks at me like—like the ogress in a fairy-tale. She does. And she doesn't mean me to have a child!'

'Listen! Just listen for an instant, dearest. All the arrangements have been made. The messengers are already on their way to London. We'll go, ourselves, the very minute you are ready!'

'For God's sake, sir!' exclaimed Lady Archibald in consternation. 'Think for a moment! Her Highness cannot go to London now, and in her condition! You wud be responsible if anything were to go wrong. It wud be worse than mad—it wud be criminal!'

'I will go even if I have the child in the coach. I will!'

'Oh, Jesus!' said Lady Archibald. 'This is pure insanity, madam! With the pains you had after dinner!'

The Princess clung to her husband, her long thin arms about his neck, her childish, pathetic face upturned to his, her eyes insisting upon the maintenance of his decision.

'I tell you I *won't* have a child here. Not with that doctor of your mother's. Not in this haunted place. It would die. It would be stolen. It wouldn't be born. Fritz, don't pay any attention to her! I *will* go!'

'Of course you shall, dearest.'

'As for the clock, madam, don't concern yourself!' said Javan, at the ordinary conversational level. 'I happen to know that someone has been tampering with the mechanism.'

At that juncture his observant eyes became aware of the merest tremor in Standring's expression of polite concern, the very slightest tensing of his body. In that instant he recalled the other occasion when he had wondered whether it had been a flicker of the candle-light or the tiny shadow of an emotion that had stirred the other's face. Accordingly he did not say that his statement was mere guess-work from the report made by Coppie some days before; but added the flat fact—

'He—they—were seen at it.'

He was immediately rewarded by another almost imperceptible quiver of the young man's countenance. Suspicion became an over-whelming certainty.

'It will be murder to take her such a journey,' Lady Archibald continued to protest.

'It is more likely to be murder if we don't,' said Frederick bluntly. 'Everything has been planned, Lady Archibald.' He sought confir-mation from Javan, who nodded. 'Messengers have been sent to Dr. Hollings and Mrs. Cannon, the midwife.'—Nod.—'We have sent to warn the Officers of State.'—Nod.—'The coach—'

Javan interrupted brusquely:

'If I may suggest, sir, it would be as well if Mr. Standring went personally to arrange about the carriage.'

'But—'

'The stables, sir, are our vulnerable spot—our very vulnerable spot. I think Mr. Standring should stay in the mews on some excuse or other until the coach is brought round to Tennis Court Lane. We want to be certain that secrecy is maintained. We want someone reliable on guard to ensure that there is no unnecessary clacking of tongues. It is essential.'

'Tell them to be quick—very, very quick!' said the Princess, and then buried her face in her husband's coat.

Standring hesitated in a pallid, limp uncertainty; looked to the Prince for confirmation of the instructions; received it in a nod; departed almost unwillingly; turned as he closed the door and cast back a look in which Javan read sudden agonized realization of a crime in which he was about to engage.

'Murder!' he said to himself. 'The place stinks of murder.'

The Prince was still soothing the trembling girl, holding her to him and stroking the nape of the long neck that was stooped towards him. His face was bent down to her head, and he was murmuring again and again, 'Courage! Courage! Courage!'

Javan approached Lady Archibald, and said in a very low voice: 'Was it Mr. Standring who first noticed about the clock?'

The Scotswoman's honest eyes studied him for a second, and then she inclined her powdered head.

'He is a fool to have said anything that might upset her!'

'A fool?' queried Javan under his breath, and turned on the Prince. 'For God's sake, sir, bestir yourself! You must be gone, and very quickly!'

The little man unashamedly kissed the fair hair that brushed his lips; he raised his face for an instant; he said almost chidingly:

'But you've changed the plan. The coach can't possibly be here for less than half an hour!'

'I have *not* changed the plan. The coach is already waiting for you in the yard of the Toy. You've got to be gone from here in five minutes. You've *got* to be!'

'He's right, Fritz,' said the Princess. 'Let us go at once! I can go as I am. A cloak. A scarf. That's all I need.'

Lady Archibald's mouth opened to protest once more; but Frederick forestalled anything she might say.

'Fetch them immediately! Not a word to anyone! We're going now.'

He strode across the room to the door of the antechamber; paused with his hand upon the latch, and asked a question in the lifting of his eyebrows.

'Standring is a traitor,' replied Javan. 'I'll wager a copper *flus* to a gold ducat! So don't waste time, sir! Desnoyers and Wrede are out there—call them in! One of them must give my man, Williams, the pass you made out for me. That's all. Hurry up, sir!'

'But you—'

'I'm your rear-guard. I must stay here for a little. I shan't be long after you . . . Now call them in, for God's sake!'

Javan felt in the skirts of his coat for the pass to the royal quarters. As he did so the silver-mounted butt of one of his pistols was momentarily revealed against the flower-embroidered back-flap of his waistcoat.

The Prince's small yellow face suddenly paled. It was as if the brief glimpse of that deadly thing brought home to him for the first time the grim reality of the danger by which they were surrounded. The slight suggestion of indecision that had lingered in his air left him. His expression hardened.

'Fritz,' his wife wailed, 'can't we go? I want to go! Can't we go?'

'We can, and, by God, we never will come back!'

In less than five minutes they were gone—although they must carry her down the dark private staircase, and support her through all the murky labyrinth of the palace. They fled in what they stood up, leaving every possession behind them.

Before ever Standring had returned to announce that the carriage from the royal mews was discreetly awaiting them in the lane by the postern gate, another coach, drawn by six horses, was thundering through the night and the mist towards London.

In the dark interior of the crowded vehicle, the Prince supported his young wife in his arms amid her pillows, whispering encouragement into her ear.

'Courage, dearest! Only a few more miles, my sweet! We are escaping for ever from *them*! We are escaping!'

She was so glad that they were escaping from *them*: so glad that her child should be born away from that haunted roof, so glad that *their* doctor and *their* servants should not be about her; but all the same, although she clenched her teeth, she had to moan with the agony of her pangs. Her whimpering could be heard above the clatter of hoofs and the rattle of wheels and the creaking of the vehicle.

Once Lady Archibald, sitting on the front seat with two of her ladies, said imperatively:

'You must stop, sir, and get Wrede to see her Royal Highness!'

So they had halted and Wrede had got down from the box and gone into consultation with the women. A large house with lights in the ground-floor windows loomed up in the darkness near by, and Wrede began uncertainly:

'Perhaps, sir, we had better not go on. This house— A first confinement—'

But she had insisted:

'Go on! Go on! Further and further away from them!'

And had willed herself not to make a sound only so long as they put more and more miles between them and the haunted red palace and the little lowering ogre King and the grey-faced ogress Queen.

'It's best to humour her Royal Highness,' said Wrede, and got back on the box beside the coachman; and Desnoyers, the French dancing-master, and the three equerries clambered again on to the footboard where the lackeys usually rode; and off they all went once more, swaying, lurching, jolting, shaking over the rutted roads.

Once she saw the trustworthy face of good Dr. Collings, and the rubicund, kind face of good Mrs. Cannon, she knew all would be well.

She would not cry out. She must not cry out. They must get there in time, out of the reach of pursuit. . . .

When Standring had returned to announce that the carriage waited in Tennis Court Lane, Javan was studying the tapestry on the walls, which depicted a naval engagement with reiterated detail of wave, and shot-torn sail, and cottonwool smoke, and ships' hulls stabbed with scarlet flashes from the gun-ports.

The young man slid discreetly, romantically, conspiratorially into the room. He was wrapped in a cloak, and from the flush on his cheek, Javan judged that he had been livening his courage or dulling his conscience by an application of the bottle.

He surveyed the desolation of the room with some surprise.

'Surely they are ready by now, your Excellency?' he exclaimed.

'Oh, yes,' said Javan, turning from examination of the hangings, and surveying the younger man with his hands behind his back. 'They have been for quite a long time.'

'But where are they waiting then?' asked the other, flabbergasted.

'They are not waiting, Mr. Standring. They should be well on the road to London.'

'On the road to London?' he stammered.

'We are to follow them, you and I,' said Javan, bringing out a snuffbox and taking a meditative pinch, 'after we have had a little talk, if you please.'

'I will warn the men, then, that we shall be a few minutes longer,' suggested Standring, about to make for the nearest door.

'I shouldn't concern yourself,' said Javan, shaking his head clearly in deprecation of the other's folly in thinking that such a suggestion could be acceptable. 'These apartments are now guarded by *my* servants. You mayn't have noticed. There are the windows, of course, but I should most certainly shoot you before you got there.'

Standring was as haggard now as any romantic who has suddenly smelled the sour earth of a newly turned grave and glimpsed the reality of hell. He saw that from somewhere a pistol had materialized in the tall man's hand.

'A charming weapon, Mr. Standring! Even an old lady firing with closed eyes couldn't fail to hit the mark at twenty paces with it.' The younger man's lips parted as though for hurried speech. 'Don't trouble to bluster, sir! I will get you to London. You shall be there—definitely. Though whether alive or dead rather depends upon your friends, I fancy. A nice subject for speculation.'

'You are mad!' said Standring, in so uncertain a fashion that it should have been superfluous for Javan to inquire: 'You honestly think that?'

He did so, however, and even waited for an answer, which he knew would never come, negligently swinging the deadly weapon to and fro beside him as though it were an innocent switch.

'Well, Judas Iscariot,' he remarked after a sufficient silence, 'the Prince was very sure of you, for I gather that he has come to your financial aid on several occasions. He's a generous little man, isn't he, even when he's hard up, himself? There was actually a matter of five hundred pounds not so very long ago. A nice round sum—but someone else promised a still nicer, still rounder sum, didn't they? And so you took the money and betrayed him, like the pimp you are!' He relieved his feelings by a fine flow of Arabic execrations, and then barked suddenly: 'And who's your paymaster?'

Standring, now yellow as old ivory, stood silent before the green lacquer chest.

'Who—is—your—paymaster?'

Standring said nothing. The sweat poured down his face. His hands trembled.

'I understand now about the death that came hunting the Prince at Crosse. I understand now about the ghost at the chapel door—

about the vanished mascot—about the clock that didn't strike. It
was far better not to have sudden death in the palace, however discreetly performed, however neatly disguised, if it could be avoided,
wasn't it, Mr. Standring? So you and your associates worked on that
child's fears until she should seek safety in secret flight. *Safety!*—
What was going to happen on that flight, sir? *Secret!*—I wonder who
in the palace knew what's been brewing, but have turned blind eyes
and deaf ears to the preparations! I wonder how many know: more
than do not, I will swear! What *was* going to happen on that flight,
Mr. Standring?'

The man in the rose-coloured coat moistened his pale lips:

'It would be better to shoot me now, perhaps.'

'A noisy business *here*, Mr. Standring. We'll see later. For I think
that in principle I agree with your paymaster. Surreptitious flight.
A lonely road. Night—with the charmingly unexpected addition of
fog. Gangs of highwaymen. Or perhaps another Jacobite conspiracy
—like that of the late Christopher Layer? Perhaps—another—Jacobite
—conspiracy, Mr. Standring! The government, I have been informed,
is very worried about the arrival of the arch-plotter in this country.
What was his name? I have even read paragraphs lately in the daily
journals about him. I wonder if he were to be a scapegoat?'

Javan meditated the point, his eyes never leaving the other's face,
and the pistol dangling from his fingers. He came suddenly alive.

'Well, to business, Mr. Standring! Let us away! Let us to business!' He raised his voice, 'O Mahmoud! O Ali! *Ta'âla hina! Ta'âla
qawâm!'*

Two coffee-coloured men in livery of blue and silver appeared
in answer to the summons.

Javan gave them an order in Arabic. They bound the unprotest-
ing Standring hand and foot; they gagged him; they wound a veil
about his face; they enveloped him in a woman's cloak, and pulled
the hood down so that nothing of his features was visible.

Two English servants joined them, and then, cloaked and muf-
fled, bearing a seeming woman with them, they went apparently
unnoticed down the private stairs to the waiting carriage by the
postern gate. . . .

The short summer night was more than half passed when the
courier arrived at the great gates of the palace on a foundered horse.

Where is the night-duty porter? Where is the night-duty page of the back stairs? Where is the Woman of the Bedchamber on night duty?

A considerable time elapses before Mrs. Titchburne—known to my Lord Hervey and other of her friends and enemies as Little Titch—has rubbed the sleep out of her eyes and put herself sufficiently to rights to come downstairs and tap upon the door of the royal bedchamber.

She knocks for a long time in vain.

She ventures to open the door at length, to put her head through the crack, finally to enter. The single candle in her hand is swamped by the darkness; the lofty painted ceiling, the immense portraits are invisible; the colossal royal bed—draped with curtains thirty feet high—looms up in the airless room like a monstrous catafalque in a mausoleum. One would not have thought that the living could sleep on such a couch—only the dead.

Little burblings and bubblings and breathings, however, told Mrs. Titchburne that Majesties were living Majesties. Courageously she approached; laid hands upon a royal shoulder.

'Your Majesty!' she said loudly.

'Titchburne? What is it? Is the house on fire?'

'His Royal Highness has sent to let your Majesties know that the Princess is in labour.'

Her every sense was now on the alert.

'Good God! Fetch me my gown! I'll go to her at once.'

'Your gown is it, madam?' said Mrs. Titchburne with full appreciation of the dramatic. 'It is your coaches that your Majesty will be needing. The Princess is at St. James's Palace.'

The small flame revealed no change in the grey face under the wide-frilled nightcap—revealed nothing to tell of shattered hopes and ruined plans. It was, however, without conviction that she said:

'You are either mad or asleep, Titch! You are dreaming!'

'Indeed, I am not, madam.'

Within the downy depths of the vast bed, there was a surging movement accompanied by inarticulate noises. Like some sea monster surfacing, the King of England slowly emerged; a tasseled nightcap—a large nose—an ugly face—an undershot jaw—an embroidered shirt.

He sat up. A stream of invective poured from him. He cast his nightcap from his head and rent it into shreds. He turned upon his wife the face of an angry goblin, and reviled her bitterly, regardless of the presence of the avidly attentive Titch.

'For all your boasted cleverness they have diddled you, you fool!' he stormed when at last he became coherent. 'So now there'll be a changeling planted on us! Your fault—*all* your fault! What are the children going to say? Haven't you done well for poor William? Oh, God!'

He relapsed into a crescendo of blasphemy.

She made no reply to him. Even now she would not believe that God could let Griffe be a father and rob William for ever of the inheritance she intended for him. Even yet she might be in time to prevent some charwoman's lusty brat being foisted on them. If she were very quick she might— What might she not do?

She rose from the bed, and was lighted by Mrs. Titchburne to her dressing-room; her attendants were called; her daughters were summoned; the carriages were ordered; she huddled on her clothes. With powder-puff and hare's-foot that forty-year-old Ganymede, my Lord Hervey, donned a complexion that should withstand the cruel grey light of daybreak, whilst his Grace of Grafton and the Earl of Essex rolled out of bed, yawning and cursing, to assist him squire the great ladies on their journey.

Barely an hour had elapsed since the arrival of the messenger from St. James's before the Queen took the road to London with her retinue in two crowded coaches.

# VI

# *The She-Mouse in the Tablecloths*

Javan was shown into a small, carpetless, uncurtained room with a barred window and so bare of furnishings as to present an almost poverty-stricken appearance. The place was, however, brightly lighted by a couple of candles on the high mantelshelf and an immense coal fire, upon which three jostling kettles bubbled and simmered. On the hearthstone stood an array of crocks from which wisps of steam arose. Linen was airing over the backs of two rush-seated chairs, and upon the rough kitchen table was a heap of white rags and other bandage material.

Desnoyers, the French fiddler dance-master, had ushered him into this unsumptuous apartment—obviously some sort of service room.

He now stood in the doorway for an instant, looking with his bony, greyish face and small twinkling eyes like a benevolent household goblin.

'Ze schild is very small eet is true, *Votre Excellence,* but she is

*parfaitement faite. Madame a souffert, mon Dieu! horriblement!
Monseigneur également!'*

'How is the Princess doing?'

'Very vell. Very vell indeed.' He nodded reassuringly, and then suddenly and surprisingly chuckled in a most elfin fashion. 'Madame vas brought to bed between two tablecloths! Zis palace!' His voice was expressive of the uttermost contempt. 'Zis palace! I say to you zat zere is no bed-linen in ze place—no bed-linen—*pas de tout!* Eet is all at ze ozzer 'ouses! Ve borrow 'ere. Ve borrow zere. 'Er Royal 'Ighness ze Princess of Vales ees bedded in tablecloths!'

From the skirts of his black moiré coat he suddenly produced a little fiddle—a kit—of the type always used by dance-masters, and played a tiny mocking air from *The Beggar's Opera,* which he apparently thought suitable to the occasion. Then with a small nod, a wide grin, and another ghostly chuckle he vanished.

Javan sat himself on the edge of the kitchen table, idly swinging a long-booted leg, and reflecting on the probable fate of the child born but an hour or so ago between tablecloths in the Palace of St. James—the child who was in direct line of the throne of England; whose coming had crushed for ever the hopes and plans of those whose fortunes were bound up with that fat butcher's boy, the Duke of Cumberland.

Then he took his pistols from their hiding-place under the skirts of his coat, and busied himself cleaning and reloading them whilst he waited.

It was not too easy a task, for his left arm was uncommonly stiff; a fact that was explained by the bullet hole drilled in the lower part of his sleeve, and the rust-red stain on the dark blue cloth. His left hand also had been grazed and was roughly tied up with a handker-chief, whilst yet another ball had travelled through the wide turned-back cuff of his coat without hurt to him, although it had been discharged at such close quarters that there were scorch marks about the hole.

'Worse than moth!' Javan commented to himself out loud, con-templating the damage to his attire.

Somewhere near at hand a door opened and shut quietly: there was a quick, light step, and the next moment the Prince appeared on the threshold. He was a wholly altered man. He no longer gave

an impression of anxiety and conscious inferiority; dignity and determination showed in his ugly yellow face—not as if they had been
assumed like a mask, but as though, being always latent within him,
they had at last burst into the light of the outer world like a child
from the womb. He extended a small, narrow hand.

'I am a father, Javan. You know, of course?'

'I do. I was very happy to hear it.'

Griffe pushed the door to.

'There are people everywhere else,' he said, and added rather
grimly: 'There'll probably be more pretty soon. I have sent a courier
to Hampton to announce that I have a child—that through *me* the
succession will go on! There will be a regular procession to St.
James's without a doubt to ascertain whether or no the child was
smuggled in, in a warming-pan. The only one we've got is one we
borrowed, and when it was brought in I made them open the lid
and show it to my Lord Privy Seal and my Lord President so that
they should know there was no deception. The two of them remained in the room all the time. There is not a living soul can throw
any doubts on Augusta being a mother, or me being a father . . . I
am a father . . . I am a father.'

He picked up a long strip of bandage, and bent over it pulling
the threads out, talking the while, and ever and anon casting quick
glances of his grey-green eyes at Javan.

'I am fatherless and I am motherless,' he said with bitter intensity,
'but I *am* a father. I swear by Almighty God the Father and by God
the Son, the Saviour, that I will be a father to my children, whatever
they may be and whatever they may do! With me the curse of
Hanover shall finish. My father—my grandfather—my great-grand-
father; they were not fathers. I will be one. God helping me, not one
of *my* children shall have to undergo the torments that I have done.'

He emphasized his words by rending the strip of linen down all
its length with a noise that set the teeth on edge.

'You are my witness, Javan!'

'I am your witness, sir.'

A vast woman with a shining red face, enveloped in a much-
crumpled apron, burst into the room, sketched the merest dip of a
bulging body—as though to indicate that this was neither the place
nor the occasion for high ceremony—collected a steaming pitcher of

water from before the fire, and departed, pulling the door to after her with a shapeless foot.

'I owe more than I can say to you, Javan,' said Griffe, making certain that the door was latched. 'You planned and braced me to action whilst I dithered. You—' A sudden thought occurred to him. 'But you were to have got here within an hour of me; instead you are many hours late. What happened?'

'I walked a not inconsiderable part of the way,' said Javan nonchalantly, 'and riding-boots are not the best footwear in the world for night marching.'

The little man's round and rather monkeylike eyes searched his friend's expressionless face; took in for the first time the rust-coloured stain upon his coat sleeve, the handkerchief bound about his hand.

'Good God!' he exclaimed, 'you are hurt!'

'No,' said Javan laconically. 'They are the merest scratches. Absolutely nothing, I assure you, sir.'

'And so you were right.'

'I was.'

'Don't ooze information, Javan! Let me have the full tide.'

'I think, sir,' reflected Javan, 'that the most interesting thing I can tell you is that Nemesis has overtaken your Mr. Standring. He has lost the end of his lovely, romantic, poetical nose. He is finding it a sad misfortune. *W-Alláhi*, when I left him by the roadside he was bleeding from what is left of his proboscis like a stuck pig and weeping as loudly as a whipped child! What he'll do when he sees his appearance in a glass, I should not care to prognosticate.'

'The double-dyed, damned traitor!'

'I thought, sir, of putting a bullet in him, but really the fate he's suffered is—for him—worse than death. I find the retribution quite a charming one.'

'What happened?' asked Griffe, sitting down on the edge of the table and thoughtfully watching the array of kettles on the fire hissing and steaming away.

'Exactly what might have been expected. The carriage slowed down at a bend in the road, most conveniently for a dozen gentlemen in ambush—or shall we say highwaymen, for I don't think we can now dignify the affair as a Jacobite plot?—to pounce out and pump the interior full of lead. Which they did. Fortunately I was already on the floor. Mr. Standring, unluckily for his beauty, was not quite so quick. He was handicapped by being tied hand and foot as well as gagged.

'My fellows at the back had borrowed a couple of blunderbusses from the landlord of the Toy. They fired simultaneously, and quite half our new acquaintances became casualties on the spot. The rest departed forthwith. The noise was like the voice of the angel in Revelation, and the horses, of course, bolted and went into the river, coach and all. I got Standring out just in time. It was really rather stupid of me to do so, but still— Since then I have been walking towards London with one of my men whilst the other went back to Hampton and fetched horses.'

'When I am king, Javan, there is nothing that you may not ask for. Anything—anything—*anything*! You see I say "When" now, not "If"?'

Griffe slipped to his feet. Upon the mantelshelf between the two tall candles was a large black bottle, uncorked. He smelled it. He smiled. It was gin—obviously for the lubrication of the red-faced woman and the other attendants upon Mrs. Cannon, the midwife. He raised it to his lips—

'Here's a health to the Augustas,' he said loudly, 'and to the man who preserved 'em!'

He wiped the mouth of the bottle with the lace ruffle at his wrist and passed it to Javan, who toasted mother and daughter and father in a mouthful of a fiery and plebeian liquor.

'I have broken away,' said Griffe. 'I am independent. I have someone to come after me. There will be others. I disown my parents. I deny my parents. I am no longer even frightened of them.' He paused before adding, 'I wonder if they—I wonder if—'

He did not finish the sentence.

Javan said:

'It is better not to wonder. We are never likely to know the truth. The only thing I know for a certainty is that Standring was well aware of what was to happen. We had literally to throw him into the coach, and he was in a state of utter panic as we approached the bend in the road by the river. It was that warned me. Behind Standring, I fancy—only fancy—is Dunscore. Beyond that all is unprofitable speculation.'

'It would have been poetic justice—'

'It is not usual, sir, to find poetic justice in the dramas of real life. Half a dozen minor villains have paid heavily. I fancy a couple of them were killed. With that we must be content. What does it matter *now*? It was the last throw: they have tossed, and they have lost. It is better not to investigate or try and exact vengeance.'

'They have tossed, and they have lost,' repeated Griffe, pleased with the run of the phrase. He inserted three fingers into a pocket of his silver-embroidered waistcoat and extracted two dice which he shook in his hand and dropped on the table between them. A pair of sixes looked blackly at them. With a satisfied smile he gathered up the ivory cubes. 'They have tossed—and I have won.'

Javan cast his eyes round the bare uncarpeted room, at the platoon of crocks and bowls, the busy kettles, and the two rush-seated chairs, and the table with its pile of torn linen.

'And now, sir,' he said, 'if you'll go off and get a little rest before your influx of visitors, I'll do a small surgery job before I return to Hampton.'

'Tonight—this morning? In God's name, why?'

'In case Shems wants me. It's the first time I've left the post completely unguarded. I dare say they can spare me some of this hot water.'

'Hollings—the doctor—or Wrede can see to it for you.'

Javan shook his head decidedly.

'Better not. Just as well not call public attention to signs of combat, if we can help it. I can do all that's needful myself. There are hot water and linen here, and I've got a penknife. The bullet in my left forearm is only just under the surface. It's done no damage. I can have it out in a whisk. Perhaps you will lend me a hand with my coat, if you please. . . .'

He had just succeeded in knotting the bandage about his arm with the aid of his teeth, standing in his rolled-up shirt-sleeves before the fire, when he heard through the door, which Griffe had left very slightly ajar, the sound of voices and approaching footsteps. They stopped outside, and a woman said:

'If it had been a large fat boy instead of a poor, little ugly she-mouse no bigger than a toothpick case, I should have had my suspicions. But now— Where is the room?'

'At the far end of the passage, madam, I fancy,' suggested a man's voice which sounded like Hervey's.

But the room was obviously not at the far end of the passage after all, for an instant later Javan heard the voices and the steps returning. The door was pushed abruptly open, and the Queen stood in the aperture surveying him, and the linen on the chair-backs, and the whispering kettles, with cold eyes.

'*Ach, so!*' she said, and came in and closed the door after her. '*Ach, so!*'

She wore the black travelling cloak in which she had made the journey from Hampton Court. Her hair was unpowdered, but dressed with sculptured severity. Her heavy face was grey with fatigue although there was a dull flush upon the cheekbones. Bowing low, Javan waited on her pleasure—or her displeasure.

'They tell me, sir,' said the Queen in a hard voice, without preamble, 'that you have been the instigator of this madness.'

'Madness, madam?' inquired the shirt-sleeved Javan in the tone of one who cannot—with all due respect—believe his ears.

'This foolish—this mad—this criminal escapade! What excuse can there be for dragging a young girl practically in the throes of childbirth on such a journey, over foul roads, at dead of night, to a house in which there is not even any bed-linen? Did nobody count the risk?'

'Various risks, madam, were taken into the most serious consideration,' Javan assured her in a deliberately uninflected voice.

She paid no heed to the implications of his reply.

'If anything had happened to the Princess and her child,' she said, 'this journey would have amounted to plain murder.'

'It might, indeed, well have done so, madam,' agreed Javan.

Again his tone was expressionless. Again she did not appear to remark anything but the bare bones of his statement.

It began to dawn upon him that she was not really aware of him physically at all. She did not see a man with a bloodstained shirt-sleeve rolled up to his elbow and a rather clumsy bandage knotted about his forearm, standing before a kettle-crowded fireplace in a sewing-room, or a housemaid's closet, or whatever it might be. She saw in him some Apocalyptical figure that had spelled utter disaster to her hopes. She was regarding him—he fancied—not with anger or hatred, or even with blame, but in despair. He had been the instrument of the God who had despised her prayers, and rejected her pleas. Her lips had said 'madness,' 'escapade,' 'risk.' But they were only hollow words without meaning, spoken automatically. What her spirit said was . . .

'All that I prayed for—'

She suddenly spoke the five words out loud, as though her mind had been following his secret thoughts, and must tell him that she knew of them.

Had murder been among the things she prayed for?

Just for the moment he would not have been shocked or horrified even if it had. He had the feeling that the erect, ungainly woman with a grey face, standing on the opposite side of the hearth, was a figure of tragedy, driven by unrelenting Destiny even as the doomed queens of Greek drama, Hecuba and Clytemnestra and Jocaste. She was not to be adjudged by the ordinary standards of morality and law.

The kettles hissed in the grate; the pallid beginnings of day showed in the square panes of the barred window opening on to Cleveland Row. The Queen no longer looked at him; her heavy-lidded eyes were turned instead towards the greyness of dawn. She remained silent.

Why had she said, 'All that I prayed for'?

She had sought him in order to pour out her anger and her disappointment, no matter on what pretence. Then almost at the moment when first she began to speak she had recognized that Fate had brought him from Africa to play his allotted part, even as she had been destined for hers in her cradle. She had started to address those words to him as one victim of the Immortal Jester speaking with another.

And then one of the kettles boiled over.

When he straightened up after attending to it, he suddenly became once more conscious of all the implications of the kettles, of the linen airing upon the chairs, of the heap of bandage material upon the table—tokens of a small life so recently brought into the world in a near-by bedchamber between two tablecloths. Conscious once more, too, of the bloodstained handkerchief at his feet—evidence of somebody's attempt to give effect to somebody's prayers!

Had this woman instigated—connived at—given her benison to a conspiracy of murder?

He said harshly:

'I trust, madam, that your prayers included one for your son, the Prince of Wales, and his wife and child.'

She did not answer him in words, but removed her regard from the smoke-grey square of the window, and surveyed him for an instant with a small and secret smile. It was a smile that made him furiously angry. Because of her prayers a horse had bolted; a wall had fallen; a barge had drifted out of control; a doll had been lost; a ghost had cried in a palace; a clock had stopped; a coach had been ambushed in the dark; and a 'she-mouse' had been born between two tablecloths.

'I wonder, madam,' he exclaimed, 'to what god you prayed!'

Even as he said those words, he knew that he—her beneficiary— had no right to use them to her. He could not use them and remain in her debt. It was not possible. By instinct rather than by conscious thought he thrust his hand into the pocket of the coat lying on the table; produced a folded document that had not left his person since he first received it; held it towards her, with a bow.

After a few seconds she took it from him without looking at it. Her eyes never left his face even for the instant when, with a flick of the wrist, she tossed the paper into the red heart of the fire.

Castle and manor, township and villages, farmlands and mountains vanished in one puff of flame. There was not even any ash to tell of them. Their destruction did not cause so much as one small extra jet of steam from the kettle-spouts. They no longer had any existence—for him . . . But then had he ever quite brought himself to believe in their reality?

In that moment of comprehension, Javan also knew that there was no hatred for him in her at all, and no desire for retribution. She had but made a gesture which had been foreordained from the beginning of time—a merely formal, ritual gesture symbolizing the vanishing of all her hopes that had involved crowns and kingdoms and nations.

He looked up from the fireplace to find that her eyes were still on him, that the small enigmatic smile still was upon her lips as though she were almost amused even at this juncture at his inability to understand.

His own expression told nothing; not even of the surprise with which he had found that there was no anger in his soul against her—and knew that there never would be any again.

All the same, as though she had comprehended, the Queen nodded at him.

'I don't think you will ever understand more than you do now,' she said. 'Not even when I am dead. Quite soon. Quite, quite soon.'

# VII

## In the Room of the Pale Horseman

ANTONIA VON PFULLINGEN, a vast amorphousness in iron-grey satin, sat with an elbow on the shimmering table and her head propped upon her hand, in her white parlour in Trophy House. Against her snowy wig and pale face two great rubies dripped from her ears. Opposite her the purple curtains had been drawn back, and the forbidding, dark countenance of the old King—an almost inhuman mask framed in the immense curls of a black, full-bottomed peruke— stared out into the dimness of a room lighted only by a pair of candles.

A sleepy Coppie fidgeted and yawned at Howell's side. It was four o'clock in the morning, and but ten minutes earlier someone had come knocking insistently at the bedroom door demanding their immediate presence below.

'There are the spoon, and the treacle, and the chafing-dish ready for you,' said Madame von Pfullingen. 'See vhat you can do!'

'It iss not the same spoon, madam,' said Howell after a quick glance.

'Vhy should that matter?'

'There was being an influence to it, madam. I do not know if this—'

'Nonsense, girl! Ve shall see. Tonight ve *must* see! Don't dare to stand with your back side to the King, bitch and fool! Vhere are your manners? Stand vith the boy at the side of the table between the King and me! So! Begin!'

There was such a sense of real urgency in the old woman's brutal voice that she made no further protest, but proceeded to carry out the ritual laid down by the Sheikh Abd-el-Emir, that prince of magicians, dwelling in the House of the Mangana in Fez, the city of magic.

It was a long time, however, before anything happened.

The room became heavy with the scent and smoke of smouldering coriander seed and frankincense, heavy with silence, whilst Coppie stared into the bowl of the spoon held in his small hand. At last he said, rather uncertainly:

'I see—I see— No, I don't see that! I *don't* see the sea. I see a curtain.'

He fell silent.

'And what do you be seeing now, little master?' asked Howell in quiet, controlled tones.

'Someone's pulling back the curtain.'

A pause. Then—

'It's not the sea. It *isn't* the sea,' insisted the child's small far-away voice. 'It's a tall room. There's a man in a sort of brown suit sitting by the fire. There are two ladies opposite him. The walls are covered with tapestry, and on it there's a man like a ghost riding on a grey horse.' . . . How well Antonia von Pfullingen remembered the room and the pale horseman on the wall!

'Somebody has just gone out of the room, and the man by the fire is laughing. I can't see his face. One of the ladies is in red and the other in bright blue' . . . The hooded eyes of the old woman were fastened on the child as though they would see through him the picture that he described. There was, indeed, such a room; and once upon a time a woman in blue and a woman in red had sat there with a man in a snuff-coloured suit.

The boy's voice suddenly sharpened: 'I can hear a baby crying somewhere—close. It must be a very tiny baby because it's a very

small noise!' . . . How well she remembered that feeble wailing!
'*I can hear a baby crying somewhere—close.*'

She needed now no magic out of Africa to conjure up that night
thirty years ago when the wails of a newly born child had been
heard in the antechamber of the pale horseman in the Leine Palace
in Hanover.

Sitting there, facing the immense portrait of the lowering man
who had been both her master and her prince, her unseeing eyes
fixed intently upon the fair-haired boy, her grandson, she gathered
in one single flashing instant the history of that night—all she knew,
had seen, had heard, had imagined—from the moment when he had
said—

The Elector of Hanover said:
'What you intend to tell me is, in plain language, I presume, that
her Highness is not going to die—after all?'

Court Surgeon Gutzkow, a rawboned young man in black, standing humbly before the grim, periwigged figure seated by the fireside,
thought to catch an inflection of regret in the bitter voice, in spite of
the studied indifference of the phraseology.

He bowed very low to his master as he replied that, in the opinion of his professional colleagues and himself, her Highness would
certainly recover; *but*— And there he hesitated very awkwardly.

'But?'

The prince set down the papers which he had been studying
upon the small table at his elbow. He exchanged a swift glance with
Sophia von Kilmansegg, a young woman in a dress of sapphire-blue
sitting opposite to him across the hearth—a handsome large creature
with jetty tresses, a milk-white skin and sparkling black eyes. He
looked from her for a second to the fiercely gipsyish woman in flame-
coloured satin beside her—Antonia von Pfullingen.

Despite the blazing logs in the fireplace, there was no real
warmth in the lofty room; candles flickered in the eddying draughts,
and among the shadows the horseman in the dim tapestry on the
walls stirred as though to the ambling pace of the pale charger
which he bestrode. The hailstorm of an angry February night beat
against the windows hidden behind long curtains of crimson velvet.

'But?' repeated the harsh voice. 'But what?'

In the opinion of his colleagues and himself, said the Court surgeon reluctantly, his Highness's daughter-in-law, the Electoral Princess of Hanover, could never bear another child.

Highness contracted bushy eyebrows over baggy eyes. His sallow countenance became a dusky red. He pursed his full lips as though to restrain his curses, for he was ordinarily a silent man. The only comment that he made aloud was in the grinding of his teeth. It was rather a shocking sound: the fancy entered Antonia's shapely head at the moment that it must be like the gnashing of the teeth of the damned that could be heard on Walpurgis Night (it was said) from the bottom of the Hell Hole in the forests near her childhood home.

The man in black explained the reason for this dynastic disaster in obstetrical terms which would have conveyed nothing to his sovereign even if he had listened to them—which he did not. His mind had seized upon the one salient fact, and he turned his regard from the obsequious surgeon to the fire, as though to avoid any possible revelation of his thoughts. In the interplay of light and shadow from the dancing flames his heavy face, framed by the black formal locks and curls of his vast full-bottomed wig, became as inhuman as the funeral mask of a Pharaoh.

So Caroline would be incapable of having another child! That was just like her. She had been an unpleasant disappointment from the very beginning. For some time already he had been referring to her as *Sa Diablesse* to his intimates. How Maximilian, his brother, would laugh—Maximilian who had renounced all rights of succession in order to save himself from the consequences of high treason perpetrated against their father! How those other brothers, too, would have laughed if they had been alive—the brothers that had hated him almost as much as they did the father who had deprived them of their patrimony!

By what tenuous thread would his line hold the sovereignty of Hanover and Brunswick, and the kingdom of England which he must so soon inherit! He cursed furiously in his heart the tormented girl lying in the great State bedchamber beyond the door of this anteroom. He cursed, too—but there was nothing unusual about his so doing—the only son who perpetually thwarted him, more often, in fact, by mischance than by design.

His mind was still revolving amid unwelcome events like a rat in a trap, when a faint particular scratching on the further door announced that his Turkish body-servant, Mustafa—who was on duty in the corridor without—requested audience of Electoral Highness. It must be something urgent to make him seek admittance.

'*Herein*,' he growled.

The man entered; remained by the door, statuelike, with his arms folded upon his chest—a lean, turbaned fellow with a thin silky moustache, his body sheathed in a long crimson coat laced with gold.

'Well?'

'His excellency the English envoy requests—'

It was the last straw.

'The English envoy be damned!' snarled the Elector of Hanover. 'Twice since dinner, Sophia, has that bastard, Howe, come thrusting his long nose into matters that are not his concern.'

'The English certainly display an almost indecent interest in the birth details of a possible sovereign,' agreed Sophia von Kilmansegg softly. She added still more softly. 'On the other hand, your Highness, their attitude is not entirely incomprehensible. Remember what was said about James the Second's son—alleged son—the "Warming-Pan Baby"!'

'A princess of *my* house,' said the Elector, 'is not going to be put on public view in childbed as though she were a pointer bitch having pups! This is Hanover—not England!'

He exploded into a spate of oaths, each uglier and fiercer than its predecessor. He took up the long clay pipe lying on the table beside him, and snapped its stem inch by inch, casting the fragments upon the fire one at a time. There was something almost murderous in the way in which he performed the operation; something hideous in the sudden frenzy of fury displayed by one who was by habit grimly restrained.

As if in sympathy with his mood, the tapestry rider on the pale horse suddenly stirred more violently than before in his place upon the wall. Antonia von Pfullingen wondered if he represented one of the horsemen of the Apocalypse; chided herself for feeling that he could, if he chose, ride out into the waveringly lighted room in presage of catastrophe.

Mustafa remained impassive. By an almost imperceptible shuffling of his feet the surgeon endeavoured to shrink out of the Elector's sight. Since he was the junior of the three Court medical men, on him had devolved the duty of bearing the ill tidings. He had not cared for the job. It was well known how terrifying could be the passions which occasionally ravaged their dourly silent autocrat.

The Elector restrained himself at length. He looked to the luscious Sophia von Kilmansegg—his half-sister by blood, though not by law—for consolation and advice. He found her now regarding him with a small smile lurking on her wide red mouth, peeping from her large black eyes. He took immediate comfort because he knew well that behind the broad snowy brow, beneath the monumental and cowlike placidity, there was an astute and conscienceless mind. She would not smile at him without good reason at a juncture such as this.

She sat there imperturbably calm, her capable hands folded on the lap of her almost indecently revealing gown of sapphire brocade. Thank God for Sophia!

The ebony and silver clock on the high mantelshelf was striking seven as Madame von Kilmansegg said in impeccable French:

'Mr. Howe has been told nothing, Sire?'

'Nobody has been told anything.'

'Then if your Highness will cause word to be sent to him that he will receive news the moment there is news; and will dispatch Court Surgeon Gutzkow about his duties with the princess, then perhaps I might venture to make a suggestion. We shall, incidentally, need Antonia's help, if you approve the scheme, Sire.'

Highness approved Antonia's presence at the conclave by a nod. She might not be much of a counsellor, and he had grown tired of her more quickly than at one time he would have thought possible, but on the other hand there was nothing in the world that she would not do for him. . . .

Half an hour later Sophia von Kilmansegg rose from her chair and swept a profound curtsy to the square bull-like figure of her half-brother.

'If you had not been so carried away by your annoyance, Sire, justifiable though it was,' said she, 'this plan would have occurred to you at once. You couldn't have helped thinking of it.'

Sensible woman! Of course he would have arrived at this magnificently simple solution of the problem the moment he had cooled down!

He smoothed a fold of his coat of snuff-coloured velvet; contemplated with complacency his out-thrust sturdy legs clad in snuff-coloured silk stockings, his shoes with red heels—sadly scratched about the toes, like all his shoes, for he was as clumsy with his feet as he was with his hands and in all his actions.

'In the event everything has turned out for the very best. The very best! God be thanked!'

He nodded vigorously in affirmation of his gratitude for the kindness of heavenly Majesty in arranging things so very, very well for earthly Highness. It was a nod of acknowledgment from one potentate to another.

Another tiny smile flickered across Madame von Kilmansegg's handsome features. Amusement was hinted at in her voice, too, when she said quietly—

'You and I, Sire, have one characteristic in common at any rate. We are both pretty ruthless.'

He found the statement a flattering one.

'It is hereditary, I believe, Sophia,' he answered rather smugly. 'My—our—father could be ruthless enough in all conscience.'

'And my mother?'

The long curls of his wig joggled against his chest as he nodded again in agreement. The sinister, raddled woman who had been his father's mistress could be—on occasion had been—very ruthless.

Sophia had brains. Sophia had magnificent brains. Antonia was as secret as the grave. Both of them deserved a small reward of the sort that they would appreciate—a reward that would cost him nothing.

'It was here *it* happened,' he said quietly.

'It?' Sophia echoed, not following his train of thought: and then suddenly realized to what event he referred; and in her comprehension brought understanding to her slower-witted companion.

The two women—the one in sapphire, and the other in flame—looked slowly round the bare room with its quivering tapestry, its polished oak floor, its ebony and silver clock, its few heavy old-fashioned chairs with high backs upholstered in dark red damask. So it was here, then, that the chestnut-headed adventurer, Philip, Count von Königsmark had been caught by the palace guard thirteen years ago, after he had left the bedroom of his paramour—wife to the grim, ugly man now before them. It was here, then, that he fell into their hands and afterwards was never seen or heard of again!

'Why do you tell us this?' asked Sophia at length.

'We were talking about your mother's ruthlessness.'

Her eyebrows rose.

'But what has this to do with it?'

'You knew that it was your mother who discovered his—their plan to elope?' Yes. Her mother had boasted of it. 'When *he* lay dying of sword thrusts on the floor—there by the door—'

He paused whilst slowly she turned her lovely head and viewed the threshold of the room as though she would picture to herself the slim, tall figure which she could just remember, lying there in its death throes under the regard of the pallid horseman, and the blood trickling into small pools upon the shining boards.

'As he lay dying,' said the Elector, 'your mother avenged herself for the insults that he had put upon her by stamping on his lips!'

He had often wished that he could have been present, and unseen, when Clara von Platen had exacted every due, to the uttermost groschen, for Königsmark's rebuff of her proffered affections.

Madame von Platen's daughter said after a short silence:

'I could believe anything of my mother, and you know it. Nothing you could tell me about her would shock me. Again, why do you tell us this?' Then enlightenment suddenly came to her. A smile curved her full red lips. 'George, you are telling us so that we can see how truly ruthless you can be! I suppose you've made certain that Güstchen knows this?'

He showed his yellow teeth in a mirthless grin at her reference to Prince George Augustus, the heir to his throne. Sophia at any rate had seen the point.

'In all the world, in all Hanover, in all the Leine Palace, Sophia, there are half-a-dozen people only who know the secret of Königsmark's disappearance—who know what I have just told you two. I fancy—I think—I *know*—that Güstchen is one of them.'

She began to laugh silently, since roaring peals of merriment were not suitable for sinister jests such as this.

'And so you forced on Güstchen and his bride the rooms where his mother was taken in adultery. Where she was held prisoner whilst her fate was debated. And where her paramour died ignominiously. George, I believe that you hate your son. Yet I cannot think that he—you don't think—it isn't possible, anyway. Or—'

She did not complete in any form that broken sentence, because she caught the answer in a sudden fleeting expression that contorted his dark face.

He contented himself by replying cryptically:

'Güstchen is his mother's son.'

She patted her sapphire dress; made small feminine preparations for immediate departure.

'We are wasting time, Sire, when time is all-important. Antonia and I will set off now . . . What it is to have loving and loyal ladies, your Highness, to assist you in your ruthlessness! . . . We should be back in less than an hour. Meanwhile you will deal, of course, with the people in there?' She indicated the room beyond the ante-room by a small nod. 'You will also persuade Güstchen, Sire?'

At the last question he burst into a sudden bellow of laughter so loud that it might have been heard in the adjoining room, where his daughter-in-law lay unstirring in a four-posted bed as immense as a burial vault, her bloodless face upturned to the crimson canopy gold-embroidered with all the blazons of all the branches of the House of Brunswick.

'Persuade!' he rumbled as though it were an enormous joke. 'I would have you know, Sophia, that we are not yet in England, and that here I am the Law, and the Law is me. Be off with the pair of you!'

Antonia von Pfullingen slipped from the room at once, but Sophia von Kilmansegg remained for a moment looking down in silence at the ugly face which even remained forbidding in its mirth. Then she said, taking up her fan—

'I do not think, Sire, that I shall ever understand about you and Antonia.'

'I do not understand, myself. But does it matter? It is already of the past, Sophia. Let us call it a spasm of middle-aged folly. At forty-seven one still has a hankering after illusions though one ought to have learned better.'

With an air of finality he took up from the table at his side the papers which he had been examining when Court Surgeon Gutzkow had sought permission to enter The Presence.

In the adjoining room, brilliantly lighted by scores of candles, the three doctors whispered together in a corner; women rustled to and fro; the pale princess moaned a little, and a newly born child whimpered—so feebly that its small cries could only just be heard through the panels of the antechamber door.

George Louis, Elector of Hanover, Duke of Brunswick and of Lüneburg, King-to-be of England, resumed methodical study of the expenses of his establishment.

They were too high. They must be cut. They must be slashed. even though they were already lower than they had been in his father's time. Why, there were no fewer than three hundred and seven persons drawing salaries and wages for duties at Court, and the annual cost of his household—apart from his seraglio, of course— was well over a quarter of a million thalers!

In the kitchen department, he remarked, the office of the *Maître d'Hôtel* employed no fewer than five clerks and a steward. It was too many. It was preposterous. Four clerks were enough. He amended the total, and was initialling in pencil the alteration when a discreet chamberlain sought permission to present himself, made sidelong entry, discreetly announced his heir, and with the skill of long habit backed from the room, silent-footed as a cat.

For a single second he looked over the top of the foolscap at his son, who stood bowing in dutiful silence at a respectful distance. He said never a word; continued his investigations into this welter of domestic extravagance.

Twenty-two cooks at wages ranging from eleven thalers to three hundred. Twenty-two of them! Monstrous!

Güstchen's face was bedrabbled with tears. Dear God, he was a soft and gutless fellow! In the brief instant in which he had looked at him, he had seen—as he was always seeing—the hateful likeness to his wife, the faithless woman whom he had divorced and kept close prisoner these last thirteen years. Sometimes he even caught himself searching Güstchen's features for a resemblance to her lover. Sophia said that it was not possible, but one never knew.

He would like to go to Ahlden where The Woman was held prisoner and wrest the truth from her, not by the deferential questioning to which the lawyers had subjected her years ago in the next-door room, but by the rack and the thumbscrew. Just for himself to know privately. His honour demanded that secrecy—just as it had demanded and obtained a divorce from her for desertion without mention of the real crime.

Seven scullions. One stoker. *One* stoker? If only one were needed, why, in God's name could not the scullions perform his functions between them?

He wondered if Güstchen—that had been The Woman's pet name for him—recollected at this moment that he was standing upon the very spot where the man who *might* have been his father had perished under half-a-dozen swords, where he was buried.

Now, he, George Louis, Elector of Hanover, was about to triumph finally over his shameless wife, over the son who *was* hers and *might* not be his! He could not keep a note of exultation out of his voice when at length he looked over the top of his papers again . . . Liveries—eight thousand thalers . . . and addressed the fair-complexioned, undershot young man in a purple coat who waited unhappily upon his pleasure.

'So I see a very proud papa before me, do I?' he said ironically. 'Now I can set the mind at rest of our most excellent cousin, Queen Anne! I can assure her that on this night of February the fourth, 1707, the Protestant succession to the throne of England has been assured in yet another generation!'

His heir, with downcast face, said nothing.

The fellow's forehead was The Woman's, and he had the same sly look in the eyes! One day—thought the older man—he would go to Ahlden amidst its swamps and see what Mustafa and Mahomet could get out of her! There should be little fight left in her after all these years.

'You have traced the family likeness in your offspring already, of course?' said the Elector. 'You have heard about Caroline, I suppose? Very well then—'

The small sound of a baby's crying came to them through the door like the distant cawing of rooks.

# VIII

## *Laughter Out of Hell*

'*I can hear a baby crying somewhere—close.*'

In the brief instant in which the words fell from the child's lips, Antonia von Pfullingen had travelled back thirty years through time to see the story of that February night in Hanover—all she knew, had witnessed, had heard of, had imagined—reflected in the mirror of her mind in its every detail.

'*I can hear a baby crying somewhere—close.*'

In that selfsame twinkling of immeasurable time her mind travels again—forward from the Leine Palace to this shuttered house within the precincts of Hampton Court. The years flash by with the speed of light. George—*her* George—of Hanover becomes King of England; is replaced by Güstchen, whom his subjects know as George the Second. Builders making alterations after the old man's death, have found Königsmark's bones under the floor of the antechamber of the pale horseman—but that, of course, has been hushed up. The prognostications of Court Surgeon Gutzkow and his colleagues have been falsified long ago, for Güstchen's wife has borne many children,

although in the future that is yet to come—is very, very near—she
will get her death from the injury caused at that first birth.

In that moment, too, wigs have become smaller and smaller, and
hoops wider and wider. Louis the Sun-King of France is dead, and
already a small George Washington is conning his first lessons in far-
away Virginia.

'*I can hear a baby.* . . . '

The child was repeating the words again. He broke off just as
Antonia von Pfullingen's mind had anchored itself in the year 1737:
broke off as her eyes had brought him back into focus, and, with a
sudden panic catching at her heart, her lips were parting to put a
stop to revelation.

He tore his regard from the silver bowl cupped in the hollow of
his hands. He raised his eyes and stared, not at her, but at the unveiled portrait in the alcove facing her. An expression of acute terror
was on his face. The great silver spoon clattered with its black content to the table. He cried in loud distress—

'No! No! He's coming out! He's coming out of the picture!'

He turned, and, in a momentary passion of terror, buried his face
against the bosom of the girl standing beside him.

Antonia von Pfullingen's heart seemed to jerk itself to a stop. She
pulled herself upright in her chair as swiftly as she might have done
thirty years before. The only lights were upon the table before the
boy, and in the dusk of the great portrait it seemed to her quick-
ened imagination that the pouched eyes of the dark man moved, that
his painted lips writhed as though his violent spirit would force
them to speak, that the body quivered as though it might burst from
the frame.

She cried out in German in a loud voice—

'No, George! No one has spoken!'

Then suddenly it seemed not only to her but also to the girl who
called herself Howell, that the quivering possibility of the other
world breaking through into this had receded; that the supper-
room had resumed its ordinariness, and that she was just a large
elderly lady with a rummer close to hand filled to the brim with the
mixture of gin and treacle known as 'mahogany.'

For a moment or two there was complete silence, as though none
of the occupants would venture to disturb the retreat of that other
world to its own circuit.

Then Madame von Pfullingen's bediamonded fingers curved round the short stem of the goblet. She raised it to her lips. She drank. She put it down completely empty, although it must have held half a pint of liquor, and sat staring into vacancy.

The viscid puddle of black treacle upon the table, where Coppie had dropped the spoon between the candlesticks, widened very slowly. The small almond-shaped flames were reflected in it in an unnatural green.

The boy recovered himself quickly. He loosed his hold of Howell's dress; cast one glance at the picture; watched his grandmother take up her glass; fixed his eyes upon the loitering puddle of treacle. His lips moved. He was not saying his prayers. He was daring the lowering portrait and its attendant powers of evil to attack him. He was repeating over and over again below his breath, so that even the girl beside him could not hear them, the words—

'Silly old walrus! Silly old walrus! Silly old walrus!'

He stopped mumbling to himself . . . Presently he gave a start and looked expectantly to the vast white face of his grandmother. At that selfsame moment she bent her head a little forward and to one side as though to catch words whispered in her ear. The child immediately withdrew his attention from her and glanced almost indifferently at the big dim portrait. It was as if he had become aware that there was a message for her, to be heard by her and none other, and that once she knew this, he had no further concern in the matter.

Antonia von Pfullingen's eyes were raised to the half-revealed countenance that looked towards her out of the heavy gilded frame. Her lips moved slightly, shaping monosyllables; her white bewigged head nodded the further to confirm comprehension and agreement.

Once she even questioned in little over a whisper:

'Aber, Georg, was willst Du damit sagen?'

And then again fell silent.

The child had taken Shems-ed-Douha's hand, and, so fortified, began to count to himself the to-and-fro movements of the girl-in-a-swing pendulum of the buhl clock upon the mantelpiece opposite him. One-two! Three-four! Five-six! At the end of the first hundred he himself was swaying to and fro a little—a very little—in time to the beat of the clock. That's how she went all day long and all night long, to and fro—to and fro—to and fro! He had lost count now. How many hundred times could it be that the little figure had swung gravely and sedately across the clock case since he had begun keeping tally?

Then of a sudden he was recalled from his rhythmic companionship with passing time. For his grandmother had returned from communing with the past. Sitting very erect, her jewelled fingers pressed against the table edge, she began to laugh. At first almost in silence; then with no more noise than the discreet chuckle of wine bubbling out of a long-necked bottle; and finally with loud, uncontrollable paroxysms of mirth.

To Shems-ed-Douha there was something horrible and obscene in this merriment at a jest retailed from the other side of the grave. But even as she speculated on the cause the laughter ceased, and Antonia von Pfullingen addressed her in a loud clear voice—in German.

'Pardon, madam, I do not be understanding.'

'Fetch him now, and very qvickly!'

The usual guttural foreignism of her speech was doubled and redoubled in her urgency.

'Fetch whom, madam?'

'The prince, girl! The prince!'

'He will not be coming for me, madam.'

'He vill. He vill. He vill. You vill just say that I vant him—I, Antonia von Pfullingen.'

'It is not yet five o'clock in the morning, madam.'

For a moment Shems-ed-Douha thought that the old woman was about to burst into unmeasured wrath. Instead she withdrew into profound meditation for some moments, clasping and unclasping the empty goblet before her with long, strong fingers that glittered with jewels. Then at length her face lightened: she spoke with a smile—

'You vill say that I am dying—I, his grandfather's friend. You vill tell him that I say to him in Shakespeare's vords—

I have a journey, sir, shortly to go;
My master calls me, I must not say no.

You vill tell him also that I have a last and most secret message from his grandfather, the old king. He vill come! He vill come!'

She chuckled and, still chuckling, raised her right hand in the smallest of gestures. Shems read the signal aright, and filled up the glass once more with the dark mixture that was her elixir.

'Now go!'

She was thinking, 'Javan will deal with this,' as her hand closed on the doorknob, when a loud and terrible voice spoke:

'Misbegotten bitch! Pay your reverence to *him*—to the King! . . .'

Behind its closed shutters and drawn curtains the Toy appeared to sleep. One only of the latticed windows on the upper floor was wide open to the daybreak mist and the silence of the outer world, its blankness starred by the small, steady flame of a candle.

'By Gooseberry,' said Coppie, 'we *have* got luck! There's a light in his room. Come on, I'll show you the way!'

The front door was ajar, but there was no one in the entrance hall or on the stairs; and when Coppie gave his customary untidy thump upon the panels, Javan's voice bade him enter.

Shems-ed-Douha went in.

Javan, with turned back, was unbuckling his sword in the window.

'This is a pretty early call, Coppie!' he commented, putting the weapon on the table, beside his pistols and an open letter.

'It's not me,' said Coppie, and therewith beat a retreat in accordance with instructions.

Javan swung round. He needed no telling whose was the cloaked and hooded figure that stood there a few feet away. He bowed low. He gave her no greeting, but said gravely:

'So you have already heard, madam! I was wondering at this very moment how best to send you word.'

'Yes, I know already, Javan,' she answered, realizing from his words and manner why he took her visit for granted. 'In fact I knew a fortnight ago that Ali was dead.'

As she spoke she threw back her hood, almost as though inviting his comment: but neither by involuntary movement nor by word did he show any of the astonishment that he might have felt at the dark and blemished face which was revealed.

'The English government at any rate have only just received the news from their consul at Rabat. They have sent it on to me,' he told her, indicating the paper on the table; and proceeded to speak of the dead Emperor with sympathy and regret.

She responded with every proper formula of custom, but all the while her secret soul was denouncing her: 'Hypocrite! Hypocrite!' It was true that she had been sorrowful, for a little, and that she had even wept a little—a very little; but now she had felt all the sorrow and shed all the tears of which she was capable. Now at last she was free—as she had always intended to be! . . . What would that freedom mean to Javan when, or if ever, he let himself think about it?

'It's not because of that I have come here,' she interrupted him abruptly.

He raised one eyebrow in lopsided inquiry and forthwith proceeded to pick up his sword again in token that he was ready to undertake her service at that very instant.

'It isn't for myself at all,' she told him, 'although I seem to have reached a dead end. The witness that I found, my one irrefutable witness, has been spirited away . . . No, I have come to ask you to fetch Griffe. Madame von Pfullingen wants him. At once. Urgently.'

It did not occur to him to question why she should have such a commission at five o'clock or thereabouts in the morning.

'He is not here. He is in London. He could not come even if he wished. The Princess has just had her baby—"a little ugly she-mouse," the Queen called it. At this juncture I assure you that it is out of the question that he should leave her.'

She had turned her head a little as she listened to him, and against the silver-radiant mist of early morning that filled the window he saw with what cunning art her face had been made one of ruined beauty. Blurred a little were its fine lines, as though youth had left it; it was nut-brown and the cheek—like the neck—marred by a great stain of a dull, empurpled red; her hair had lost its midnight sheen, and was of an almost lustreless chestnut. Yet in that quick instant he knew, beyond the possibility of doubt, that had she really been as she appeared to be, and what she pretended to be, he would have cast himself and everything that he had at her feet. But she was *not* such as she seemed, and his wide estates had gone back to the land of dreams. And anyway—

'So Griffe is a father, is he? and in London?' said Shems, not unaware of the pattern of his thoughts. 'I saw him from the Trophy House last evening walking towards the palace, so I suppose he and Augusta eloped?'

'They did. I only got back from St. James's a few minutes ago.'
She nodded her head as though well satisfied.

'That is well done, indeed. But what did his mother say?'

'She has said a good deal,' remarked Javan succinctly, adjusting
his sword-belt and the hilt of the weapon to the slit in the side of
his coat. 'But there is nothing she can do. Even if we forgot about
bed-linen, we made very sure that every regulation attending the
birth of a possible heir to the throne should be carried out. There
were two impeccable Ministers present in accordance with protocol.'

'We?'

'I have not been uninvolved in the affair, madam.'

'I might have guessed that you would fill in your spare time
knight-erranting for someone.'

He made no reply to the observation, but said instead:

'Have you any idea why the old woman should want Griffe?'

'When I say that I think she has a message for him from the
other world I really believe it. It's possibly a warning, although she
laughed a great deal over it—and I'm certain that she was neither
mad nor drunk.'

'Laughed?' exclaimed Javan.

'Yes. It was rather horrible,' said Shems-ed-Douha. 'She laughed
as though she were enjoying some joke that involved torment—
something that had been retailed to her by the Evil One himself.'

'Well, she will have to enjoy it by herself. There's no possible
way of getting hold of Griffe. And as for a warning, the danger is
past. He has a child to succeed him. The line of succession is established. No one dare do anything now.'

'All the same it may be something of immediate importance.
She said she was dying. It may be the truth—I don't know. Javan,
will you come back with me? Perhaps she will tell you as his friend.'

'Of course, if you think it will be of any use. At once.'

At length he had succeeded in adjusting his sword to his liking
—a slow process with a rapidly stiffening left arm. Now by some
rather clumsy movement he attracted Shems-ed-Douha's attention
to it. She remarked the bullet hole drilled through the wide cuff,
the dark rusty stain a little higher up.

'Where will knight-erranting lead you in the end, Javan, I
wonder?' she commented, as Coppie, weary of waiting, poked an
inquisitive face round the edge of the door.

'As long as it doesn't leave me nearly noseless like your Mr. Standring, I don't much mind,' he replied.

'Oh, sir,' said Coppie, being quite enchanted, 'have you really blown off the end of Mr. Standring's nose? with your silver pistols?'

And he eyed with respectful admiration the deadly things lying upon the table in the window.

'No, Coppie,' Javan confessed, 'his friends did it for him. It was a sad mistake on their part, and a sad loss on his. . . .'

They entered unnoticed through the door in the outer wall of Trophy House, crossed a narrow flagged yard, and then plunged into a dark labyrinth of passages. No porter was on duty in the wide low entrance hall; and Franz, the saturnine footman, with his hands folded on his lap, sat staring at a solitary candle in the small ante-room to Madame von Pfullingen's parlour.

The man rose to his feet as they entered. He moistened his lips as though they were too dry for him to speak; his dark, secret eyes flickered from Shems to the door of the parlour—from Javan to the door: his hands were trembling.

'She sent for pens and ink and paper a little while ago,' he said in a very low voice. 'I took them in. There was no one there but her. I have not gone away from here at all, and no one has gone in but me. All the same I heard someone laughing with her—roaring with laughter! Laughter out of hell!"

'It is past cockcrow, Franz,' Shems-ed-Douha reassured him. 'It is long past cockcrow. The little master shall keep you company whilst I take the general to see the countess.'

Antonia von Pfullingen did not heed their entry. She sat at the head of the table, to their left, staring fixedly at the portrait facing her. Sconces on either side of the picture lent a certain warmth to the dusky features, and emphasized the yellowing varnish on the foaming cravat and the regal cloak of ermine dotted with black tail-tips like caraway seeds. The white room was almost daffodil-hued with the innumerable lights.

Madame von Pfullingen's beringed hands rested on the edge of the wine-red mahogany. A silver inkpot with a quill pen in it and a sheet of paper covered with writing lay before her. A goblet full of dark liquor was well within reach, and Shems-ed-Douha noted that the tide had receded in both the heavy, square-cut decanters.

'You are nearly too late, very nearly too late!' said the old woman at last, and turned her head slowly—as though reluctant to let the portrait out of her sight—towards the girl and the man standing before the closed door.

Her hooded eyes studied for a few seconds the oak-tanned face and deep blue eyes of Javan Tierce, the blemished mask that the girl she knew as Howell offered to the world; and then she said sharply:

'But vhere is Fritzi—vhere is the prince? Vhy is he not come? Who is this gentleman?'

Shems was Howell once more, and bobbed a small, respectful curtsy before she spoke.

'He will be explaining to you, madam,' she said. 'He iss General Tierce, the Prince's friend. They do be saying, madam, that he has saved the Prince's life three times.'

Madame von Pfullingen made no comment. For an instant her fierce eyes studied the tall figure that bowed respectfully to her; then they turned to the portrait as though for consultation.

'Vell, sir,' she said at length, 'and vhy did not the Prince come himself vhen he had my urgent message? Vhy did he send you?'

'The Prince is not here, madam. He is in London. He became a father only a very few hours ago. He cannot very well leave his wife.'

'A father!' echoed Madame von Pfullingen. 'Fritzi a father!'

Her grim face suddenly crumpled into a smile. She chuckled. She burst into a roar of delighted laughter. Her body shook with the violence of her mirth, and the tears streamed down her powdered cheeks.

'And vhat does the Qveen say about it?' she asked when at last she was capable of speech.

'Her Majesty remarked in my hearing, madam,' said Javan, 'that the child was no bigger than a toothpick case—a poor, little ugly she-mouse!'

'And she opened and closed her hands like talons as she spoke,' said Antonia, illustrating the action graphically, and grinning. 'Just as if she vould tear the little thing in pieces! I svear it . . . Girl, be off vith you! Ve don't vant you listening to our talk vith your great ears hanging out like the flaps of elephants!'

The brutal arrogance of the command infuriated Javan. He cast discretion to the winds.

'If you wish to give me a message to his Royal Highness, you will give it in this lady's presence or not at all, madam. She is—'

Shems-ed-Douha laid a quick, restraining hand upon his sleeve.

'Your mistress?' asked the old woman, completing his unfinished sentence.

'Not in the sense that you mean, madam.'

With her hand still resting in warning upon his right arm, Shems spoke in her own natural voice:

'As General Tierce says: Not in the sense that you mean, madam. In fact, I am—I was your son's wife. I was the wife of Count Louis Anton von Pfullingen.'

The countess's heavy pale face was a study in swiftly changing expressions. Javan thought to see astonishment chase anger, and amusement chase astonishment. There was, however, no sign whatever of dubiety. Eventually Antonia took up her glass and drank; was silent for two or three minutes—an interminable time in which Javan, like Coppie earlier in the evening, found himself watching and counting the rhythmic beat of the little swinging lady in the clock case. At last she said, cudgelling her memory, with a frown:

'Jane—Jane—Ja-ne—'

'Jane MacGillivray. Against whom you trumped up a charge of theft. Who was flogged at the cart tail through the streets of Kingston, and was sentenced to seven years' transportation to the American plantations.'

'And Louis, the besotted fool, bribed the beadle to vhip you so it vouldn't hurt!'

'Poor Louis, who hanged himself afterwards!'

'He hanged himself,' agreed Madame von Pfullingen, nodding gravely.

And then she started to laugh again. Her earlier merriment was as nothing compared to her present mirth. She fell back in her elbow chair and burst into peals of laughter. Her vast body trembled like a jelly with the paroxysms.

'You find then, madam,' said Javan very loudly, 'false charges, public whipping, transportation, and the suicide of your son a fit subject for mirth?'

'Those who bear the name of von Pfullingen, in whose veins is the blood of princes, do not mate vith servant-maids. This young voman has paid the penalty for her presumption. But I vill make it right for her. I have made it right. This letter'—she spread a big shapely hand upon the sheet of paper lying before her—'vill do all that she vants. You vill see that it is delivered after I am dead? Upon your honour, sir!'

'I will see it is delivered. Upon my honour.'

Madame von Pfullingen turned her jetty eyes upon the tall girl waiting silently by the table. Malicious laughter was in her regard.

'I am old and heavy, madam,' said she, 'and so you must forgive me if I do not pay you due reverence. Madam, you are not my son's vife or vidow! If you had your rights, madam—and you von't get them!—you vould be the Princess of Vales.'

Javan stole a sidelong glance at Shems-ed-Douha. Her expression was unchanged; she said in the tone of remote disinterest—

'In that case, madam, who is Griffe?'

'He is my son and George's.' She paused to rumble with merriment. 'He is half-brother to the man who is supposed to be his father! He is brother-in-law to his mother!' She rumbled with laughter yet once again. 'He is uncle to his sisters!'

Javan said—

'So you and your lover inflicted a changeling and a bastard on his son!'

'Sir, there is no bastard!' said Madame von Pfullingen. 'I vas George's wife. He married me secretly several years after he divorced Sophia Dorothea. He found he could get me no other vay! The Prince of Vales is the lawful son of his father, King George the First, Elector of Hanover.'

'But why was the incredible thing done?'

'Ask her! Ask this other Princess of Vales! She vill tell you vat sort of a child Caroline and Güstchen produced to be the heir to kingdoms and principalities.'

'Louis,' said Shems, 'was a cripple and a hunchback, a gentle, unhappy, timid soul whose life you made hell upon earth! whom to all intents and purposes you murdered! whom you drove to self-destruction!'

'He vas a poor fool,' said Madame von Pfullingen indifferently. 'Vhen George—my George—saw vhat Caroline had produced; vhen he heard that she vould never have any more children; vell, our Fritzi vas just a month old and out at nurse! Vhat easier than to exchange them? Vhy not? Ve did . . . I like to think that my son—

*our* son—vill vun day be King of England and Elector of Hanover.'
She repeated the phrase very slowly, savouring all its magnificence;
'King of England and Elector of Hanover—my son! How George
hated Güstchen! He always saw the face of his faithless vife in
Güstchen's face. He vas glad to have another son who should vun
day be King and Elector!

'And what did the other mother say? the other father?'

'Vhat dare they say, girl? In Germany a prince *is* a prince. In
Germany a secret *is* a secret. In Germany you do not talk about the
secrets of princes. For thirty years ve kept dark the fate of Königsmark. For thirty years, too, ve have kept dark, even from them,
whose child vas put in the cradle beside Caroline's bed, and vhat
happened to theirs. George left Fritzi behind in Hanover all those
years to be out of harm's way. He vas on the road there to tell him
the good joke vhen he died. A good, good joke!'

'You think that Fritzi would appreciate the joke, madam?' Javan
was impelled to ask.

She ignored the question, and continued, patting the sheet of
paper lying before her on the table:

'Now I tell Caroline the good joke in this letter. It is time to do
so. After thirty years she can do nothing—nothing at all. I tell her
that I vas the vife—the secret vife of her husband's father. I tell her
of the baby who grew up to hang himself from his bedpost. I tell
her how he married a servant girl, whose father kept a village school.
I tell her how that girl vas transported to America for a theft she
didn't commit. I suggest to her that she gets a free pardon for this
other Princess of Vales. I think that she vill laugh—laugh very much!'
Her regard travelled back to the picture. 'It has been a very, very
good joke, George! How ve have laughed! . . . And now you have
called me as you alvays said you vould! George, I come!'

So saying, she rose slowly in her place, levering herself up by
the edges of the table, and pushing the chair back from her. Then
she curtsied deeply—very deeply—to the grim representation of the
King.

She did not rise again, but fell forward on her knees so that her
head and shoulders rested upon the table almost in an attitude of
prayer. Then with a gurgle—it seemed—of laughter she died, and
her body crumpled to the floor and became just a shapeless rag-bag

of iron-grey and violet and black satin. Her powdered wig fell off, revealing the naked baldness of her skull, white as bone.

For a moment Shems-ed-Douha stood looking down on her; then she turned and, with a rattle of rings, drew to the purple curtains and blotted out the lowering, bull-like face of the first George.

Javan went to the head of the table. He stooped and encircled one of the old woman's wrists with his fingers. It was pulseless.

'God have mercy on her,' he said.

Shems-ed-Douha did not echo the prayer. She came quietly up the room to the other side of the fallen figure. She put out a long slim hand, and took up the letter to Queen Caroline, and read it, and then, before Javan realized what she would be at, held it to the nearest candle.

The paper caught light, flared in yellow flame, curled into black and brittle ash. She did not let it fall until it had burned to her very finger-tips; and then the last small corner fluttered down upon the glittering blot of spilt treacle upon the table.

'So now you cannot fulfil your promise, Javan!' was all she said.

He made no comment, but—

'Did you realize, before you destroyed it, what that letter meant as proof of the innocence of Jane MacGillivray?'

'Of course,' she answered almost scornfully. 'But how could one add more misery to the unhappy Queen? She was robbed of her child by *that* man. She was given a changeling in its place, the child of them who hated her! Doesn't it almost sound like incest? Her husband's half-brother to be brought up in place of her own baby, to inherit the titles and possessions that should have gone to a child of her own body! She must have suspected it. It is far better that she should never know what happened to her own son, that Griffe should never know, and that that precious pair should snigger over their private joke by themselves—in Hell!'

'Nothing can be undone now,' said Javan.

'Nothing—not even by the ways she *may* have tried! *May* have tried, Javan! Only "may"! But could you ever blame her, knowing what we know now? What would I have done, had I been she? Should I, too, have done what she *may* have done? And other women, would they not do all they could to disembarrass themselves of so monstrous a burden?'

For an instant Javan looked down on the thing that lay almost at his feet—the splendour of grey and violet and black satin, the glitter of gems upon the half-open hand which seemed to be clutching at the white froth of the fallen wig, the almost obscene nudity of the shining skull. He stepped back so that it should be out of sight.

He remembered the grave, tormented face of the Queen, a figure of Sophoclean tragedy, in the shabby, whitewashed service-room at St. James's; but he remembered, too, the anxious tragic mask of Frederick, and the trembling hands of Augusta.

'Poor Queen!' he said, 'and—poor Griffe!'

'Poor Louis!' said Shems-ed-Douha with emphasis, and she, too, surveyed for a second the crumpled body of her who had been wife to a king; and then averted her gaze as from a distasteful object.

'It was her wickedness to him—calculated, continued, monstrous —that made me first—was it love, or was it pity?—him. I was very, very young! . . . For seven years I have waited for the day when it should be made manifest that Louis and my father were justified in their belief in the girl who once upon a time was me. I have wanted that more than anything in the world . . . Well, the day has come—and gone!'

A day had come and gone for him, too! reflected Javan.

'You will not wait here any longer?' he asked.

She shook her head.

'I have no purpose now. I will take Coppie back to Crosse today. As soon as the coach can be got ready.'

# IX

## *The Defeated*

JAVAN REACHED Vicar's Close early in the day to the intense gratification of Mrs. Garlicke, who had nothing more interesting in the
street to engage her attention than the Honourable Mrs. Foley's
ancient sedan-chair, which, being of a rusty black and ornamented
with rows of brass-headed nails, looked as though it were in attendance upon an undertaker.

He dismounted and gave his horse to Williams, and quietly went
up the worn steps to the Close. The long shadows of the young
morning lay among the silver birches of the churchyard and barred
the flagged pathway; the upper windows of the drowsing houses
were luminous with pale gold; the air was full of the noise of con-
fabulating birds. The front door of Tregallion House stood wide
open, although no one appeared to be about, and he could glimpse
the watery shimmer of the four tall hourglasses upon the oak chest
in the dusk at the back of the hall.

As he turned from the scene, he heard his name pronounced

and saw Mrs. Foley, wrapped in a thick cloak, moving tortoiselike towards him.

'My dear general,' said she with a bleat of pleasure, 'welcome back to Crosse! Welcome back, indeed! When Miss Jane arrived we flattered ourselves that you would not be much longer absent. But a whole week has passed since!'

Javan explained briefly that certain final formalities in connection with imperial business had taken longer than he had anticipated. He was conscious, however, that the Honourable Henrietta's attention to his reply was a mere polite show, and that there was another matter upon her mind.

'Monstrously irritating, sir!' she agreed as soon as he had done. 'I have been awaiting your return with great—very great—anxiety. It would be quite true to say that you are the one person of all my acquaintance whose advice I sadly need. You may possibly recall, sir, our little conversation at my "evening" just before you went to London?'

'We discussed a good many things, ma'am,' hedged Javan, fearing some unremembered commission. 'What was the particular subject in your mind, may I ask?'

The Honourable Henrietta's faded grey face emerged slowly from the shelter of the capacious hood of her mantle.

'Marriage was the topic, sir. You said, I fancy, that a man was allowed four wives by Mahometan law?'

'That is so, ma'am.'

'A-ah!' sighed Mrs. Foley with intense gratification. 'My memory has not played me false then. May I ask, my dear sir, if such a ceremony could possibly be performed in this country?'

For a wild moment the idea passed through Javan's mind that the venerable leader of the social life of the Close was herself contemplating matrimony with a Mussulman.

'There is nothing to prevent it being performed, I imagine,' he said rather doubtfully. 'The basic business is the mere giving of a dowry and a simple declaration of consent before witnesses. That's all. I am afraid, though, such a marriage would not be valid in England, even if polygamy were permitted.'

'No matter! No matter!' declared Mrs. Foley. 'It would be a great relief to my mind, all the same. A very, very great relief!' She projected her head from her carapace of frieze and then drew it back two or three times just as though she were a tortoise divided betwixt curiosity and fear: decided eventually on further—rather embarrassed—revelation. 'The fact is, my dear sir, that my maids—my four maids!—are—have—in fact—my manservant, Letchworth. Well, the fact is—in short, I should be less concerned, if I felt that the—unions —could be recognized. In any sort of way, you know, sir. It would be comforting to me to think that *somewhere* in the world everything would be accounted quite proper and regular. Even a Mahometan recognition—I mean no offence—would be gratifying. After all, in good King Charles's day there were a number of serious divines who strongly advocated that polygamy should be recognized by the Anglican Church. At the present I fear my friends appear to consider that I am condoning immorality; but Letchworth is an invaluable servant, and I am very much attached to him and my maids, and if— But, of course, you see my point! They are all quite agreeable. They understand my views. If only, sir, you could see your way—'

'I might discuss the matter with the Princess if you permit, ma'am?' suggested Javan very gravely.

With another outward darting of the head Mrs. Foley expressed her gratification . . . Now she must not detain him any longer . . . If he would call on her as soon as he had had word with her Imperial Highness, it would be most kind—most kind! . . . She continued on her way to her chair under his escort.

With a vast interest Mrs. Garlicke watched the Turkish general hand the old lady into her funereal sedan. He turned a trifle as he kissed the mittened fingers, and she saw his sunburned face in silhouette, with the irregular features and expression of melancholy good nature that had reminded her before of the princes of a vanished dynasty. Even the smile, with which he viewed the stately progress of the vehicle down the street, recalled the exiles.

Mrs. Garlicke sighed for the good old days as he mounted the steps to the Close, and then turned, much to her astonishment, not into Tregallion House, but into the pathway to the church. . . .

Javan did not, indeed, pause for an instant outside the sundial-guarded home of Coppie and his grandfather, but walked—almost as though it had been the whole object of his travel—through the graveyard under the whispering birches, past the west door of the church, to the solitary tomb of Count Louis von Pfullingen.

The grave was held very secret by the weeping ash beneath which it stood. The foliage of the lofty branches cascaded about it to the ground, completely enclosing it beneath a dome and within walls of living filigree. He entered the green luminosity of this chantry, and looked once more upon the moss-stained chest of stone and the inscription that might have been—

What might it not have been? . . . He stood there for a very long time lost in deep thought—so lost that he was unaware that someone else had come and stood watching him, holding aside the curtain of leaves, until she spoke.

'I knew that I should find you here,' said Shems-ed-Douha. She was regarding him—he found—with a grave, small smile, her tall, slim figure wrapped in a cloak of dark violet.

'I knew that I should find you here,' she repeated, and came into the chantry, and faced him across the tomb, touching the discoloured slab with her fingers almost as though in a caress.

Her action gave him a tiny prick of an emotion akin to jealousy, of which he was immediately ashamed.

'But how did you even know that I had returned, madam?' he asked quickly, hat in hand.

'Not by any magic, Javan. You told me I might expect you this morning, you remember? So, contrary to all of your rules, I have been sitting in your room waiting for you. I could hear you just now, but not see you. Well, what is your news?'

He was embarking on an account of various financial and legal operations in London when she checked him abruptly:

'I mean news of Griffe.'

He hesitated before he presented her with his budget, as though doubtful whether it were fitting to speak of the one prince over the sepulchre of the other.

'Louis would have had a fellow-feeling for him,' she assured him, reading at once what was in his mind. 'After all they both were changelings. They would have liked each other. I know. Go on!'

'Well, Griffe has won, and won all along the line, madam.'

'Louis would have been glad for Griffe's sake . . . And "Jane," not "Madam"! . . . Tell me more!' she commanded, her grey eyes studying his down-bent mahogany face.

'The fact is,' he answered her, 'that the people of England—the plain people—seem to have learned, or else have guessed or imagined something of what has been going on. They have taken Frederick to their hearts as the innocent and long-suffering victim of a most cruel oppression by unnatural parents. He is the most popular figure today in all England. If anything were to happen to him, the prophets think that the dynasty would fall.'

'He has a nation on his side, then! Louis had only me.'

Once again she touched the stone of the tomb as though to tell the poor ghost of the presence of her whom it had loved.

'The Court and government,' he continued, 'of course, have not failed to show their resentment in a hundred gadfly ways. The Duchess of Ancaster has lost a pension, because her husband remained loyal to him. One of the royal lamplighters has been dismissed because he continued to work for him. The sentries have been taken from before his door. A soldier was threatened with flogging for saluting him. The ambassadors have been told that they will be *personae non gratae* if they visit him. The peers and the privy councillors, too, have been warned of serious consequences if they don't keep away.

'He's not to be allowed to take a stick of furniture from his quarters—not even trunks to put his or Augusta's wardrobe in! "Clothes-baskets are good enough for them!" said the King, and the Queen's *obiter dictum*, I am told, was: "I hope in God I shall never see him again!" But they'll never dare do anything desperate. Never. They are frightened of the temper of the people. When it was proposed to remove the baby from the care of its mother and father—'

'The newborn child? Oh, God! They never proposed that?'

'The scheme indeed was mooted, madam—'

'Jane.'

'—Jane! But it was rejected immediately when Walpole, the Prime Minister, remarked, "If anything happens to the little animal the world will accuse the Queen of murdering it for Cumberland's sake." '

'The Queen would never murder a child. Never! Never! Never!'

'She would not,' he agreed; added grimly, 'She would, however, have a precedent for its substitution by a changeling! A dead changeling from the rookeries of London would be even easier than a live one!'

She made no comment, but asked:

'How, at any rate, is the child—the "she-mouse"?'

'It's a lusty little creature, and Griffe is a very proud father. The child is—'

At this moment a question that had never occurred to him before suddenly darted unbidden through his mind, and he paused involuntarily. Shems-ed-Douha's eyebrows rose a little at the outward tips; the merest shadow of a far-distant smile touched her face: she spoke at once, as though he had said the thought out loud.

'No, Javan, we had no child—Louis and I. He was practically a dying man when I married him. Though even then, as you know, in the end he found death too slow in coming for him. So far as he's concerned, you've helped to perpetuate no injustice.'

They stood in a long silence facing each other across the altar-shaped tomb of the hunchback who had been a prince, who had been stolen from a palace, who had wedded a serving-maid, who had hanged himself from a bedpost. The great curtains of the pavilion shivered and whispered in a small errant breeze. Upon the flagstones of the path a thrush tapped briskly at a snail-shell. The clock in the church tower struck the half-hour. Then she said suddenly and almost violently—

'Don't pity him, Javan! It is pagan to pity him who is one of the victorious dead! Pity the defeated living—his mother, who has seen a changeling thrust into her cradle, and her own children plundered of their rights! If I had had a child and been robbed of it, as she was, I should have hired bravoes and poisoners, and myself committed murder without a moment's regret. You don't understand women, Javan. Not at all! . . . And now, Javan, if you have any pity left, spare me a little! I badly need it.'

He thought she was referring to the sacrifice which she made in destroying Antonia von Pfullingen's letter to the Queen; but she corrected him before he had said more than two words.

'Oh, not that!' she said. 'There was nothing else to be done. That letter was the most wicked thing ever set upon paper. It was a screech of triumph straight from Hell over a poor mother! She gloated over the telling of the cruelties she had done to Louis, just as she had gloated over the doing of them. Every word was barbed, and every sentence poison. I would do what I did again . . . It isn't that, however. It's much more humdrum. It's very simple. I'm destitute.'

'Destitute!' Javan repeated. 'Destitute of what?'

'Penniless,' she elaborated. 'I'm penniless in all my characters—empress, princess, countess, and servant-maid! A woman with many pasts and no future.'

He stared at her to see if she were serious.

'I don't understand.'

'It's quite easy to explain. When I got back to Crosse I found that Zadana had disappeared with everything in the strong-room that I possessed! . . . Now say that you were always warning me against keeping my gold and jewels in the house! Say it! I shan't blame you!'

He denied himself that poor satisfaction, however, and awaited the remainder of the tale in a frowning silence.

'She just went! She told them at Old Palace that she had to carry out a special mission on my instructions. She even borrowed a hundred guineas "against possible emergencies" from Mr. Tuke—who appears to have had a *tendresse* for her—and then vanished off the face of the earth.'

'W–*Alláhi!*' ejaculated Javan, 'But what has been done about it? Why wasn't I sent for? Isn't there any clue?'

'It was already too late to do much by the time I returned. She'd been gone a week. Tuke notified the authorities for me at once, but we really can't have a public hue and cry, even if it would do any good—which it wouldn't. She is supposed to have been seen dressed as a man in Gloucester!' —It struck Javan that Shems-ed-Douha spoke almost as though she saw an irresistibly comic side to the crime— 'She's said to have been disguised as a doctor with black clothes, round wig, and gold-topped cane. But there's been no trace of her since. She probably changed her appearance and is long since out of England in the guise of a merchant venturer, or a Quaker, or even an old lady with my diamonds sewed inside her stays. After all, Bristol is only a few hours away from Gloucester, and London little more than two days.'

It was very true. With a week's grace Miss Mott might well be on her way to the ends of the earth—Miss Mott who considered all forms of travel lowering to the dignity of the genteel female! Miss Mott who was so very 'Attic'!

'I still think that you should have sent for me,' declared Javan. 'The woman ought to hang as high as Haman!'

She shook her head.

'It would have been of no use. Zadana has learned her lesson.

She is a very astute woman. She found herself once before in the shadow of the gallows—like me—'

'No!' he said loudly. 'No.'

'But yes! The girl I can never escape from now, was once as close to the gallows as I am to this tomb.'

He was about to start further protest, but she stopped him:

'Zadana, I tell you, was once nearly hanged because of a very small slip. So there'll be no slip this time.'

'And you knew all this, and yet trusted her as you did?'

'Perhaps as a convicted criminal myself'—he again made a quick gesture and exclamation of denial— 'I had a fellow feeling for her. After all, hers was a very different crime from vulgar theft. She was sentenced to death—the sentence was later commuted—for attempting to poison the mistress of the house in which she was employed as governess. She apparently took great exception to her manners and overbearing behaviour.'

'I fear the Close would not approve such "ultraistical" conduct on the part of Miss Mott.'

'Not at all "Attic,"' agreed Jane, nodding her lovely head. 'Well, she and I were the only survivors when the transport was wrecked on the coast of Vled de Non . . . From then she was constant companion and tutor. She taught me all the manner of things that would give me my background in the very far-off future I looked forward to in those days in Morocco—the things that are the essential social and mental equipment of a princess living in a civilized country in a snug and semiroyal retirement.'

Javan did not speak for a moment; then he said very formally:

'Don't you realize that the enormous fortune that we have stowed away in this country for Mulai Ali is now yours—legitimately yours?'

'It is not. I am not entitled to it. What Ali gave me personally was mine, and justifiably mine. But that belongs to the Emperor of Morocco, whoever he may be—Mulai Abdullah, I suppose—not to me.'

'But at least you could recover all you have just lost through Zadana's theft—and with it your ambition!'

'Even if I hadn't lost that ambition, Javan, I still should have nothing to do with Ali's hoard. My future was never going to include him. I never intended returning to him from Europe. I'll confess it now. You would never have got me back. I would have rather died.

I can draw quite properly on the fund for the expenses of the household for a reasonably short time. And that is all I propose to do. Anything else would be dishonest.'

As she spoke she lifted her regard from the weather-stained slab of stone between them and looked directly at him. There was questioning as well as an appeal for comprehension—and, perhaps, for more than comprehension—in her grey eyes; but his serious face was bent, and all his attention seemed to be concentrated in a worried way upon the winged head of a cherub carved in bas-relief above the inscription on the tomb. She slowly looked away.

In the new long silence that followed, the bell of the church clock chimed the three-quarter hour; the thrush renewed its attack upon the recalcitrant snail-shell; the pale golden glow increased within the leafy chantry of Louis Anton, Count von Pfullingen; a labourer with a scythe upon his shoulder approached and passed out of earshot, his iron-tipped shoes ringing upon the stones. . . .

Javan spoke at last, abruptly and without looking up

'The position is very serious, you know, madam.'

'Jane.'

'Jane. Have you got no plans at all?'

She looked at him a little whimsically:

'You think—and I dare say you are right—that a woman-servant who has been transported for theft may find it difficult to obtain reasonable employment?'

'For God's sake—'

But she interrupted him, speaking with the brisk, bright air of Jane Tierce, that imaginary niece.

'I told them at Tregallion House to make some coffee for you, when I heard you talking under the window. I thought a cup would do you good—more good than the brandy of which I had once to complain!—before you changed your clothes or lay down. Come along, and I will give it to you!'

He glanced at her quickly in a rather puzzled way, and then thanked her in a preoccupied manner. He accompanied her through the churchyard to the deserted Close with a grave, unsmiling face, which she inspected narrowly and unobtrusively from time to time, at first with unhappy speculation and then with a dawning realization of the truth.

Without encountering anyone they entered the hall and ascended

the stairs to Javan's dark-panelled parlour with the bare buffet con-
fronting an empty hearth and a stopped clock; and the crookedly
hung picture of a storm-driven ship facing the sunlight and silvered
foliage framed in the open windows.

The room looked less inhospitable than usual today by reason of
a vase of red roses and a tray gay with cups and coffeepot of Staf-
fordshire stoneware upon the table, and an open book lying face
downwards on the ledge in a window-place.

In a niecely way she poured out his coffee and made him sit
down, and then helped herself and seated herself in the chair in the
window, whence she subjected his dark, irregular face to a searching
scrutiny of which he was most uneasily conscious.

In Shems-ed-Douha's mind a guess became a certainty. As it did
so, without preface, without prelude she posed the question in her
most Vicar's Close manner:

'Do you believe in witches, Javan?'

Struggling as he was with conflicting thoughts and emotions, he
was inclined to resent in his mind the intrusion of Jane Tierce and
her seemingly purposeless remark. Nothing of this showed, however,
in the inquiring face, the uplifted eyebrow with which he answered
her.

'Listen to this,' said Niece Tierce, holding up the shabby little
leather-bound book. 'I was reading it while I was waiting for you
to come. It's Sir Thomas Browne's *Religio Medici*. This is what he
says:

'"I have ever believed, and do know, that there are Witches: they
that are in doubt of these are obliquely and upon consequence a
sort, not of Infidels, but Atheists."'

'I am no atheist,' said Javan, 'if unbelief in the witchcraft of the
Princess Shems-ed-Douha is implied in the term.'

She turned her head very slowly—for she was sitting sideways
to the window—and looked steadily across the room at him for a
moment. In the long glance of those grey eyes he knew beyond cavil
that there was, indeed, magic—a very great magic—about her. And
then she bowed her head over the cup that she held cradled in her
hands against the folds of the violet cloak.

'I will give you, Javan, one last display of my magic, without
pools of ink and invocations and the burning of coriander seed. First
of all, I will look into the past for you . . . I see a paper, Javan,

with great red seals upon it. A paper which spelled honour and
security and rank and return to civilization. A paper which you
always carried with you, as a child carries its most prized possession.
. . . You haven't got it any longer.'

The last five words were pronounced so quickly, and she looked
up at him so quickly, that she caught the astonishment and admis-
sion of the truth in his expression. Nothing of the triumph that she
felt showed, however, in her voice or in her face: she said in an even
tone:

'You gave up the honour and security and rank that were yours
by right because you could not accept them from the hands of the
Queen of England, the unscrupulous enemy of *your* friend. Just as
the girl MacGillivray would not accept the restoration of an un-
stained past if it should involve more bitter anguish for the Queen
of England, the mother of *her* friend. A pair of fools, Javan?'

'Perhaps so, madam.'

'And now, having looked into the past—the very recent past—for
you, I will read your mind. You are wondering how a man who has
nothing but his sword can be of any material use to a Princess of
Morocco who has been a Countess von Pfullingen and, almost, a
Princess of Wales. Isn't that so?'

He said nothing for a while and a sidelong glance showed that
he was apparently staring out of the window over her head at the
dark bulk of the church rising above the swaying birch trees, like a
ship of stone in a sea of foliage. She suddenly knew that his regard
had returned to her; and then he said in a taut voice:

'I believe, madam, that you might be convinced I am not an
"atheist" if you could read for me the mind of one Jane Mac-
Gillivray—'

'Jane MacGillivray has noted that you concerned yourself very
deeply some half an hour or so ago with the marriage of four of
Mrs. Foley's maidservants. It is her view that you might concern
yourself more fittingly with the question of *her* marriage.'

'By Old Gooseberry, sir,' said Coppie later in the morning to Mr.
Tuke, 'I think I ought to tell old Mrs. Garlicke, don't you? She'll be
as sick as a walrus because she didn't see anything . . . Perhaps
she'll tell the man in the shop to give me some of those lozenges
made of onions and honey.'

# AFFINITY OF THE 'GRIFFE'

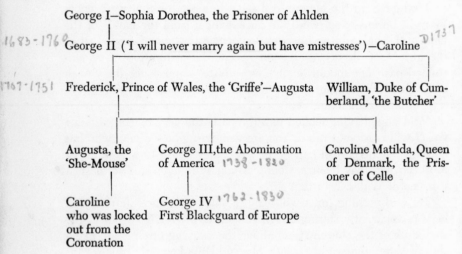

George I—Sophia Dorothea, the Prisoner of Ahlden

*1683-1760* George II ('I will never marry again but have mistresses')—Caroline *D1737*

*1707-1751* Frederick, Prince of Wales, the 'Griffe'—Augusta     William, Duke of Cumberland, 'the Butcher'

Augusta, the 'She-Mouse'     George III, the Abomination of America *1738-1820*     Caroline Matilda, Queen of Denmark, the Prisoner of Celle

Caroline who was locked out from the Coronation     George IV *1762-1830* First Blackguard of Europe

Date Due

~~Due~~ 28 Days ~~From Latest Date~~

28 DAYS

| Date Due | | | |
|---|---|---|---|
| SEP 6 1975 | AUG 1 0 1978 | | |
| OCT 3 0 1975 | JAN 2 2 1979 | APR 1 1985 | |
| NOV 4 1975 | FEB 1 0 1979 | NOV 25 1987 | |
| JAN 1 7 1976 | AUG 4 1979 | | |
| MAR 9 1976 | APR 1 5 1980 | | |
| NOV 2 0 1976 | JUL 2 5 1980 | | |
| JUL 3 0 1977 | AUG 1 5 1980 | | |
| FEB 4 1978 | SEP 3 1980 | WITHDRAWN | |
| MAR 4 1978 | AUG 5 1983 | | |